Acclaim for Suzanne Adair

Paper Woman
winner of the Patrick D. Smith Literature Award

"...a swashbuckling good mystery yarn!"
–The Wilmington Star-News

The Blacksmith's Daughter
"Adair holds the reader enthralled with constant action, spine-tingling suspense, and superb characterization."
–Midwest Book Review

Camp Follower
*nominated for the Daphne du Maurier Award and
the Sir Walter Raleigh Award*

"Adair wrote another superb story."
–Armchair Interviews

Regulated for Murder
"Best of 2011," Suspense Magazine

"Driven by a desire to see justice done, no matter what guise it must take, [Michael Stoddard] is both sympathetic and interesting."
–Motherlode

Books by Suzanne Adair

Mysteries of the American Revolution
Paper Woman
The Blacksmith's Daughter
Camp Follower

Michael Stoddard American Revolution Thrillers
Regulated for Murder

Paper Woman

Suzanne Adair (signature)

Suzanne Adair

A Mystery of the American Revolution

Acknowledgements

I receive help from wonderful and unique people while conducting research for novels and editing my manuscripts. Here are a few who assisted me with Paper Woman:

The 33rd Light Company of Foot, especially Ernie and Linda Stewart

The Sisters in Crime Internet Chapter, especially Lonnie Cruse, Marja McGraw, and Jeri Westerson

The folks in the print shop at Colonial Williamsburg

The Atlanta chapter of ABANA, especially Tom Davanhall

Dr. Larry Babits

Carl J. Barnett

Marg Baskin

Barclay Blanchard

Karen Breasbois

Dr. Ed Cashin

J. B. Cheaney

Larry Cywin

Bonnie Bajorek Daneker

Peggy Earp

Mike Everette

Jack E. Fryar, Jr.

Tom (Blue Wolf) Goodman

Mark and Sherilyn Herron

John (Winterhawk) Johnson

Nolin and Neil Jones

Geoff Kent

Henry Kinard (a ghost)

Isabel Alcobas Kramer

Judith Levy

Gerry Marcin

John Millar

Patrick O'Kelley

Dr. Betty Owen

John Robertson

Dr. Anthony J. Scotti, Jr.

Dr. Christine Swager

Elaine Terna Weller

Joyce Wiegand

John Mills Williams, Sr.

Mike Williams

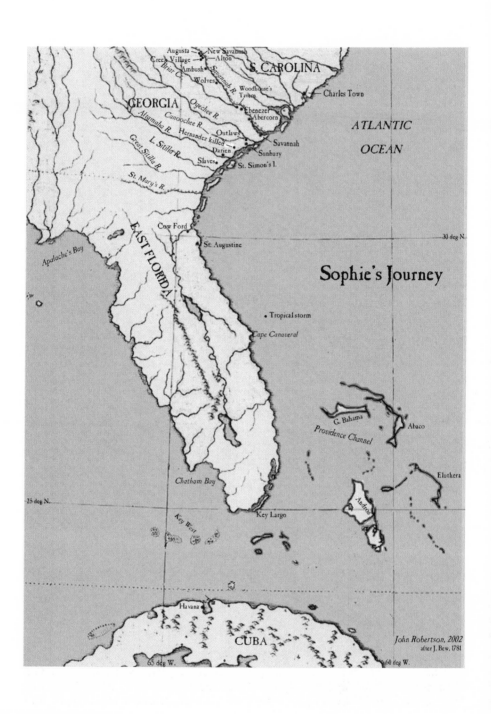

Augusta · New Savannah
Creek Village — Alton
Briar C. · Ambush · Savannah R. · Wolves
S. CAROLINA
Woodhouse's Tavern
Charles Town
GEORGIA · Ogechee R.
Canoochee R.
Altamaha R. · Hernandez killed
Great Stilla R. · L. Stilla R.
Outlaws
Darien
Slaves
Ebenezer
Abercorn
Savannah
Sunbury
St. Simon's I.
St. Mary's R.
ATLANTIC
OCEAN
Cow Ford
30 deg N.
Apalache's Bay
EAST FLORIDA
St. Augustine

Sophie's Journey

· Tropical storm
Cape Canaveral

G. Bahama
Providence Channel
Abaco

Eluthera

Chatham Bay

25 deg N.
Key West
Key Largo
Andros

Havana
CUBA
John Robertson, 2002
after J. Bew, 1781
65 deg W.
60 deg W.

Chapter One

IN THE JUNE twilight, Sophie Barton stopped strolling with her brother to assess the number of soldiers present by the blaze their scarlet uniforms made along the perimeter of the crowded, open-air dance ground. One of those redcoats' musket balls could be destined for her father. More likely, Will St. James would end his life in the customary manner for rebel spies: his body swaying from a noose, his face an indigo twist of agony. Either prospect gave her a bellyache the size of a cannonball.

If she kept an eye on him, maybe she'd limit his antics for one night. She craned her neck in search of him. Burning pine knots in metal baskets on poles frisked mystery across the faces of soldier and civilian, merchant and farmer, musician and servant. There was her sister, Susana, brewing tattle into gossip with the help of several other goodwives. But Will was nowhere in sight.

Beside her, David aped an accent straight from Parliament. "Madam clearly prefers a sedan chair to walking amongst the vulgar herd." Sophie rolled her eyes. "Or perhaps Madam prefers a candlelit ballroom on the Thames?" Mischief reigned in the handsome face of her tall, lanky brother.

"You silly goose." Who wouldn't prefer London to Alton, Georgia? Still, she'd never turn her nose up at one of Zeb's dances, guaranteed to enliven a Saturday night. She'd even worn her favorite blue wool jacket for the occasion, the one with enough boning to make her look buxom.

David scanned her up and down. "By Jove, you do clean up nicely."

"The first such compliment ever you've paid me."

He dropped the accent. "You don't dress like this to pull the press. What's the occasion?"

There Will was, but damnation, he was talking with stout Zack MacVie, his assistant chairman for the Committee of Safety. Never mind that Will had formed the Committee to maintain a militia and promote local trade. Put

MacVie and her father together, and sedition happened. "I'm weary of dressing in ink." Seizing David's hand, she towed him after her.

Near straw sheaves along the perimeter, they caught up with Will. MacVie saw them coming and slipped away into the crowd, a scowl on his swarthy face. Ignoring sweat that escaped her mobcap into a wisp of dark hair on her neck, Sophie prodded trim on her father's green silk waistcoat. "Remind me on the morrow. I shall mend that."

"Thank you." His voice was taut. Supervising one of his "special editions" at the printing press all Friday night with his rebel friends had transformed him into a grizzled and winter-worn wolf — gaunt, yet potent for his small stature, and gray-eyed like his son and two daughters.

The fresh lampblack and varnish on his hands might as well be blood. She resisted glancing at her own hands, likewise stained from setting type on composing sticks and fitting lines and woodcuts into galleys.

Across the dance ground teeming with townsfolk, committee treasurer Jonah Hale signaled Will. Annoyed and alarmed, she turned and grasped his shoulder. "You know, I'd *so* enjoy the first dance with my father." Warmth replaced the hunted look in his eyes, and hope leaped to her heart. Not long ago they'd listened to each other, supported each other's ideas. Alas, they hadn't discussed much of anything in recent months. They had to live under the same roof. The war. The damned, wretched war. "Please," she whispered. "Lie low tonight."

Stubbornness sealed his expression and drove out the warmth. He passed a critical eye over her attire. "Where's your beau?"

Her blank look transcended to vexation. How exasperating that both her father and sister read courtship into chess games and business discussions. "Major Edward Hunt *isn't* my beau."

With a grunt, he shrugged off her hold and strutted for the company of Jonah, skeletal fingers of bitter black smoke from a nearby torch grabbing for and just missing him. David occupied the void beside her, but it didn't dull the despair filling her soul. "Father despises me."

"Nonsense. The old man doesn't hear me, either. Take my advice. Don't cluck over him tonight."

"But —"

"Enjoy yourself. He's going to do what he damned well pleases." David's voice dropped in disgust, and shadows darker than his hair roamed his expression. "What fools in the Congress and Parliament."

"Yes, how unfortunate they won't listen to each other."

"Four years after fifty-six congressional peacocks strutted around their imagined independence, it's become a cause of holy proportion for both sides." A roguish grin dispelled the gloom on his face. "But I know I can dance a tune with the prettiest lady in Alton, even if she's my big sister."

What a sight they'd make, too, with David dressed the dandy in lace and fine linen, and she in her mother's garnets.

"Hah! Quit wrestling that smile off your face. Makes you look like you've eaten pickled turnips." David glanced to the right. "Guess who's back in town."

The glee on his face was a clue. "Uncle Jacques?" Many of the townsfolk called the old Frenchman "Uncle." She darted a look around, her heart lightening. "Here at the dance tonight?"

David aimed her for the sidelines. "With Mathias and Mrs. Flannery." At the sight of the wiry gnome standing near a sheaf of straw, Sophie tidied her apron, petticoat, and jacket, self-conscious that she'd flushed. David chuckled. "Do hurry. You just might claim him for a dance."

Jacques le Coeuvre packed the Red Rock Tavern to capacity whenever he turned up, for the community was eager to hear the latest installment of his wild and often preternatural excursions. Starting with the Indian massacre of redcoats at Fort William Henry back in '57, he'd landed himself in the middle of more adventures than any man ought to. In July of '77, he'd finagled his way in to witness the nineteen-year-old Marquis de Lafayette volunteering his services to a skeptical and chilly Congress in Philadelphia. Six months later, he'd enthralled listeners with tales of bloodying his tomahawk at Saratoga.

Sophie kept her skepticism about scrappy Jacques's "spying" to herself. People who'd lived as long as he had deserved to embellish their youthful years. Just before she reached Jacques and his half-Creek nephew, elderly Widow Flannery took her leave of them. A grin split the Frenchman's weather-beaten face. "Sophie, *belle* Sophie!"

After exchanging an embrace with Jacques, who smelled of brandy, garlic, and dusty hunting shirt, she winked at Mathias Hale, a blacksmith like his two half-brothers. He looked quite polished that night in a fine brown wool jacket, waistcoat, and breeches. "Your uncle hasn't changed a bit."

"He boasts of a new scar." Warmth softened the obsidian of Mathias's eyes. "Jonah brought me his horse earlier and said he was too busy to replace a shoe, so I shan't have your hoe and pot repaired until Monday."

But he'd walk all the way across town to give her back the hoe and pot. Sophie returned the warmth of his serene smile.

"So David is just back from Wilmington today. How was his trip?"

Wry amusement brushed her lips. "The master of piquet and one and thirty has new tales of glory for you."

"I shall look him up tonight." Perhaps Mathias had spotted David charming a smile from a shapely, young widow, because his tone became droll. "Or tomorrow. Sophie, may I have a dance with you later?" She smiled and nodded assent. "Thank you." He grinned and bowed, then sauntered off.

She inspected Jacques from head to toe. A bit more gray at his temples. "You slunk into town two days late for Elijah Carey's funeral but just in time for another dance."

"We French have such instinct about parties, *non?* But had I attended the funeral, I am afraid my respect for *Monsieur* Carey might have been out-weighed by memories of the — er — masquerade."

She laughed. "My goodness, Susana and I thought about it during the funeral, and the Careys admitted they did, too!"

"There, you see? The town biddies milled the prank to such extent that Carey and your father are now legend. You have to admit it would not have smelled so scandalous had *Madame* Carey not taken two hours to realize that it was Will in her husband's clothing."

Sophie, David, and Susana had hooted together over the "masquerade" for months, wondering whether their father would have pushed the joke so far as to climb in bed that night twenty years earlier with the wife of miller Elijah Carey. They finally decided that although their father had his share of vices,

Mrs. Carey hadn't been one of them. No, Will St. James, now a widower for a decade, still wore his wedding band.

Will. She glanced over the grounds without seeing him. By then, more than half of Alton's forty-man garrison of redcoats was present for the dance. Fiddle scratch from two players warming up atop a wooden platform rose above the buzz of folks on the dance ground already surrendered to the lure of liquor and long shadows.

Jacques slipped his hand into hers, reclaiming her attention. Black eyes aglitter, he took his leisure inspecting her from head to toe. "Like fine wine, you grow more delectable with each passing year."

She smiled. Typical Frenchman. "Pshaw. You've just come from a bottle of brandy at the Red Rock."

"*Mais oui!* It does my old heart good." His gaze took in her bosom, and his smile became a leer. "I suppose I am too late to claim a dance from someone as slender and graceful as you."

"Not at all, but my father has the first dance."

"Of course. May I have the second dance, then?"

"You may."

"And perhaps the sixth also?" He wiggled his eyebrows. "And the twelfth? I feel the most fortunate man alive."

She laughed and hugged him again. "I'd love to dance with you all night."

"Ah, for a moment, I thought the whispers I heard were true, that an English is courting you." Misinterpreting the exasperation on her face, he gripped her hand. "*Non, non*, not an English pig, Sophie! Tell me it is not so."

Behind her, she heard Susana's squeal. "Uncle Jacques!"

He released her hand, and while he and Susana embraced, Sophie slipped into the crowd. She didn't enjoy watching her younger sister favor Jacques. It came too close to ingratiation, as if Susana imagined the Frenchman had a fortune stored somewhere, and she could earn some of it by flattering him. And when it came to Edward Hunt, she knew Jacques wouldn't accept her explanation of chess games and business discussions either.

From the platform, the mayor's voice boomed across the crowd. "Welcome everyone to Zeb Harwick's fifteenth dance. Let's thank our fiddlers for coming." Applause followed. "And let's thank Zeb for making all this possible." More applause and enthusiastic shouts of "Huzzah!" The wealthy cattle farmer had given them all a magical three-hour reprieve so they could forget debt and disease and the frightening way Loyalists and Whigs were bashing each other's brains out in neighboring South Carolina. "First tune tonight is a reel. Grab your partner!"

Noise escalated as people swarmed from the sidelines to the dance ground, rousing the smells of dung and straw, rosewater and sweat, and onions and whiskey. Sophie searched in vain for Will. One of several British privates standing near the ale scored a fourteen-year-old girl for the first tune and guided her to a line with a flourish.

Sophie smiled at the girl's blush, remembering being fourteen, remembering her wedding the following year to blond-haired, blue-eyed Jim Neely, the apothecary's apprentice. The year after that, she'd borne her daughter Betsy, and her first husband lay in his grave, dead of pneumonia.

The town hornsmith stuttered out an invitation to dance, and she glanced at his fingernails. She couldn't help it. No one else chewed fingernails to nubs the way he did. She thanked him and declined. His bow spasmodic, he hastened on to the next eligible female.

Across the ground, two more soldiers found partners. Then Lieutenant Dunstan Fairfax strolled into view. Hands clasped behind him, the russet-haired young officer assumed position well away from the beverage table to interrogate the crowd with his stare. By convention, officers didn't mingle with their men during social occasions. But one look at Fairfax, who displayed all the sentiment of a suspicious swamp cat, convinced Sophie that the dance didn't constitute a social occasion for him.

The mayor began walking three lines of dancers through steps. Privates escorted women out to the dance ground past her father, who was conversing with MacVie. Sophie had best grab Will for the dance.

Within twenty feet of the two men, she realized they were arguing and halted in time to hear MacVie snarl to Will, "...just you and Jonah, eh?" A warning look from Will silenced his associate. Both turned, MacVie sneering at her, Will tense.

Awkwardness squeaked her voice. "The first dance, Father."

MacVie gestured beyond the straw sheaves and stalked off the dance ground. Regret wove through Will's tension. "I apologize. Something's come up." He spun on his heel and followed his cohort, leaving Sophie speechless.

She whirled about in a huff. By then, just about everyone was lined up with a partner. Fairfax caught her eye and started toward her, and she cast about in panic. Gods, no. She didn't want to talk with him, and she sure hoped he didn't want to dance with her. Handsome as he was, the thought of him getting too close reminded her of the way she'd felt when David dropped a live lizard inside her shift years ago at the fair.

She signaled a fifteen-year-old lad to join her in the line closest to the ale. Seeing her partnered for the dance, Fairfax retreated, and the fiddlers fired up an introductory four measures. Ten minutes later, after Sophie and the boy traveled up the line and then halfway back again, the fiddlers wound down the tune. People applauded, thanked partners, and scrambled about for the next dance, merry and flirtatious.

Sophie spotted David in conversation with Widow Reems. David sure did like widows. Will had vanished. So had Jonah Hale. She noticed even more redcoats on the grounds. Lieutenant Fairfax was questioning MacVie, who often whittled woodcut artwork for the newspaper. Interrogation couldn't have happened to a nicer person; in MacVie's world, women should be silent and servile — probably a factor in his failure to find a wife. Still, her uneasiness returned. A charred woodcut had been left in the fireplace after last night's print run. With hindsight, she wished she'd insisted that her servant clean the fireplace that afternoon.

Bearing the smile of a diplomat, tall, blond Edward Hunt met her halfway to the sidelines. "Good evening. You look lovely tonight." He took her hand and escorted her off the dance ground, the scarlet of his uniform like a beacon. People gawked at them and whispered, grinding grist in the gossip mill.

The mayor's voice cleared the hubbub. "The second one is a minuet. Grab your partners, friends, and let's get started."

Edward clasped her hands in his. "I'd dearly love dancing with you, but I fear my schedule doesn't permit it."

"No? You've given your men leave to attend the dance."

His sapphire-hued gaze roved over her bosom before returning to her face. "Good soldiers, each of them deserving of a few hours leisure."

"And you don't deserve such leisure?" Fairfax drew up at attention behind the major, a hound awaiting the command of his master in the shadows, and just close enough to hear their conversation.

"Commanding officers see little of leisure." To her surprise, he lifted her hand to his lips. "I shall return later, perhaps in time for the final dance." He released her hand, bowed, and pivoted toward the lieutenant. The two stepped over straw sheaves, headed out of the torchlight toward the horses. Still bemused by Edward's kiss, Sophie remained where she stood, her ears trained on his query to Fairfax: "MacVie?"

"Nothing. Just like St. James." No emotion colored Fairfax's voice.

"Carry on. With good fortune, we shall have all we need by midnight."

"Sir."

Their voices dwindled, and the sputter of a torch swallowed the rest of their conversation. She chanced a look at them, but they'd already passed from silhouettes into secrecy. *We shall have all we need by midnight.* Anxiety parched her mouth and fluttered her stomach. She paced the sidelines and searched the crowd. Where was Will St. James?

Chapter Two

JACQUES TROTTED OVER for the second dance, his expression stern. "*Belle* Sophie, there you are, and finally free of the company of pigs." A beguiling smile creased his face. "Let us make merry, eh? I will show you how the French dance a minuet."

Popular "Jacques-Lore" held that decades earlier, before bandits butchered his parents and a Creek family adopted his young sister, Madeleine, the Frenchman had learned his dancing in Paris. Jacques decorated Sophie's minuet with wild swings and twirls, leaving her laughing and breathless. Clearly, some lore about him must be true.

For the third tune, she found herself appointed David's partner by virtue of her ability to pick up dance combinations quickly. They demonstrated a dance called a "waltz" that he'd seen in Williamsburg. Couples joined in. When she could spare a moment, she glanced over the crowd. Three rebels present at the previous night's printing run had disappeared, and Will was still absent.

The waltz wound down, and several fellows thumped David on the back with approval, their faces flushed with dancing and ale. David nodded at them, then he led Sophie to the sidelines, where he pitched his voice low. "You really stir matters up with Major Hunt."

"Too many people have nothing better to do than mind my business. Have you seen Father in the last quarter hour?"

"Forget about the old man. You wouldn't be vexed so by gossip were you on a course that carried your heart with it."

"Hearts." His sober expression drew a chuckle from her. "Hearts have nothing to do with this."

"To the contrary, it's clear the major's quite taken with you."

"Oh, poppycock."

"Join me for a short walk."

Her hand on his elbow, she strolled with him toward Zeb's barn, aware that Lieutenant Fairfax watched them leave together. They passed a dozen men near the barn shrouded by night and the haze of tobacco smoke. One said, "Buford surrendered. That scum Banastre Tarleton butchered men who lay down their arms."

"They were asking for it up there in the Waxhaws," said a second man.

"Asking for the likes of 'Tarleton's Quarter'? Bah! Who expects no quarter after surrendering? I tell you, carnage like Buford's Massacre will continue."

"Buford's Massacre" they'd labeled the military action on May twenty-ninth, five days earlier. How orderly had Continental Colonel Buford's surrender been? Sophie suspected that news of the massacre disturbed a few redcoats, too. More unsettling was the fact that it had occurred in neighboring South Carolina. Was Georgia next?

David steered her away from politics and around the corner of the barn, where he regarded her in the darkness. "If Major Hunt isn't your beau, what do you expect from his attentions?"

"Intelligent conversation. A glimpse of someplace — anyplace — other than Georgia."

"And what does he expect from you?"

"A reasonably challenging chess game. Discussions on Plato, Socrates, and expense accounting."

"Good gods!" David howled with laughter. "He's positioned for a grand look at the operations of the printing press."

"Naturally. But never fear, I'm thirty-three years old and immune to the follies of girlish infatuation."

"Let us hope so."

"And I don't care what color coat he wears. He's a hundred times more interesting than the men of Alton and Augusta."

"Of course he's more interesting than Georgia stock, but you aren't in love with him."

"What of it? He isn't in love with me, either."

"You're certain of that, are you?" Concern clipped David's tone. "Look at you. That jacket compliments your figure so well, and with Mother's garnets at your ears and throat, you look positively elegant. I've watched you turn the heads of half the men of Alton tonight. Everyone's smitten, Sophie. Are you going to tell me you dressed up just to improve your mood?"

"Yes, I did dress up to improve my mood. As I said earlier, it's a pleasure to wear something other than ink."

"Major Hunt wasn't ogling ink when he kissed your hand. Suppose he declared his love for you and offered to take you away from Alton to his estates in Hampshire? You'd be guaranteed to wear something other than ink there."

Sophie found it easy to dismiss similar sentiments expressed by her sister and father. However, David wasn't a raving rebel, so his intimation sent her reexamining the situation. Given the academic and business topics of their conversations, Edward had to be just passing his time in Georgia in the company of an intelligent woman. He wasn't about to make any grandiose offers to her. Not with the class distinction. She shrugged off her disquiet. "Your question is hypothetical, so I'll answer hypothetically. If he fell in love with me, I might fall in love with him, too."

"*You?*" Her brother snorted. "No. You'd be feeling gratitude, not love."
She scowled. David understood her just a little too well. She'd read every
book she'd gotten her hands on, so she knew there was a big, bold world out
there. Too bad she couldn't see more of it than the Georgia colony. "Faugh,
managing our business and extra projects out of Augusta and Savannah is
sheer drudgery! I'm sick of Alton. It's little more than stinking swamp. The
men gripe about whiskey and livestock, and the women natter on and on about
babies and baking. I want something else. I want *life!* I've never seen mountains or the ocean. I'd give anything to travel the way you've done, and pluck
purses over piquet, but women aren't supposed to gamble or travel —"
"Or operate printing presses?" His teeth shone in a brief grin. "Come now.
You know most women, especially Susana, envy you for running that press. To
be sure, they consider you eccentric and too independent, but don't believe for
a moment that all they want from life is babies and baking."
She swatted at a whining mosquito. "I daresay if women ran the world,
there'd be far fewer wars."
"Undoubtedly. But you shan't stop this war by dallying with a nobleman
you don't love. Your good fortune has been to outlive not one, but two un-
desirable spouses." He paused. "I've never faulted you for sending Betsy to
grow up with Sarah and Lucas in Augusta. But I often wonder how you've kept
yourself these seven years since she went away, particularly now that she and
Clark are expecting. Don't you want to play the doting grandmother come
Christmastime?"
Sophie had just about convinced herself that seven years of alone wasn't so
bad because she'd grown accustomed to it. But David's words raked over and
exposed an ancient ache in the cellar of her heart. She'd never enjoyed living a
day's travel away from her only child, even though she'd seen it as a necessity
seven years earlier, when she'd fostered Betsy with her cousin. "Well, yes. Yes,
of course I look forward to being a grandmother." And being with Betsy again,
sweet Betsy. The ache compressed her heart.
"Sophie, you're lovely and vivacious. You've intelligence and wit. Living
with the old man and his crazy notions day in and day out, running the press,
keeping the accounts straight — how does that feed your soul?"
Amazed, she blinked up at him. In the St. James family, certain sentiments
weren't vocalized easily. "It — it doesn't."
"What does feed your soul?"
"I'm not sure."
"Well, perhaps you'd best think on it. I shan't lecture you about duty. The
gods know what a pimple Alton is on the arse of civilization, and I'm the last
person you'd hear advising you to remain here out of *duty.*" He paused again
in search of words, and she sensed him fidgeting. "To be sure, Major Hunt is
a fine fellow. But if ever you truly love a man, I shall encourage you to follow
your heart." Dancing had loosened hair from the purple, silk ribbon at the
nape of his neck. He tucked the errant strand behind his ear and edged back
toward the barn's corner. "Now, I've a widow to dazzle tonight. Shall we return?"
"You go. It might do me well to stand out a dance." He nodded and headed
back for the torchlight.
With a sigh, she waved off the query of another mosquito and scratched

behind the ears of one of Zeb's hounds that trotted over to check on her. Then she ambled further around the barn, flitting fireflies her escort, her heartache subsiding into disillusionment and dissatisfaction. Where was her place in the world? With her seventeen-year-old married daughter in Augusta, awaiting grandmotherhood? At the printing press in Alton, growing more distant from her father the longer they lived together? Sophie didn't feel like she belonged anywhere anymore.

A man's murmur delayed her turning the corner. She didn't want to interrupt a lovers' tryst. In the next instant, she realized that the man wasn't speaking English, so she pressed herself against the rough siding of the barn and peeked around the corner. Overcast sky silhouetted five shapes of darkness — four bare-chested, top-knotted Creek warriors, their earrings and nose rings tinkling in the muggy breeze, the fading light glinting off their shaven heads, and a fifth man in colonial dress, his back to her.

She squinted. Was one of those warriors the horse trainer, Runs With Horses, adoptive cousin to Mathias? The racket from the crowd prevented her identifying a voice, so she withdrew. Only Jacques and his nephews spoke Creek well enough for lengthy conversations. So who was out there with the Creek? And *why*?

Hairs on the back of her neck prickled, the feeling she got when someone watched her. She retreated along the barn, turned the corner, and almost collided with Lieutenant Fairfax. "Ah, madam. Your brother returned without you. I thought to assure your safety."

Sure he did. "Thank you, Lieutenant." Since he didn't budge, she maneuvered quickly around him toward the dance ground.

Inside the ring of torchlight, the back of her neck prickled again. Fairfax snarled, "I would speak with you, Mrs. Barton."

She whirled on him with the haughtiness she invoked to bring a peddler's price down. "Speak with someone else."

His eyes took on the appearance of pale green hailstones hammered from the heart of a thunderstorm, and he towered over her, not at all possessed of a peddler's suggestibility. A thousand times worse than a live lizard down her shift, the seethe of inhumanity in his eyes made her want to cower. Somehow she found the strength to jut her chin.

To her astonishment, MacVie bounded over, grabbed her hand, and dragged her after him. "She promised *me* this dance." They tacked onto the middle line, her rescuer pale despite whiskey on his breath. He darted a glance over her shoulder. "Ghoul."

On the sidelines, Fairfax cornered another rebel crony, Sam Fielding. The redcoats must have kept the shop under surveillance all night. If Fairfax singled her out, he'd interrogate her in much the same manner. Rather than rescuing her out of kindness, MacVie schemed to keep her apart from the lieutenant.

Her gaze on the hog farmer sharpened. Will was still absent, as were several accomplices from the previous night. "Where's my father? I've not seen him since you two argued."

"I don't know." Nonsense. Her father, Jonah Hale, and the gods only knew who else were up to no good. Fairfax was there to gather leads. The other soldiers were there in case trouble erupted. And Edward — was he off tracking down rebels who operated a printing press in the middle of the night? The swarthy man flashed sharp, yellow teeth. "But take my advice, Mrs. Barton, and stop asking so many questions."

"But Mr. MacVie, I'm full of questions."

"Aww, just like the child who questioned what was down the well, leaned over too far, fell in, and drowned."

Was that MacVie's idea of a threat, patriot-style? She sniffed. "I can swim." He bared his teeth again and stubbed the toes of her left foot three times before the dance was over.

While the mayor talked the mob through a circle dance, and the pathetic hornsmith prowled for a partner, Sophie skirted the ground to where Mrs. Reems and David huddled, enmeshed in each other's gazes. Just before she reached them, David trailed his fingers down the widow's forearm.

"David," she whispered from behind.

He sighed and faced her with a waxen smile. "Make haste."

She launched into a summary of the evening's weird events. After five seconds of it, David patted her shoulder. "Relax and enjoy yourself." He waved to someone. "Would you be so kind as to partner my sister for this dance?"

The hornsmith bounded over and proffered his nail-gnawed hand. "Mrs. B-Barton, I'm d-delighted to be your p-partner."

She forced a smile at David, who turned his back on her and re-engaged Mrs. Reems, and then at the hornsmith, who guided her onto the grounds. Not soon enough, the dance ended and she hobbled off, both feet bruised. The mayor's voice boomed: "Next one's a quadrille. Sets of four couples." Quadrilles could be complicated. Her punished feet begged her to rest.

Her brother-in-law, John Greeley, stomped over. "Susana reminded me you and I haven't had a dance, even though a bloodyback *is* courting you." Dousing her retort was the sight of Fairfax tracking her. Like the folk-tale girl who danced to death in a pair of magic slippers, she took John's hand. He trotted her out, and his meaty, cooper's hands routed her through the dance with all the subtlety of maneuvering tobacco hogsheads and corn barrels.

When the tune was over, Sam Fielding interposed himself between her and Fairfax. "How about *our* dance, Mrs. Barton?"

By then, she knew the script. "Of course, Mr. Fielding."

Fairfax knew the script, too. His eyes iced over again. "May I have the *next* dance, Mrs. Barton?"

"My apologies. I'm taken for the rest of the evening."

Jacques focused on her for the following tune and honed his flirting skills. Laughing, forgetting her sore feet, she danced up the line with him, and at the top, Fairfax and a townswoman jumped to become their neighbors for the next thirty seconds of music.

The lieutenant emerged from an allemande with Jacques and caught Sophie up into a swing. "Where is your father at this moment, Mrs. Barton?"

"Isn't he here? If not, I've no idea where he is."

"What did you print last night on the press?"

"I printed nothing."

"Do you expect me to believe you were asleep all night?"

Her mouth tightened. "I don't care what you believe."

A smile devoid of warmth rippled his mouth. "Major Hunt has a blind spot when it comes to you. I suffer no such affliction."

"How reassuring."

His smile lingered when he handed her back to Jacques. Not once had his stare strayed to her bosom. "Such a pleasure dancing with you at last, Mrs. Barton."

Chapter Three

DURING THE BREAK, people thronged to the beverage table to slake thirst or bolster inebriation. Everyone ignored lightning undulating on the western horizon and a thunderstorm grumbling in the swamps, threatening to roll east to the Savannah River and give them a good soaking down. The air stank like the yeasty insides of a cattle farmer's boots. Fanning away gnats, Sophie discussed her garden with Widow Flannery, who promised to send over some potted herbs.

With Mrs. Reems ornamenting his elbow, David meandered Sophie's way. "Huzzah! You're enjoying yourself."

Sweat gleamed on Widow Reems's big breasts, pressed so high in her bodice they looked ready to explode, a feat all the boning in the world would never accomplish for Sophie due to lack of volume. She aimed a tart smile at her brother. "I'm having a delightful time."

"Jolly. And don't worry about the redcoats. Fairfax is interested in two Spaniards who came to the dance looking for the old man."

"Spaniards? Where?" She looked around, noting the absence of Fairfax and all but five redcoats.

David shrugged. "We've probably seen the last of those Spaniards."

As if adventuring with rebels wasn't enough, Will St. James must also dabble in dealings with Spaniards. With Spain having declared war on Britain, small wonder that Fairfax bayed out his pursuit. She scanned the crowd again and turned back on David.

"Now, now, let's banter about the possibilities on the morrow. I've other thoughts to occupy me tonight." Smiling down Mrs. Reems's cleavage, he kissed her hand before strolling her away.

Soon after the dance resumed, an empty-handed Fairfax returned with his men, sweat streaking their scarlet coats. Preoccupied, the lieutenant paid only cursory attention to the return of several Safety Committee members and spent the rest of the event conferring with soldiers and studying the crowd.

Grateful for his waned interest, Sophie sat out a dance. Committee scribe Donald Fairbourne plopped down on the sheaf next to her. "Evening, Mrs. Barton." He jammed a piece of straw in his mouth and gnawed it, watching the dancers.

"Evening, Mr. Fairbourne." She regarded his damp hair and mud-caked shoes. "Were you caught in rain on the way over?"

He glanced at his shoes, the straw dropping from his mouth. "I was gardening and lost track of time. Would you care to dance?"

"No, thank you. What were you planting?"

"Perhaps the next dance then." He shoved himself up.

She watched him stride to Susana, intuiting that he'd hastened off to avoid discussing his muddy shoes. Charley Osborn, another rebel, claimed her for the next tune, his hair damp, his shoes muddy, his response to her queries just as evasive as Fairbourne's had been. The hair of rebels Measure Travis and Peter Whitney was dry and their shoes clean, thus dashing her theory that her father and his associates were competing with two Spanish fortune hunters to recover lost treasure from the swamps. But she'd have wagered six loaves of her molasses bread that those Spaniards figured into the Safety Committee's intrigue.

During the following dance, MacVie stepped on her left foot twice, as if penalizing her for curiosity. She doubted her father had anything in common with the odious hog farmer beside the rebel cause. At the end of the tune, she hobbled to the sidelines, sweaty, irritable, needing a good night's sleep, but certain she had everything in perspective. A pox on rebels and redcoats and everyone else whose small minds played at secret missions. Regardless of who eventually won the war, the sun would continue shining, and the Georgia colony would continue to resemble hell. Unfortunate that the men with the small minds weren't the primary casualties of war.

When the mayor announced the final number, she didn't check for Edward Hunt. She didn't care whether he'd returned. Over the course of the evening, her interest in him had waned. He belonged to the group of people who thought themselves clever that night by being dishonest with her. Eccentric, overly independent widows couldn't be bothered with such games.

"Don't tell me you're going to sit out the waltz."

She tilted her head and cocked an eyebrow at Mathias Hale, having concluded that it must have been him outside talking with the four warriors. When she, David, and Susana were children, they'd run hoops through the dirt streets with the three Hale brothers. Now Jonah, tangled in rebel intrigue, never jested with them anymore. And Mathias had his own little game going with the Creek. "My feet were stepped on too often tonight."

"Have I ever stepped on your feet?"

Feeling obstinate, she looked away. "I'm tired."

He leaned over and whispered, "You're sulking."

Her gaze swiveled back around to challenge his. "You should have invited your four Creek friends to dance."

Eyes hardening, he stared at her several heartbeats before he whispered, "They don't like European dances."

After a night of subterfuge and lies, she'd given up expecting anyone to admit to anything, let alone trust her with secrets. She mused why Mathias, of those at the dance that night with clandestine dealings, had trusted her. Clearly his stakes were on a different plane. "How unfortunate."

The guard in his expression retreated. Straightening, he extended his hand. Up on the platform, the fiddlers meandered into "Give Me Your Hand," a tune by the Irish harpist Rory Dall O'Cahan. Sophie took Mathias's hand.

They danced without conversation. Taller than his uncle by several inches but just as wiry, the blacksmith led her around without stepping on her feet or colliding with anyone. When the fiddlers finished, thunder boomed closer. A cool downdraft fluttered torches and stirred a murmur through the applause. Rather than lingering and socializing, people hurried off the grounds, eager to return home ahead of the storm.

Sophie spotted Susana and John herding their six children for the horses and wagons. "Pardon me, but I must help my sister. Good night." After a curtsy for Mathias, she retrieved her kerchief and fan and bustled after the Greeleys.

The major caught up with her at the family's wagon just after she lifted Susana's little girl inside to Mary, the St. James's servant. "A moment, please!" Lightning illuminated the contrition on his face and the distaste of the Greeleys.

Vexation pressed Sophie's lips together. "Visit me at home on the morrow. We're off. We've no desire to get drenched tonight."

"I shall make sure you're home ahead of the storm."

Expelling annoyance, she motioned Susana to go on without her. Her sister glared from Sophie's earrings to the pendant at her throat, and acid stung her voice. "Wearing Mama's garnets. Such airs you give yourself lately. Must be the company you keep." Then she turned her back on Sophie to settle down children scampering over each other like squirrels hitting upon a cache of acorns.

Damp wind smelling of swamp, sand, and Piedmont red clay whipped Sophie's petticoat. Edward Hunt seized her hand. When they reached his horse, he vaulted into the saddle, and he and a private hoisted her up behind him. A tepid raindrop splashed her cheek as she wrapped her arms around him. They trotted for the road, passing wagons. When she glanced at the four accompanying soldiers, lightning illuminated a sheet of rain sweeping over Zeb's barn. The major spurred the horse into a gallop.

A quarter-hour later, ahead of the rain but followed by thunder, they arrived at the St. James house and print shop. The town stank of livestock, rotten fruit, and wood smoke. From the direction of the Red Rock Tavern, south of Town Square, came avian screeches and human cheers from a cockfight in progress. Two soldiers saluted their commander and rode south on the dusty main street lined by most of Alton's two-dozen wooden buildings — businesses on the ground floor, residences upstairs. The other two dismounted with their commander and Sophie.

Will's hounds, Achilles and Perseus, crawled from beneath the porch, shook off, and ambled over. She and Edward Hunt petted them before he escorted her to the porch, where she turned to him. "Thank you for bringing me home ahead of the rain."

"You're most welcome. May I come in for a moment? I've a matter to discuss."

"My sister and her husband will arrive before long."

"I don't need much time."

She nodded. He instructed his men to wait on the covered porch, removed his hat, and opened the door. They entered the stuffy darkness of the shop, where the St. Jameses also had a small post office and sold Will's almanacs, magazines, books, and maps. Thunder rattled the house. She closed the door and reached for the shelf beside it. The absence of the expected candle made her recall that she'd given the holder to Mary to clean. Scowling at the servant's laziness, she groped her way to the pressroom. "I've a candle in here."

Sharp and musty, the odors of ink and lye hung in the air. With the lantern lit, she faced Edward, who'd followed her in. His gaze ranged over the clutter of ragpaper and the half-opened drawers of type before he set his hat atop a cabinet. "Are you assembling the galleys for Wednesday's paper?"

More thunder crackled, and the front window shook. "Yes."

"What will you print about the military incident on May twenty-ninth in the Waxhaws?"

The formality in his carriage indicated the all-business nature of the visit. "What's being called Buford's Massacre? I shall state facts — an engagement between regulars and militia from Virginia commanded by Buford, and His Majesty's provincials commanded by Tarleton — with the provincials victorious."

His nod was curt. "That's all that need be said about it."

"They're calling the engagement a massacre because Buford's men were supposedly cut down after they'd surrendered. Why did that happen?"

"I wasn't there. Without details, I cannot presume to know what invokes specific decisions of my superior officers."

"Could something like that happen here?"

"I've no comment."

"But would you cut down men who had surrendered?"

His smile was meant to be reassuring. "You're speculating, making yourself uncomfortable. We protect our colonies. We don't slay the King's friends."

Yes, it made her uncomfortable, but it made Major Edward Hunt uncomfortable, too. Buford's Massacre could happen anywhere. Were conditions right, it could happen in Alton, under his command. He was, after all, a soldier, and soldiers did what they were told. Her responsive smile felt wooden. "You're right, of course. It's foolish for me to alarm myself."

From the way his shoulders relaxed, she knew she'd said what he wanted to hear. He approached her, his expression agreeable. "I've never told you before, but the hue of your eyes reminds me of dawn in Hampshire."

A flush tingled her cheeks. No one ever said things to her like that. Most of the men from Georgia were so ordinary.

"Perhaps even the luster of silver."

How charming, especially when her father had once told her that all his children had eyes the color of common slate and hair like coal. "You flatter me, sir."

He leaned over, extinguished the lantern, and captured her hands in his, brushing his lips over her fingers. "Edward," he whispered. Then he kissed her palms and wrists. His lips delivered intriguing moisture and softness between her forefinger and thumb, the sensation contrasting with memories of two husbands' clumsiness.

A thunderclap faded, and a horse nickered. He murmured, "My darling, you have enslaved me."

She swallowed, uneasy at his departure from their intellectual relationship, her stomach fluttering again, and withdrew her hands to fumble for the lantern. "I must make sure the windows are —"

"I'm sorry about tonight." He recaptured her hands and reeled her to him, just the outline of his face visible. "I wanted to dance with you."

"You had your priorities." Her unease deepened. Where was this leading?

"I shall make it up to you. My temporary assignment in Alton is over. I'm returning to England. Come with me. Let me take you away from all this barbarism."

She gaped at him in the darkness. Disbelief and instinct almost caused her to recoil. "This comes as quite a surprise."

"Have you misunderstood my attentions?" He grasped her shoulders. "I'm in love with you." He slid his hands down her arms and around her waist. After brushing his lips over her collarbone, he trailed them down where her shift peeked from the neckline of her jacket, and his hands guided her hips against his. "Kiss me."

Her lips opened for his, and from the way his loins performed with hers, she fancied he knew far more of the act than porcine grunting atop a woman. Mechanical response stirred within her body, too long asleep, and her initial shock ebbed, but her brain nagged that his charm obscured something. She turned her face aside. "You're going home?"

His lips pursued her throat. "When my replacement arrives."

"But this war is far from over."

"My elder brother died. I've inherited the family estates."

The slow percussion of raindrops pattered the roof while kisses traveled to her temple. She frowned. He must be feigning his fondness, hoping she'd tell him about rebel printing runs. "Surely the Crown can ill afford to lose your military expertise. And I really must close all the windows."

He pressed her hips to his again. "The Hunts are well-regarded in Parliament." Translation: He, like other officers weary of a war with no end in sight, had used wealth and Parliamentary connections to buy his way out of the American conflict. "Let me show you what civilization is. Come with me."

One little detail hadn't yet been discussed. "As your wife." She made it a statement, not a question.

"Ah." The tempo of his kisses slowed, even as the rhythm of raindrops quickened. "Well, there's a financial empire at stake with my fifteen-year-old cousin, Beatrice, having come of marriageable age, and —"

"Wait a moment." She wiggled out of his embrace. "You're saying you want me with you as your *mistress.*" Certainly not a slight to a woman's worth, and a more desirable arrangement than matrimony when the man was grateful to be in the company of his mistress, having come from a shrewish wife and whining offspring. But Sophie's thoughts spun. How in the world could she have so misread him? Worse, had she misread herself?

"Not to worry. I shall arrange a fashionable townhouse in London for you."

He nibbled the knuckles of her right hand. "My duties in Parliament will take me there at least twice a month. We can be together during those nights."

Edward did indeed sound as though he belonged among the "grateful." Plus, two mediocre marriages, eight years of widowhood, and a measure of financial independence had made Sophie indifferent toward matrimony.

But anxiety lurched around in her stomach. In the American colonies, where a woman could manage a plantation or operate a printing press, weren't she and Edward sharing an illusion of equality created by their intellectual relationship?

And there was the matter of that age difference between Edward and Beatrice. "How happy will you be married to a girl who's younger than my daughter? You've almost a quarter-century more life experiences than she. Believe me, I know. My first marriage was at fifteen."

"That's why I need you. You and I discuss Plato and Euclid and Shakespeare." He kissed her left palm. "You understand what operating a business is about. Operating estates is like that, but on a grander scale. Beatrice and I have little in common."

"Except consummating a financial empire and placating friends in Parliament."

"Sophie, would you stay here running the press for the rest of your life? Between the Creek, Spaniards, French, and roving outlaws, Alton could be a pile of rubble within five years."

"Within five years, your cousin will have borne you children, and you'll have that bond with her. Where will I be?"

"I know you aren't happy here." He grasped her shoulders again. "You've never tasted fine wine or felt silk against your skin. You've never been to the Drury Lane theater or heard a symphony. I'm offering you a way to experience all that."

She considered treasures beyond her economic reach: fine wine, silk, symphonies, the theater. She also thought of the times she'd collapsed into bed, bone-tired from a printing run. Edward's offer provided splendid passage out of Alton, a dream women in her position would lunge for with no reservations. It was just the opportunity she'd been waiting for, wasn't it?

What would happen if her intellectual parity with him didn't survive crossing the Atlantic? She sighed, still disoriented, confused. "I shall consider it."

"What's to consider? Ah, you don't love me, do you?" He paused, reflecting. "It's hard to love in circumstances where you're preoccupied with survival. If you freed yourself from those fears, you might grow to love me. And with that thought —" He kissed her left hand again. "I shall bid you good night."

The rain had slackened, so Edward retrieved his hat, and she walked him out the front door. Halfway back to the pressroom, she paused, sniffed, and frowned at the faint redolence of squashed strawberries. When she groped her way into the dining room, her shoe skidded on something slippery. She fumbled a lantern lit and held it up to view the bowl of strawberries she'd put on the table earlier and at least a dozen berries on the floor. With the lantern held high, she headed for the stairs. At the foot of the stairs she spotted a man's boot print: a man who had stepped in strawberries.

Her stomach tensed, and her gaze leaped up the staircase. "Father? Are you there?" Receiving no answer, she returned to the dining room and noticed another boot print. An explanation spiked a chill through her. Burglary! During the dance, the thief had entered through the back door, bumped into the table, spilled strawberries, and proceeded to the stairs, leaving two strawberry boot prints behind.

And for all she knew, he might still be in the house with her that moment.

Chapter Four

SOPHIE RUSHED TO the front door and flung it open, but the soldiers had already ridden off into the steamy night sprinkle. After shutting the door, she braced herself against it until her knees stopped knocking. Then, anger coating her fear, she squared her shoulders, marched into the pressroom, and flung open the cabinet where Will kept one of two sets of pistols in the house. No thief was going to steal her family's property.

At the foot of the stairs, she reexamined the print, made by a man with larger feet than her father's, so the culprit had probably been taller. The lantern held aloft, she crept to the landing, loaded pistol ready, her breath sucked in soft gasps.

For a dozen heartbeats, she listened to the sough of wind, creaking boards, and raindrops spattering the roof from branches of fruit trees. Then she nudged bedroom doors open, one by one.

No one jumped at her from the four bedrooms. However, someone had searched her room and her father's room — drawers left ajar with their contents jumbled, furniture repositioned, beds mussed.

Loath to verify the plunder of her mother's jewelry in her own room, she found it untouched, as were Spanish doubloons and two century-old horse pistols in her father's room. Baffled, she lit Will's bedroom lantern. What was he searching for, the stranger who violated their privacy earlier that night?

Instinct wailed that something was missing, something small but not insignificant. She glanced over the nightstand and retraced steps she'd made earlier, when she'd shut her father's window before leaving for the dance. Her gaze returned to the nightstand. Had a peculiar book been sitting there? *Confessions* by St. Augustine, a gift her father mentioned receiving that afternoon from his friends in Philadelphia.

She searched the floor around the bed to no avail, still wondering whether she remembered seeing *Confessions* there at all. When she straightened, fear and anger ebbed, replaced by a muddle of emotions. Why would an intruder steal a book? More perplexing, why would Will tolerate such a book when he didn't even keep the family Bible in his bedroom? With titles such as *Common Sense* by Thomas Paine and *On Secular Authority* by Martin Luther dominating his library of revolutionary thought, a book about self-denial looked mighty odd.

The major question of the night resurrected itself. Where was Will St. James?

Voices out front drew her to her bedroom window. John trundled down from the driver's seat of the Greeleys' wagon, parked in the muddy street. Leaving the loaded pistol behind, she trotted downstairs and opened the front door. In slogged Mary the servant, bronze hair plastered over her jacket and down her back. "Got caught in the rain, Mrs. Barton."

Sophie brushed past her into the humidity of the porch. "John, we've had a burglar!"

"Oh, for god's sake," said Susana, shaking water from her mobcap out of her eyes. "Is the villain still there?"

"No."

John climbed into the driver's seat. "What did he steal?"

"One of Father's books, I believe."

Susana and John burst into laughter, and Susana added, "We're exhausted and drenched, Sophie. Report the theft to your precious redcoat on the morrow." She laughed again. "And here's an excellent caption in your newspaper. 'Book-Stealing Scoundrel Burgles Newspaper Editor's House.'"

John snapped the reins. "Heigh! Get up!" With a jerk and a creak, the wagon rolled through the mud and off into the night.

A puddle of water had collected beneath Mary, who looked woebegone. Sophie closed the front door and flung her hands up. "Well, don't just stand there. Get yourself into dry clothing."

***

"Mrs. Barton! Wake up! Please, wake up!"

From somewhere below, Sophie heard pounding on a door and the hounds barking. She fended Mary's hands off her shoulders and bolted upright, trying to shake the fuzzies from her head.

Terror writhed across Mary's face by candlelight. "There's two Spaniards at the back door calling for your father. We'll be ravished and murdered! By *Spaniards!*"

Spaniards. Sophie shoved the girl aside and climbed out of bed. "Take hold of your wits. Have you ever fired a pistol?"

"Wh-what? You want me to sh-shoot them?"

"Never mind. Just stay out of my way." Flinging a shawl over her shift, she grabbed the pistol and Mary's lantern. After verifying that Will wasn't in bed, she padded downstairs ahead of her shivering servant.

With the pistol hid behind her, she hung the lantern beside the back door and opened it. In the yard, Achilles and Perseus growled at two Spaniards who stood shoulder-to-shoulder on her step. The men's glowers transformed into leers at the sight of her, and her fingers flexed on the butt of the pistol. "For what purpose do you interrupt our sleep?"

The man on her right murmured to his partner, "*La hija del Lobo.*" The daughter of the Wolf. The Wolf. Was that some sort of alias for Will? A lie wouldn't hurt. Her voice sliced the damp night air. "Speak English, for I understand no Spanish."

The smile of the other man broadened. He muttered to his companion, "*Es muy bonita,*" before addressing her. "*Señora,* we have urgent business with *Señor* Will St. James."

"It will wait until the morrow. Begone." When she shoved the door with her foot, his hand blocked it from closing. She whipped out the pistol, cocked it fully, and leveled the barrel at his nose, hoping he couldn't see her heart pounding in her throat. Both Spaniards' eyes bulged in shock. "Away, or I'll blow someone's miserable brains from here to Madrid."

They backed from the door, their stares on the pistol, the dogs still growling. She slammed the door shut with her foot and extinguished the lantern. "Mary, drop the bars across both doors." If Will came home, he'd have to sleep in the stable.

Mary complied, and Sophie peeked out the dining room window, but it was too dark to see much. She strode into the shop and peered out the windows while Mary barred the front door. Nothing.

"A-A-Are they gone?"

Sophie sighed, certain the girl was twisting her fingers in her shift. Having an indentured servant had seemed a good option to slavery, which Sophie abhorred, but Mary possessed neither spine nor brains. "I hope so. Make sure all windows on the ground floor are closed."

Back in the pressroom, she lit a lantern and loaded another pistol. She and Mary secured the house, and she sent the girl up to bed, forcing herself to remain awake another hour. The Spaniards didn't return, and the dogs calmed.

Still, when she trudged up to bed at two o'clock Sunday morning, she carried the pistols with her. In the doorway of her father's bedroom, she paused to whisper, "What's become of you?"

***

"Mrs. Barton! Wake up! Please, wake up!"

Not again. Sophie moaned and rolled over in bed, opening one eye. This time, at least it was daylight.

Mary set a towel and pitcher of water beside the washbasin. "Major Hunt is downstairs asking for you, and he brought that — that unpleasant Lieutenant Fairfax and a dozen soldiers!"

Dread clambered over Sophie. "Inform him I'll be down in five minutes. Then help me dress." Mary curtsied and scurried out. Sophie rolled from bed, tied her hair back with a ribbon, and sloshed water in the basin. By the time Mary returned, she was already blotting off her face.

Edward appeared to have passed the night in the same restless state she had, and his expression filled with duty when she entered the shop. Fairfax, too, had bags under his eyes, but vitality blossomed across his face at the sight of her. Outside, a sea of redcoats blocked her view of the street. She said, "May I serve you gentlemen something to drink?"

Edward shook his head. "I would speak with your father. Where is he this morning? His horse isn't stabled."

"I don't know where he is. He didn't come home last night."

He extended his arm in Fairfax's direction. From a leather portfolio, Fairfax withdrew a broadside. Edward showed it to Sophie. It depicted a redcoat bayoneting a kneeling militiaman, and the caption read, "Tarleton's Quarter."

She touched her fingers to her mouth in horror, unable to tear her gaze from the gruesome image. "Ye gods." So that's what the Committee had printed two nights before. "How horrid."

His expression hard, Edward handed the broadside back to Fairfax. "We found ten of them posted about town. Since the print run lasted most of Friday night, there were clearly more than ten printed. Where are the rest?"

"I've no idea. I'd nothing to do with it."

This time Fairfax handed him a newspaper. Edward held it out for her, and she examined it. "Last Wednesday's paper."

He nodded. "You supervised the printing?"

"Yes." She glanced at Fairfax. His eyes glittered. His face held the rapture of a saint who has communed with angels. The ache in her belly flared like dry kindling on a banked campfire.

Edward directed her attention to an advertisement for Zeb's dance. "Notice the crease in the lowercase 'e' of Mr. Harwick's first name."

"Yes." Her mouth dry, she sensed what was coming.

"Examine the broadside again. What do you see in the lowercase 'e' of Colonel Tarleton's name?"

"A crease in the curve." She silently lambasted her father for not having been more cautious.

"Would that not imply that these documents were printed by the same hand?"

She lifted her chin. "Yes, but I've already told you I'd nothing to do with the production of that broadside."

Edward returned both papers to Fairfax. "Where were you during the print run two nights ago?"

"Asleep upstairs."

"While eight men crowded the pressroom the night before last and printed copy after copy of a broadside, you never woke up?"

"I sleep soundly."

"Weren't you curious as to your father's visitors?"

"Why should I be? His business is his own."

"I shall ask you again. Where is your father right now?"

"I told you I don't know."

Fairfax stepped forward, his face angelically beautiful. "Sir, allow me a few minutes alone with her. I assure you I shall find out everything she knows about the rebel operations."

Unable to hold Fairfax's unearthly stare of frigid green, she sought humanity in Edward's eyes. "Cease this foolish prattle. You *know* King George is my sovereign."

Fairfax's nostrils twitched. "False loyals profess fidelity to His Majesty even as the noose is draped round their necks."

Edward sounded bored. "Fairfax, as you were." The lieutenant subsided into silence, a rare hound with the intelligence to curb his barking instinct, but

Sophie stayed tense. Edward scrutinized her. "Show me your lowercase e's."
"Of course. I'll even help you find the creased letter, but it's circumstantial evidence." Pivoting, she did her best to flounce into the pressroom, despite her fluttering heart. Edward followed and observed while she sorted through a tray of vowels. "Someone burgled my house last night while I was at the dance."
"What was stolen?"
"One of my father's books."
"I believe you know far too much about the dealings of these rebels to be considered innocent."
She barked a laugh. "My skill at deducing what's missing from my house makes me suspect. How logical. What if I said two Spaniards came banging on my door in the middle of the night?"
"Spaniards." An edge cut his voice. "What did they want?"
"Will St. James. My loaded pistol convinced them to conduct their business in broad daylight." Shutting the tray, she turned to him and deposited an "e" in his hand. "Here's the evidence with which I may be damned."
His hand closed about the letter. "I hate arresting you, but you've been a passive accomplice in rebel operations."
"He's my father. Am I supposed to betray my own blood?"
"Your 'own blood' has vanished and allowed you to be implicated in his stead."
She unclamped her teeth. "I presume you've arrested those who assisted my father at printing?"
"Unfortunately not. After being questioned, they've not admitted to wrongdoing."
And they had no circumstantial evidence against them. Enraged that culpability for rebel operations had fallen on her, she wondered if she could shift the blame where it belonged. "How may I prove my innocence?"
He wrapped the "e" in cloth, tucked it in his waistcoat pocket, and withdrew a small piece of paper. It bore a scrawled list of numbers beginning *seventeen, four, twenty-five, sixteen, forty-nine, eleven.* "Does this mean anything to you?" She shook her head. "It's a cipher intended for your father."
"How do you know that? And where did you find it?"
He ignored her questions. "Our expert on codes has yet to break it." He handed her the paper. "Decode it within a day. Give me your word that you'll not try to escape, and I shall let you remain under house arrest while you're working on it."
She gaped in dismay from the numbers to him. "What makes you think I can succeed where your expert failed?"
"You know your father better than we do. Your success will convince me of your innocence and exonerate you. Otherwise, I must escort you to jail."
"But you still haven't told me how you know the cipher was intended for my father. How do I know you aren't just sending me on a fool's errand?"
His voice quieted. "Trust me. I'm allowing you house arrest, and that involves considerable trust on my part."
She comprehended the risk he took. No one had made that kind of sacrifice for her. Softness unfolded in her soul. "I appreciate your trust. I shall give it my best endeavor and not attempt escape." She paused. "But don't ciphers

require a key?"

"Indeed." He motioned her to follow him back out into the shop. Along the way, she wondered how the pressroom fireplace had come to look so tidy overnight. Near Fairfax, Edward faced her. "The key to this cipher is in a book by Saint Augustine."

Sophie's jaw dangled. "*Confessions*? Why, that's the very book stolen last night! If you wish me to succeed, you must find a copy of that exact edition for my use. I doubt anyone in Alton has such material. You might have luck in Augusta."

"Lieutenant, give Mrs. Barton the book."

Fairfax stared at Edward as if he misunderstood. "Sir?"

Sophie stared at Edward, understanding at last. The softness in her soul withered to ash, and a dank sense of violation spilled into the void. Glancing to the base of the stairs, she spotted the strawberry boot print. She stared at Edward's boots: the same size. She could also count on the soldiers to extract any evidence the confiscated charred woodcut yielded. Why didn't they violate her house Friday night and arrest eight men in the act of sedition? Perhaps it was more convenient to arrest one woman on circumstantial evidence.

Anger flooded her soul. How dared Edward do this to her?

He passed her the copy of *Confessions* he'd removed from Will's night-stand. "Mrs. Barton is under house arrest."

"Sir, I remind you of regulations concerning rebel spies —"

"Thank you, Lieutenant. She has agreed to decode the message in exchange for the privilege of house arrest."

"Sir, the regulations are clear. No privileges may be —"

"You will select two suitable men and station them here, within the St. James home."

"But, sir —"

"Lieutenant, need I remind you of your role as my subordinate?"

The volcano capped itself, and non-emotion resumed residence on the face of Fairfax. "Sir." He stood at attention.

"Mrs. Barton requires no interruptions, no visitors."

Sophie gripped the book, white-knuckled with fury. "What of my brother? Surely you know he has no dealings with rebels."

"One ten-minute visitation with David St. James."

"Sir."

"And secure all firearms." Edward leaned closer to Fairfax and lowered his voice until she could barely distinguish his words. "El Serpiente was here last night looking for St. James." El Serpiente — alias for a Spanish spy? "The men chosen for this assignment must *protect* Mrs. Barton." Edward straight-ened and regarded her. "I leave you now in the capable hands of Lieutenant Fairfax." He glanced at the time on a watch from his waistcoat pocket. "I shall return for the deciphered message on the morrow at precisely eight-thirty." After a short bow, he exited out the front door.

"You will surrender all firearms to me immediately."

Sophie repressed a shudder at the thought of being in Fairfax's "capable" hands for a full twenty-four hours. Perhaps if she cooperated, he'd leave her alone, and she'd only have to deal with the two soldiers. "This way."

Chapter Five

SEVENTEEN, FOUR, TWENTY-FIVE, sixteen, forty-nine, eleven...Numbers in odd positions of the cipher increased, but those in even positions followed no pattern. Sophie decided she might as well assume the message began on page seventeen.

If he fell in love with me, I might fall in love with him, too. Could she love a man who'd burgled her house and arrested her? Could she *sleep* with him? Did he love her? What did she want from him?

Back to the cipher. At the desk in her bedroom, she copied the fourth word on page seventeen to a sheet of paper, and the sixteenth word on page twenty-five, and so on before realizing the scheme was too obvious. Next she copied first letters of words. Gibberish. She inverted the order of letters. More gibberish.

Ensign Baldwin knocked on her door. "Mrs. Barton, your brother has arrived. Shall I admit him?"

She sprang up and yanked open the door. "Yes, straight away." David trod upstairs, and she motioned him inside.

He shut the door and sat on her bed. "News of your arrest is all over town. What the deuce is going on?"

"I shall be jailed on the morrow if I don't decipher *this*." After showing him the cipher, she summarized the past twelve hours and finished with, "Did you see the broadside?"

"Oh, yes, posted around Alton this morning, so townsfolk have seen it, too. Despite efforts to hush the affair, the broadside keeps reappearing. No one can catch the perpetrators."

"What did you think of the broadside?"

"Definitely not MacVie's best artwork." With a beguiling smile, he dodged her swipe at him. "Seriously, the full story has emerged from the Waxhaws incident. Colonel Buford invited massacre upon his men — first by refusing to surrender, then by continuing to fight after raising the white flag."

"The fool."

"No greater fool than Colonel Tarleton, who allowed his soldiers to hack men to pieces. Sanity has fled both sides. Your arrest confirms fears of Loyalists that the redcoats prey on their own. It also confirms the convictions of rebels that everyone's a patriot."

She grimaced at the implication. "I don't fit the profile for a heroine. I complain far too much."

"True, but you could still end up being a martyr."

They locked gazes, and a rare furrow appeared between his eyebrows, sign that he'd leaped from the happy-go-lucky wagon of his life into the carriage of concern. A lump formed in her throat before she rose and fumbled through papers on her desk. "So tell me, what do you make of this?"

He shrugged at the numbers. "The old man is in over his head. Sit in his room awhile. Let him tell you what it means."

"I cannot decipher it. I shall be jailed on the morrow."

The furrow between his eyebrows deepened, and he stared through her. "Jailed? I've a hunch not."

Baldwin rapped on her door. "Your ten minutes are up, Mr. St. James."

"A hunch, you say?" she whispered.

David rose, and the furrow disappeared, replaced with his familiar complacency. "A feeling I get when the cards are right. Players around the table change. Captain John Sheffield and Lieutenant Michael Stoddard arrived in town this morning. Hunt will be returning to England, and Fairfax will be transferred to the Seventeenth Light in South Carolina." He hugged her. "So chin up. You'll triumph."

***

She ate dinner in the dining room while pondering the change in the garrison's command. Back up in her room, she paced and tried more decoding schemes, but they resulted in gibberish. She kept wondering whether Captain Sheffield would dispense with house arrest and jail her after Edward left town.

Her patience grown short, her bedroom grown warm, she leaned out the window for a view of the town. Goats roamed loose pilfering neighbors' garden greens, and chickens flitted out of the way of two boys running a hoop in the dirt street. Wood smoke dulled the sky. Years of sun and rain had bleached the wood buildings to a uniform gray. How drab Alton looked. She pulled back inside and sat on the bed. Was Hampshire more colorful? Not that she need waste time wondering, for surely Edward's offer had become void.

Conversation in the shop preceded the tramp of boots up the stairs, a rap on her door, and an unfamiliar man's voice. "Mrs. Barton, I must speak with you." Shoulders squared, she opened the door to a dark-haired British lieutenant in his mid-twenties, mild-featured despite a cluster of pimples on his chin. He stood at attention, looking beyond her. "Lieutenant Stoddard at your service, madam. I regret to inform you that your father met with foul play, we believe sometime between ten last night and two this morning. As neither your sister nor brother can be located this moment, we require your attendance at the scene to confirm identification of the body."

In the first second, the news speared her with panic and fear. Then she clamped down on it. Will St. James — dead? Absolutely not. A deep suspicion that the redcoats were baiting a trap carved through her. She glowered at Stoddard. "As you wish." He turned on his heel, and she followed him downstairs, the cipher forgotten.

***

Their destination was on Zack MacVie's property. Feeling her neck branded by summer, she adjusted her straw hat, dismounted the sweating horse just outside a copse of hardwoods, and handed the reins to a private supervising horses.

Nearby, Mathias Hale stood with Edward, the scarlet of Edward's uniform vivid against the lush countryside. Although she couldn't pick out their conversation, she watched Mathias pivot and bow his head against his horse's saddle, and her confidence sputtered. Could Will truly be dead? Dread seeping into her heart, she hastened after Stoddard, who made for the copse.

He stomped vines out of her way. Upon entering the cool shade, she passed a tethered horse, then her nose was assaulted by the stench of charred meat. While her eyes adjusted to shade, she spotted sheets draping three bodies. What devilry was this? Had there been *three* murders? Memory of Mathias's posture of grief knotted her stomach.

Both lieutenants were afoot among the moldering leaves of the copse, and Stoddard addressed Fairfax. "I didn't expect to find you here. What brings you this way?"

Fairfax took position above the gore-soaked sheet near Sophie. "I'm solving murders and appreciate your leaving the premises before you destroy evidence. Sir."

Sophie flushed at Fairfax's rudeness. Stoddard closed the distance between them and swelled his chest. Although he was Fairfax's height, the russet-haired lieutenant outweighed him by at least twenty-five pounds, all of it muscle, making Stoddard look scrawny. "I was given charge of this investigation at one o'clock. *You* and your commander have been transferred from this garrison. Sir."

"How unfortunate. Sir. I presume you've skill solving crimes?"

"I've tracked down burglars and livestock thieves."

"Capital. Such depth of experience should stand you on firm ground in the realm of violent death."

"And *you've* skill solving crimes of violence?"

"Four cases of arson, three abductions, five murders. I no longer count the burglaries and livestock thefts." Fairfax glanced beyond her and came to attention, mockery departing his expression.

Leaves rustled behind Sophie. Edward interposed himself between her and the nearest body, diplomacy smoothing his tone. "No need for concern, Mr. Fairfax. I believe we can turn the investigation over to Mr. Stoddard with confidence."

Sophie shuddered. Being stationed in frontier Georgia offered an ambitious junior officer little opportunity for advancement. Fairfax must have jumped at the chance to perform early investigative work. Now that Stoddard was going to take all the credit for solving the crimes, he was fuming.

Edward turned to her, the gravity in his expression ringing sincere for an officer who dealt with murder, and lowered his voice. "I wish I could shield you. Not one, but three men lie slain here."

Compassion tugged at her heart at the thought of Mathias. "Who?"

"Jonah Hale, his throat slit. A Spaniard, flayed alive —"

"A Spaniard?" Flayed alive. Her stomach protested.

"The murderer left his face untouched. I ask you to verify whether he was one who threatened you last night."

She nodded, lightheaded of a sudden. "I shall do my best. And what —" She gulped. "What of my father?"

"Burned at the stake."

No, this was unreal. She gaped at him, horrified. Will St. James burned at the stake. Jonah Hale's throat slit. A Spaniard flayed alive. The Indians were well known for such gruesome executions. Disbelief and betrayal rattled her, and she clenched her jaw to keep from mentioning Mathias's meeting with four Creek warriors the night before. She'd experienced firsthand the power of circumstantial evidence and refused to implicate the Creek when many were quick to blame them for anything that went wrong. Besides it was quite possible the murderers *intended* to implicate the Creek. "Show me the Spaniard while I still have my mettle."

Edward led her to the body guarded by Fairfax, which lay twenty-five feet from the other two bodies. At a gesture from Edward, Stoddard stepped back from the corpse. Edward nodded to Fairfax. "His face." Fairfax knelt, fanned away an arabesque of flies, and uncovered the head.

The dead man had been the one who labeled her "Daughter of the Wolf." Sophie's skin crawled at the torment twisting his expression. Surely a corpse's face shouldn't retain such agony. It was unnatural, diabolical. "Yes. He was at my house last night." Who could be so barbaric as to kill another human being meticulously, with such torture? She wished she'd done the Spaniard a favor by blowing his brains out with her pistol.

Edward studied her. "What time did he come to your house?"

"One in the morning. Where's his partner?" She realized her hands were shaking and pressed them together to still them. "And is — was — this man El Serpiente?"

"His partner is El Serpiente, and we don't know where he is. Let's finish this business so we can bury the bodies." Edward walked off, his boots crunching leaves and twigs.

Her attention shifted from the dead Spaniard to Fairfax, and her stomach torqued. Tenderness wreathed the lieutenant's face as he draped the sheet back over the corpse's head — the kind of fondness one reserves for an object of devotion. He noticed her observing him then, regained his familiar non-emotion, and rose. She backed away in revulsion and hurried to Edward, who had paused beside the second body, leaving it covered.

The third sheet-covered body drew her attention, and a mechanical part of her brain registered details. A scorched post nearby about five feet tall. A zone cleared of grass and leaves around the post. Six buckets of dirt. Someone had planned it well enough to take precautions against the fire getting out of control.

Edward shook his head over the second body. "We all know Jonah Hale was a rebel. St. James might have betrayed them, and they took his life. Perhaps he and Hale betrayed the group. Or perhaps the Spaniards killed St. James, and Hale, seeing the blaze, hastened over and met his death at their hands. Ah, but who killed the Spaniard?"

Her neck tingled, and she resisted an urge to gape at Fairfax. She really didn't want to know what was going on inside his head. Fortunately, Fairfax had untied and mounted his horse. "I've picked over the area well in the last hour," he snapped to Stoddard from the saddle. "Do let us know whether you find evidence. And, by the by, there is a cure for pimples. You find yourself a lusty wench and plough her every day and night for a month straight — but I don't suppose you'd know about the plough, having spent so long with your own shovel buried in guano."

Stoddard held Fairfax's gaze, and even through Sophie's personal jumble of emotion, she couldn't help but admire the dark-haired lieutenant's professionalism at expressing only detachment. "My benefactor raised peregrines, not seafowl."

Edward's mouth tightened, and steel infused his tone. "Mr. Fairfax, you may fetch the surgeon now." He then guided her to the third body, where the stench of incinerated flesh dangled her on the edge of retching. Still, her nose tried to identify another stench that the fire almost obscured. Edward lifted the sheet.

The thing beneath it looked like a sketch she'd seen of a pharaoh's mummy, shriveled and blackened. The mechanical part of her brain took control again, sweeping her scrutiny the length of the body, past charred clothing, up along the withered face and familiar shape of the nose and brow, back to the incinerated waistcoat and crispy remnant of trim she'd promised to repair. No, this wasn't real!

She gagged. Tears cresting her eyes, she bolted from the stench to the edge of the copse, dragged her apron over her mouth, and half-sobbed, half-gagged several times. Her tears dried up, yet she kept shaking. That burned thing had looked demonic, not human. It wasn't Will. He couldn't be dead. She'd just talked with her living, breathing father last night. The cremated abomination wasn't Will, no, no, no!

Desperate for the release of tears, she squinted toward the sun and blinked, but tears didn't come. Mathias still stood beside his horse. She didn't blame him for not rushing home to tell his stepfather. Old Jacob Hale adored his son, Jonah.

Edward joined her, his face haggard. "We found this on the body." He showed her a blackened ring. "His wedding band?"

Her heart wrenched again. "We never understood why he kept wearing it. He could have remarried."

"Do you want it back?"

She extended her hand and closed fingers over the ring when he dropped it onto her palm. She imagined feeling her father's heartbeat trapped within the ring, pulsing a whisper: "Not dead."

Her chin jerked up. "It appears you no longer need my assistance with the cipher."

"To the contrary, we need you to decode it more than ever. In return, we shall place as much priority as possible on bringing your father's murderer to the gallows."

The cipher's decoded message might hold a clue to Will's murder, but it was more certain to provide information of rebel espionage. Heartsick, she envisioned the Crown's idea of justice as contingent upon first trussing up a spy ring. "I'm unable to work on it today. Please tell Captain Sheffield I shan't have the translation ready —"

"Sophie." He rubbed his neck. "Promise that we shall have your coopera-tion. Promise you'll stay in your house."

"I've already given you my word on the matter." Grief and outrage plunged her ahead. "Folk will want to pass along condolences to me. Am I still denied visitors?" He hesitated, and she ground her teeth in desperation. "I've sworn to you I'm innocent of dealings with the rebels! Allow me to come to terms with my father's — with this catastrophe. Allow me visitors."

"Very well. You may have one visitor at a time for five minutes, and a sol-dier must be present during each visitation."

Such a decision wouldn't go over well with the garrison. Edward would have to soothe Fairfax, that watchdog of regulations, and minimize the wildfire of gossip through the ranks about the colonial frill who'd enchanted their com-manding officer. Perhaps Edward did love her. "Thank you."

"I shall visit you this evening."

She wished he needn't bother. She didn't covet the company of someone who'd burglarized her house, and she wasn't in the mood to hear Edward re-tract his offer from the previous night. But he'd allowed her extravagant privi-leges. "Don't bring Mr. Fairfax."

A dry chuckle escaped him. "I shan't."

Her father's ring tucked in her pocket, she walked over to the horses, where she paused behind the blacksmith before resting her hand on his shoulder. "I'm sorry. I shall miss Jonah." Her throat shuddered. A childhood friend murdered. Tears gathered in her eyes, only to be dammed up again. She squeezed her lips together and sniffed.

Mathias swiveled and embraced her, his voice a whisper. "My condolences for the loss of your father, a friend to all who —" He broke off. She felt tension in his body soar, as though at any second he would dissolve into lamentation, but he maintained control. "I shall find who murdered him and avenge his death."

Did he speak of avenging Jonah or Will? "Stay clear of the soldiers," she whispered.

He coughed with derision before grasping her hand and walking with her a few feet from the horses. "Three enemies of the Crown are dead," he said, low. "Don't expect the redcoats to trouble themselves solving the murders. As far as they're concerned, justice has been served." Determination fired his expres-sion. "If we want answers, we shall have to find them ourselves. But you've been arrested."

"House arrest. A cipher supposedly intended for my father fell into Major Hunt's hands. In exchange for decoding it, I exonerate myself from involve-ment with the rebels."

"Ah." He glanced over her shoulder. "Mr. Stoddard draws near. You and I must speak again."

"I'm allowed no privacy with my visitors."

He wrapped an arm about her shoulder and raised his voice for Stoddard to hear. "Take heart. You aren't as isolated as you believe." After releasing her, he retrieved his rifle and reins and hoisted himself into the saddle. With a nudge, he sent the horse eastward, back to town and the Hale smithy.

Stoddard brought her the horse she'd ridden. In the seconds that she watched the diminishing figure of the blacksmith on horseback, she concurred with Mathias. The redcoats wouldn't exert special effort to solve the murders. That meant it was the responsibility of the St. Jameses and the Hales to bring the killers of their loved ones to justice. Plagued by doubts of her father's love in his final months, she resolved that moment to find his murderer and show herself a worthy daughter.

Chapter Six

RANKLED OVER BEING implicated for the broadsides, stunned by her father's death, Sophie clung to composure while receiving condolences in her dining room. Who killed Will St. James? The redcoats had motive to arrest and imprison him, but burning him at the stake just wasn't their style. Indeed, the manner of his murder, hallmark of someone hell-bent on revenge, made his rebel cohorts, the mysterious El Serpiente, and the Indians suspects. So, suspects she had aplenty, but as for their motives —?

Private Barrows entered the dining room with a sour look. "A savage is outside. Says his name is something like As-say-see-cora." One shoulder jerked with dismissal. "Shall I get rid of him for you?"

She sat forward. "Assayceeta Corackall?" Runs With Horses, son of Madeleine le Coeuvre's adoptive sister, Laughing Eyes — what brought him to Alton? He seldom ventured into town.

"That's the fellow. You want to see him?"

"Please."

Barrows looked surprised. "But everyone thinks the savages killed those men."

Foreboding twined with her grief. She stood. "Please."

In contrast to the thud of Barrows' boots, Runs With Horses glided into the kitchen, his moccasins a whisper on the wood floor, his earrings and nose ring silent. Lines of dotted, charcoal-colored tattoos ornamented his bronze, shaven head and encircled his topknot of blue-black hair. A bandoleer of tiny charcoal tattoos extended from left shoulder to right hip, continuing over the portion of his right buttock visible outside his breechcloth and coiling down his right leg like a rattlesnake. He halted about two feet from her and bowed, the sigh of arrows brushing together in his quiver and a rancid whiff of bear grease the non-visual harbingers of his arrival. "Nagchoguh Hogdee." Paper

Woman.

The Creek slit enemies' throats, and flayed them alive, and — heaven forbid — burned them at the stake, but until she had a motive, she'd grant them the courtesy she'd always given them. "You honor my house with your visit, Assayceeta Corackall."

"As you have honored the house of my mother." Behind him, Barrows leaned against the doorjamb yawning, bored with condolences, perplexed by her choice of company. "The people send well wishes. The journey of Will St. James separates from yours for awhile, but Creator will again unite your paths."

Hardly the speech of a murderer or enemy. Intrigue gleamed in the onyx depths of Runs With Horses's eyes, sending a shiver through her. On a deep level, she sensed he wasn't just spouting Indian-speak. "And how do you know this, friend of my house?"

With peripheral vision Runs With Horses ascertained Barrows' inattention and reined back disdain. "We saw his spirit pass through the forest last night."

Yes, they would have, after all the times her father had visited the village. She bowed her head, by then certain the Creek weren't involved in Will's death. But unless the murderer was found, they'd be blamed. Sorrow thickened her voice. "You bring me great comfort. Thank you for your kindness."

Barrows escorted the warrior out. Sophie's attention wandered all afternoon. Susana drenched her sleeve with tears during her visitation. David kept a tight cover on his grief. Between two visits from Alton's undertaker, thirty townspeople paid their respects. She kept wondering what secret mission was worth dying for in such a horrendous manner. The redcoats, the rebels, the Spaniard: who killed Will? Through her head wove that column of numbers in the cipher.

Back in her bedroom Sunday evening, she studied the cipher while nudging ham and hominy around a pewter plate with her fork. With a sigh, she shoved the plate aside and cleaned her teeth. Then she set the supper tray at the top of the stairs. Jollity from Mary and both soldiers carried upstairs. Will's death created little stir in Mary's life, for it was Sophie who managed the finances. "Mary! Fetch my plate. I'm done with supper."

"Right away, Mrs. Barton."

In Will's room, Sophie eased into the rocking chair and thought about rocking Betsy, all full of squalls, brawls, and life, her dark hair tousled and damp. Five years later, she'd rocked a boy babe, born too soon, until his hold on the earth slipped away. Then she'd laid him to rest beside his tiny twin who'd never mewed signs of life.

There'd been no solace from Richard Barton, her second husband, away on business in North Carolina when she'd borne the twins in Augusta. He was always away on business, even when he was home. As soon as she could travel, she'd returned to Alton with little Betsy, where her family had given her the solace she needed. Not just her family, she recalled, but friends as well. The Carey brothers and their wives stammered out platitudes. Newlywed Joshua Hale and his wife were full of trite little sayings about life and love. Jonah Hale had mumbled out an "I'm sorry," then scurried off because he was still mourning his wife, who had succumbed to yellow fever earlier that summer — Jonah, whom she'd never see again. Sorrow clutched the back of her throat and receded without leaving her the relief of tears.

The visitor who stood out most in her mind from that time was Mathias Hale. Unmarried after his Creek wife, Stands Tall, had died in childbirth, he'd sat quietly with her one morning. When she'd asked him why he didn't speak, he'd said, "I figure by now everyone has said all the words and still not made it better, so I'll sit with you and not say anything." His stoic presence bolstered her more than anyone's shallow attempts at cheer. Mathias, she reflected, had always been anything but shallow.

The current of memories carried her farther back to a summer afternoon eighteen years before, to one of her earliest memories of Mathias's depth. A scant two weeks before she was to marry Jim Neely, she and the girls stole clothes from the boys at the swimming hole. On the opposite side of the pond she discovered and swiped Mathias's clothing. A good sport about it, he traded repartee while she returned articles of clothing one by one, starting with his left moccasin.

When he'd bent to help her disentangle her petticoat from brambles, across the ropy muscles and Creek tattoos on his left shoulder she'd seen an outrage: faded scars, legacy of his stepfather's wrath. Why did Jacob Hale beat him? Had Mathias let the fire in the forge go out or been slow with the bellows? Not likely. Jacob had never taken to his stepson, no flesh of his own. But still, that was no reason for Jacob to beat him.

Didn't his brothers know their father beat him?

Mathias had regarded her then, expression composed, precursor to his solace over her twins. Of course his brothers knew. How could they not know? *Sophie, do me a favor and don't say anything about it,* he'd said. *In fact, just forget about it.*

Sophie returned to Sunday, June 4, 1780 in the dusk. How peculiar that sitting in her father's bedroom should call to mind Mathias's depth. Yet something told her it wasn't coincidence.

She pulled the wedding band from her pocket and scrubbed scorch marks off with her fingernail. Tears pressured her throat, but when she waited for relief, the flood didn't come. Instead, a blaze in her insides burned the tears away. She didn't want to weep. With her bare hands, she wanted to strangle every redcoat, rebel, and Spaniard she could find. Will couldn't be forever gone. She expected him to stomp in through the back door at any moment calling for his supper. Exhaling despair and bewilderment, she closed her eyes, and another memory trickled into her head: Will with six-year-old Betsy on his knee.

***

"Grandpapa, what's your favorite animal?"
"A horse. He's smarter than most men I know, and he'll tell you who's the master."
"What's your favorite color?"
"Green. It's the color of the deep, untamed wilderness."
"And your favorite number?"
"Three, for my three children and three grandchildren."

***

Anxious, Sophie rose, pocketed the wedding band, and brushed her fingertip over one of three painted wooden soldiers ornamenting a bookshelf. Three clay pots of different sizes each contained tobacco for Will's pipe. On his desk she found quills for his inkpot and three seals. A shudder wove up her back and stirred her imagination. *Three.*

Back in her room, the door closed, a lantern lit, she opened *Confessions* to page seventeen and wrote the third letter of the fourth word. Next to it she wrote the third letter of the sixteenth word on page twenty-five, and from page forty-nine, pulled the third letter of the eleventh word. By the time she'd ferreted out twelve third letters from the book, she'd cracked the cipher. Those letters spelled "Don Alejandro."

Night settled over Alton while she dipped her quill in ink and extracted the message one letter at a time. Then she sat back and whispered, "Gods." *don alejandro de galvez awaits you midnight june seventeenth near old fort beware the serpent*

She knew who "the serpent" was. Had Will been supposed to meet a Spanish lord at midnight on June seventeenth but been killed by the serpent? "Don Alejandro" might know something — if she could talk with him.

Many forts in North America could be reached by a man on horseback within two weeks of leaving Alton. Where was the "old fort?" She correlated the page-word pairs with the letters to make sure she hadn't missed any, but she'd used them all. Edward wouldn't have kept any of the message from her. Perhaps Will had known his destination in advance. Or perhaps the clue to his destination was conveyed in another manner.

She rolled her head around to work kinks from her neck, picked up the book, and examined scratches on the front and back covers. None of it looked like secret code. The soldiers had slit the covers, hoping for clues. She examined the spine, still amazed that her father would tolerate material from a "damned Papist" in the house. And St. Augustine, of all people.

The chill slid up her backbone again. St. Augustine. *San Agustín.* Wasn't there an old Spanish fort at St. Augustine in East Florida?

Having acquired East Florida from Spain after the Old French War, Britain had booted most Spaniards out to Havana, then concentrated military attention on the thirteen colonies. The garrison and residents of St. Augustine formed a stronghold of the king's friends. The city hardly sounded like a haven for a meeting between a rebel courier and a Spanish lord, unless the meeting was facilitated by an agent in St. Augustine. How likely was it that a spy for Spain resided there?

The Congress was desperate for support from another European power like France. Spain had declared war on Britain in June of the previous year, then intrigued with France. But Spain hadn't made an official alliance with the American rebels. Even though rebels in the southern colonies won smaller battles, such as that fought not far from Alton at Kettle Creek the year before, the entire southern Continental army had surrendered to the redcoats just three weeks earlier in Charles Town. The Crown also held Augusta and Savannah. The rebels needed more direct intervention from Spain. Earning approval of a Spanish lord who had the ear of King Carlos couldn't hurt the rebel cause.

Time to make Edward aware that she'd cracked the code so he could exonerate her, and she could find out what else Mathias had needed to tell her. The folded paper in hand, she headed downstairs, entered the front shop, and stopped short, stalling a conversation between Barrows and Fairfax. Both men looked at her. What the deuce was Fairfax doing there instead of Edward? She slid the paper toward the pocket of her petticoat, but Fairfax missed nothing. "Barrows, it appears Mrs. Barton has completed her assignment."

"Yes. Inform Major Hunt that I've decoded the cipher."

"Excellent." He strode forward and shot out his hand. "I shall convey it to him."

"I'll give it to him when he arrives here tonight."

"Unfortunately, he's occupied with new issues." Was that worry in his tone? "He's unavailable to meet you tonight. Give me the translation."

She hesitated a second too long. Seizing her upper arm, Fairfax propelled her against the wall, where he pinned her wrist. With a gasp of pain and astonishment, she released the paper. He snatched it, still restraining her. "Mrs. Barton, can it be that you don't trust me?"

Fear and anger twisted round each other in her soul for a second or two before the same anger that parched her of tears crushed the fear. Fairfax would love to cow her. Rather than yielding to her desire to jam her knee into his groin, she glared at him. "Whatever gave you that idea?"

He released her. "I'm glad we understand each other. What have we here? Ah, Gálvez. Do you know who the Gálvez are?" She shook her head. "They've distinguished themselves in military service to the Spanish monarchy. Don Miguel: counselor of war. Don José: minister of the Indies. Don Matías: captain-general of Guatemala. Don Bernardo: brigadier-general and thorn in our side in West Florida. While I've not heard of Don Alejandro, the family is quite large. Cozying with the powerful Gálvez. How well this fits with our anticipation of rebel activities. I'm intrigued. How *did* you break the code?"

He thought she lied and was feeding the redcoats a story they expected to hear. Anger firmed her jaw. "My father's favorite number is three. Every letter in that message represents the third letter in a word in *Confessions*. Each word is identified in the list by page number and word number on the page."

"Show me an example of this scheme."

Turning about, she exited the shop, but it was too soon to breathe relief. Fairfax followed her up to her bedroom. By lantern light, she opened the book to page seventeen and brought the paper with the column of figures close while he spread the translation open on her desk. "You see, the third letter of the fourth word is a 'd,' and if you turn to page twenty-five, the third letter of the sixteenth word is an 'o.'"

"I see that. Where is the location of the 'old fort' specified in the translation?"

While heading up the stairs, she'd decided it would be a cold day in hell before she let Fairfax in on her hunch about St. Augustine. "Did I receive all the cipher to translate?"

"Yes, of course."

"Then that's the full message. I see no destination."

Angelic radiance transforming his expression, he stepped toward her, but she refused to retreat. His gaze tarried over her face, as if her resistance intrigued him. "Are you being honest with me?"

"Work it out for yourself. No destination is mentioned."
He regarded her a moment longer before sitting at the desk. While he flipped pages in *Confessions*, she walked to the window and leaned on the sill, longing to feel a breeze on her skin. After a few minutes, he stood and tucked the papers into a breast pocket. "Thank you very much." He swept from her room.

She descended to the shop in time to hear him tell Baldwin and Barrows, "For no reason must she leave the house tonight."

Eyes wide with incredulity, she stomped toward them. "I've performed my duty! I'm no longer under arrest. I must pay my respects to Jacob Hale."

"You'll stay in the house. Conditions have changed."

She balled her fists. "*What* conditions?"

"Someone manufactured a rumor about the garrison that those idiotic savages believed and took issue with. Major Hunt's orders. You remain in the house until he resolves the matter. On the morrow, I'm sure you'll be allowed to pay your respects."

The story was the biggest pile of hog dung Sophie had ever smelled. The Creek near Alton were of White-Stick persuasion, not Red-Stick. They'd been a peaceful people during her whole lifetime. Were that not the case, she and other residents of Alton would never have received invitations to join the Creek for certain festivals. No, she was *still* under house arrest. Fairfax had merely dressed it up in different clothing. "I must talk with Major Hunt."

"I shall relay your message. We protect the King's friends, Mrs. Barton. Remember that Baldwin and Barrows are here as a service to you. Good night." With a bow, he was out the front door, only to return in seconds, a clay flowerpot in his hand. "This was on your front porch. Someone sending condolences, I presume."

"Widow Flannery. Last night she promised to send me something for my garden." Sophie retrieved the pot from him, yellow daisies in dark soil. Odd, she could have sworn Mrs. Flannery had told her she'd send *herbs*, not daisies. "Thank you." Then she watched Fairfax leave again and finally let out that slow breath of relief.

Chapter Seven

MARY WAS FETCHING water from the well out back near the kitchen building when Sophie noticed a sliver of oiled paper protruding from the soil in the flowerpot. She held the pot closer to the lantern in the dining room, dug out the oiled paper, and unfolded it to find a strip inside displaying a cipher similar to the one she'd just decoded. Bewildered by the find, she jumped at the sound of Mary clattering to the back step with a full bucket and jammed the oiled paper and cipher in her pocket. Her expression composed, she stretched while the maid set the bucket on the table. "I'm for bed. Turn in after you've watered these daisies."

"Are those two soldiers spending the night?"

"Yes."

"Well, then, at least we won't have to worry about Spaniards or Indians causing us a fright in the wee hours of the morning."

Hearing the clack of dice on the counter in the shop, Sophie smiled with irony. "Such a comfort."

She poked her head into the shop and bade the men goodnight before heading upstairs, feet dragging in pretense of weariness. But behind her closed bedroom door, she rushed to the desk and spread the new cipher open. Fairfax had left *Confessions* on her desk. Did the new cipher use the same key?

Within minutes, its message emerged: *serpent knows all old fort too dangerous leave immediately for havana woman in black veil awaits you church of saint teresa.* Her imagination leaped.

If Don Alejandro hadn't already been diverted to Cuba for the meeting, he might still expect to rendezvous with a messenger in St. Augustine. She could pose as the messenger, meet the Spaniard, and learn who'd murdered her father and Jonah Hale. Perhaps she'd even help bring the murderer to justice.

Ah, but embracing such a plan required freedom, a horse, and supplies.

She had none of that. She slumped in the chair with a ragged sigh, admitting the crazy, reckless nature of the scheme.

Brooding, she rose, stuffed the new cipher and translation into her pocket, dimmed the lantern, and lay back on her bed. The night was moonless, the atmosphere heavy with moisture. No breeze ventured inside her window. Sweat gathered between her thighs, in the crack of her buttocks, and in her armpits. She'd have been far more comfortable undressed to her shift, but intuition prodded her that the night wasn't over.

For the information in the new cipher to be legitimate, the courier must have gotten skittish at the sight of soldiers at the house and decided to drop the pot off without drawing attention to himself. The Red Rock closed at two in the afternoon on the Lord's Day, so the courier would have had little chance to hear that the recipient of the flowerpot was dead. Therefore the probability was good that she wasn't dealing with a false encryption, and she could trust the cipher.

Who was El Serpiente? A Spaniard, surely, but from his actions, no ally to rebels or redcoats. She stared at the ceiling. Her imagination, stimulated by books and business, yet bound for years by scant contact with the educated world, ran amok. So many different interests collided in the American War, but she had yet to see any nation concerned for the *people* in the colonies. What sort of world were these "interests" bequeathing to her daughter and unborn grandchild?

Uncanny quiet held the night outside her window, crickets and frogs reluctant to complete the melodies they started, reminding her of more immediate concerns. Fairfax's story about the Creek was absurd. Knowing her discomfort with him, Edward wouldn't have sent him to her house. Something had happened to Edward. Perhaps Captain Sheffield had had to assume command of the garrison. She knew nothing of Sheffield, but she'd observed Edward's sensible leadership style contributing to calm, fair relations between soldiers and civilians in the four months since his arrival. The repercussions for Alton, if he proved unable to exercise his leadership, might not be pleasant.

Again she thought of his offer from the previous night. She couldn't expect a better offer anywhere. She had little money and was thirty-three, a woman with gray in her hair and autumn in her womb. But she didn't love Edward. If she never grew to love him, how satisfied would she feel with her life?

Even thornier was the issue of class. And in England, Edward would court and marry someone Betsy's age and beget children upon her. Soon enough, Lady Hunt would develop finesse at the non-intellectual means of taming her husband. When it came right down to it, most males responded to that non-intellectual persuasion with a predictable deficit of common sense. Did Sophie want to be in the middle of all that?

Something scraped her window, so she rolled over and looked out. Dark as the night had grown, she discerned an oblong blot of midnight that lifted and scratched at her window frame.

Fright ignited in her chest, and she sprang from bed. Someone had scaled the side of the house and was balanced atop the porch, trying to enter though her window. Time she took advantage of the soldiers' duty to protect her.

"Sophie!" whispered the shadow. "Sophie!"

She hesitated. Was it someone bringing secret word of her father's murderer, perhaps? She crept around the bed and flung aside the curtain, where her gaze lodged on a Creek warrior balanced on the porch roof and clinging to the side of the house. A scream tightened her throat, but before it could escape the man stuck his turbaned head inside. "Shhhh! It's me!"

Voice recognition routed out terror. "M-Mathias!"

Earrings tinkling, the blacksmith glanced down at the ground before turning back to her. "I must speak with you. You're in danger. May I come in?"

She backed away, and he crawled inside accompanied by the scent of pine straw. Seldom had she seen him dressed like a Creek, and she tried not to gape at the picture he created with feathers and shells, turban, tomahawk and knife, breechcloth, leggings and moccasins. She yanked the curtains closed. "What in the world are you doing out there?"

"The Creek have surrounded the garrison and number over one hundred and fifty."

Her gape magnified. So Fairfax hadn't been fabricating the story. One hundred and fifty Creek warriors. Many must have been summoned from Red-Stick villages. "What's happened? Have the colonists given offense?" Heavens, some clod of a farmer must have flung the gauntlet and openly accused the Creek of the murders.

"No, our business is with the British alone."

Our business. Well, at least he was clear about his allegiance. "But King George and the Creek have a treaty —"

"Treaty? Bah! What is the worth of King George's word if his soldiers will impersonate others to kill hundreds of people?"

"What are you talking about?" Sophie frowned.

"They've schemed with outlaws and mercenaries to impersonate the Creek and massacre the townspeople."

"That's a rumor. Lieutenant Fairfax spoke of it tonight. There's no logical reason for the soldiers to do such a thing."

"Did logic figure into 'Tarleton's Quarter?'"

"Oh, come now, the redcoats don't usually massacre their prisoners, and I still haven't heard how this hare-brained rumor originated."

"British intelligence reports that Spain has launched an offensive to capture Georgia and Florida later this summer —"

"British intelligence?" She looked askance at him. He hadn't picked up that tip standing over an anvil. What maelstrom had Will plunged into with El Serpiente and Don Alejandro?

"Britain is sending seven hundred more troops into Georgia with no time to expand the barracks at local forts."

Mathias wasn't given to flights of fancy. Rather, he had summoned the mindset of a Creek warrior. "You cannot believe that Britain will butcher loyal subjects of the Crown, just to accommodate soldiers! Major Hunt would never consent to such wickedness."

"It appears that's why he's been recalled to England."

"Recalled? But he told me that — that —"

"That he'd inherited family estates and bought his way out?" Mathias ejected a short, soft laugh. "Not all who wear the uniform are warriors. Major Hunt belongs on his Hampshire estate, not on the battlefield."

Not only had Edward burgled her house, but he'd lied to her about his reasons for returning to England. She lifted her chin to stop her lower lip from quivering with disillusionment.

"Tonight all hundred and fifty warriors will make sure the soldiers don't impersonate *us* for such an atrocity. Let Whites massacre each other if they must, but we won't be cast as villains."

This was madness. Her heart stammered a beat. "You're going to kill Major Hunt!"

"Only if he doesn't cooperate."

Sophie reflected that Lady Beatrice had best keep her betrothal options open. "I still don't know why you're *here*."

"I'm here to ensure your safety."

"There are two soldiers downstairs charged with that duty."

"If we aren't satisfied with Hunt's explanation, both of them are dead, along with as many others as we can find tonight."

For the first time, she noticed his quiver of arrows and bow. "You plan to guard me until the danger is passed. Why?"

"A month ago, Will asked me to protect you if danger ever came to Alton and he wasn't here." Ah, so her father knew at least a month in advance that danger was coming. Mathias took a step toward her. "I gave him my word I would do it."

"But *why*?" she whispered, although she knew at the core of her soul.

"In all my life, few have given me respect. Will dealt me far more respect than my stepfather, as have you, your brother, and sister. It's a debt I can never repay."

A solid enough rationale, one that stood on its own, but after almost two decades, she suspected Mathias's own agenda played into it. It dawned on her then that his offer was an avenue to freedom from the absurd house arrest. "If all you say is accurate, I'm not really safe here. I must leave."

"Those two soldiers won't let you go, and I won't attack them unless it becomes necessary to protect you."

"We don't have to let them know I'm leaving. I can get out the window if you help me."

He propped fists on his hips. "Where would I take you?"

"To the Creek village."

"That's the first place the redcoats will look." From his expression, he realized the obvious with his next breath, and he sealed his lips briefly over scorn. "Ah. They'll see only what we wish them to see."

Better still, perhaps the redcoats wouldn't find her in the Creek village because she'd be miles away to the south, en route to St. Augustine. Now that she'd gotten that wild scheme in her head, she couldn't turn it loose. Grasping for it was far easier than embracing the finality of her father's murder.

Somewhere in the distance, they both heard the report of a musket, followed by others. In the room below, Barrows's voice rose. "Did you hear that? Zounds, it's war with the Creek!"

Sophie seized her tote sack and threw in toiletry articles, hair ribbons, and an extra shift and pair of stockings while Mathias climbed back out the window. Ensign Baldwin stomped across the shop floor. "Shut the windows. Block the doors."

Out of intuition, she also threw the copy of *Confessions* into the tote sack.

Then she diapered her petticoat together, slung the tote over her shoulder, extinguished the lantern, and went to the window.

Mathias clung to the side of the house and whispered, "Crawl out like this. Get your balance on your stomach the way I'm going to show you, and then ease your legs over the side. I'll wait on the ground and help you down." She watched him roll onto his stomach, wiggle to the edge of the porch roof with his legs dangling over the side, then drop out of sight.

Holding her breath, she crawled outside and balanced on the roof. She eased the window shut, dropped her tote over the edge, and let out her breath. Then she rolled onto her stomach, slid her legs over the edge, and scooted backward. While gripping the planks with her hands, she heard the approaching gallop of a horse. "Mathias?" One of the planks splintered. She clawed the roof for support.

He caught her about the waist as the plank gave way, as Fairfax rode up, reined his horse back from a gallop, and vaulted from the saddle. No doubt about it, the British lieutenant saw a Creek warrior trying to spirit away a helpless, senseless woman from Alton that he'd captured and slung over his shoulder. "The devil — savages! Baldwin! Barrows! To arms!" Achilles and Perseus sprang up from the porch and began barking. Fairfax's infantry hanger sang with a metallic *shhhling*, freed from its scabbard, while he sprinted toward Sophie and Mathias.

Sophie found herself dumped hard on the ground beside the porch. From inside the house, Mary screamed, and Baldwin hollered, "Barrows, douse the light! Assume position!" Sophie realized the two soldiers had misunderstood Fairfax. Rather than rushing to the lieutenant's aid outside, they prepared to repel hoards of Creek warriors from breaking into the house.

Meanwhile, the blacksmith staggered backward, beyond reach of Fairfax's first swing, seeking the cover and shadow of fruit trees along the side of the house. Out of sight from the front windows, Sophie collared Achilles before he could lunge for the two men. Both hounds barked and whined.

The curved sword's second whoosh through the air curtailed when the blade embedded in a tree trunk. Growling, Fairfax yanked at it. Mathias grabbed a branch and swung his legs around. They caught Fairfax in the chest and knocked him away from the trees and the hanger. Fairfax reached for his knife. Mathias slammed a fist into the pit of his stomach. Then he brought both fists down on Fairfax's right kidney. The lieutenant landed belly down on the ground and didn't move.

Sophie rose, her tote on her shoulder. The dogs' barking subsided, and they circled around, confused, curious, sniffing at Fairfax and Mathias. "Are you hurt?" she whispered to Mathias when he staggered over.

Breathing hard, he shook his head. "Even better, I doubt he recognized me."

"He knows you were Creek." She stroked both hounds. They pranced back to the porch, toenails clicking on the boards. "Taking me to the village isn't wise. Hide me in the smithy."

Adjusting the quiver, he whispered back, "I am *not* leaving you in Alton tonight."

"Gods, but you're stubborn."

His smile gleamed in the starlight. "The pot calling the kettle black, eh?"

She turned back to the dogs to hide a grin. "Down," she said, her voice low. Achilles and Perseus flopped down with sighs, relieved that the activity was over. "Stay."

Mathias signed for her silence. Then, hugging the deepest shadows, they crept west, out of town and into the rolling, lush wilderness of pines and hardwoods peopled by the Creek Confederacy.

Chapter Eight

THE FIRST TIME she awakened, night had not yet surrendered the land. Unable to see more than dark, she lay still, heart pounding with disorientation. Musty scents of deer hide hammock and fiber blanket deepened her confusion. In the distance a dog barked, competing for nocturnes with crickets and frogs. Above her, a mockingbird experimented with Monday predawn. Not far away, a man snored bass to the bird's soprano.

Sophie recognized the interior of a wattle-and-daub house of the Creek village. The snoring came from beyond a partition near her hammock: Hawk In The Sun, who was husband of the village's ambassador and *Isti Hogdee* — Beloved Woman — Laughing Eyes. At Laughing Eyes's groggy mutter, his snoring curtailed with a grunt. He grumbled, and they grew quiet. Sophie smiled at the familiar routine of urging a snoring husband to roll on his side. She drew the blanket over her shoulder and eased back to sleep.

Daylight awakened her the second time — daylight and a conversation in Creek between Jacques le Coeuvre and Laughing Eyes. Curious, she rose and pushed the window shade aside.

Outside the lodging house, Jacques gestured east toward Alton to emphasize a point. He wore a hunting shirt, trousers, tomahawk and knife in his belt, and moccasins. A thin strip of leather held his shaggy salt-and-pepper hair in a braid down his back. Over his shoulder draped his haversack, and he carried his musket. No doubt about it, he was ready to embark on another adventure, rub shoulders with celebrities. Envy crawled through Sophie.

Laughing Eyes nodded to him, the creases on her face deepening. Almost three decades earlier, while in her late twenties, she'd begun taking Mathias with her on visits to the Europeans, allowing her adoptive sister's son to absorb the art of diplomacy. Ayukapeta Hokolen Econa, they soon named Mathias: Walk in Two Worlds. Naked from the waist up that morning, the Beloved

Woman wore a knee-length skirt of floral print. Strands of shells and beads adorned her neck and bosom, and a myriad of flowers twisted through the plaits of her black hair.

All those flowers triggered Sophie's memory of her stroll home from the swimming hole that afternoon. Mathias had stolen her mobcap, snagged wildflowers, and twined them into her braid. Silly with summer, they'd made each other laugh by convoluting sentence structure to an approximation of Shakespearean English. A poetic side of him emerged that she'd never expected. Along the way, the dark of his eyes had softened whenever he looked at her.

Had it been eighteen years since then? It seemed a hundred. At what moment in time had they turned from giddy youths into duty-bound adults?

Jacques referenced the garrison, and Laughing Eyes responded something about warriors. Sophie listened with diligence but didn't know enough Creek to understand. Vexed, she eased the shade back in place and began dressing.

Instinct told her there'd been no bloodshed in Alton the previous night. The Creek village would be hopping with activity otherwise. Finding no sign of a struggle in her bedroom, the soldiers would conclude that she'd left of her own volition, violating house arrest. With Fairfax insisting he'd been attacked, the incident would appear schemed between Sophie and the Creek. The redcoats wouldn't take that lightly. What had she unleashed?

While she was drawing on her stockings, Jacques rapped on the door of the hut. "*Belle* Sophie, you are awake?" She stuffed her stockinged feet into shoes, set the partition to one side, and opened the door. A blend of pleasure and relief wove through his expression. "Ah, it is good to see you safe and well after last night. May I come in?"

She stepped aside. "And where are you headed today?"

His expression darkened. "Anyplace where trouble is not, and that does not include Alton this morning."

"You'll not attend the funerals at ten?" She closed the door behind him.

He shook his head. "Bad luck, my old heart tells me, to leave town the same day I attend a funeral, even the funeral of my nephew." He paced the interior of the hut. "What possessed Mathias to bring you here last night?"

Chagrin gnawed her. "I coerced him. He wanted me to be safe. Where is he?" Mathias had disappeared within minutes of depositing her into the hands of his mother's adoptive sister.

Jacques sneered. "He is in Alton, convincing English pigs that no hostages were taken during that gross misunderstanding. I do not know how the rumor originated among the Creek, but I am certain that no one was slaughtered to make room for troops."

She expelled relief. "Mathias thought the real reason Major Hunt was surrendering command to Captain Sheffield was because he'd been recalled to England for refusing to commit atrocities."

"Bah. Hunt is wealthy. He bought his way out of the war."

"I presumed as much. Then why did Mathias so misread the situation?"

"The rumor infringed on the sacred honor of the Creek people." The sneer contorted Jacques's upper lip. "Even if the rumor vanished with the light of day, that lieutenant was knocked out after he charged the Creek warrior with you —"

"Hah. Fairfax attacked Mathias with his sword."

"As far as the pigs are concerned, you escaped arrest. And although no one was injured in the confrontation in town last night, the Creek are now suspect of breaking their treaty —"

"I cannot go back to Alton, Uncle Jacques!" She threw up her hands.

"Soldiers are on their way here. You must return to Alton, or the Creek may be charged with abetting your escape." He grumbled, "And already the whispers I hear are foul, that the Creek murdered those three men."

Time to enlist qualified help for the cause. She seized his upper arm and lowered her voice. "I'm leaving for St. Augustine today. Find me a good horse and some supplies."

"Eh? Have you hit your head, *belle* Sophie? St. Augustine is more than a week away by rigorous travel over terrain no woman dare journey alone —"

"Get word to David that I require his company."

Scowling, he shook off her hold. "What is all this about?"

"Solving the murders of my father and Jonah."

Disbelief faded from his face, and he studied her. "Perhaps you had best explain everything. Keep your voice low."

She told him about the ciphers, showing him the second one and *Confessions*, and related the visit of the Spaniards two nights before. The Frenchman's eyebrows bristled like caterpillars, his beady gaze stung, and the veins in his ropy neck stood out. "St. Augustine belongs to George the Third. Sophie, you cannot go. You are a woman."

She stamped her foot. "I run a printing press. My aim with a musket is excellent. I ride a horse better than most men in Alton." From his expression, she wasn't getting through to him. Exasperated, she realized her argument wasn't convincing because in her heart she hadn't accepted her father's death. "Jacques, the redcoats won't solve the murders! Someone did them a favor and rid Alton of rebel spies. Don Alejandro de Gálvez is a lead in the murders. He may be in St. Augustine. If the soldiers are on their way here now to find me, you can either help me get to St. Augustine, or you can hand me over to them." She braced her fists on her hips. "I'll not return willingly to Alton today."

"St. Augustine is a different world from Hampshire."

"Then perhaps I shan't be followed to St. Augustine."

His expression thawed. "*Belle* Sophie, you may find the companionship of more than your brother on your journey."

★★★

Inside the Moon Lodge, the smell of menstrual blood blended with that of sweat, flowers, and a grass-and-herb smudge. Two-dozen Creek women of various ages lounged around a fire pit, the interior of the lodge dimmed by smoke. Some were naked above the waist. Others wore floral print shirts like the one Two Rainbows had loaned Sophie. They gossiped while having their hands and feet massaged or their hair combed and braided. None seemed concerned that eleven redcoats had ridden into the village a quarter hour before and begun nosing around.

Three women entered bearing platters of cut fruit and corn cakes. They served the food as if the menstruating women were goddesses — which they were in Creek civilization, exalted and one with Creator during their menses.

Imagining the townsfolk of Alton treating menstruating women with honor made Sophie want to laugh. That idea had slim chance of generating approval among those who regarded work as a moral good.

With a swirl of skirt fabric, Two Rainbows, younger wife of the medicine man, pivoted from the small window. "Nagchoguh Hogdee, a lieutenant comes." The Creek woman sashayed to the opposite side of the fire pit and sat facing the doorway.

Her back to the door, Sophie shifted on her mat and willed the muscles in her neck to relax. Surely Lieutenant Stoddard wouldn't invade the Moon Lodge. Strands of shells and beads around her neck chuckled, blended with the earthy murmurs within the lodge. Earth, she told herself, I am earth as the other women are.

Jacques's voice, steeped in indignation, closed on the lodge from the outside. "What can you be thinking?"

"The Moon Lodge is the only place in the village we haven't searched."

Dismay and panic tore through Sophie. That was *Fairfax* outside with Jacques, not Stoddard. Fairfax had received movement orders. Why hadn't he left for South Carolina?

"Uhchulee Nagonúhguh gave you his word that Sophie Barton is not here." She almost smiled at the semantic game the medicine man, Old Tale, had played with Fairfax. No, Sophie Barton wasn't there, but Nagchoguh Hogdee was.

Indignation in Laughing Eyes' voice rang distinct. Old Tale said something in Creek. "*Monsieur* le Coeuvre," said Fairfax. "Please be so good as to translate for me. I could have sworn this fellow spoke the King's English."

And so he did when he felt like it. The smile plucked at Sophie's mouth. She fanned a fly away from her face.

"Uhchulee Nagonúhguh reminds you that the Moon Lodge is a sacred place and that great Mico George has thus far respected the customs of the people in this village —" A snarl penetrated Jacques's tone. "— English pig."

Fairfax's voice lowered. "Curious, *Monsieur* le Coeuvre. I detected neither the Creek words for 'English' nor 'pig' in the fellow's statement."

Jacques lowered his voice, too. "Translation is a delicate and subjective art, impacted by the judgment, personal experience, and prejudice of the translator — English pig."

Oh, gods. She closed her eyes a moment. Jacques le Coeuvre had just elevated himself to the top of Fairfax's dung list.

"Tell the medicine man I follow orders to search the *entire* village for Mrs. Barton."

The incongruity of the situation jolted Sophie. Fairfax should be headed that moment to South Carolina for his next assignment. Technically, neither Edward nor Captain Sheffield was his commanding officer. Neither should have sent him on such a search.

Fairfax paused the duration of a heartbeat. "While King George does not wish to infringe on the customs of natives, Mrs. Barton is a subject of the Crown, has violated arrest, and must be taken into custody if she is here."

Wood clattered and feet shuffled outside — warriors stepping before the lodge with spears. Movement within the lodge stilled, and conversation ceased. Jacques dripped acid into his voice. "You will have to get past *them* first. Now look around you. At least a dozen warriors have you targeted. Even King George is not mad enough to proceed on your course. Stand down, Lieutenant, or you will die."

Seconds dragged by while Fairfax considered. "*Monsieur*, extend King George's gratitude to the people of the village for cooperating in this matter." The women in the hut returned to their tasks. "Oh, and *Monsieur*, I encourage you to use better judgment at translations in the future as your personal prejudice may predispose you to making enemies." Gravel and grass crunched beneath the lieutenant's retreat. Jacques spat.

The trembling in Sophie's hands quieted. She'd expected Fairfax to open the door and look around. But, when threatened by warriors, even someone as unyielding as he couldn't help but feel the negative pressure of transgressing the cultural and sacrosanct boundary of the Moon Lodge.

As she assessed the elements within the lodge — native women, smoky dusk, earthy smells — she reflected that Fairfax was looking for a woman who held herself apart from the Creek, not one who had removed her mobcap and let her hair riot across her shoulders and back like a "savage." *They'll see only what we wish them to see*, Mathias had said the night before. Would Fairfax have recognized her, had he opened the door? The British mouthed policies of protecting the natives, but they hadn't the slightest idea who the natives really were.

Jacques tapped the door, his voice low. "Nagchoguh Hogdee."

She rose and cracked the door open. "Are they gone?"

"*Oui.*"

She opened the door several inches. Over his shoulder she took in activities in the village plaza — children scuttling a ball around in the dust with dogs chasing them, two men returning from a lake with fish, several other warriors negotiating with traders. The ordinariness of it soothed her. "Thank you."

He inclined his head. "Your brother should arrive within the hour. Mathias will rejoin us at noon with transportation and supplies. And I have requested that Zack MacVie meet me here in the village."

"MacVie?" She grimaced, recalling how he'd stepped on her feet at the dance to discourage her sleuthing. Then she remembered he was second-in-command for the Committee of Safety. Her zeal over the St. Augustine lead had made her overlook the potential complicity of her father's cronies in his murder. Not a one of them had stopped by to pay his condolences on Sunday. They might very well have double-crossed him. "Leave no stone unturned."

A wicked smile twisted the Frenchman's lips. "Ask the correct way, and MacVie will volunteer information."

She nodded. "If we go to St. Augustine, I shall need a man's hat and clothing." Jacques arched an eyebrow at her. "I shan't slow the party by riding a horse in a petticoat."

His eyes twinkled. "You are a wanton, *belle* Sophie."

She grinned. "Has it taken you thirty-three years to recognize that?"

"Not at all."

Chapter Nine

FINGERS INTERLACED BEHIND his head, the hammock swaying beneath him, David contemplated flies scooting around the ceiling of the guest hut in the heat of the day. "Havana."

Sophie gave the hammock a push. "Have you been there?"

He regarded her with amusement. "You know I'd have told you if I'd wandered off to Havana. Now who'd have thought the old man would go to a place so exotic?"

"Ben Franklin goes to Paris." She pushed the hammock again. "I've heard he's courted more women in Paris than there are women living in Massachusetts, Pennsylvania, and New York."

"Three cheers for old Ben. Still, Paris isn't tropical. This is a once-in-a-lifetime opportunity."

"Does that mean you want to come along?"

"They have women, whiskey, and whist in Havana. I'm in."

"But it isn't certain that we'll go to Havana. We'll likely go only as far as St. Augustine."

"They have women, whiskey, and whist in St. Augustine, too."

She smiled. David was such an uncomplicated man. "Of course, should we need to go to Havana, there's the issue of passage aboard a ship."

"The card tables of St. Augustine are generous."

"I didn't plan for you to subsidize the venture."

"And how are *you* going to pay for it?"

"I have some money hidden away at the house."

Clearing his throat, he sat up and rubbed the back of his neck. "Uh, your supply is now in the hands of our enterprising younger sister."

"*What?*"

"Along with Mother's garnets and the old man's doubloons and horse pistols. For safekeeping, she said."

Anger balled Sophie's fingers into fists. "'Enterprising?' You mean 'thieving,' don't you?"

He pushed himself out of the hammock and gave her shoulder a squeeze.
"Calm down. I was witness to her taking it. That way, at least you know where
all of it is, and she can't claim your servant stole it." He spread his hands.
"Look, you aren't an heiress sitting on a fortune. The *first* lesson you need to
learn if you go off on this adventure is to accept the generosity of others when
it's offered.

"The *second* lesson you must learn is that you won't always be in control.
Dash it all, you've had that printing business under your thumb your entire
life. Month after month, year after year, those columns in your ledger have
added up perfectly and balanced. But your debits and credits will be fouled
by the time you get to St. Augustine. If you go on to Havana, forget about ever
balancing anything."

Indignation yielded to reflection, smoothing the pucker of her lips. "You
think my life is boring."

"Abysmally so."

"I agree."

"Then why have you been chasing the perpetuation of abysmal boredom on
an estate in Hampshire?"

She frowned. Edward's offer was the fond fancy of so many women. Why
hadn't she accepted it Saturday night? "I'd be lodged in a townhouse in London, not in Hampshire."

David rubbed his chin. "Oh. That's a different offer and a point in Hunt's
favor. You wouldn't be bored in London unless his money ran out or he lost interest in you. But somehow I just don't see you in London." He took her hand
and patted it. "My dear sister, you've set this ship a-sail on the open seas and
given her a bearing. Let others trim the sails and tack to keep her on course.
The ship will find harbor, I assure you. And don't worry about the print shop.
With six brats running around, ink creates an appealing diversion for Susana
right now."

"You must be joking. She hasn't touched that press in fifteen years." But
Sophie knew her absence was just the opening Susana had been waiting for.

David's grin took a bawdy bend around the corners of his mouth. "I suspect
it's like climbing in the saddle after you've been out of it awhile. Comes back
to you with hardly a hitch."

She pulled away to hide a blush. David wasn't talking about horses. Eight
long years it had been for her. "What would *you* know about being out of the
saddle?"

"It was an intelligent guess."

Outside the hut, they heard MacVie approaching. "Better not be wasting
my time with this, Jacques. I got a fence to repair before the new hogs arrive.
And that ghoul, Fairfax, is harassing me."

Sophie caught her brother's eye. "Let me handle this."

Jacques opened the door for the hog farmer and assumed a position just
inside. MacVie removed his hat, nodded to David, and stared at Sophie. "Mrs.
Barton! We heard you were kidnapped." His gaze encompassed her loose
hair and the strands of beads and shells atop Two Rainbows' shirt, and his lip

curled. "Perhaps something worse than kidnapped."

She clasped hands behind her back and regarded him with a cool eye. "When was the last time you saw my father alive?"

He looked at the ceiling and hummed several seconds before returning an indulgent smile. "Oh, nine o'clock Saturday night."

"Where?"

"At the dance."

"You didn't encounter him alive after the dance was over?"

"No." He wiped his nose on the back of his sleeve.

"When did you last see Jonah Hale alive?"

"About the same time as Will, right after the dance started." His tone hardened. "Why are you asking questions?"

"Where were you between ten Saturday night and two Sunday morning?"

"Not that it's any of your business, but I was at the dance, and then Donald, Charley, and me had a couple rounds at Donald's house before I went home to bed. Find fault with that."

"I will. We suspect you of complicity in my father's murder."

His face contorted. "How dare you say that? He was my friend!" He bared teeth. "I don't care if you're his daughter. I don't owe you anything."

She ignored his statement but not the sentiment. MacVie despised her, so she'd best watch her back. "Some friend you are. You never came by Sunday to offer condolences. Not a one of you rebels did. And you seem to have forgotten that I witnessed an argument between you and my father just before the first dance. I overheard you say to him, '...just you and Jonah, eh?' He and Jonah are now dead. Coincidence? I think not."

"I don't have time to listen to your foolishness —"

"I shall be blunt then. You rebels betrayed my father and Jonah Hale because you were bought out by a Spaniard known as El Serpiente."

The momentary widening of his eyes indicated surprise and panic galloping through him. Zack MacVie, defender of the patriot cause, had been nabbed. "E-El Who?"

"You're such a terrible liar. Two Spaniards came looking for my father at our home early Sunday. One was flayed alive on your property not long after. The other was El Serpiente." She balled her fists. "You know him."

MacVie darted a look around the hut, his fingers clenching and unclenching. "How much of this do the bloodybacks know?"

She smiled again. She liked seeing him off balance. "I don't owe you anything."

"I knew it! You're a flaming Tory with a redcoat lover!"

Of course a flaming rebel would view a neutral as a flaming Tory. "You're an ignorant, arrogant hog farmer who hasn't any sense. You fancy Lieutenant Fairfax stupid. You've no inkling of all he knows, or what he'll do to confirm his suspicions." She must have struck a nerve, for MacVie sucked in a breath, and his swarthy face paled at the mention of his favorite ghoul. "Out with it! Why did you kill my father and Jonah?"

"I-I didn't do it." His shoulders sagged, and he hung his head. His hands shook, though whether from rage or fear she wasn't sure. "El Serpiente killed them. I had nothing to do with it. None of us did. We weren't bought out, no matter what you think."

"Liar. Why would a Spaniard kill a rebel?"

He jutted a sullen lip at her. "All I know is that he has his own interests in this war."

More subterfuge. It sure looked as though they'd be chasing El Serpiente to St. Augustine. "Have you any idea where El Serpiente was headed?" MacVie shook his head in negation, but she doubted he was ignorant of the meeting in St. Augustine.

Jacques crossed his arms high on his chest. "You claim he murdered Will and Jonah. How do you know it? Did you see their murders?"

MacVie regarded the ceiling again. "I was coming home from Donald's house and saw flames on my property. I rode over fast, thinking a fire was spreading. That's when I saw Will tied to the stake and the Spaniards watching him burn."

David's jaw hung slack. "Didn't you try to stop them?"

"No. Will was already dead."

"What about my nephew? Was he dead, too?"

"Yes." MacVie refused to look at them. "Lying there on the ground. I figure the Spaniards got both of them."

Sophie raised her hands, elbows bent, in a gesture of exasperation. "What were my father and Jonah doing on your property at that time of night?"

"How should I know?"

"Why didn't you tell the soldiers you were a witness?"

"Oh, indeed. They know I've no love for their poxy king. They'd have charged me with the murders, just to lock me up."

"A pleasant thought. What time did all this happen?"

MacVie glowered at her. "One-fifteen, one-thirty."

Her eyebrow shot up. Impossible. The Spaniards had been to her home looking for Will at one o'clock. There wasn't enough time for them to have him mostly burned at the stake by one-thirty. "Who flayed El Serpiente's partner?"

He gulped and blanched. "I don't know. Sneaked away to my home after that so as the Spaniards didn't catch me."

MacVie at least suspected who'd killed the other Spaniard. If any portion of his tale was true, he'd had good reason to sneak away from the gruesome site so he didn't get caught, too. Only one person in Alton made his face pale. "I'm surprised you haven't leaped to avenge the murder of your fellows."

He pondered several seconds. "El Serpiente ain't traveling alone."

"His accomplice was flayed alive."

"Aye, but — but he has two others."

From how quickly he blurted it, she knew he was lying yet again. "Oh? You saw them? Where?"

"No. I overheard him at the murder site telling the other Spaniard where they were all going to meet and camp last night. North, he said, to discourage pursuit."

"Ah, you speak Spanish, then?"

Puzzled, he frowned at her while he worked out the logistics that the two Spaniards wouldn't have spoken English to each other. "Aye, a little. So you see, it ain't safe chasing him. Besides —" MacVie grew moody. "Glory ain't for everybody. Some of us got to stay behind and pick up the pieces when things go wrong."

She acknowledged the shrewd expressions of both David and Jacques, reading in them the same suspicions she held. They'd have to bring MacVie along on the chase for El Serpiente because the farmer knew too much about them and had become a liability. Dragging an unwilling traveler with them wouldn't be fun. No, they needed to give MacVie incentive to join them.

She allowed disgust to curl her lip. "What a coward you are. Well, Jacques, David, and I won't crawl on our bellies. We're going after El Serpiente. He has almost a two-day lead on us, so either you agree to help us catch him, or we hand you over to the local authorities. And believe me, after you milksops who call yourselves 'Patriots' allowed me to be blamed for printing those broadsides, nothing would give me more pleasure than to turn you over to the British."

"You got nothing on me, and you know it."

"Oh, don't I?" She took her time walking a circle around him. "Your wits are addled. Must've been from watching that Spaniard being flayed alive early yesterday morning."

Color drained from his face, and his hands trembled again. "I d-didn't see it. I w-went along home to bed."

"Lieutenant Fairfax would love hearing how much you know about *that* murder. And did you know I saw you carve the woodcut for that broadside in the pressroom Friday night?"

"All right, all right! I'll go with you!"

"Your change of heart gratifies me. Your primary task will be to find the site where El Serpiente camped last night with his two accomplices. We leave in an hour. Before then, you'll help gather supplies. Jacques or a Creek warrior will accompany you to make sure you don't stray from the village to warn the rest of the Committee before we go."

"When do I get my musket and knife back?"

"When we decide you're cooperating with us."

"Ah, no, I'm not going on any trip with you unarmed —"

"You do as you're told!" Apprehension bombarded her at the lethality of MacVie's glare. She lifted her chin. "Don't just stand there. Hop to it!"

He jammed his hat on his head and stormed from the hut with Jacques following him out. David flopped into the hammock with a grunt of discontent. "He's going to be more trouble than he's worth."

Chapter Ten

MATHIAS ARRIVED TEN minutes later, dressed in hunting shirt and trousers, leading his horse and Jonah's gelding. While he unloaded gear outside the guest hut, Sophie noticed the grip of fatigue and grief in his expression. "Five o'clock in the morning Fairfax showed up on my doorstep! He must never sleep."

Contempt contorted Jacques's expression. "Not the only body function he omits."

Sophie paused from stroking Jonah's gelding to wag her finger at the Frenchman. "You've made an enemy of Fairfax."

David's eyebrows rose. "Indeed? I'd sooner have the devil himself as my enemy."

"You think I should fear him, eh? You were not at the Plains of Abraham, when honorable French blood ran in rivers." Jacques lifted his gnarled hands heavenward. "You did not see the jewels of Auvergny, Bretagne, and Lorraine crushed."

That story had certainly circulated a few times. Noticing the glaze in David's eyes, Sophie nudged him to polite attention.

"And you did not kneel beside the body of your beloved Montcalm and weep. After Quebec, David, I fear no English pig."

"No, I don't suppose you would, Uncle Jacques."

"And perhaps I've slid my dagger between the ribs of a few of them since the Old War, eh?"

"I don't doubt it, Uncle Jacques."

"My hand itched to do the same this morning." Jacques mimicked Fairfax's accent and carriage. "'Mr. Hale, if you suspected the savages' plans in advance, why did you not inform us of it?'"

Mathias straightened. "Stop stomping it into the ground."

David tongued a piece of straw. "You have to admit the redcoats asked enough questions at the funerals this morning to become annoying." He patted the gelding. "Didn't you attract attention by fetching Jonah's horse and all this gear?"

"Samson's been in my stable since Saturday afternoon, when Jonah brought him to me to replace a shoe."

Jacques eyed his nephew with skepticism. "How do you know you were not followed out here?"

"I didn't leave with both horses at the same time, and I took an indirect route."

"Good." Jacques's nod was curt. "As soon as we divide the gear and supplies, we are leaving with MacVie."

Mathias stared at David and Jacques. "Zack MacVie? You're going somewhere with that patriot pustule? Where?"

Samson nosed Sophie, and she continued stroking his neck. He'd be a good traveling horse. "I decoded the cipher. My father was to have ridden to St. Augustine, presumably to speak with Don Alejandro de Gálvez on behalf of the rebels." Shock hiked Mathias's eyebrows an inch. "Yesterday evening, I intercepted another message warning him that someone called El Serpiente knew of the mission, so the meeting had to be diverted to Havana."

"Havana?" He shoved a tinderbox back into a sack. "What danger makes a sea voyage to Cuba desirable?"

"El Serpiente's companion was the man who was flayed. MacVie claims El Serpiente killed my father and Jonah. He's agreed to help us find him. As soon as he returns, we're off."

His gaze rocketed from her to Jacques and David. "*We*? You aren't taking Sophie, are you?"

She smiled. "I think Samson and I have reached an understanding about the journey."

He scowled. "No! It's lunacy to take Sophie. She could be killed or violated or injured or abducted or tortured or —"

"Mathias, my good fellow." David removed the straw from his mouth and tossed it away. "You sound like a father."

She pinned Mathias with a stare. "Or a husband — without the marital amenities, I might add."

Anxiety bulged his eyes, and he cast a desperate look at David. "You're her brother. Talk sense into her, for god's sake! She'll be safe here with the Creek."

David waved away the plea. "You didn't see her with MacVie. When he returns with your cousin, ask him if he feels his anatomy's been damaged."

A frown darkened Mathias's expression. "Witty repartee doesn't qualify her to make such a journey. You can't take her with you."

"Because I'm a *woman*? Since it bothers you so much, you don't have to come with us."

"Sophie, be reasonable." Mathias gestured south. "The wilderness is full of savage animals and outlaws. Your odds of surviving this preposterous journey unscathed aren't good."

"Then come with us and increase our chances of success."

"I don't understand you."

She crossed her arms and drummed the fingertips of one hand atop her upper arm. "You've *never* understood me."

David's eyes bugged. "Bloody hell!"

Jacques marched Mathias away. "All this time I thought you had learned the wisdom of not arguing with a woman."

David stepped in front of Sophie, blocking her view of uncle and nephew. "Astounding. With my experience at reading faces around card tables, I cannot believe I've missed something between you and Mathias all these years."

Her nostrils flared. "This is the wilderness, not a card table. And there's nothing between us to miss." Nearly two decades of "nothing" seemed to have borne that theory out.

He nodded with perception. "So 'nothing' is the problem."

"Exactly."

"Wilderness, like card tables, has a peculiar way of turning 'nothing' into something. We're taking MacVie along. Make your peace with 'nothing' so it doesn't interfere with our finding this snake fellow and returning intact." Flicking lint off the sleeve of his fine jacket, he strolled off.

She looked in the direction Jacques and Mathias had taken. "Blast it all, Mathias," she muttered. "Speak up, man. Is there something you want from me?" And she mused over more memories of that summer afternoon, eighteen years earlier...

***

"The Cherokee say this was built by the Moon Eyes." Mathias crawled away from the grotto's entrance, mist from the deluge clinging to his hair and eyelashes, and sat angled to Sophie.

An aromatic scent arose from the carpet of pine straw. She'd heard of the Moon-Eyed People — forest-dwellers for eons before Indians — and of similar structures farther north in Georgia and the Carolinas. Craning her neck back, she examined ivy on the low, rocky ceiling. "Why was it built?"

Humor wove through his expression. "To keep us from getting drenched in that rainstorm out there."

"That's as good a purpose as any." She smiled at him. "When do you find time to read all that Shakespeare?"

"Before dawn. I sneak downstairs so I don't wake anyone."

"Really? So do I. You've never made fun of me for reading so much."

"Why should I do that? Reading brings you the world."

She leaned toward him. "Can you keep a secret?" He nodded. "I'm managing the ledgers for the print shop now."

Admiration flooded his expression, evoking a thrill in her. "A good move on Will's part. David's not the slightest bit interested in the business. So what has Jim to say about it?"

"I told him I promised to help Father until he found an apprentice." She laughed. "He doesn't know I plan to operate the press after we're married."

He studied her. "What will you do when Alton grows too small for you?"

"Whatever do you mean? Running the business is a tremendous opportunity. How many women are so fortunate?"

Laying the palm of his hand on her head, he pinched his countenance to resemble a mystic on a mountaintop. "Within a few years, you'll discover that Alton and business fills such a small portion of your mind that you'll be stifled with it."

The warmth of his benediction felt good. *"Just as blacksmithing already fills such a small portion of your mind."*

"Why do you say that?" His fingers spread apart and partook of the texture of her hair as if it were a delectable substance.

"You walk between the worlds of the white man and the red man, Ayukapeta Hokolen Econa." She sighed at the caress. Jim had never stolen her mobcap or put his hands in her hair. *"You've two full lives to lead, respect, and explore."*

"Indeed, I've been summoned by Creator, granted more than one life to respect and —"

"Explore," she whispered.

He examined a flower, plucked from her hair. Longing and regret occupied his expression. *"Respect."*

"Is that the way of it in your other world, too?" Certainly not from the rumors she'd heard. Why else would Christians be so desperate to clamp their morality on the Creek?

He twined the flower back into her hair and brushed her lips once with his forefinger. She closed her eyes, savoring the touch. The pine straw rustled, and she opened her eyes to find him supine, regarding her. *"What are you thinking, Sophie?"*

She traced her fingertips the length of his cheek. *"That my world is full of unfairness."*

"You see, Alton has already grown too small for you."

She slid down beside him, and he folded her to him, his thumb stroking the palm of her hand. Her cheek pressed to his chest, she listened to the paean of his heartbeat above the tumult of rain.

At length he rose on one elbow to study her, face embedded in shadow, and she laid her palm against his cheek. He caught her hand in his, brushing his lips on her palm and wrist before grazing her lips with his. Her voice emerged husky. *"This isn't fair to you. I'm to be married in two weeks."*

"It doesn't matter," he whispered, the warmth of his breath stroking her lips apart.

***

Outside the guest hut, she inspected supplies. A sewing kit. Soap. Bedrolls and canteens. An extra musket with spare flints and a musket tool, a powder horn and shot pouch, and a cartridge box. A map. Knives, tinderboxes, tomahawks. Mathias's rifle and bow and arrows. She fingered the quiver.

It doesn't matter. At first it hadn't seemed to matter. One of many guests at her wedding to Jim Neely, Mathias had wished the newlyweds well. The first time she'd suspected that the grotto of the Moon Eyes *did* matter was six months after Jim's death, when she'd returned to Alton after spending those months in Augusta with infant Betsy at her cousin Sarah's house, after Sarah had introduced her to handsome, blond-haired, blue-eyed Richard Barton. In the ensuing years, Mathias's courtesy and concern only reinforced her intuition that the grotto of the Moon Eyes had mattered very much to him. But like most men, he was afflicted by the inability to open his mouth and tell her so.

Handsome, blond-haired, blue-eyed Edward Hunt had had no difficulty telling her she mattered to him. Did she still matter to him after escaping? Had she ever mattered, or had he been using her to gain information about the rebels? Surely her journey to St. Augustine would slam the door on any favor from him.

With the arrival of Captain Sheffield, knowing he was free to return home, perhaps Edward had taken the initiative and slammed the door. She envisioned him thanking the heavens he'd bought his way out of the godforsaken war in the colonies. Loss prodded her soul. Was she certain she wanted to go to St. Augustine?

Unable to make sense of her conflict, she returned to her inspection of supplies. In addition to the cooking pot, she found dinnerware, eating utensils, and a sack of staples: beef soup squares, coffee, salt, pepper, maple sugar, and cornmeal.

David led his horse over, his gear packed, his grin toothy. He'd changed from his fine clothes into a hunting shirt and trousers. "Is everything in order, General?"

"All I lack is suitable apparel, and if I don't get it by departure time, I shall steal Uncle Jacques's spare clothing. He's about my size, don't you think?"

David pulled out the tool kit for his fowler and sniggered. "I dare say Jove himself shall hurl thunderbolts at us if we allow Jacques le Coeuvre to ride around Georgia naked."

She mustered a cheery expression. While her brother unscrewed the worn flint on his fowler, he whistled the ballad "Barb'ra Allen." Hoping he wasn't trying to make a point with his choice of tunes, she examined the stock of herbs. Yarrow to stop bleeding and heal wounds — she hoped they wouldn't have to use that one. Chamomile for headaches and upset stomachs.

David broke into his baritone. "They bury'd her in the old churchyard, Sweet William's grave was nigh hers. And from his grave grew a red, red rose —" He waited for her to look up at him before flashing a devilish grin. "From hers a cruel briar."

Sage to soothe itching. Mosquitoes, chiggers, ticks, and poison ivy. Delightful.

"O, they grew up the old church spire, until they could grow no higher. And there they twined in a true love knot —" He paused again, screwing the new flint onto the fowler with gusto, the grin consuming his face.

An acrid smile captured her lips, and she responded with her own mezzo-soprano. "The red, red rose and the briar."

"You know, Sophie, I've a concern preying upon my mind."

"Ah, I figured you were backing into something with 'Barb'ra Allen.' What's troubling you?"

"Major Hunt."

She wrapped the herbs and stood. "He's halfway to England in his heart by now. I'm sure he cannot leave Alton soon enough."

"I wish I could agree with you." Gaiety abandoned his face.

She swallowed. "Whatever do you mean?"

"It's what he said to me this morning after Jonah's funeral. He apologized for not knowing your whereabouts, or being there last night when Fairfax failed to apprehend your 'abductor', or treating you with the utmost delicacy and consideration after you'd served King George in the highest capacity by breaking the cipher. It was almost like watching a Catholic flog himself. He was quite sincere. He's in love with you, Sophie."

Frowning, she scratched at her temple, distressed that she seemed to have to choose between Edward and family honor, even after Will was dead. Was this about family honor? Was she being a naïve fool? Perhaps Edward did love her, but when was the last time she'd felt that Will had loved her? "Shall I become his mistress just because he loves me? I'm not responsible for making him feel better."

"No, that's not what I meant." David gnawed his lower lip. "I've a peculiar feeling about him. He may be a mediocre soldier, but he possesses great tenacity and determination."

"A statesman, then. He'll do well in Parliament."

"There's one more thing I must say. Mathias is right. This is a fool's journey. If you knew what's out there in the wilderness, you'd stay here." His cheeks paled. "By all the gods on Olympus, *I'd* really rather not be going. I'm not tagging along for some visceral delights I imagine at a card table in East Florida or Cuba. I'm in because you're my sister. So think hard about staying here."

Her resolve never wavered. "I'm going."

"Damn, I knew you'd say that."

"*Bonjour!*" Jacques sauntered into their midst bearing a bundle of fabric. "Or should I say *Buenos días*? For you, *belle* Sophie." He lobbed her the bundle: two pairs of trousers and two hunting shirts with a brimmed hat sandwiched between. "All we lack now is that rascal, MacVie, with the rest of the staples."

"Thank you, Uncle Jacques." She hugged the clothing to her chest. "What do I owe you — Ow!" David had stepped on her foot.

A leer glittered in the Frenchman's eyes. "*Payment?* You wish to discuss *payment?* I am always willing to discuss *payment* when lovely ladies believe themselves in my debt."

David's "I-told-you-so" expression backed her toward the hut. "Never mind. I shall go change now." She entered and shut the door.

Outside, she heard Jacques: "I stand ready to assist you, should you need help with the trousers."

Chapter Eleven

"TWO O'CLOCK." DAVID pocketed his watch.

Hairs escaping from Sophie's plait tickled her sweaty neck, suggestive of mosquitoes. "Where is that blasted hog farmer?"

Jacques tapped his overturned pipe in his palm. "This little piggy went to market, this little piggy ran home."

"Squealing 'wee, wee, wee' all the way home while being shot through with Creek arrows — ah, at last." Sophie exhaled relief. MacVie approached leading his horse laden with sacks of deer jerky and dried fruit. Mathias, accompanied by Runs With Horses and his similarly tattooed younger brother, Standing Wolf, followed with their horses.

The quartet halted before the hut, MacVie glum. Mathias said, "My cousins and I are going with you." He brushed past Sophie and began loading gear on his horse.

"Thank you." She sidestepped to tug once on the blacksmith's plait of long, dark hair. "*All* of you."

"I gave my word." Expression dour, he secured his bedroll.

"But if you don't dispose of that conservative countenance, I shall leave you behind."

Smug humor enlivened the Creek brothers' faces. Mathias regarded her for a few seconds before his expression softened, and a smile relaxed his lips.

The seven distributed the load of gear and supplies among the horses. Sophie removed her hat to drape her haversack and cartridge box over her shoulders. "Mr. MacVie, show us where you believe El Serpiente camped last night. North of here, you said." She replaced the hat and took up Samson's reins and the spare musket. Since MacVie had little incentive for honesty, what he showed them in the remaining six hours of daylight could reveal much about the rebels' motives and schemes.

They mounted their horses, a subdued MacVie in the lead, Sophie riding between David and Mathias. Once she glanced behind, but by then, the forest had already swallowed the Creek village. A nameless something called to her from beyond her conflict, a siren that she sensed had little to do with family honor or a nobleman's affections but much to do with her own soul. A piece of herself waited out there, ahead. The thought of a summons wielding such power frightened her a little, but she knew she couldn't rest until she found it.

***

Late afternoon, they crossed Butlers Creek west of Augusta and found remnants of a recent campsite. Evidence of three people with horses included broken twigs, churned ground, and human and horse turds. Antsy, MacVie gestured around. "The Spaniard and his two allies camped here yesterday to mislead pursuit. Let's go back to Alton before we chance on them."

Mathias rose from an examination of hoof prints, motioned Sophie, Jacques, and David to him, and said, low, "The trio headed south. If El Serpiente continued on to St. Augustine without delay, he'd be in the swamps near Briar Creek tonight."

About thirty miles south-southwest of Augusta. Sophie regarded him. "When is our earliest chance to overtake them?"

"Probably two days hence, near where Briar Creek meets the Savannah." Mathias's attention shifted to MacVie, who'd slunk closer, and the four of them turned to glare at the rebel.

MacVie spread his hands to encompass the abandoned campsite. "You asked me where they camped last night. Here it is. Don't you trust me now?"

Sophie propped her fists on her hips. "Not even as far as we can throw you."

Anger trapped his tongue a moment. "Someone — someone needs to put you in your place!"

"Watch your mouth, MacVie." David took a step forward, Mathias at his side.

"Gentlemen, please." Through the shield created by her brother and the blacksmith, she stared down the farmer, hoping he couldn't tell how he frightened her. "Mr. MacVie, have you any idea who are El Serpiente's accomplices?"

"Two men from Boston. Friends of John Adams."

The more he talked, the less sense he made. Why would two friends of John Adams take up with a Spaniard who'd killed a fellow rebel? When would they get the truth from MacVie?

David snapped, "What are their names? Did you meet them?" MacVie shrugged again. David shook his head and looked at Sophie. "Let's intercept the Spaniard quickly. The mosquitoes haven't fancied me yet, but I'm not fond of the idea of giving them several days to change their minds." Sophie, Mathias, and Jacques agreed. MacVie scoffed at all of them.

An hour later, a couple miles west of New Savannah and the postal road, they stopped for the night in a pine-scented dell. Mathias, Runs With Horses, and Standing Wolf vanished into the forest with bows and arrows as soon as they'd unsaddled, rubbed down, and picketed their horses. Sophie performed the same tasks for Samson, then helped clear the site. They'd seen no pursuit, but they'd be cautious and build just enough of a campfire to cook supper. A pity she couldn't have the sanctuary of wood smoke. Although bird and cricket nocturnes filled the vicinity, so did the less-welcome whine of mosquitoes.

Standing Wolf dropped off three writhing, large-mouthed bass. Sophie dressed the fish and skewered them on green willow wands. Into the aromas of fried johnnycakes and roasting fish, the hunters returned with seven rabbits between them and the reassurance that the party hadn't been pursued.

By the time night tangled the forest in a turgid blanket, little remained of the rabbits and fish but bones. Jacques knapped the flint on his musket. David prodded the coals with a stick. Moths waltzed low, singed in the heat yet lusting for light. Fireflies flitted at the boundary of night, and pink heat lightning pulsed the sky. In the distance, an owl hooted, and some small critter emitted a scream of mortality.

MacVie stashed his pipe away, heaved himself up, and belched. "I got the first watch. You with me, Jacques?"

Standing Wolf came to his feet. "*I* will join you."

MacVie's tone soured. "Whatever delights your heart." He stomped off into the brush. Standing Wolf slipped into the foliage after him.

Half a minute later came MacVie's cry of astonishment. "Aaaach! What do you think you're doing, interrupting Sir Reverence by sneaking up on me? I got enough trouble making it happen without the comfort of me own jakes. Begone, you tattooed whoreson, or I'll give you a face full of it!"

Belly laughter rocketed around the campfire. MacVie certainly wasn't concealing his resentment.

***

A hand prodding her shoulder awakened her to pre-dawn coolness amid the pewtery glow of starlit forest and the stink of rancid bear grease. The whisper from a crouched shadow belonged to Mathias. "We must move on. We've company out there."

All thought of sleep vanquished, she sat. David and Jacques shuffled bedrolls together, and two grease-slathered shadows murmured among the horses. "Where? Do they know we're here?"

"Camped a mile away, just off the postal road. A party of a half-dozen civilian men. They don't know we're here yet."

"Good." She indicated the snoring MacVie. "A connection?"

Mathias grunted. "I recommend that we don't wake him until the last second. Maintain silence all the way to breakfast."

She groped for her shoes and smiled without mirth. "Let's tell him we're being tracked by redcoats."

"I'm expecting that development, too. The Fates are fickle, especially in the forest."

He moved away on moccasin feet. With a swivel up to her knees, she smoothed out blankets and assembled the bedroll. Then she saddled Samson and loaded her gear.

Fearful of being nabbed by soldiers, MacVie fumbled his bedroll together in haste after being awakened. The party mounted horses and resumed the journey southbound. With Runs With Horses in the lead, Standing Wolf and Mathias melted into night to create a false trail, rejoining the group twenty minutes later. Mosquitoes bombarded Sophie's hands, face, and neck. Irritated to be the only one under attack, she considered slathering on some of the

Indians' bear grease.

They paused at seven Tuesday morning for deer jerky and dried pears before paralleling the Savannah River and the postal road by a mile to the west. The rolling hinterland made the going slow and fatigued the horses.

By noon, south of Alton, MacVie recovered enough mettle to gripe. Since they were approaching Mack Beans Swamp, he said, they ought to use the road and give the horses a break. He ought to get his weapons back, too. And didn't they trust him enough yet to tell him their destination?

With the noontime sun beating down, the group headed toward the road. Half a mile from it, while the rest of the party dismounted in an oak grove and ate more jerky and dried fruit, Runs With Horses and Standing Wolf set off to scout the safety of the road.

MacVie claimed a patch of grass near the horses, stretched out in the sultry cicada-song, and snoozed, hat covering his face and just visible above the long grass. David, Jacques, and Mathias conversed in quiet tones, weapons in hand. Holding her loaded musket, Sophie walked to and fro to ease the stiffening of muscles in her inner thighs.

David and Jacques meandered to the periphery of camp, the brown of their hunting shirts blending with the bark of trees. Mathias migrated over to her. "Muscles sore from riding?" She nodded. "Give it a couple days. You'll feel better."

"You're not trying to talk me out of this journey anymore."

"Rather late for that." He glanced over her shoulder, and she, following his glance, glimpsed MacVie's black hat. Mathias lowered his voice and infused it with humor. "When you set your mind to something, stopping you is like halting a runaway horse team."

"The pot calling the kettle black indeed."

"True, and as I join the ranks of cantankerous old men like my uncle, I shall be entitled to ever-increasing stubbornness." After a mutual chuckle, the amusement on his face faded, replaced by sobriety. "Sophie, now see here —"

The report of a firearm bounced off the trees. She clutched her musket, and Mathias pushed past. "MacVie, on your feet — ah, damn his eyes!" She swiveled to see the black hat left as decoy in the grass. Then she dashed for the horses.

David yelled, and another shot sounded much closer. Several more close shots, and she reached Samson, who, with the other horses, shied about. Out in the woods, she heard Creek battle whoops. Jacques exulted, "*Vive le Montcalm!*" and followed it with his own whoop. Mathias sprinted past the horses and discharged his rifle. A man screamed. Alerted by peripheral vision, she pivoted to spot MacVie, his right arm recoiled, an eight-inch knife in his hand.

She hit the dirt. In passage, the knife clipped her hat from her head and pinned it to a tree not far behind her. Terror rebounded her to her feet, musket in hand, to find him gripping a tomahawk. "Will can't help you now, wench. This is between you and me." Yellow teeth bared, he charged her.

She shrieked, hauled up her musket, and fired point-blank into his pelvis. Hot blood spewed everywhere, including her arm, and he flopped on the ground, screaming. Horses whinnied.

A tattooed blur of rancid bear grease wielding a tomahawk leaped over him and vanished into the dense tree growth, followed by a man's screech of terror from the trees and another Creek whoop. MacVie began bleating his epitaph, his dark eyes imploring, agonized. Sophie threw down her musket and gagged at the sight of death and the stenches of blood and burning black powder. The pulse of blood from his severed pelvic artery slowed. A rattle took up residence in his throat. She backed into Samson, spun about, and leaned against the horse, drinking in his familiar warmth and smell. Grabbing the saddle, she gagged again and almost vomited.

She heard a final, distant report from a firearm. Then the forest, including MacVie, quieted. Her right sleeve, sprayed with blood, grew sticky. She clung to Samson's saddle, and they calmed each other.

In the distance, David yelled, "Sophie! Sophie!"

Mathias sounded at least as frantic. "Near the horses!"

Fowler in hand, David crashed through underbrush and emerged at the horses. "Ye gods — Sophie!" He dragged her around and clutched her. "How much blood on your arm is yours?"

"None," she squeaked into his shoulder. Beneath the stink of sweat, blood, and black powder, she smelled David's familiar scent. She started trembling again. Two years earlier, she'd fired pistol shots out her dining room window to chase bandits off her property. She'd heard the pain of one hit by a ball, but she hadn't *smelled* it. And she hadn't killed him. Her stomach lurched.

David set her out at arms' length. The sight of sweat spiking his hair and runneling through dirt and powder on his face pitched her from nausea into a burst of hysterical laughter. Never before had she seen her brother in such disarray.

Mathias bounded onto the scene, drew up short at the sight of the body, and sprinted for her. He caught her up in an embrace made awkward by the fact that it included his rifle. "Your arm — you're hurt!" He dropped the rifle and took her face in his hands. "I shouldn't have left you. I promised, gave my word. Forgive me."

An elemental tremor grazed her at the touch of his callused hands on her face, the first time in all her life that a man had held her face. From the earnestness in his black eyes, she doubted Mathias had needed *any* convincing from Will a month before. It led her to wonder: What had her father intuited all these years that caused him to assign Mathias as her protector? David, however, required no guesswork. Wiggling his eyebrows, he ambled away.

After a moment, flustered, she guided Mathias's hands off her face. "I'm all right. Really."

David stood over the body and grimaced. MacVie's blood had attracted blowflies. Sophie looked away in haste, her nausea returning. "H-he threw a knife at me and missed, then came at me with a tomahawk, so I —" So she killed him, a human, her neighbor, someone she'd bartered and danced with. "I shot him."

David sounded on-edge, disgusted. "I took care of Donald Fairbourne." He hadn't enjoyed killing. "Charley Osborn and Pete Whitney ran afoul of Uncle Jacques's tomahawk."

"I shot Measure Travis." Mathias retrieved his discharged rifle, his teeth jammed together. He hadn't enjoyed killing, either.

Alton's rebels had been disbanded — almost. David glanced at Mathias. "Sam Fielding ran away eastward. Sehoyee Yahuh gave chase."

Standing Wolf — where was he? The expression on David's face mirrored her realization that Jacques and the two brothers were missing. Twigs snapped. They spun about, Mathias reaching for his tomahawk, David ready with a knife.

Jacques and Runs With Horses walked into view towing the Indians' horses. Standing Wolf limped, bloody-legged, between them. Dark satisfaction filled Jacques's eyes when he spied MacVie's body. "Excellent. We need not worry about that one escaping." His ropy neck rotated to allow him sight of Sophie's hat pinned to the tree. He scowled, freed the hat, and tossed it to her. "That dog MacVie stole my extra knife — and my second tomahawk!" He knelt, whisked MacVie's purse from his waistcoat as if purse cutting were second nature to him, and retrieved his tomahawk. "I presume that is not your blood, *belle* Sophie. You are using your arm much too well."

Still shaky, she approached Standing Wolf with Mathias. "Did you find Sam Fielding?"

The warrior scowled. "His feet and dagger were too quick."

David gestured dismissal. "He isn't worth hunting at this point. If we don't intercept El Serpiente by tomorrow night, we'll have to wait for him in St. Augustine. Let's get out of here before scavengers assume we're trying to compete."

Standing Wolf leaned against a tree, his expression stoic, the gash in his thigh oozing. Mathias and Sophie inspected the wound, and she straightened to look in the Creek's dark eyes. "We'll dress it quickly so we can leave. You may need stitches later." He nodded, impassive over his injury.

Mathias muttered to her, "Why did they ambush us? Can it be that they did help El Serpiente murder Will and Jonah?"

That theory held water better than others, but it still contained too many holes. Little would make sense until they tracked down and interrogated the man known to them only as El Serpiente.

Chapter Twelve

PICKETED NEAR THE road, the mounts of Donald Fairbourne, Peter Whitney, Measure Travis, and Charley Osborn grazed. Churned grass, hoof prints on the road, and a dropped haversack testified of Sam Fielding's frantic flight northward on horseback. Having confiscated the dead men's supplies, the travelers divided their money. Then they took the road south after a detour into the thicket to discourage pursuit, the extra horses plus MacVie's roped behind them, the empty saddles discarded.

Mathias scouted a mile ahead in the sweltering afternoon, warning the party into concealment from marching militiamen and, later, from several families with wagons. Runs With Horses ranged a mile behind to verify lack of pursuit. By dark, they'd put more than thirty miles between them and the noontime carnage.

The drenching of afternoon rainstorms was a mixed blessing, washing away evidence of their passage, yet promoting activity of insects. Camped a mile from the road on Perkins Bluff, they ate a meal from their stores and banked down the campfire after it provided light for Mathias to stitch Standing Wolf's thigh.

Sophie collapsed on her bedroll, exposed skin smeared with bear grease. Her inner thigh muscles felt like throbbing jelly, and bruises and insect bites mottled her skin. Although she'd changed shirts and washed the blood off, her right arm still felt sticky. Most of the dead men had families. Three nights earlier, she'd danced with MacVie.

Every time she closed her eyes, she saw blood spray, heard screams and moans, and smelled death. Revulsion and regret pirouetted through her soul and ground at her stomach. The worst part about it was realizing she'd make the same choices again.

For an hour she listened to men's snores before she pushed her blanket off and stood. From the direction of the road, a red wolf howled. She hobbled a circle around the coals and swung her arms, wishing her mind would quiet.

Jacques materialized from the surrounding foliage. "A problem, *belle* Sophie?"

"I'm too tired to sleep. I'll take your watch for you."

Chuckling, he cradled his musket and meandered to her. "*Non.* I am wide-awake. I have relived the times Pierre, Jean, Auguste, Claude, and I made a glorious team for Montcalm, cutting down the English pigs. Back in '58 we built a rockslide. When the pigs triggered it, those who were not swept off the mountainside screaming were crushed beneath boulders." He chuckled again.

"We were reunited at the side of Colonel Prescott near Breed's Hill five summers ago, but we had claimed our most excellent victory days before that. We discovered the route some pigs were taking to Boston, and we disguised a pit in the road filled with sharpened sticks. While we watched, a half-dozen pigs marched into it and impaled themselves." He sighed, enraptured, oblivious to the disgust filling her face.

Having witnessed the Frenchman in action, Sophie no longer dismissed his war stories as figments of an old man's imagination. Another wolf howled from the direction of the road, closer to the campsite. One of the pack answered from beyond the road. "Uncle Jacques, the French War is long over."

"*Au contraire*, we are still fighting it, and we will not stop until arrogance has been wiped from English faces."

The west shadows around the campfire emitted Mathias, concern on his face. "Sophie, you cannot sleep?"

She shook her head. "'Out, damned spot.'"

"Ah." He sighed, his face filling with regret, and nodded. "'What's done cannot be undone.'"

Jacques frowned. "Whose secret code is that?"

"Shakespeare." Mathias's gaze met hers, and she knew that he commiserated with her sense of loss. She fished out a smile for him, enjoying the "secret code," wondering if he'd intended a double meaning in his quote.

Disdain curled Jacques's upper lip. "The Bard — bah! What is wrong with Racine or Molière, eh? I shall translate for you the wit and wisdom of Alceste in *Le Misanthrope.*" He cleared his throat and adopted a swagger straight from the Comédie Française. "'The more one loves, the more one should object to every blemish, every least defect'." Sophie's efforts at restraining a grin were almost undone when she realized Mathias also struggled to submerge his humor. "'Were I this lady, I would soon get rid of lovers who approved of all I did, and by their slack indulgence and applause endorsed my follies and excused my flaws.'"

A wolf howled less than a quarter mile west. Picketed together, the horses shifted about, ears pricked, nostrils examining the breeze. Mathias said to Jacques, "Pardon me, Alceste, but we've camped across a favorite wolf route."

Annoyance speared Jacques's expression. "I shall make sure the horses are secured."

Sophie imagined indignation seasoning the howl from the wolf that sounded off next. His fellow, just as close, voiced his displeasure. She looked at Mathias. "They sound quite close."

"They'll get closer."

"Are we in danger?"

He motioned her to help him build up the fire. "We won't provoke them, and their food supply is abundant this summer."

Runs With Horses joined Jacques at the horses. David and Standing Wolf rose. Needing no explanation for the sonata swelling around them, they faced outward, listening, weapons ready.

At least eight individual melodies of wolf-song flavored the night while the pack encircled them to protest invasion of their territory and insist on their departure. Eager to comply, the horses struggled with the instinct to flee while responding to the assurance imparted by Runs With Horses's touch and murmurs.

Her back to the crackling fire, Sophie glimpsed the glint of green eyes in the foliage and lifted her musket. Gooseflesh raised on her arms and neck at the raw emotion hurtling through her. Fight or flight — was she the hunter or the hunted? The green eyes subsided into night. She relaxed and exhaled a shaky breath. Near her, Mathias said, "He's assessing for his leader."

The pack elevated their chorus to a din, members pacing just beyond the reach of firelight. She let the butt of her musket slide to the ground and, balancing the barrel against her pelvis, covered her ears. For another minute or two, the pack maintained the racket, ancient warriors in ceremony around a sanctuary they could neither enter nor leave. At last, resignation punctuated the howl of a wolf farther away — the leader summoning the pack to more productive activities. After voicing final opinions on the intruders, each wolf rejoined the leader and the night.

Runs With Horses had calmed all eleven horses, but Sophie stroked Samson because she'd never been so close to wolves in the wild. Her ears still ringing, she watched Jacques wiggle his forefinger in his ear with an expression of distaste. "One thing is certain." He switched fingers and ears. "The night will seem very quiet now."

★★★

Cirrus curtains draped Wednesday's steamy sunrise. Sophie tightened a strap on her saddle and wondered when she'd sleep well again. What slumber she'd snatched had been splintered by visions of MacVie's agonized face and a dream wolf — gaunt, gray, and winter-worn — that circled her and howled with laughter. "*La hija del Lobo*, no daughter of mine. It isn't *me* you should track. Frightened yet? Go home to your beau before it's too late!" How utterly macabre.

Next to her, David secured his bedroll to his saddle. From the purple smudges beneath his eyes, she knew the loss of their father had overtaken him, too. But by that evening, the Fates willing, they'd catch El Serpiente, and perhaps they could close a door on the murders of their loved ones.

She muttered, "I keep going over it in my head, but it makes no sense. Why do *you* think MacVie and the rebels wanted us dead? Were they bought by El Serpiente and trying to assure his safe passage to St. Augustine?"

"If so, I'm glad those buggers are dead, but I just don't swallow it. To be truthful, I'm not sure Fairbourne wanted to kill me. From the look on his face, he might have settled for scaring me off, driving me back to Alton. I've no idea who made the first aggression — it all happened so fast — but it's no use speculating or casting blame. Fairbourne's dead.

"And that the old man is gone, too — I mean, there's a part of me that refuses to believe it." He choked off and gritted his teeth before releasing a fey laugh. "It's so odd that he's gone the same week as old Carey, as if the two of them sat down together and plotted it out — the two peas in the Alton pod."

Like a second masquerade for both men. "Elijah must have had a St. James in his ancestry. Or maybe Father had a Carey in his."

David's smile withered. "Insanity. Rebels murdering each other, mysterious Spaniards wandering into it and being flayed alive. It's a black, bloody masquerade, that's what it is. Mathias got a look at the old man's corpse. He must have been unconscious or already dead when they burned him because his arms were straight, not contorted from being tied to restrain him. As if that suggests the killers were humane. But there's nothing humane about murder. And we're still missing a crucial piece to the puzzle."

She couldn't have agreed more. She studied him. "Had you killed someone before yesterday?"

His hand on the saddle hesitated, and he didn't look at her. "Eight years ago. I was all of twenty-three."

"What happened?"

"It was a stupid thing — really, *I* was quite stupid."

She voiced her instincts. "There was a woman involved."

Joyless laughter escaped his nose. "A married woman."

"You dueled with her husband?"

"Yes. I will never fight another duel." So that was why he preferred widows. "Killing is wretched business. You never forget that last look on their faces."

No, she'd never forget MacVie's eyes when she shot him. Even though her own survival had depended on killing him, she couldn't rejoice at being the survivor, not while the deed was fresh and a portion of her soul sleepwalked with Lady MacBeth. She wondered how soldiers and militiamen could kill repeatedly. All those sets of eyes, damning and beseeching.

David shook his head. "I find no glory in killing another." He glanced over her shoulder. "Monday afternoon, when Uncle Jacques flaunted his enmity over Fairfax, I thought him a fool doting on memories of the Old French War. Then I saw him go after Peter yesterday. If he and Fairfax ever come to blows, Fairfax will have far more on his hands than he expects."

With a shiver, she recalled the angelic radiance on Fairfax's face Sunday morning, when he offered to interrogate her. "Unfortunately, so will Uncle Jacques."

***

By nine, cumulus cluttered the humid atmosphere, heralding afternoon thunderstorms. Concealed in the thicket just off the road, Sophie, David, Jacques, and Runs With Horses awaited the scouts. Standing Wolf, whose thigh gave him no cause for complaint, reported the road empty at least a mile to the south. Mathias rejoined them a few minutes later from the north. "Three peddlers are headed southbound. If we let them travel with us, we'll hear news."

Jacques narrowed his eyes with suspicion. "They will also learn about us."

David pushed his cocked hat up on his forehead. "Not if we allow them the

stage. Peddlers love to talk about themselves."
Sophie said dryly, "Any Spaniards among them?"
The others stared at her a moment. Then Mathias grinned. "A good point.
I didn't see a Spaniard."
"Well, then, if you didn't see a Spaniard, and you didn't recognize any of
them, let's invite them to join us. David, you spin a story about us traveling
to — uh —"
"To Savannah. To deliver horses to my sister. And Bear Tracker here and
his brother are horse trainers."
"Plausible enough. Just don't give it too much detail. It's hard keeping
track of lies."
He winked. "Especially in the boudoir."
Jacques wiggled his eyebrows. "*Mais oui!*"
Peddlers Harry, Rob, and Tim and their packhorses soon caught up with
them, and David's congenial nature encouraged all three to set aside their
road-wariness. Paunchy Harry relaxed and gabbed about his fabrics. Spindly
Tim's business was deer hides. And red-haired Rob peddled herbs.
Sophie made herself inconspicuous. From the peddlers' cursory glances
at her, they'd assumed her a scrawny boy, and she liked it that way. Besides,
between their bombast and David's coaching, she couldn't have wedged in a
word. But also, the agony from her thighs, ten times worse than that on Tuesday, forced her to concentrate on staying in the saddle.
From time to time, a peddler would glance at the road behind. David finally
said, "You expecting company?"
Harry's laugh was nervous. "Ah, no, at least I hope not."
"Sounds like you're running from a cuckolded husband."
Excitable laughter burst from Tim. "Imagine the likes of *you* cuckolding
some doxy's old man, Harry."
Harry scowled. "Why laugh? I got me a doxy in Charles Town, Augusta,
and Savannah — more than I can say for *you.*"
David flagged off the bicker. "See here, we don't want to catch a ball meant
for your hides, so out with it, lads, on the looks behind."
Rob licked his lips. "It ain't a jealous husband. It's them soldiers we passed
yesterday."
"Ah, the militiamen. We passed them, too, with naught but a nod of greeting."
"No, there was a party of ten redcoats headed south on horseback. They'd
stopped about thirty miles or so back. Nabbed a fugitive, they had, and were
interrogating him."
Sophie forced her facial and shoulder muscles to relax and noticed Jacques
attempting to do the same. But all those years of card playing had been a boon
to David's theatrics. He slapped the pommel of his saddle. "Jolly show! I say,
it's about time the redcoats rounded up criminals and made the land safer."
"True," said Harry in a grudging tone, "but criminal or no, I didn't like what
I saw and heard yesterday. Off to the side, a lieutenant was flogging a fellow.
As we rode past, there stood the major, calm as you please at the roadside,
giving us a good day like he'd just stepped out of a meeting with Parliament,
la-dee-dah."
Rob grumbled. "Like it was all in a day's work for them to thrash the poor

lout around."

Tim said, "He enjoyed flogging him, the lieutenant did."

Loathing punctuated Jacques's mutter. "English pig."

Sophie shuddered. In his desire to escape the previous day's carnage, Sam Fielding had hopped from the frying pan into the fire. The word "mercy" wasn't in Fairfax's vocabulary. As for *why* Edward Hunt and Dunstan Fairfax had elected to give chase, she surmised the quest must have become personal for them.

The back of her neck tingled with apprehension. Any soldier who defied movement orders risked a court-martial. Lieutenant Fairfax must be damned certain the quest would score him glory vast enough to excuse his defiance. Will St. James and Jonah Hale had been murdered for that glory. She stared ahead, southward, as if she could see past the hundreds of miles that separated her from St. Augustine. Her neck tingled again.

"To be perfectly honest with you folks," said Harry, "we'd like to pick up the pace a bit. You're good company, but we'd rather not run into *them* again."

She wondered what the peddlers would think if they knew dead men's horses were roped behind them. David rotated his head to evaluate the others in his party. "These fellows want more speed of the journey. That meet with your approval?"

She thought he'd never ask. They mumbled their agreement. Biting her lip against the throbbing in her thighs, she kicked Samson into a gallop. And the party of nine flew south on the postal road beneath the congesting cumulus of late morning.

Chapter Thirteen

NEAR BRIAR CREEK and the Savannah River, the road sloped out ten feet into dark swamp muck. The terrain stank of sulfur and stagnation, like dozens of farting cows. Beneath overwatered, undernourished trees, Sophie mopped sweat off her neck and slid the soggy kerchief beneath her hat to blot at the hairline. Gnats and flies persecuted the sweaty travelers and tired horses.

In that location back on March 3, 1779, British General Prevost had battled with General Ashe, resulting in two hundred drowned Whigs. She wondered what possessed the men to fight in a place where anyone could drown in seconds by walking the wrong path. Surely they could have agreed to find solid ground first. Women would have done so — but women would probably have found *common* ground and left the scene without resorting to a battle.

During the day, the peddlers had figured out she was a woman, but none had so much as leered at her. Their manners might be attributed to the presence of her five companions. However, she received the impression that none of the peddlers was the sort of fellow to abuse a woman. For random travelers encountered on the road, she could have done far worse.

Rob fidgeted. "Those friends you said you was waiting for out here ain't going to show."

Harry jutted his chin at the western sky, where towering cumulus churned and boiled higher during the time they'd waited at the junction. "I don't like the looks of the weather."

Rob spread his hands. "There's a tavern and trading post at a crossroads a few miles south. They got a decent ale with beds and clean sheets if your money's good. You can even get hot water. And the roof don't leak."

Sophie and David exchanged a look of dejection. Mathias and his cousins had scouted into the snake-infested swamp and found no sign that anyone had preceded them to the area — if their guess had even been correct about El

Serpiente's itinerary. With a thunderstorm threatening and the evening approaching, they'd have to push on.

David beamed at the peddlers. "You fellows have the wisdom of it. I'll buy you a round of ale for being such good sports and waiting with us."

The peddlers' spirits perked up at the mention of free brew. Everyone began mounting horses. Sophie stroked Samson's neck. "Five more miles, hey, boy? I'll find you oats and dried apples if you'll just give me five more miles." Samson's tired, dark eyes regarded her with understanding, so she hauled herself back into the saddle, clamping her teeth together against the agony in her thighs. "Good boy." She took a deep breath and trotted him after the others. "This hurts me far worse than it hurts you."

***

Pipe smoke blue-hazed the candlelit common room of Woodhouse's Tavern — a sturdy timber building, the only watering hole for miles — and muted its yeasty, sweaty stink. At one of the rough-hewed tables, six men huddled over dice while several others pondered backgammon. A fiddler scratched out "The Star of the County Down" while a red-haired matron with an Irish accent mangled the tune for her red-haired, Irish family. Men talked over tankards, and women mended socks or embroidered by candlelight at the table next to Sophie, sleepy youngsters nestled against them.

The only woman in the room wearing trousers and a man's shirt, Sophie was also the only woman in the room cleaning a musket — anomalies that other women had difficulty comprehending, judging from inquisitive glances aimed her direction. They probably hadn't blown a man's guts open and stood their ground against wolves in the past thirty-six hours, either.

In the shadows, Standing Wolf and Runs With Horses murmured with Creek warriors from a nearby village. A weary-eyed David leaned against the stone fireplace with his tankard, ignoring Harry's pleas for a card game. Mathias was out back in the forge helping the elderly blacksmith repair the Irish family's wagon wheel, and Jacques lurked around the kitchen.

Widow Woodhouse slid a tray before Sophie and unloaded a bowl of stew, fresh bread, softened butter, and a tankard of cinnamon water on the table. Then, she hiked up her petticoat and straddled Sophie's bench, wobbling it. "I do wish I spoke more French. That father-in-law of yours well knows how to make an old woman remember her girlhood."

Father-in-law? Jacques had spun some crazy story to capture the widow's favor. Sophie sniffed the repast.

Her amiable face rosy, Mrs. Woodhouse tucked gray hair beneath her mobcap. "*Voulez, voulez, voulez.* I could hardly get my work done for him trying to butter the bread in the oven, if you take my meaning."

Hard to miss Jacques's meaning when he spoke that kind of French. Mouth watering, Sophie set her cleaned musket aside and picked up her spoon. "This smells delicious."

"Eat, child. You're nothing but skin and bones. Got you some hot water started. Should be ready in half an hour. I'll show you the tub out back soon as you've supped."

Sophie swallowed a mouthful. Not enough salt, but after two days of deer jerky, she didn't care. "Thank you."

"Need laundry done? My granddaughter could use the work."

"Umh-umh," said Sophie, her mouth full of bread.

"Got extra oats for the horses in the morning. Poor beasts look half-starved, too."

"Umh-umh."

The proprietress regarded the collection of people, then looked back at Sophie. "So good to have a common room full of decent guests like this. Makes me glad to help travelers."

"Umh-umh."

"A pleasant older gentleman passed through here just after noon, two young fellows with him. All polite. They ate up quick and rode off southbound but left me a decent tip." All right, all right, Sophie acknowledged the hint about a tip. She noticed the widow's expression cloud. "They wasn't at all like that Spaniard who came through about four o'clock."

Sophie coughed up cinnamon water. "Did you say a Spaniard?"

"Aye. He frightened me. You know, sometimes you can tell when a man has killed people. This dreg had me fingering my pistol. I was never so glad to get rid of a patron as him."

So El Serpiente was only about two hours ahead of them. Sophie cast an eager glance in David's direction, but in the next instant estimated the effort they'd exert to overtake the Spaniard and slumped in her seat. She and her party, horses included, were exhausted. If they took up pursuit without rest, each of them might as well shoot themselves in the foot for all the progress they'd make. But an emergency meeting that evening and a pre-dawn start for the morrow were in order.

"Your business must seem dangerous and frightening sometimes with patrons like that Spaniard and his companions."

"Companions? Hah. He was traveling alone. Scum like that don't have friends."

Hadn't MacVie said El Serpiente was accompanied by two Bostonians, "friends of John Adams"? What had happened to them? Perhaps MacVie had lied about them, and El Serpiente traveled alone — yet the campsite near Butlers Creek displayed evidence of three travelers. Even more pieces were missing from the puzzle than they'd assumed, but one thing was certain. Mrs. Woodhouse was observant. With the redcoats less than a day behind, Sophie's party couldn't afford to stand out in her memory by asking peculiar questions about travelers who'd preceded them. "Sorry. I misunderstood." She took another bite of stew. "Delicious. Don't forget our blacksmith."

"I fed him first. Such a kind fellow to help my brother with the wheel. You're a lucky woman."

Why was she a lucky woman? Then, recalling the widow's comment about Jacques being her father-in-law, she realized the story the Frenchman had spun. Jacques needed his mouth gagged. Sophie sweetened her smile. "We're lucky for your hospitality."

Mrs. Woodhouse patted her shoulder. "You need anything else, you let me know. Oh —" A conspirator's twinkle entered her eyes. "I save the little room in the corner upstairs for special guests. You can have it tonight."

Gratitude surged through her. Despite the stress of the past few days, her menses had started right on time, and she was cranky enough to tell her male companions to ride off without her. A night spent alone without their snores would be a delight. "Thank you."

"Cozy in there. Just enough room for the two of you." With a wink, the proprietress heaved herself up, retrieved the tray, and lumbered back to the kitchen.

Oh, hell. Jacques had woven quite a web, the old fool. Annoyed, she nevertheless plowed into her food. She was better off straightening out the sleeping arrangements on a full belly.

The fiddler finished the tune, and the Irishwoman was welcomed back to her seat by polite and obligatory applause from patrons. Tankard in hand, David pushed up from his bench and headed for the fiddler, with his height clearing the low ceiling by only a foot. Sophie motioned him over to tell him about El Serpiente, but he waved her off.

After David spoke with the fiddler, the man sawed out bars of music that sounded vaguely familiar, and naughty. David nodded approval, initiating the first bawdy song of the evening. The entertainment would degenerate from there and run the women and their children out of the common room and upstairs to bed.

Sometimes when David got rolling, he was difficult to snag off the stage. Sophie's lips pinched over a burst of displeasure and prudence. She'd grab him between songs, allow other guests to become the center of attention.

The fiddler fired up his introductory measures, and David, saluting her with his tankard and a wicked grin, sang:

A lusty, young smith at his vise stood a-filing.
His hammer laid by, but his forge still aglow.
When to him a buxom, young damsel came smiling
And asked if to work in her forge he would go.
Jingle bang, jingle bang, jingle bang, jingle heigh, ho!

A match for the smith, so away they went thither.
Along to the young damsel's forge they did go.
They stripped to go to 't, 'twas hot work in hot weather.
She kindled the fire and soon made him blow.
Jingle bang, jingle bang, jingle bang, jingle heigh, ho!

She lowered her gaze to the stew, a flush sweeping her neck and cheeks. Jacques had a collaborator. She needed to shut both of them up. Chatter and clatter dwindled so the men could enjoy David's baritone. When it came time for the refrain, they chorused it with such vigor that she was certain the tavern walls would cave in for the "jingle banging."

David circled the room for the next two verses. Women gathered children and bustled out. He wiggled his eyebrows when he reached Sophie on the fifth verse.

Six times did his iron by vigorous heating
Grow soft in her forge in a minute or so,
And often 'twas hardened still beating and beating,
But the more it was softened, it hardened more slow.

All the men swung their tankards in the air and roared, "Jingle bang, jingle bang, jingle bang, jingle heigh, ho!"

She collected her dishes and musket and hauled them from the common room, chased out by the closing verse:

The smith then would go, quoth the dame full of sorrow,
"What would I give could my husband do so?
Good lad, with your hammer come hither tomorrow,
But pray, can you use it once more ere you go?"
Jingle bang, jingle bang, jingle bang, jingle heigh, ho!

Out in the kitchen, she surprised Jacques with his hand on Widow Woodhouse's hip. Sophie set the dishes on the counter, juggled her musket and wagged a finger at him. "That is unconscionable!"

He withdrew his hand looking insulted. "At our age, we need no chaperone, *belle* Sophie."

"You know what I mean. You and my brother are scheming."

His face crinkled with a leer, and he listened to David's second song for a moment. "He has an excellent singing voice, *non?*"

"It's gone quite far enough, thank you. Step inside to the hallway. You and I must talk."

He kissed the widow's hand in apology. "I will return soon, *mon fleur.*" Mrs. Woodhouse sighed and fanned her face with her apron. Sophie flounced from the kitchen.

While David commanded patrons' attention through more ribaldry, she motioned Jacques down the hallway. They paused before a window, and through waning daylight she glanced at the forge out back, where a blacksmith's hammer bent scarlet metal with a rhythmic plunk and thud. She propped her musket against the wall and turned on the Frenchman. "El Serpiente passed through here two hours ago."

"*Mon dieu*, such incredible news! How did you come by it?"

She packed ice into her tone. "By *not* having my hand up Widow Woodhouse's petticoat like some slimy old satyr."

He grinned. "You would be amazed at the volume of secrets petticoats conceal."

"Mrs. Woodhouse divulges *useful* secrets in response to other stimuli."

"We must tell the others immediately. Fetch your brother and the warriors, and I shall fetch Mathias —"

"I shall fetch the others." She grabbed his upper arm. "*You* fetch David. The matchmaking game you and he are playing is neither just nor kind."

"*Belle* Sophie, how much longer are you going to fight it?"

"Fight *what?* There's nothing there, Uncle Jacques. Otherwise Mathias would have shown me by now."

"That all depends on what you are looking for from him."

She released him. "Untangle the sleeping arrangements."

"But it gives me such delight to be your father-in-law."

"Don't ruin my friendship with him."

His lower lip jammed into his upper lip. "It must be your monthly time."

"*Uncle Jacques.*"

"Very well." Expression long, he headed for the door to the common room, where he paused with his back to her. "Let us discuss your news outside. No interruptions, no eavesdropping."

"Five minutes. We'll meet you and David behind the forge."

Chapter Fourteen

DARKNESS DULLED SOPHIE'S view of the Woodhouse's yard from the tiny window of her room. Washed of trail grime, she'd earned sleep in preparation for resuming the trek at four in the morning. Yet when she stretched out on the bed, sleep evaded her.

Far to the north, her sister grumbled over the printing press. Not so far away, Edward swatted mosquitoes and pined for mosquito-free, thunderstorm-free Hampshire. Miles to the south, the serpent pressed on to St. Augustine: El Serpiente, the blackguard who figured somehow into the murder of her father. And Zack MacVie's damning, beseeching eyes chased her.

Visualizing Will's face almost released her tears, but again they dried up. In the final months of his life, as the silence and awkwardness swelled between them, there'd been too much they hadn't said to each other. Now they'd never have the chance for those conversations. Memory of the dream wolf taunted her: *no daughter of mine.* When had he stopped loving her, and why?

The anguish in her soul drilled down to an ancient depth, and a seventeen-year-old memory trickled into her mind from the day after she returned to Alton with infant Betsy. Although she hadn't yet mentioned it to a soul, Richard Barton had proposed marriage to her two nights before, in Augusta. "I'll consider it," she'd told him.

"What's to consider?" He'd studied her, astonishment rolling across his handsome face. "Don't you love me?"

That exchange seemed hauntingly familiar to her now.

But seventeen years ago, she'd forestalled giving him her answer for a few days. She had unfinished business in Alton.

***

The thud of a hammer shaping hot metal came from the shop behind her.

She settled Betsy in the sling and smiled up at her father in the sunlight. "A quarter hour."

Will studied her from the driver's seat of the wagon, his gray eyes discerning and shrewd. "A quarter hour." He lifted the reins and paused. "Sophie, you look lovely."

Oh, gods, she hoped so. "Thank you." She waved him off. Betsy cooed from the sling. "Soon, my love," she whispered.

Dusting off his hands, a leather-aproned Jacob Hale limped from the forge into the shop at the jangle of the bell, while the sounds of smithing continued from the forge. Arthritis had already claimed his left hip, but his stern Presbyterian visage relaxed at the sight of her. "Mrs. Neely, how good to see you! What's it been, a year since you left? You shouldn't have stayed away so long. It's almost as though you were hiding in Augusta. Now, who's this?" He helped her extricate Betsy from the sling and held the baby. "A beautiful child. Look at all that dark hair. Hmm." He glanced back and forth between Sophie and Betsy, and she held her breath. "I believe she's going to look exactly like you when she grows up. I don't see a speck of Jim Neely in her, God rest his soul."

She exhaled and grinned. "Everyone says that."

He handed Betsy back to her and jiggled the baby's fist, curled around his forefinger. "Wa-wa-goo-goo. How strong that grip is, little one. If you were a boy, I'd say that fist was meant to swing a blacksmith's hammer."

Sophie forced her jaw to relax. "Now really, can you imagine Betsy a journeyman?"

"No, no, no. Wa-wa-wa-goo-goo-goo."

She cleared her throat. "Um, who else is here? I'd like to show off my pride and joy before my father returns."

Formality drew over his face. He straightened and jutted his chin toward the forge. "Mathias."

"Well, then, I shall just walk on back —"

"Don't take up much of his time. He has a substantial amount of work to finish."

"All right." She turned away to hide her irritation. He always had a substantial amount of work to finish, twice as much as Jacob, Jonah, and Joshua. When he returned from visiting his Creek family, he had three times as much work. Yet somehow he managed to get it all done.

She hesitated in the doorway of the forge, the heat intense, the dusty smell of red-hot metal drenching the air. Faced away from the doorway, Mathias probed the living glow of the forge with tongs, sweat seeping through his shirt and waistcoat. Her gaze strayed to his left shoulder. Outrage scored her soul again. Scars should never have been on his shoulder that summer afternoon the year before.

He pivoted to the vise, a glowing spear of metal captured between the tongs, and spotted her in the doorway. "Sophie?" he whispered.

She smiled. "Hello."

Metal abandoned on the vise, he seized a towel and rushed forward, mopping his face, mirroring her grin. "How wonderful to see you again! You look marvelous. Say, is this Betsy?"

"Would you like to hold her?" Oh, please say yes.

"*May I?*" *He brushed soot off his leather apron.*
Ecstatic, she handed Betsy over. "*Ba-ba-ba.*" *Betsy gazed up at Mathias.*
"*Da-da-da.*"
"*She's beautiful, just like her mother.*"
Hunger in his eyes spiraled across the distance between them and coiled around her heart. "*Thank you,*" *she whispered.*
"*Ironic. She doesn't look a bit like Jim. Just like you.*"
Now was the time to speak. She parted her lips.
Movement snagged her eye, someone entering the forge from the outer door. A gangly, young Creek woman waddled forward in the beautiful, clumsy way of pregnant women and stood beside Mathias.
At Sophie's blank look, he said, "*My wife, Teekin Keyta. Did no one tell you?*"
Teekin Keyta — Stands Tall. "*No.*" *Sophie produced an even voice and bobbed a curtsy.* "*How do you do.*"
"*This is Sophie Neely. She's a childhood friend who has been living in Augusta. She stopped in to introduce us to Betsy.*"
Stands Tall glanced between Betsy, Sophie, and Mathias. "*Betsy looks like her mother.*"
Understanding shone in Stands Tall's eyes. Oh, gods, she knew. Change the subject, quickly. "*And when is your baby due?*"
"*Two months.*" *Mathias handed Betsy back.*
"*Congratulations. I'm sure you'll both be very happy.*"
Will waited in the wagon in the shade across the street when she emerged from the shop. He helped her aboard with Betsy, climbed back up, and twitched the reins. The wagon swayed. "*Something bothering you, Sophie?*"
"*Why didn't anyone tell me Mathias Hale had gotten married?*"
"*Obviously it must have been an oversight. Sorry.*"

***

She stared at the ceiling. It wavered and blurred while the storm built inside her. Then she rolled onto her stomach, buried her face in the pillow, and yielded to grief in racking sobs. That was it, the moment when spirit departed the communication between father and daughter. Why hadn't she seen it before? All those years her father had known about Mathias, and likely her mother had, too, but they'd never lectured her about her choices. Alas, by now the smile she'd worn for her husbands fit her face too well. She might even produce it for Edward Hunt and perpetuate her own masquerade.

Will had never stopped loving her. He'd grown frustrated with her choice of men, for his approval had gone to Mathias. But she'd been blind to it. Futility and irony forced out another onslaught of tears. Well meaning but naïve, her father hadn't recognized that Mathias was only interested in being her friend. Surely she would have noticed by then if he'd wanted more — wouldn't she have noticed? Her sobs dwindled, and she pondered.

A generation had passed in eighteen years, enough time for two people to diverge in interests and beliefs, to shake off childhood fascination and release into the past one afternoon of intimacy. After all that time, she and Mathias still kept each other's confidences, enjoyed each other's company. Was that all he'd ever wanted from her?

What did she want from him? Her fingers lifted to her cheek, recreating the sensation of his hands on her face from the day before, the touch that conveyed a feeling so unique that she'd no name for it yet, no kin in the repository of her experiences.

She shivered. Whatever the touch had awakened, it wasn't worth ruining a friendship.

Weariness ripped a yawn from her, and she rolled onto her side. As she slid into sleep, the certainty sneaked over her that the afternoon at the forge had also been the moment when two giddy youths had become duty-bound adults.

***

Standing Wolf's hushed voice penetrated her peculiar dream about sharing the bed with Jim, Richard, and Edward: "Nagchoguh Hogdee. We talk. Quickly." She rolled up, groped her way to the door, and cracked it open to the bear-greased shadow outside. "Ten redcoats on horses with one extra horse headed south on the road, five miles north of here."

She gaped. "This moment?" From her estimation of how long she'd slept, surely it wasn't past three in the morning. Edward must have driven the patrol much of the night to have covered such ground. That meant ten exhausted soldiers and eleven exhausted horses were less than an hour from the tavern. "Thank you. Wake the others, starting with my brother. We leave in fifteen minutes."

After she'd stubbed her toe twice on the bed, she lit the candle to finish dressing. With luck, they'd have at least a quarter-hour lead on the British. From the taste of her own fatigue, she knew Edward and his party would have to rest before resuming pursuit.

Only after she'd pulled on her stockings did the significance of the eleventh horse in Edward's group strike her. The horse must be Sam Fielding's, *without* Sam Fielding. The soldiers, deeming him useless at tracking their fugitives, must have decided he was more trouble than he was worth. She shuddered.

A yawning Mrs. Woodhouse met them out in the stables ten minutes later, lantern held high, two bundles beneath her arm. "I wish you folks could stay another hour and a half. Porridge with raisins and cinnamon for breakfast, starting at four."

Edward loved porridge with raisins and cinnamon and would be most appreciative. Sophie smiled. "You've been so kind, but we're running behind schedule."

The widow extended wrapped trail bread to a sleepy-eyed David, then motioned Sophie closer to hand her the second bundle. "I figure you could use some extra rags. Cannot say I blame you for running off your husband last night. I never wanted *mine* in the bed when my monthly time was upon me."

Sophie glanced around to Mathias, who leaned half-asleep against his saddle, and almost hoped the widow would spin a tale for Edward Hunt of a menstruating, musket-toting martinet. After all, why should General George Washington be the primary source of legends during the war? "Thank you, Mrs. Woodhouse."

With the extra horses roped behind, the travelers walked their mounts from the barn into the frog song of the yard. Mrs. Woodhouse's cur padded circles around them, tail wagging in adieu. A waxing quarter-moon silvered the swamp and showed the southbound road deserted. The widow waved. "Visit us again, especially you, *Monsieur*."

"*Au revoir, cherie*." Jacques blew a kiss.

"*Vive le Montcalm*," David said under his breath, eliciting a grin from Sophie.

At the road, Sophie, who rode MacVie's mare for a day to give Samson a break, surveyed the five men. "Anyone see why we shouldn't put as many miles as possible between us and the redcoats by taking the road until dawn?"

David sounded awake at last. "No arguments here."

Sophie's heels tapped the mare in the ribs, and she felt the horse leap forward, eager for the canter she paced her in. Overhead, Vega, Deneb, and Altair steered the Summer Triangle and the heavens full of stars westward. And a shooting star curved southward through the cosmos, blue-white beacon to East Florida.

Chapter Fifteen

DAVID SETTLED HIS hat on his head. "Surely we've lost the redcoats in the swamp. And I dreamed last night that Fairfax was eaten by an alligator."

Jacques paced near Runs With Horses and Standing Wolf. "After that English pig is court-martialed and sentenced for ignoring movement orders, he may wish he had been eaten by an alligator. But the palates of alligators are more discriminating."

"Amazing what you'll eat when you're hungry." A turkey buzzard landed on a limb of the pine above David and regarded humans and horses with dispassion. He flicked his hand at the bird. "Begone. We aren't ripe enough for you yet."

Sophie pushed up from where she'd been studying the map. "Have you gentlemen considered who the soldiers are pursuing?"

Jacques shrugged. "Us. So we remain in the swamp."

Mathias stood with the unfolded map. "They may also be chasing El Serpiente. But it's getting swampier, and I don't enjoy sharing a route with so many hungry water moccasins. My cousins and I are unfamiliar with this terrain. Unless we return to the road, we'll still be picking our way through swamp two weeks from now, too late to stop any meeting in St. Augustine."

David rubbed his hands. "I cast my vote for the road."

Jacques's expression clouded. "Do not say I did not warn you. This part of the road is far from deserted."

Sophie winked at Mathias. "Well put, Ambassador Hale."

"Thank you, General Barton."

She studied their location on the map, peered through tree branches at the sun, then folded up the map. "We've enough daylight to find a campsite south of the Canoochee River."

"Better still, an inn in Savannah — Huzzah!" David reached for his horse's reins, a jig in his step. "Savannah, Savannah, on a Friday night. Savannah, oh, Savannah on a Friday night."

She cocked her eyebrow at him while handing the map back to Mathias. "Surely we announced our whereabouts to the redcoats back at Woodhouse's Tavern. Would you do so again in Savannah?"

"Dear sister, do you know how many inns there are in Savannah?"

"Dear brother, do you know how many redcoats there are in Savannah?" In response to Mathias's tug on her hand, she glanced to where he held her hand palm up. "Is something wrong?"

Amusement enlivened his dark eyes. "I couldn't help but notice. The lampblack and varnish are disappearing."

She studied both palms, amused by the thought that Lady Beatrice's hands, in contrast, would be soft and white, the nails trimmed and polished. "Why, so they are. I suppose that means Paper Woman has retired. What sort of name shall I take now? Wolf Woman? Musket Woman?" She chuckled. "Swamp Woman?"

Mathias tucked the map beneath his arm and took her other hand in his. "All Women," he whispered.

The warmth and gentleness in his expression quieted the restlessness in her mind and the words on her tongue. She followed the luminous guide of his dark eyes into a realm where the quest and all her irritations and terrors receded. Imagining again the feeling of his hands on her face, her soul resonated with understanding. Then she heard Jacques's voice: "Now we know why the swamp steams," and she spied David and Jacques leering.

Infusing her expression with what she hoped was silly charm, she withdrew her hands and prodded the map beneath Mathias's arm. "Don't lose our location on the map, Ambassador."

His eyes twinkled. "No, General, I don't believe I shall." David and Jacques whooped with satisfaction.

Late afternoon found the party south of the Canoochee River and Savannah and north of the town of Sunbury. Westering sunlight glinted on the sweaty black shoulders of slaves trudging through rice fields, and on musket barrels of white overseers astride horses. Everyone Sophie saw — slaves, redcoats, Indians, colonists — wore a forbidding expression. Every tree they passed bore a broadside denouncing the acts of renegade bands of Whigs or Loyalists. She kept her head bowed and averted her gaze from other travelers. The subdued posture they adopted blended well with that of area inhabitants.

Early in 1779, the redcoats had overpowered two hundred Continentals holding the small, earthen Fort Morris, which protected Sunbury town and port. They'd then dismantled the fort and wharf, destroying what supplies and equipment they couldn't carry off. Their actions incensed local plantation owners, who were forced to haul their produce twenty-five miles or more to the port of Savannah.

David had related tales of Savannah's Committee of Safety plotting in back rooms of taverns, burning effigies of King George, rioting in the streets, and dressing like Indians to dump British imports into the harbor. The miasma of fear, desperation, and hostility hovered in the air — palatable, clammy, fetid — made concrete when David, in the lead, brought their party to a halt at the top of a rise. Beside the road a hundred feet south, a group of two-dozen civilians had clustered around the trunk of a tree. Nailed to the tree was one of Will's "Tarleton's Quarter" broadsides.

A man lunged forward and ripped the broadside off. "Whig rubbish! I'll wipe my arse with it!"

Another man shook his fist at him. "Murdering redcoats. Kill us all in our sleep, just like that butcher, Tarleton!"

"Lies! It wasn't *redcoats* who raped my niece and held her for ransom! It was Whig scum like you!"

"King George is the liar, and you're the nockhole for believing!"

"And it's Whig bum-fodder like you what printed these broadsides!"

"Where's the tar and feathers, lads? I say we give these Tories some new clothes!"

Approval resounded from half the crowd, and the mob congested. A pistol shot rang out from within the knot of people. Sophie and the others galloped the horses back north on the road several hundred feet before heading west into the marsh and paralleling the road by a quarter mile. Brother killing brother, neighbor against neighbor, father betraying son — and not a redcoat in sight. That seemed the way of the war in the southern colonies.

Quite a difference from the day before, when they'd traveled without incident to their campsite between New Ebenezer and Abercorn. Alton, too, was tame in comparison. Not for the first time on the journey did she realize how fortunate she'd been to live so sheltered a life. And she thought with longing of her safe, comfortable bedroom and her safe, comfortable vocation at the printing press.

Mathias, scouting ahead, found a ridge of dry land half a mile from the road, sheltered by a grove of pines. After the horses had been unsaddled and rubbed down, he and the Creek brothers disappeared to hunt with their bows. Jacques led the horses down the ridge for water. Sophie and David built a fire.

Although she'd no difficulty lighting the resinous pinewood, she'd have given three armloads of it in exchange for a couple of seasoned hardwood logs, for fire devoured the pinewood and gave them more sparks and pops than heat or light. She and David were forced to forage in the gathering dusk for more firewood. She returned to the fire ahead of him, dumped a load of branches, and began feeding them into the flames.

A twig snapped behind her. Snatching up her musket, she rose, pivoted, and peered into the surrounding foliage. "David?"

"Damn," said a man, "look at that. It's a *woman*."

She faced the voice, musket raised. "Show yourself."

Response slurred from the opposite side of the foliage. "Tad, you reckon we ought to leave anything of her for Ben?"

Laughter rumbled from several men in the foliage. Fear chilled her. She cocked the musket fully.

"Man, I don't know." That voice sounded slurred, too. The men were drunk. "You reckon she knows how to use that musket?"

"She's looking like she's used it before."

Mere threats with her musket might not be enough with these men. Zack MacVie's screams of agony haunted her memory and flooded her with nausea. The thought of killing another human was almost as horrifying as that of being assaulted. Her hands began shaking, and she silently implored the men to back off.

"What the hell, there's six of us and one of her. Who's had the least whiskey? Jed, go on out there and coax that musket out of her hands."

"Kiss my arse, Hoppy. She's too old to be worth having my jewels blown away."

"Yah, and I like 'em with big bubbies."

"Jove bugger the lot of you. I say she can't aim that thing worth shit. I'm getting me that oyster basket."

A man tottered from the foliage unshaven, reeking of whiskey. Terror commanded Sophie's reaction. Two seconds later, a leer still pinched the left side of his face as he collapsed, the right side of his face blown away. With her discharged musket, she clubbed the groin of the closest bandit who leaped out at her. He doubled over in torment. The other four wrested the musket away and pinned her arms behind her.

Breath stinking of whiskey and rotting teeth slammed her face. "She *is* awful old and skinny."

"Release me!" She thrashed for escape, and pain shot through her shoulders.

"Shit, why bother Ben with her?" Fumbling with the buttons on his breeches, the bandit tottered, his sneer revealing blackened teeth. "I'll empty my own stones in her —"

"Sophie!" The back of the bandit's head dissolved in a spray of bone fragments, brains, and blood, and he sagged to the ground. A snarling David charged through the black powder smoke, knife raised.

She twisted and jammed her heel into the instep of one of the men holding her. He howled and turned her loose. Another man whipped out a pistol and aimed at David. The third man pinned her arms again. She screamed. "David, look out!" The report of the pistol echoed through the trees. David cried out in agony, dropped his knife, clutched his left upper arm, and fell to his knees. "David!"

"Son of a stinking slut — Ben warned you about wasting ammunition!"

"Kiss my arse, Tad! He was going to spit me on that knife!"

"How many more of them are there?"

"I don't know."

"Let's get the hell out of here."

"Without their money?"

"Those two weren't traveling alone. We're probably outnumbered. Take the old nag's musket, and let's begone."

"With the old nag?"

"Why not? Ben may want her after all."

Like hell. Arms still pinned behind, Sophie stomped for another instep. When she missed, she tried to wriggle free. One of the other men seized her plait and brought the point of his knife within six inches of her left eye. "You cooperate, or I put your eye out."

She ceased struggling, her gaze fixed on the knifepoint, her gut churning.

"That's better. Wheezer, on your feet, you whoreson!" The man kicked the leg of the bandit who was still incapacitated on the ground from her blow to his groin. Without waiting to see whether he revived, the trio marched her from the campsite and down the ridge.

On marshy moonlit ground, they halted long enough to bind her hands behind with a kerchief, long enough for the pistol-toting bandit to reload. Stinking of sweat, he waved the pistol in her face. "Make any trouble for us, and you're carrion." He spat near her feet for emphasis.

They marched her across the tall-grass salt marsh eastward. When she stumbled and fell, bruising her left shoulder, they hauled her to her feet and shoved her onward, ever deeper into the nightmare. Terror kneaded her stomach. She tried not to wonder what size reception she'd entertain at her destination or anticipate her fate with the entire gang.

Chapter Sixteen

AFTER A HIKE of a quarter hour, they entered another pine grove. Sophie smelled horse dung, wood smoke, whiskey, and human waste. Staggering into the cleared circle around their campfire, she tallied a couple dozen bandits before one of her captors gave her a shove that sprawled her into a noisome mass of pine straw. "Look here, Ben, we brought you an oyster basket!"

A heavyset, oily man heaved himself up off a fallen log and approached her, eyes bloodshot with whiskey and fatigue. He yanked her to her feet, jerked her head back by her plait, and groped her breasts through her shirt. "Bloody old and skinny, but I reckon she'll do for me. And you boys are welcome to her afterwards."

Stinking of diarrhea and whiskey, Ben wheeled her around and paraded her past the men, who shouted their suggestions for his sport. Terror coiled in Sophie's stomach and rotated dark specks through her vision. This wasn't a nightmare from which she could awaken. No one was going to rescue her. She'd be violated by the mob for hours, unless she found a way to rescue herself. Her brain clutched for something she'd read earlier that day on a broadside, a caption about rebels exchanging a kidnapped nobleman for one of their own destined for the gallows. Did she have the presence and mettle to pull off a bluff? Anything was worth a try.

She honed an imperious edge on the British accent she'd heard so often. "Release me this moment!" Thank heaven her voice didn't betray how she shook. "None of you is man enough to recognize a woman nobly born!"

The command in her tone sliced through enough of the mob's derision to taper off some of the noise.

"A woman nobly born?" Ben roared with laughter, turned her loose, and leered at his men. "Sure, and next we'll entertain Lady Pitt, the Duchess of Chatham, or perhaps Queen Charlotte herself. Tad, where'd you find this doxy? In a tavern?"

"Eh, no, Ben. At a campsite about a mile and a half away."

"You killed everyone who was with her, right?"

"Eh, no, Ben. Sly shot one of them, but we ran off before the others showed. Here's the woman's musket —"

"*What*? You bleeding idiot, you left a trail for them to find, and you bring me a bleeding musket?" Ben whipped a knife from his belt and flung it. Tad screamed, the knife embedded in his chest, his hands clutching at the shaft, his body convulsing. Keeling forward onto one knee, he succeeded in prying the knife out. Heart blood spurted forth. Sophie closed her eyes a moment and shuddered over the bandits' idea of discipline.

Ben waddled over, kicked a gurgling Tad aside, wiped his knife off on Tad's clothing, and shoved it back into his belt. He dragged another bandit by the shirt closer for scrutiny and flung him toward the trees. "Stand watch with Rabby. You, too, Jed. You boys got the least whiskey in you."

The two trudged off to patrol the perimeter, taking their muskets with them. Ben snatched up Sophie's musket, swiveled his gaze around the group grown silent and sullen, then headed back over to her, drawing up so close that his foul breath coated her. "What's your name, woman?"

She held his stare, not knowing whether he could tell how her stomach still heaved. Since he seemed familiar with the names of British nobles, she raked her memory for the name of one who supported the cause of the colonists. Lennox, the third duke of Richmond, perhaps. "Lady Sophia Lennox."

Ben's eyebrow rose. "Lennox? As in Charles Lennox, the secretary of state?" She nodded.

A brigand across the fire sounded apprehensive. "Ain't Lennox partial to the patriot cause, Ben?"

Another outlaw spoke out. "Yeah, if she's a Lennox, we can't touch her."

"Been sticking up for us, Lennox has. The gods know we need more of his kind over there."

Ben bellowed with laughter. "Cow piss!" He slapped Sophie's shoulder. "'Lady' Lennox, suppose you explain to me what an English gentlewoman is doing out here in the middle of the night dressed like a man?"

Was her bluff actually working? The bandits around the fire were paying attention. She lifted her chin and maintained the imperial accent. "I am returning to Savannah from St. Augustine with my escort of *twelve*. As for why I'm dressed like a man, well, I invite you to don stays and a petticoat and see how comfortably you can travel in such a manner."

Bandits guffawed. "Ben, we'd like to see you in a petticoat." "Yah, Ben, with stays jamming your teats up your nose." "Wag your arse on the wharf. See what money you fetch!"

"Shut up, you bung-hole cleaners!" Ben began pacing. "Didn't you hear her? She had an escort of twelve."

"All we saw was one. And Sly shot him."

Sophie's heart had ceased hammering enough for her to drill Ben with a glare. "It might be expedient for you to consider me a candidate for a prisoner exchange." She slathered haughtiness into her tone. "And I remind you that should you consent to such an exchange, it behooves you to leave me unmolested while I'm in your custody."

A sneer imprisoned Ben's face. After flinging down her musket not far from the edge of firelight, he swung his fist in the direction of several of the bandits. "Barney, haul your arse over here and tie her Ladyship up!" Dear gods, her bluff had worked! "Sol, get out there and help Gabe with the horses. The rest of you, do what you got to do to get your miserable hides sober. We're marching out in a quarter hour. *All* of you, no more whiskey until the morrow!"

Within a minute, she found herself sitting, hands and feet bound, at the edge of camp, her musket forgotten on the ground about six feet from her. Adrenaline ebbed. She felt cold, drained. Her memory revisited MacVie's face and that of the bandit she'd shot, lingering on the sight of blood on her brother's arm, the contortion of agony in his expression. David, oh, David.

A bandit staggered over and retched into the bushes near her. The stench settled over her like a sticky cloud. While he staggered back to the campfire wiping his mouth, another bandit pissed on the ground nearby. She drew her feet up closer to her body to avoid getting splashed. The night seemed to have no end.

Rustling in the bushes drew her attention over her shoulder. She caught her breath when a pair of dark eyes materialized in the bushes, and Mathias lifted his finger to his lips. She took a deep breath and let it out slowly, almost unhinged with relief. Caught up with departure preparations, the mob had ceased paying her direct attention. A gentle tug and loosening of the rope binding her hands told her Mathias was cutting her free.

From somewhere out in the trees, she heard the approach of multiple horse hooves, a pistol report, and a man's scream of pain. More screams — human and equine — erupted from beyond the trees. Then seven sword-wielding redcoats thundered into view on horseback, Lieutenant Dunstan Fairfax at their lead.

Fairfax's voice roared through the campsite: "Tarleton's Quarter!" Scarlet archangel from the abyss, he dismembered or beheaded four bandits. Through geysers of blood, their heads bounced and rolled, and their bodies collapsed, twitching. Horror punched the breath from Sophie's lungs and paralyzed her, even as the rope fell away from her hands.

Drunken bandits scattered, bellowing with panic. A few managed to discharge their pistols at the soldiers, but terror torqued their aim awry. Swinging their blades like scythes, Fairfax and the six soldiers mowed the band of brigands down. Severed arteries spurted. Bandits writhed and screamed.

Mathias sprang from concealment into chaos, a single slash of his knife freeing her feet. Two bandits charged Sophie and Mathias with knives. Mathias yanked her to her feet and thrust her musket into her hands. She clobbered a bandit in the head with the butt while Mathias kicked the knife from the other's hand and kneed him in the groin.

She scurried into the bushes with her musket, but not before a backward glance rewarded her with the sight of Edward and two other soldiers riding into the clearing. The blacksmith caught up with her. "Go! Run like fire!"

They sprinted for the moonlit marsh, galvanized by the pounding of pursuit, and emerged from the pine grove into moonlight. Sophie tripped over the body of a bandit with an arrow through his throat. As Mathias heaved her to her feet, a sword-bearing Ben barreled from the grove and was upon them. "Whore of Babylon, I'll cut your scrawny teats off!"

She screamed. The *schlick* of an arrow silenced when it pierced Ben's throat. The bandit gurgled and sagged to the grass, thrashing.

Bow in hand, Standing Wolf emerged from behind a lone tree, while Runs With Horses trotted their four horses over. Mathias shoved Sophie up into Samson's saddle. Her limbs beginning to tremble, she kicked the gelding into a gallop and, with her companions, fled the massacre in the grove.

At the ill-fated campsite, she spied her brother propped against his saddle, bare-chested, near the dying fire. A bloody knife nearby, Jacques finished bandaging David's arm and sat back, satisfaction on his weather-beaten face. She rushed to them and threw her arms about David, who clutched her with his right arm. "Sophie, oh, gods, Sophie, are you all right?"

She doubted she'd ever be "all right" again. "Yes. Let me see your arm — broken?"

Pallid-faced, he struggled up to a sitting position and shook his head. "Mere flesh wounds."

Jacques laugh was harsh. "How like a brother to not worry his sister. I pulled a ball from his arm."

David gritted his teeth. "None too gently, I might add."

"Uncle Jacques, did you get all of it out?" Her words sounded distant to her. She felt distant, as if she were teetering on the fringe of humanity.

"Of course, *belle* Sophie."

"Thank you." She shook out David's shirt, then stared at the bloodstains on it.

"Unfortunately I have performed such grim service many times before, once on my own leg at Saratoga." He grinned at David. "You want to see the scar, eh?"

Even through his pallor, David managed a gusted laugh. More stories of valor from the annals of Jacques le Coeuvre. "No. I'll take your word for it."

Mathias strode past the body of the outlaw David had killed and knelt beside David. "Our redcoat friends are about a mile in that direction butchering bandits. They were making quick work of it, so I cannot imagine them wasting time before they look for us. Can you ride?"

"Jove's jewels, the mongrel didn't shoot my bum, you know."

Mathias helped him stand. "I don't want you bleeding to death on the road."

"As I've never been a martyr, I'll let everyone know if I start bleeding to death." He snatched his shirt from Sophie. "Let's go."

Chapter Seventeen

TWO HOURS LATER, beneath a half moon and firmament of stars, they guided the horses to firm ground west of the road. A groan escaped David's lips when he slid from his saddle, and Sophie led him to moonlit grass. "Sit. I'll care for your horse tonight."

"Thank you." He folded his long legs beneath him. "I hope we left the whole bloody lot of redcoats behind."

Jacques yawned. "We should be back on the road by sunrise."

Sophie said to her brother, "Help me remove your shirt so I can change the bandage."

"My arm doesn't need more prodding tonight."

"If gangrene sets in, you'll be shuffling cards one-handed. Off with your shirt!"

Mathias led his horse past. "You'd best do as General Barton orders. Wounds like that fester."

Cursing under his breath, David eased his shirt over his head. "The rotten luck of it. I could have been at a Savannah card table tonight plucking purses and drinking whiskey."

Well she knew he might have enjoyed Savannah. *She* might have slept in a bed at a decent inn. She'd voted to bypass Savannah and pitched them into that snarl of outlaws and redcoats — gotten David shot, and nearly gotten herself violated by a gang — and she'd had to kill a *second* man, not that she wanted to dwell on that at all. She unrolled David's bandage. How naïve she'd been to insist on making the journey. Were her companions humoring her: a "general" with no field experience?

Eager to embrace a caregiver role, she re-poulticed and re-bandaged David's wound before seeing to their horses. The others made a fire and boiled water, and she prepared a mug of willow bark tea to ease David's pain. To the rest of the pot, Jacques threw in a soup square, dried vegetables, and the two dressed rabbits caught before the party abandoned the first campsite. The aroma soon had the five men milling about in anticipation.

Her appetite gone, Sophie trudged to a creek fifty feet from the campfire. Screened in the long grass, she stripped and sponged off sweat, horse, grime, and crusted menstrual blood. But neither caring for David nor wearing clean clothing improved her spirits. She felt empty inside and not quite real, as if she weren't awake — sleepwalking, indeed, like Lady MacBeth, now with two men's blood on her hands.

While she pounded away at soiled rags and clothing, Mathias ambled out, making himself heard in advance, and crouched near her. "Plenty of stew left."

"I'm not hungry." She wrung out her shirt.

"You haven't been eating enough."

"Yes, I know. I'm so skinny that even bandits debate whether I'm worth ravishing."

A growl burst from his throat. He snatched the wet shirt, flung it on the ground, and shook her once. "Quit blaming yourself! We agreed to stop back there. Mistakes happen. You were tired, your attention wandered —"

"My brother got shot, I nearly got..." Her voice squeaked out of a throat tightened with tears, and she attempted to twist away from him, humiliated because her tears wouldn't be dammed this time. "It *is* my fault! I should have listened to David, and we should have stayed at an inn in Savannah." Her voice went shrill. "You were right! I should never have come! I don't know what I'm doing out here." Tears rolled down her cheeks. "I've killed two men, bungling my way through it!"

"Sophie, each one of us here has killed at least two men."

"But how can you and the Indians kill and be done with it? You don't like to kill. I saw it in your face Tuesday."

His shoulders slumped, and his voice thickened with remorse. "None of us enjoys killing."

"Yet you leave it behind you like ashes at a campsite."

"What would be the point of dragging it with us? We carry too much in this life as it is. We — Indians — thank Creator that we were the survivors of a deadly encounter, and we move on. If you expect to complete this journey, Sophie, you must find your own road past killing MacVie and that bandit. At your life's end, you will stand before Creator and the lake of spirits and speak to all, not only of your sorrow but of the wisdom you learned on this journey."

She stared at him, his ideology stark, meaningful, piercing. Then her remaining composure crumbled into sobs, and he tucked her against his shoulder.

Had it been merely a week ago, Friday night, that she lay in her bedroom, listening while rebels printed broadsides? Those horrid broadsides popped up everywhere, poisonous toadstools of the press, fertilized by bloodlust and rage.

Colonists were falling upon themselves in a frenzy of bloodlust, forging a nation founded on insanity. They might demonize the likes of British such as Banastre Tarleton, but it was only to thwart themselves from looking in the mirror and seeing the Demon Ultime reflected back at them.

Why had she thrust herself into such a morbid quest? For family honor? For sweet Betsy and her unborn child? For herself, because she was bored with life in Alton? If so, surely she was just as crazy as every rebel in the Congress was.

"I want to go home." Tears congested her voice.

"We *all* want to go home." He pressed his cheek to her tears and wrapped his arms about her waist, folding her into the hearth of his body, his touch communicating that it made even less sense to turn around and go home than to keep pushing forward. They'd already traveled more than halfway to St. Augustine.

He held her through the search she made of her soul for a corner in which she could bind desolation, terror, and hopelessness. Somehow, she had to keep pushing forward and not allow any of it to bind her, not even when she'd had to kill two men. She didn't have to like any of it, but she *did* have to move forward. Mathias was right. She carried far too much with her.

Moonlight silvered the marsh. Frogs throated night, and crickets chirped. An ancient memory stirred in her brain. Earth, salt, musk — a man's flesh and fire forgotten for eighteen years. Clay to clay, the curves and angles of their bodies sought each other, shifting and sedimenting together until a scarce-remembered fit emerged. She breathed in cadence with Mathias and the nocturne of the marsh.

His cheek caressed hers. Lips parted, she tilted her face toward his until the corners of their mouths brushed. An elemental ember of forge-fire fanned back to life and swelled between them. In wonder and delight, she tilted her head further. Lips hunted for each other, and she tasted the moisture of his mouth.

He pulled back from her, his hands fumbling for hers, covering them with his own. Through resonance pulsing between them, he shook his head, denying his thirst.

"No?" she whispered, baffled. Every nerve in her body vibrated to close a circle left ajar for eighteen years. Why did he push her away?

"All the handsome men you've chosen, with blond hair and blue eyes."

She gripped his hands, trying to shut out a flood of memories — images of handsome blond-haired, blue-eyed Jim Neely, Richard Barton, and Edward Hunt. "I haven't chosen Edward Hunt."

"Ah, but he's chosen you, and he's everything Alton is not. How can any woman turn her back on a protector in Parliament? I know what he offered you. David told me. I can give you nothing like that, Sophie." Moonlight starkened torment on his face after he pulled free of her. "At least I know you consider me your confidant and comforter." Pain and confusion knotted his voice, her heart. "That's more than will ever be said for any of *them*." He strode back to the campfire as if he couldn't escape quickly enough.

***

Sophie lay on her bedroll, her gaze following meteor trails, a list of attributes grinding through her brain. Edward: intelligent, handsome, wealthy, enchanted by her. Mathias: intelligent, successful, confidant, friend. The analysis allowed her scant sleep, and when she did sleep, she dreamed of men's faces floating on the surface of a lake of spirits, their eyes damning and beseeching her. The party broke camp predawn Saturday with Sophie feeling every sore muscle in her body.

Did Edward imagine Lady Beatrice stupid, just because she was fifteen? Why, if *Sophie* were Lady Hunt, she'd hire someone to follow Edward and get to the bottom of any frequent visits to London. A lifestyle of silk gowns and theater visits must be exquisite. But if she became Edward's mistress, contention with a noblewoman the age of her daughter was inevitable, and not an experience for which she was eager to cross the Atlantic.

As for Mathias, she didn't understand the reasoning by which he'd arrived at the conclusion that he could only be her friend. It seemed obvious that if she'd "chosen" Edward Hunt, she'd have stayed with the victorious redcoats at the bandits' campsite instead of escaping. Mathias surely hadn't factored much logic into his decision-making.

Damned if she understood men.

No such perplexity saddled David's mind. The willow bark tea had allowed him to awaken well-rested and eager to move on. By late morning enough of his personality returned for him to canter his horse up beside hers and give her a wink of sarcasm. "You look like the cat dragged you home and left you on the doorstep."

"Thank you."

"I'd like to think it was fresh air and exercise doing you so much good." Swiveling, he glanced at Jacques, who rode ahead, and Standing Wolf at the rear. Mathias and Runs With Horses were out scouting. "I really think it's a certain *nothing* we discussed on Monday, before starting our journey."

She stared ahead, her brain exhausted. "You're right. It's nothing. I won't waste my breath talking about nothing."

"Maybe I'll discuss it with Mathias, then, because I couldn't help but notice after you two returned from your stroll last night that nothing was clearly wrong."

She glared. "Keep out of it, or I'll punch your arm."

He cringed. "Ooh. I was just trying to help."

"Help someone else. You're about to ruin a friendship."

"There are ways aplenty to encourage such a friendship —"

He broke off to the sound of a horse galloping in from the south. With no time to seek cover, they pulled to the roadside and readied weapons. Mathias thundered into view and reined back his mount. "Quickly! There's a man left for dead about a mile down the road!"

They kicked their horses into a gallop and followed. Minutes later, they arrived on the scene — grass trampled and torn, a dead saddled mare, and a raven-haired young man sprawled supine near the horse in the humid shade of a lone pine, blood darkening the right side of his well-tailored waistcoat.

At their arrival and dismount, the man's eyes flickered open. He lifted his head, dark eyes full of pain and determination, hand closing about the handle of a pistol holstered at his hip. Robbery hadn't motivated the attack. Bandits would have stripped him and taken his weapons.

David caught Mathias by the upper arm. "Watch yourself. He thinks we've come to finish him off."

Jacques knelt beside the mare. The man's gaze wandered back and forth between Standing Wolf and Mathias. "Indians. At least not redcoats." He sank back, hand still clutching the pistol.

Redcoats. Interesting. Sophie wondered how old he was. He reminded her of her son-in-law, Clark. So young.

David spread his hands. "Let us help you."

The man dropped his hand away from the pistol and nodded. David and Mathias approached with caution. Jacques whispered, *"Belle* Sophie," and directed her attention to the man's saddle. "Made in Boston, the excellent work of a patriot saddle maker named Herman Stone. I recognize it."

Her attention sprang to the wounded man. "A friend of John Adams?" The Frenchman nodded. She looked from the empty road north to where Mathias knelt beside the man in the grass, David standing behind him. "How Fairfax would love to get his hands on him."

"We need not let that happen."

They agreed silently before she approached the pine. Mathias had opened the man's waistcoat to blood soaking the right side of his fine shirt. He groaned while Mathias pulled the shirt from his breeches. Blood rimmed a shot hole below his ribcage. The blacksmith poked his finger through a rip in the front of the shirt and one in the back. "The ball passed straight through you, front to back."

"He killed my horse and left me for dead."

Mathias studied him. "Who attacked you?"

The young man looked away. "A highwayman, of course."

Of course? Mathias and Sophie regarded each other a moment, and she read his acknowledgement that the man had lied. This wasn't the work of highwaymen. Why would a wounded man protect the identity of his attacker? A chill teased her neck.

Mathias offered a curt nod. "We've no way to tell what the ball nicked inside you. How long ago did this happen?"

"Mid-morning. My two companions and I had just taken a break."

Two companions. The puzzle grew more complex. MacVie had said El Serpiente was traveling with two Bostonians, but by Mrs. Woodhouse's account, El Serpiente had been traveling alone. And hadn't the widow also commented on a party of three men who'd passed through before the Spaniard and left her a decent tip? "So you were wounded no more than two hours ago." Sophie sank in the grass near the man's left shoulder.

Hearing her voice, he regarded her with perplexity. "A woman?"

"And you're a friend of John Adams."

His eyes widened in astonishment. "Who are you?"

"Good Samaritans."

David leaned over, his right hand braced on his knee. "We're on the trail of a man known as El Serpiente. We want to question him about a murder. What's your name?"

Expression closed from his face, but not before they'd seen a flash of panic in his eyes. He rotated his head back to stare at pine branches above, lips clamped shut. A frown dragged from Sophie's brow to her lips. "Suit yourself. We've redcoats tracking us no more than four hours behind. Cooperate with us, and we'll get you to safety. Don't cooperate, and we'll let them have you." The man's cheeks paled further. "And by the by, the British lieutenant's disposition doesn't portend any displays of leniency from him toward wounded spies."

"My name is Stephen Hawthorne," whispered the wounded spy.

She doubted he gave his real name. "A pleasure to meet you, sir. Given the urgency of the situation, I think it prudent to bandage you and see whether you can ride one of our spare horses."

Caution edged Hawthorne's expression. "I shall try."

"Good. While we're tending your wounds, it only seems fair if you tell us some information about El Serpiente, since from your expression you obviously know him." She smiled. "We've come almost literally through hell and high water to find him."

Chapter Eighteen

WHILE JACQUES KNELT to inspect the saddle of the dead mare, Mathias pressed a doubled cloth to Hawthorne's injured side. His face blanching with pain, Hawthorne leaned back on his left hand to hold the wadded cloth in place so Mathias could bandage his midsection. "I was traveling to St. Augustine with companions. That's all you need to know."

Sophie's eyebrows shot upward. "And their names?"

"I'm not at liberty to tell you."

Jacques's hand sneaked to one of Hawthorne's saddlebags. What was that wily old Frenchman up to? She said, "It's useless for you to dodge our questions. We know you expected to meet Don Alejandro de Gálvez in St. Augustine."

David sucked a gasp, and Sophie stared at a pistol suddenly grasped in Hawthorne's hand, leveled at Jacques. Pain clipped the spy's voice. "I thank you to keep your hands off my property. I appreciate your assistance, but it is discourteous of you to take advantage of my incapacitation and snoop."

Diplomacy stretched Jacques's lips over his teeth. "My apologies." He stood, keeping his hands in view, and when the pistol motioned, stepped away from the horse carcass to where Standing Wolf stood out on the road.

Sophie eyed the saddlebags. What was Hawthorne protecting?

He holstered his pistol and glanced at her. "Very well, yes, a meeting with Don Alejandro was arranged for us in St. Augustine."

"Will Don Alejandro then plead the cause of the Continental Congress to King Carlos?" She studied Hawthorne's noncommittal expression. "Spain has yet to ally herself formally with the Congress, but it's clear from the way she's intrigued with France for half a year that she's determined to thrash Britain."

Hawthorne granted her the ghost of a smile. "Spain will divide with France the spoils from this war."

"Spoils?" Sophie echoed the smile, even while intuition prodded her. He wasn't what he seemed. Something in his accent, perhaps. "Spain would dearly love to have East Florida back. She was the first European nation to claim the territory." She listened to his response.

"The Congress shall return East Florida to Spain, who has, of late, seen the value of intensifying military activities against Britain. One of my companions bears intelligence from the Continental Army. He will meet with Don Alejandro to discuss how Spain's strategies might be synchronized with ours."

"With *yours?*" Cynicism brushed Mathias's tone. "What is left of the Continental Army after the fall of Charles Town?"

The young man looked south. "We shall fight to free this country from King George's tyranny until the last of us falls."

Hawthorne might be from the North, but his mindset matched that of rebels from Darien, Georgia to Williamsburg, Virginia. Ironic that those who strove to oust the government, rather than defend or reform it, envisioned themselves the "patriots."

David's tone was quiet and firm. "Sir, we're in the position of protecting you. You owe us an explanation of who we're protecting you from and what's in your saddlebags."

His chin lifted. "I've told you all you need to know."

"Not quite." Sophie pulled the second cipher from her haversack and showed him the numerical sequence. "This cipher was intended for Will St. James, except that it arrived the day after he was murdered in Alton — we suspect by the serpent."

Hawthorne's sulk intensified. "You expect me to decode it?"

"No. I've already done so. It instructs him to meet in Havana, as St. Augustine has become too dangerous. The serpent knows about it." Hawthorne's lips compressed. "El Serpiente." She returned the cipher to her haversack. "Who is El Serpiente?"

The young man studied her, obstinate, and made a faint gesture of dismissal with his head. "As you've deduced, La Habana is our alternate meeting location. We've no idea whether El Serpiente knows it's the secondary site."

La Habana. How interesting that he gave Havana its Spanish name. And it was obvious he didn't want to tell them more about the Spaniard. Sophie glared at him. "El Serpiente. Who is he?"

He sighed. "He's a trained assassin from a Spanish faction called *Casa de la Sangre Legítima.*"

David's expression soured. "'House of the Rightful Blood.' What is it they think is so rightful about themselves?"

"They resent the influence of French Bourbons on Spain and believe that Spain, allied with France in the Old War, has lost enough to Britain in North America. They commissioned master assassins last year to infiltrate the coalition between Spain and France. Five came to America to assassinate Spanish and French representatives and anyone who gets in the way."

David expelled a hard breath. "Jolly. That's ever so damned jolly. Here we've wandered into the midst of it all."

"Their signature execution is to slit the throat of a victim from ear to ear."

Mathias's eyes bulged for a second. Then emotion slid from his face.

Hawthorne said, "Two assassins were killed in the northern colonies last year. Three continue the mission."

Jacques ambled over. "*Au contraire*, Alton claimed a third just last week. He was flayed alive."

Suspicion pierced the pain on Hawthorne's face. "Who would do such a thing?"

Sophie resisted the urge to look northward along the road. "We're not certain. The assassin's body was found near the bodies of two other men."

Mathias glowered. "My brother was one of them. His throat had been slit from ear to ear."

Hawthorne bounced his glance around the party. "It sounds as though an assassin got him, but I wouldn't know for certain."

Would they ever have their suspicions confirmed about who had murdered Will, the other Spanish assassin, or Jonah? Hawthorne talked in circles, and they didn't have time to dawdle and question him more. Since Mathias had finished with the bandages, Sophie stood and brushed off her hands. "Let's see if you can ride. I apologize we've no leisure to brew you something to ease your pain."

His features distorting with pain, the young man accepted Mathias and David's assistance in standing. Then he insisted on transferring his saddle and saddlebags from the dead mare to Donald Fairbourne's horse. Mathias checked his bandage, but no fresh blood soaked outward from the wounds. Helped into the saddle, the spy took the reins despite bloodless lips. Not while he was conscious was he letting the redcoats have him or what he transported.

Runs With Horses caught up with them as they resumed their trek south on the road to report the absence of soldiers for several miles back. In Creek, Standing Wolf updated his brother on Hawthorne. The rigors of horseback sealed the Bostonian's remaining strength into silence. They walked the horses a few minutes to make sure the young man wasn't going to collapse. Then they increased their pace to a trot. Mathias resumed scouting southward, and Standing Wolf dropped behind.

David sidled his gelding up to Samson. Sophie assessed her brother's preoccupied expression. "How's your arm?"

"My arm? Oh, *that* arm. Hurts like the deuce." He nodded toward Hawthorne, twenty feet ahead of them, and murmured, "I don't know how he stays in his saddle without whimpering."

She lowered her voice, too. "Weren't you ever fervent and idealistic when you were a puppy?"

"Possibly about women, but I doubt I'd ride with two holes in my side for any woman. And definitely not for a cause."

"There's more to him than meets the eye."

"Or ear."

"You heard it, too. His accent."

"He wasn't born in Boston."

She nodded. "He speaks Spanish words with such clear vowel sounds. I wager he was born in Spain and raised and educated in Boston."

"And Hawthorne's an alias. Something else doesn't make sense. He was shot from the front, but his horse was shot from *behind*. Who shot him, El Serpiente? Was the assassin responsible for both shots?"

"Maybe he had help. He mentioned a fifth assassin."

"We should have checked the site for more evidence." David gnawed his lower lip. "The morning you were under house arrest, I told you the old man was in over his head. We're in over *our* heads now, too. A Spanish spy with saddlebags full of the gods know what, a redcoat patrol behind us — bah! I say we exit this perilous stage."

She sighed. "Alas, we cannot back out yet. We've a moral obligation to get Hawthorne to safety. Darien, perhaps."

"If he remains alive as far as Darien. You realize the very fact that we're chasing the old man's killer makes us look like we're in bed with the French and prime prey for those assassins." He shook his head. "Damn the war."

A quarter hour later, Mathias trotted his horse back to report that the tracks showed El Serpiente's horse had slipped a shoe. The Spaniard needed to find at least a hammer and nails, if not a farrier or a smith, before he continued much farther. No trading post was marked on the map in their vicinity, and the settlement of Darien was more than an hour away. The assassin was on foot not far ahead. They could encounter him before noon. And Mathias saw no sign that he had an accomplice.

Mathias and Runs With Horses checked their weapons and rode southward to discover the assassin's whereabouts. Dry-mouthed, Sophie made sure her musket was loaded. Jacques and David readied their own weapons and Hawthorne's pistols. Then they proceeded after Runs With Horses and Mathias.

In another quarter hour, Mathias rode back to them. "Looks like an abandoned trading post about a mile ahead, set back from the road. We tracked El Serpiente headed that way." His gaze roved over them and came to rest on Sophie. "Watch yourselves."

The five rendezvoused with Runs With Horses and arrived at a building shaded by pines and live oaks. At one time, underbrush had been cleared all the way to the road, but foliage had encroached on the structure after its abandonment. Aside from cicadas strumming the noontime and an occasional crow caw, Sophie heard nothing other than movements of her party. Tracks in the sand leading to the building revealed that a man on foot and a three-shoed horse had preceded them. However, there was no sign of man or horse.

Jacques and Mathias helped Hawthorne dismount just outside the cleared brush. Mathias motioned the young man to wait there and caught Sophie's eye. "Stay with him."

Still partially concealed, Mathias, David, Jacques, and Runs With Horses spread out to encircle the building, firearms ready. Hawthorne leaned against his saddle, exhaustion escaping his lips. She reached for her canteen. "Water?" she whispered. He shook his head no, his face devoid of color.

He couldn't travel much farther. "You're better off lying down for now." She kicked together a pile of pine straw, eased him onto it, and stood in time to glimpse Jacques and Runs With Horses disappearing behind the building.

Hawthorne grew quiet. Musket in hand, Sophie walked past him, her horse, and those of the others to the four extra horses and gave each of them a pat.

A twig snapped in the palmetto brush behind her, and she spun about. With no time to raise her musket, she found herself staring down the barrel of a pistol not four feet from her; and above the pistol gleamed the fatigue-rimmed black eyes of El Serpiente. Fear beat her pulse into staccato.

Grime and sweat streaked through stubble on his face, matted his hair, and sullied his clothing. He stank of sweat and horse. "*La hija del Lobo.*" His upper lip twitched with sarcasm. "French-loving fools."

"You've misunderstood —"

"Drop the musket." When she hesitated, hatred snarled his lip. "*Now!*" He cocked the pistol She swallowed and let the musket drop. "*Bueno.* Untie the last two horses."

Horror and outrage flooded her. Why did he need *two* horses unless he planned to take her hostage? "I won't go with you."

"Then you die now —"

The report of Hawthorne's pistol rang through the brush, the ball passing between Sophie and the assassin. While the horses skittered in shock, Sophie snatched her musket and dove for cover in the palmetto underbrush on the other side of the horses. El Serpiente fired his pistol, Hawthorne screamed, and she cringed.

She took aim on the Spaniard. Dread stayed her trigger finger and dribbled sweat down her back. The flint had fallen from her musket.

El Serpiente whipped out a knife, his attention focused on her. With the musket useless for firing, she prepared again to use it as a club. Squared off with the assassin, she heard Mathias from the direction of the abandoned trading post: "To the horses! Quickly!"

Rather than leap into the brush for her, the assassin lunged for the nearest horse — that of Charley Osborn — sliced through the rope guiding the horse, and vaulted onto the animal barebacked. Reins seized, he jabbed his heels into the horse's sides, spun him about, and galloped back toward the road. Mathias's rifle shot sheared his hat from his head and skimmed his scalp, shattering branches and showering man and horse with splintered pine.

Sophie's knees wobbled when she recalled the sight of the assassin's knife. "N-no flint!" she croaked when her brother and the blacksmith sprinted over to her. That instant, she remembered the rest of it. "Hawthorne! Ye gods!"

Blood seeped through the right upper portion of his waistcoat, the smell of it mingling with that of pine straw to form a dusty and acrid stench. While the four other men gathered around, Sophie knelt at his side, helpless. "Stephen Hawthorne, thank you for saving my life!"

He moved gray lips. "In my saddlebags — it was split between the three of us. You must help le Comte Dusseau take it to Don Alejandro, *por favor, te suplico.*" He lifted his right hand and clutched her sleeve, his Spanish heritage tumbling from his lips. "*Mesón de Dragon y Phoenix en San Agustín...busca a Luciano de Herrera.*" His voice began failing, and he forced out final words. "*O la casa de mi tío, Don Antonio Hernandez, en La Habana...*" His body relaxed, and his eyes searched the sky without sight, a glaze settling over them.

When his hand fell away from her sleeve, dejection and loss smothered Sophie. Another man dead. Good gods, was there no end to the violence? The sound of an approaching horse dragged her to her feet. Standing Wolf reined back. "Redcoats. Four miles away."

At that proximity, the soldiers would have heard the firearm reports. Runs With Horses rushed over to rope the horse they'd loaned to Hernandez. Sophie retrieved her musket, mounted Samson, and headed the gelding out, realizing when she reached the road that she hadn't glanced at Hawthorne's body again. Perhaps she was indeed capable of leaving violent death behind, but she was certain she'd never grow inured to it. Damn the war, the bloody, wretched, useless war.

Chapter Nineteen

THEIR FIRST GLIMPSE into Hawthorne's saddlebags didn't occur until mid-afternoon. Whatever the rebel had been protecting with his pistol wasn't obvious among his personal articles, spare clothing, food, and extra ammunition. After they'd set up camp for the night south of Darien, they inspected his property again, and Sophie wondered whether he'd been crazy. To her eye, there was nothing about his belongings to defend.

Jacques sat near firelight with the saddlebags. Knife in hand, he prodded seams, scraped surfaces, and whistled through his teeth. Soon he motioned the others over and handed each a pistol ball.

Sophie rolled hers between finger and thumb before holding it closer to the firelight to examine a section Jacques had scraped off. Beryl green winked at her from the heart of the ball, invoking an initial thrill of wonder: an emerald disguised as ammunition.

Jacques insisted that they divide the collection of twenty-four emeralds between them before he and Standing Wolf left the circle of firelight for their allotted watch. Mathias hunkered down on his bedroll to patch a moccasin, and Runs With Horses sharpened his knife. Sophie continued cleaning her musket. Then she cocked the unloaded musket, aimed it at the ground, and pulled the trigger. To her satisfaction, the new flint sparked. But by then, her wonder over the emeralds had waned.

David, who had paced awhile, sat near her and flipped a twig into the fire. "I doubted the lure of military intelligence alone could provide adequate persuasion for the likes of the Gálvez family. Curse Hawthorne for taking advantage of us."

Mathias said, "Too late for curses. He's dead."

David glared at the campfire. "If the total bribe was split among three couriers, they'd some seventy emeralds to wave beneath Don Alejandro's nose.

Where did they come by it all? The Congress hardly has two pennies to rub together and cannot even send supplies and soldiers to the rebels in Georgia."

Mathias shrugged. "Maybe it's another loan from France."

"France is destitute, too." David caught Sophie's gaze and lowered his voice. "Four emeralds apiece will keep us content for awhile. Haven't we discharged our responsibilities to Hawthorne by now?"

"Those emeralds are a burden, not a blessing. And we haven't caught the murderer yet. We go on to St. Augustine."

David watched Jacques slip into the ring of firelight to light his pipe before he said, "So we mark ourselves as rebel couriers by handing the emeralds over to a Gálvez?"

"We won't give them to a Gálvez," said Sophie. "We'll track down this Comte Dusseau person that Hawthorne mentioned and transfer the onus onto him. Let him decide what to do with the stones. At that point we discharge our responsibilities. And I wager he'll supply us with information about Father's murder in return."

More tension infiltrated David's expression. "Dusseau. Who the hell is he?"

Jacques stood. "Comte André Yves François Dusseau, a young man well-connected with the Marquis de Lafayette."

"Charming." David tongued the information with a twist of sarcasm. "And who was Hawthorne's *other* traveling companion?"

His question hung almost as palpably in the air as Jacques's tobacco smoke. "Another spy. There is certainly no shortage of spies in *this* land." The old Frenchman strolled back out into the foliage.

David's sigh sounded brittle. "Well, at least Hawthorne told us where we might find Dusseau. The Dragon and Phoenix Inn in St. Augustine. I wonder why he mentioned an uncle, Don Antonio Hernandez, in Havana, but didn't say anything about the woman in the black veil at the Church of Saint Teresa."

Mathias shrugged. "Rendezvous plans change."

"Horse shit. The whole affair reeks worse than a Savannah bawdyhouse in August. And who's that Luciano de Herrera fellow we're supposed to seek in St. Augustine?"

Sophie said, "I don't know, but I've no desire to meet Herrera or travel to Havana. The way the Fates have operated thus far, I shouldn't be a bit surprised if a Spaniard turns out to be an agent for the Dutch and absconds with all the stones to Holland."

"Ah, Holland, jumping on Britain's back along with France and Spain." David's chuckle was raspy. "You know, Sophie, you should pen your memoirs of this adventure."

"No one would believe it, even if I were a man."

He rose. "All right. I'm for sleep if my arm will let me."

She studied him. "Is it worse? I can brew you more tea."

"It was quite bearable until you poked at it before supper and changed the bandage."

"Very well. You may change your own bandage from here on."

"Thank you." He massaged his lower back. "Peter's gelding is odious. I shall be glad to have my horse back on the morrow." He walked off to clean his teeth. They were lucky to have extra horses, even those with cranky personalities, to give their own a break from the saddle every few days.

She set her musket aside and ambled to Mathias. "May I join you?" He nodded, still sewing his moccasin, so she crouched beside him. "If the flint hadn't fallen out, I'd have shot him."

"You're alive and well, and that's what counts." He slid the moccasin on his foot and set the kit aside, eyes like obsidian. "Clearly it wasn't his time. Besides, he's *mine*."

"But it may have been his dead partner who killed Jonah."

"That makes no difference."

No, it didn't make a difference. She licked her lips. "I think I figured out what happened that night." He studied her with expectation. "Jonah — with Fairbourne, Travis, Osborn, and Whitney — got the fire going around Father's corpse. Jonah stayed behind to make sure the fire didn't get out of control. Whitney and Travis headed straight to the dance. The other two left to clean up first.

"The Spaniards came upon the scene, and one of them killed Jonah. While they were poking around —" She pressed her hands together to calm their shaking. "Lieutenant Fairfax found them and shot El Serpiente's partner in the knee."

"Fairfax." Mathias's eyebrow shot up.

"Unable to escape, the second assassin was left behind to Fairfax and his — his interrogation."

Plausibility sifted into Mathias's expression. "Explain why you think it was Fairfax."

"MacVie was terrified of him. I suspect he saw him torturing the Spaniard. The next morning, Fairfax and Major Hunt came to arrest me. I could tell Fairfax hadn't slept. At one point, he offered to interrogate me, and he appeared enraptured, even affectionate, at the thought of it. That afternoon, when I went to identify the dead Spaniard, he interrupted Stoddard's investigation and tried to run him off. I suspect he was looking for evidence he might have left behind in the dark, perhaps a button torn off his coat while subduing the Spaniard. And he looked at the corpse with such affection, as if he were delighted by that agonized face —"

"And Hunt did nothing about it."

"I doubt he knew."

"Of course he knew. How could he *not* know? Have you forgotten how frightened the peddlers were of the redcoats? Have you forgotten how much Fairfax enjoyed killing those bandits last night? Fairfax the machine, and Hunt the spineless: what an excellent team they make."

The hiss of venom in Mathias's voice astounded Sophie, almost obliterated her own quiet instinct that Edward would never willingly choose Fairfax on his "team." "So logically you've assessed it." Her nostrils expanded. "I wonder why you've not dedicated the same deductive skills to another incident last night with the bandits."

"How do you mean?"

"Had I wanted to become Edward Hunt's mistress, I'd have stayed behind with him instead of fleeing with you, and I'd never have crawled out my bedroom window a week ago — also with *you*."

He regarded her coolly. "Will you continue to flee from him when he asks you to marry him?"

She tittered. "He won't do that. He plans to add to his estates and wealth by marrying a fifteen-year-old cousin."

"He's in love with *you*, not his cousin. If he marries you instead, he's still far from penniless. You'd turn your back on that? The very sound of it is majestic. Lady Sophie Hunt."

Humor drained from her heart, replaced with chill and loss. Mathias seemed to be encouraging her to return to Edward. "I don't love him."

"You didn't love Jim or Richard, either."

She searched his emotionless face, not comprehending the wall between them. "I admit to making imprudent decisions when I was young, but I'm a bit older and wiser now."

"And how is accepting the protection of Edward Hunt an imprudent decision? Through him, you'd spend the rest of your life in comfort and luxury, something few in Georgia can expect of their lot."

Confusion wrung her soul. If only she'd deferred accepting Richard Barton's proposal another month. But she'd no way of foreseeing that the following month, Stands Tall would be dead, along with her unborn child. No, Sophie'd had Betsy to think about, Betsy to protect. Betsy. Sweet Betsy.

She lifted her chin. It was time. "England is a long way from Georgia. How can I move to England when —" She made sure her voice held low. "— when every year, Betsy looks more and more like her grandmother, Madeleine le Coeuvre?"

While incredulity swelled across his expression, she was certain frogs stopped croaking, crickets ceased chirping, and the world paused rotating. She held her breath in nervous anticipation. Surely now Mathias would comprehend why she hadn't leaped to accept Edward's offer, and the two of them could begin to talk at last. But instead, he scowled, pushed up from the blanket, and swept out into the night with his rifle.

Anger boiled in her chest: disbelief that Mathias could *still* not understand. How dared he run away? She jogged after him, her peripheral vision granting her a view of David's curiosity. Oh, how her brother would tease her on the morrow.

Moonlight broke through clouds and permitted her to spot Mathias striding southward through palmetto-strewn swamp grass. She halted and cupped hands around her mouth. "I'm not going to run the rest of the way to East Florida after you!" She wasn't sure whether she felt relief when he stopped and waited for her.

When she reached him, he remained facing south. "I cannot believe you've *never* told me. In all of eighteen years, you never told me." Sadness weighed down his voice. "Did you never realize how much I wanted children?"

"Then why didn't you remarry?"

"Great gods, Sophie, I lost my mother and first wife to childbirth. I didn't think I could lose a second wife that way."

"Well, you have a child."

"No. I never had her. I wasn't there for her birth. I never rocked her to sleep, heard her first words, watched her first steps, or played with her. Now she's an adult, and I wasn't even at her wedding! I've missed having *everything* a father should have had."

She glared at his profile. Damned if he was going to make her feel guilty for her choices. He had a right to feel loss, but she'd done the best she could to provide for Betsy, and Betsy had turned out to be a decent, sensible woman. "Not everything. You and I shall be grandparents in December." He faced her then, expression knotted with deepened incredulity and betrayal. "If you so desire, I shall open the door for you to talk with Betsy."

He spread his arms in a gesture of being overwhelmed, and she heard lamentation in his voice. "Betsy won't accept me!"

"That depends on how you approach her. She never knew Jim Neely, and Richard Barton wasn't much of a father to her."

"You'd be honest with her about us? You act proud of it."

She felt doubt and self-recrimination crawling around in his soul and smashed her lips into a line. Damn. At least she'd been loved by *her* father. "Exactly what about my daughter should shame me into silence? I will never be shamed to have given myself to a fine young man in the grotto of the Moon Eyes. Nor will I ever be shamed to have borne his daughter or to have sought protection for her with two other men.

"Perhaps you expect me to be shamed because your stepfather drilled into your head that your heritage somehow makes you subhuman. If you really must know the truth, why in eighteen years I never told you that you're Betsy's father, well, it's because I've never forgotten those scars on your back. Jacob and his religion would only have made your life more miserable had he known you had an illegitimate child. That's why I sent Betsy to Augusta. I didn't want him seeing Madeleine in her."

His expression grew guarded. "The opportunity for Betsy, you, and me to resolve this muddle is forever gone, Sophie. You never tried to talk with me about it."

This muddle. She felt ill. "How could I have talked with you about Betsy? You never gave me a chance. Since Richard's death, you've scurried away from me."

"'Scurried away?' Not so. I was rebuffed. I've never been able to pierce that phalanx of handsome, blond-haired, blue-eyed men orbiting you."

"What phalanx? Edward Hunt is the first since Richard —"

"At the harvest festival, right after Joshua's first son was born, Andrew Barton had you perched on his elbow the entire time. You wouldn't even dance with me —"

"My feet were sore! And Andrew Barton became a phalanx of men after that, eh?"

"For years I watched you select suitors with whom you never shared yourself. I finally decided that all you wanted from any man was this much." He showed her his thumb and forefinger spaced but a quarter inch apart. "I gave up."

"You don't give up at anything. This imaginary phalanx of blond men helps you to keep me out at a distance!"

"*You* keep all the men who might have a sharing relationship with you out at a distance."

Baffled, angry, smarting, she scowled at him. "That afternoon in the grotto wasn't fair to you. We were both hurt by it, and I'm very sorry. I'm also sorry that I kept the truth about Betsy from you. But I won't be responsible for your fears about me today. I have my own fears about you to deal with.

"As for my selecting suitors with whom I've never shared myself —" She showed him her thumb and forefinger spaced but a quarter inch apart. "That's how much affinity I've had for them, so why bother sharing? How sad to feel the affinity we still have for each other after eighteen years, but we're unable to nourish it because we're so busy being afraid."

She waited for him to respond, but he stared at her as if her words had paralyzed him. Rolling back her shoulders, she headed to camp, where she cast herself on her bedroll and yanked the blanket over her head.

Her heart thrashed about like a caged hawk. Mathias's energy, his passion, burned within him, hot as the heart of any forge, so hot it glowed dark. All her life it had spoken to her in a language her soul understood but couldn't voice. Small wonder she'd kept his confidences through all the years, rejoiced when he mediated between the worlds of the white man and the red man, and acknowledged the things of importance to him. Small wonder she'd been bored with other men. Her soul thirsted for each next contact with that passion, attuned as it had somehow become eighteen years before by one afternoon of intimacy.

Did he not feel it? How could he *not* feel it? All that passion had resonated through his fingertips last Tuesday afternoon when he, despairing for her life and safety, had taken her face in his hands and told her without telling her that he cherished her.

Cherished, yes. She had been desired by many men, and her body had been in the legal possession of two men, but in her entire life, only Mathias Hale had cherished her. Of all the men she'd known, only he had captured her abiding respect. Now that she finally recognized it, he wanted nothing to do with her. Oh, how very bitter.

Chapter Twenty

AT MIDNIGHT, DAVID woke Sophie to assume watch beneath an overcast sky. A muscle in her neck knotted as she trudged through mist with her musket to the edge of the pine copse. A breeze from the east drifted drizzle down her neck.

Runs With Horses joined her. "Listen. What do you hear?"

Wind rustled palmettos and pines. A brook dribbled over stones. An owl hooted. And men were talking near the road. "Redcoats?" she whispered. With their military discipline, would they have prattled so?

The warrior sniffed the wind. "No. We go see."

She followed him, her footsteps almost as quiet, and they crouched in a thicket. Dark skin on eight people in the road — one doubled over on hands and knees — offered little contrast to the night. She whispered, "Runaway slaves." The Creek nodded.

A woman's sob broke from the person on hands and knees. "Cain't — cain't go no more!" Her voice twisted with pain.

A stocky man knelt beside her. "Baby's coming, Moses!"

"Massuh ain't more'n half an hour behind us. I ain't letting him catch me again. We cain't stop."

Another man said, "Got to leave Lila behind."

"Yeah, Ulysses. 'Mon with us."

Lila wailed. The man at her side stood, a full head taller than the other men. "Cain't leave her! G'wan without us!"

"You sure?"

Lila arched her back. "I got to push! I got to push!"

"I said git!"

The six backed away. "Good luck," said the one called Moses. He and the others sprinted south.

"Ulysses, the baby killing me!"

Sophie moved to rise. "I must help her."

Runs With Horses grasped her arm. "Runaways are desperate. Slave catchers are worse."

"You'd want *your* child born in the middle of a postal road?"

He considered. "We first make sure the others are gone."

They waited another half minute before rising from concealment. During that time, Lila moaned and rocked herself. Crouched at her side, Ulysses didn't spot them until they were upon him. He leaped up, knife drawn, teeth flashing a snarl. "We ain't going nowhere with you."

Sophie stood her ground, right hand upheld in greeting, even though his size made her feel more like running in the opposite direction. "Let us help the woman. We've a fire and blankets."

The whites of his eyes glittered. "Ain't never heard of no slave catcher being a woman. You ain't slave catchers."

"No, we aren't."

He sheathed the knife at his belt. "We be much obliged for yo' help, then." He bent over and put his arm about Lila's shoulders. "Folks going to help us. Got to walk to their camp."

The woman struggled to her feet. Another contraction seized her. Sophie went around the left side of her to help Ulysses. Above the stink of the woman's sweat, she detected the almondy odor from her bag of water. Back-to-back contractions, her water broken, her pushing instinct in place — the baby was on the way. "A little farther, and you can rest." Lila panted and nodded.

Runs With Horses sniffed north. "Listen."

From Darien came the baying of hounds. Lila moaned. Ulysses tensed. "They coming for us!"

Sophie looked at the warrior. "Wake the others. We must throw off those dogs." Runs With Horses dashed westward.

Sophie and the Negroes followed more slowly. Halfway to camp, Standing Wolf, Runs With Horses, and Mathias met them. They sent Ulysses to the road with the Creek brothers, while the blacksmith assumed support of Lila's right side.

David rose from where he and Jacques had fed the fire with dry wood, amazement in his expression at the sight of Lila. Sophie gestured to a blanket. "Pull that blanket near the fire."

"I got to push! I got to push!"

David gulped. "Right away."

Lila dropped to the blanket on all fours, panting through another contraction. She gasped, "The baby's head. I feel it."

Jacques whispered, "*Belle* Sophie, I hope you know what you are doing."

Her brain muzzy from lack of sleep, she rolled up her sleeves and regarded him. "Does *anyone* really know what they're doing at a time like this?" The Frenchman shrugged and joined David in loading weapons. Sophie knelt on the blanket with the big-boned, young Negro woman. "Let me see how far along you are." She motioned Mathias to support her back and eased her into a sitting position. Beneath Lila's soiled petticoat, a two-inch-diameter circle of the baby's head crowned. "I can see the baby, Lila. I want you to push with all your might next time."

Tears rolled down Lila's face. "It hurts so bad."

"I know."

"The baby tearing me up inside."

"I know."

Lila's belly stiffened with a contraction, and her spread legs trembled. "Now, I got to push! Oh, Mama, I got to push!"

"Deep breath and push! Mathias, bring her forward!"

Lila screwed up her face and bore down, exposing more of the baby's head, squeezing out clear fluid and a little blood. When the contraction passed, she collapsed against Mathias, gasping. "You got to promise me. Please don't tell Ulysses."

"Shh. Save your strength. You're almost done."

"The baby be the young massuh's. Promise not to tell."

What difference did it make? A baby was a baby. "I promise." From the direction of the road, she heard the hounds. Weapons in hand, David and Jacques waited, facing the road. The wind favored their party, so the slave catchers wouldn't smell burning wood, but if those hounds followed their scent off the road, or they heard Lila cry out —

"Young massuh come ten — maybe twelve — times when Ulysses not there. He kill Ulysses if I tell."

Indignation smoldered within Sophie at the unknown male who had indulged himself with Lila. "Forget about it and birth this baby." She rolled up a rag and pushed it in Lila's mouth. "Bite down and scream into it so they won't hear you."

Lila's belly knotted. The rag trapped her wail. Sophie hissed, "Push!" Her scream muted, Lila bore down again, and the baying of hounds swelled. "Harder!" The baby's head slid out face down and rotated to the side. Sophie held it in her hand. To her, the baby looked very much like Lila and not at all like the spoiled son of a plantation owner. "Another good push like that, and you'll have the shoulders out."

The hounds sounded even closer. David and Jacques cocked their firearms. Then the predatory overtones in the baying transformed into confusion. Jacques slapped his knee and chuckled. "What?" Sophie glanced over her shoulder at him. "What did you do?"

"What every good chef knows to do, *belle* Sophie. A dash of *poivre* enhances the flavor of food."

Pepper. They must have seasoned the area in it. That ought to keep the hounds busy.

Another contraction gained momentum. Lila writhed against Mathias, words muffled. "Ain't gonna have this baby. Ulysses won't want me when he see it."

Oh, hell. Sophie scowled. "You nit, if he didn't want you, he'd have left you behind. Stop talking! Deep breath. Push!"

Lila bit the rag and bore down once more, legs quivering, to squeeze out the baby's shoulders. Sophie guided the slippery mass of girl baby into the world trailing umbilical cord, cradled the infant lengthwise on her lower arm, and massaged her back while Lila spat out the rag, panted, and trembled. The little girl coughed, wriggled, and gave a lusty cry.

Mathias tucked a blanket roll beneath Lila's back and eased her down before scooting aside and standing. Lila reached for the baby, and Sophie handed her over. "She's beautiful. Good job." Lila, already busy counting the baby's fingers and toes and cooing into her face, hardly seemed to hear Sophie.

David grinned. "That looked mighty easy."

Sophie glowered at him. "Men always say that." She wiped her hands on the blanket, stood, and walked about, rolling muscle kinks from her shoulders. How long had Lila pushed? Ten whole minutes? Both times Sophie had delivered, she'd pushed for an hour. Lila must be one of those women made to have babies.

Mathias strolled past and paused. "Nice job, General."

He'd made an excellent assistant. "Thank you, Ambassador."

"You tried to tell me that day at the forge." She blinked at him without comprehension. He lowered his voice. "Betsy. You'd planned to tell me I was her father, but Teekin Keyta was there." Concession filled his expression. "I assumed you never tried to talk with me about it. My words were harsh. Please accept my apology."

Awkwardness crawled over her. The last thing she wanted from him was groveling when she felt less than noble about her own erroneous assumptions. She nodded.

"I remember your expression. You didn't know I'd married Teekin Keyta. You kept quiet about Betsy to protect me, perhaps to let me find happiness with my wife."

She squirmed. "It seemed the honorable thing to do."

"How hard that must have been for you. Betsy needed a father. You needed a husband, but I wasn't — *Richard* was available."

For several seconds they stared at each other while years of missed opportunity thrashed about her soul. Then the wind of the present zephyred through reminiscence and regret. They must talk more later. The wilderness had quieted, and Jacques listened to it at the edge of the firelight. Sophie asked him, "Where are the dogs?"

His eyes twinkled. "Gone. Southward."

Relief sagged her shoulders. In her peripheral vision, Mathias moved back to the fire, but the door between them was open.

She cut the baby's umbilical cord and tied it off with a strip of rag. While Mathias swaddled the newborn in clean rags, Sophie helped Lila deliver the afterbirth. Mathias handed the baby back to her mother, and Sophie studied him. He'd known how to support a newborn's head, something few men knew. Perhaps he'd celebrate the birth of his grandchild after all.

Runs With Horses, Standing Wolf, and Ulysses soon converged on camp and confirmed that the search party had continued southward on the road. His grin silly, Ulysses played with the baby's fingers and kissed the infant's forehead. "My little girl." He also pressed a kiss to Lila's cheek. "My woman." Lila looked at Sophie, and a shy smile touched her full lips. So much for Ulysses not wanting Lila or the baby.

With the parents enraptured over their newborn, David motioned Sophie, Jacques, Mathias, and the Creek brothers close for a conference. "What are we going to do with them now?"

"Take them with us," whispered Sophie.

Standing Wolf stiffened. "Slaves can be dangerous, and —"

"Yes, your brother reminded me of that." She sighed. "We've extra horses. Those people won't get far alone with that baby. And Lila's tote bag hasn't any food. I checked."

Mathias frowned. "I wonder where they're going. Fort Mose in East Florida? I'm not sure it's still there. They'd be taking their chances with the Lower Creek. They could be welcomed into a tribe but just as easily be enslaved or killed."

Jacques removed his hat to wipe sweat from his forehead. "They will not wish to stay here. The man might be of help to us in our travels, especially with those redcoats not far behind."

"I say we take them with us, if they're willing to go." Sophie looked at David. "What do you think?"

"I think I should like to sleep in a bed for a whole day after whiskey, a pork roast, cards, and a handsome woman."

She swatted his chest in annoyance. Mathias glanced back at the Negroes. "They're watching. Let's ask them what they want."

"You do the talking." David winked. "Ambassador."

When the six disbanded their huddle, Ulysses crouched and watched their expressions for clues. Not by any stretch of the imagination was the man stupid. No doubt he'd honed the art of deciphering expressions as a survival technique. His goal was freedom with his wife and baby. They mustn't forget he carried a knife. "Lila and me be much obliged to you folks for helping us. What yo' names?" Sophie and her companions remained silent. Ulysses licked his lips. "Never mind. You folks running, too."

Mathias cleared his throat. "You heading to Fort Mose?"

"Yessuh, near St. Augustine, it run by escaped slaves. All you got to do to get in is become a Catholic. Lila and me got no problem with that."

"It was destroyed about forty years ago by the British."

"Yessuh. We heard they built it back."

"There have been recent rebel forays into East Florida. What if your sanctuary isn't standing when you get there?"

"Indians sometimes help runaways."

"And Indians sometimes enslave or kill runaways."

Ulysses's jaw became obstinate. "Yessuh. Everywhere we go, we taking our chances. Ain't going back to the massuh."

"Very well. We've extra horses. You may ride with us if you agree to some rules first."

"Thank you, suh."

"Follow our orders. Don't wander off. Don't snoop in our property or take what belongs to us. Assist with camp chores and sentry duties. Help defend us, if necessary. Understood?"

His head bobbed. "Yessuh." Lila nodded, dark eyes large.

"Good. I'm Mathias, and that's Jacques. David. Sophie. Sehoyee Yahuh. And Assayceeta Corackall."

"Mistuh Mathias, I only got a knife." The Negro's biceps rippled beneath his sleeves. "Who do I defend you against?"

The blacksmith's tone was nonchalant. "Bandits. Spanish assassins. Loyalists and Whigs. Redcoats."

Disbelief creased Ulysses's brow, and he blotted sweat off his forehead with his sleeve. "Yessuh, you running, all right. You be running from everybody in this land. Any chance you running from them camped redcoats we sneaked around earlier?"

Sophie pared emotion from her voice. "How many were there?"

He swiveled his gaze to her. "Ten, Miz Sophie."

They just couldn't seem to get far enough ahead of Edward to breathe easy. "Let's just say we're avoiding *all* redcoats."

"Yessum."

***

After she'd nursed the baby, Lila was up and about and stabilized enough to travel. Had she still been on a plantation, she'd have been back in the fields at daybreak, the baby with her in a sling. Sophie found herself pondering the significance that out of all the children she and Mathias had conceived, only the child they had begotten together, Betsy, had survived.

The drama of the birth and the proximity of the soldiers chased sleep from all of them. After a cold meal, they packed up and moved on at three in the morning, even though lack of sleep dragged at all of them. They paced the horses, with Runs With Horses and Standing Wolf scouting before and behind. Ulysses and Lila rode well, despite having blankets for saddles and no stirrups. Lulled by the warmth of her mother and the motion of the horse, the baby slept.

South of St. Simon's Island just after dawn, Runs With Horses rode back, expression grim. "Slave catchers return."

They headed west, downwind, into a thicket of palmettos and live oaks a hundred feet from the road. Jacques brought up the rear spreading pepper. Everyone dismounted, readied firearms.

To the east, sunlight sparkled on the Atlantic Ocean, and salt flavored the air. Sophie heard the jingle of metal, the whine of hounds, and the crack of a whip, followed by a man's hoarse command: "Get up, you colored rat!" She squinted at the road. Ulysses wrapped an arm about Lila, and they trembled.

Three men on horseback dragged six roped Negroes. Bringing up the rear were three more men on horseback and five hounds. One of the hounds scented the other party and bayed, only to be neutralized with sneezing when he encountered the pepper. A man dismounted and kicked the beast out of the brush back onto the road. "Move, worthless varmint!" Another such encouragement, and the dog obliged and galloped north. The man remounted his horse and caught up with the rest of his party. Sounds of their passage dwindled.

Ulysses and Lila clutched each other breathing hard, the baby between them. "Your people?" Sophie whispered. He nodded.

David walked over beside her. "We cannot help them. We need them to spread word to our pursuers that we've not been seen on this road. You understand?"

"Yessuh." Ulysses swallowed. "Yessuh, we do."

Chapter Twenty-One

AT THE CAMPSITE Sunday evening in East Florida, south of the St. Marys River, Lila flopped onto a blanket with almost no strength to nurse her infant. Ulysses staggered about trying to help with chores but was so dazed from lack of sleep that he was ordered to the blanket with his wife and daughter. The runaways deserved honors. In one day, they'd covered mileage that would have challenged a cavalry unit.

Since David was still mending from the pistol wound, Sophie and Jacques built the fire while Mathias and his cousins hunted. Wood smoke clashed with a breeze reeking of seaweed, dumping the taste of smoked brine into Sophie's throat. "Gods, it's hot."

"And it stinks worse than London." Jacques inspected her, his expression pensive. "What is between you and Mathias? For two days, you have not spoken with each other except to argue."

She fanned off mosquitoes that the limpid breeze failed to flush — mosquitoes twice the size of Alton's. "It's none of your business — or David's, either, so you may tell him that."

"It is my business if I see it disrupting the mission. So you tell me the problem, and I will act as your messenger, *oui*?"

She scowled. "Jacob Hale's the problem. And the poor judgment of Madeleine for marrying him."

Jacques flinched as if she'd slapped his jaw. Old sadness haunted his dark eyes, and his shoulders slumped. "*Belle* Sophie, let me share a story with you." He escorted her to the edge of camp. "For half a year after the ambush, I thought Madeleine was dead. Then I heard she had been the sole survivor of the massacre. I spent three years tracking her from New Orleans into Georgia and found her with the Creek, married to Toókóhee Nókúse.

"The brother of our dead father died, and Madeleine and I inherited the family wine estate. In Bordeaux I dealt with my aunt, the administrator." He glowered. "A foul woman with such airs about herself. She had respectable spouses picked out for my sister and me.

"Fearing Madeleine would lose her inheritance, I told Aunt that she had married a colonist. Aunt wanted to see her, meet her husband. By the time I returned to Georgia, the smallpox had claimed Toókóhee Nókúse. Madeleine agreed to return to France with me. I thought we would have Aunt's blessings at last. Then Madeleine told me she carried Toókóhee Nókúse's child. Mathias." Jacques rubbed his hand over his face.

Understanding and sadness crept through Sophie. "Jacob seemed respectable, successful. You convinced her to marry him."

Jacques nodded. "We did not foresee that he would grow fanatic for a god who curses women and people with other gods."

"Did your aunt disown you and Madeleine?"

"*Non.* I sailed back to France with the story that Madeleine was pregnant and could not travel. Aunt's health was failing. She accepted my story. In exchange for her blessings, I was to marry a girl from a minor aristocratic family."

"You're *married?*"

Slyness creased the corners of his eyes. "Two weeks before the wedding, Aunt died. Back I went to America, before the girl, her father, and the village priest could tie me down for vows."

Aware that her jaw dangled in surprise, Sophie close it. "You and Madeleine still inherited the estate?"

"We inherited the estate."

"Well, how do you like that? Susana was right about you concealing a fortune somewhere."

"Bah. Men have made bigger fortunes here overnight. But I will be certain to tease her about it when next I see her." They both snickered a moment before Jacques sobered. "My nephew isn't at rest with himself."

"True. He's created masterpieces at the forge and built a bridge of peace between two civilizations, but he allows himself little pride in his accomplishments." Why had Mathias told her two nights before that he had no material assets to offer her? "Does he know about the estate?"

"*Mais oui. Bien sur.* Mathias does not hunger for wealth of substance. He hungers for wealth of spirit. Something to fill the treasury of his soul, the companionship of people who appreciate his worth and accept him as he is. And a partner."

"Many of us hunger for that. How hard it must have been for him when Teekin Keyta died."

"*Oui*, but she was not his partner. He did not love her."

She frowned. "He married her. I thought surely —"

"For at least ten years I have wondered." Jacques caught her hand in his. "Your daughter resembles my sister."

She pondered who else besides her parents might have seen the resemblance. Jacob Hale? Jonah and Joshua? David and Susana?

Jacques nodded, wise. "I see. We will leave it at that."

"Yes," she whispered. "Let's leave it at that."

***

They broke camp Monday before daybreak, everyone sensing the journey's end by the following evening. With dawn came the view of cattle ranches and indigo plantations to the west, palmettos cluttering the sandy soil, and curtains of moss choking live oaks and cypress trees. Dawn also brought company. The broad avenue they traveled, known as the King's Highway, led to St. Augustine through the Crown-held settlement of Cow Ford, supporting far more traffic than the road between Augusta and Savannah.

Early that afternoon, with sun and humidity smothering them like a giant forge, they crossed Thomas Creek. A mile south, soldiers had blockaded the highway in both directions. Before they reached the roadblock, David, riding at the rear, trotted his horse and the horse he towed up front. "All right, everyone follow my lead."

Jacques, riding beside Sophie, chuckled. "Your brother never ceases to amaze me with the fiction he spins."

She regarded David's sweaty back. "You wouldn't believe the number of times our parents swallowed that fiction."

"I would indeed."

They pulled up before wooden barricades. A sweat-drenched ensign emerged from a scrap of shade shared with several other soldiers. "Good afternoon. Sorry to detain you, but we've a bit of trouble in these parts with cattle thieving the last week." He swelled his chest, face florid in the heat. "Bother. It's the most those rebels can manage."

Indignation screwed up David's expression. "My property agent never told me East Florida had that sort of problem with rebel scum. I shall box the fellow's ears when I see him next."

"The problem is but infrequent, and we've hanged quite a few of the thieves."

"Jolly good show." David layered on the ire. "Cattle thieving. Hrumph. Fortunately my concern is with indigo."

"Ah, yes, sir." The ensign nodded to a scribe, who dipped his quill in an inkwell and readied paper. "We're recording information about all travelers in the area. Please state your name, destination, and business."

"Daniel Hazelton. That's my sister, Sarah, her husband, Mark, and his father, Jonathan."

Sophie refrained from glancing at Mathias. So she was his wife *again*. He must be squirming.

"We've brought household slaves and native guides to help us through Georgia and East Florida." The ensign eyed Lila's baby. "The baby came Friday night, five weeks early."

"I hear a great deal of riding will do that. I take it you're from the Carolinas, then?"

David nodded. "North Carolina."

"And your destination and business in East Florida, sir?"

"Cow Ford. I'm not satisfied with the returns I'm getting from naval stores, and frankly, the winters in North Carolina are bloody cold. Far worse than what Mother England hands out. Been researching indigo. My agent has property picked out for us to inspect. If we like what we see, I shall sell my business, buy into indigo, and move south."

"Very good, sir. I wish you success. You may proceed. Thank you for your time." The ensign stepped aside, pulling the barrier open with him. Sweat streamed down his face. "Oh, I should advise you that the summers in East Florida are as ferocious as you claim the winters in North Carolina to be."

David laughed and motioned Sophie and the others through. "This heat is marvelous." While sucking in a deep breath, he straightened in his saddle and slapped his palm to his chest. "And that salty air — so invigorating!"

From the revulsion on his face, the ensign found East Florida an antechamber to hell. "It isn't even the hottest part of the season, yet."

"Excellent! This venture sounds better and better!" The ensign shook his head in disbelief, and David paraded his gelding past. "Oh, can you recommend an inn of distinction in Cow Ford?"

"Try the Lark and Dove, sir."

David tipped his hat. "Many thanks. Good day!"

They passed northbound travelers waiting at the blockade, and David caught up to Sophie beaming as if he'd dropped live lizards down the shirts of a few redcoats. "How was I?"

"A consummate liar." The smirk she'd been holding back seized her lips. "I take it we shan't be staying at the Lark and Dove tonight."

"Indeed, no. Major Hunt might search the Lark and Dove to his heart's delight, but we shall be long gone from town."

***

Cow Ford, named for a narrow point on the St. Johns River, had sprung up near ruins of Fort Caroline, site of the Spaniards' massacre of French Huguenots two centuries earlier. Sophie and the others stepped off the ferry Monday afternoon and assessed the kaleidoscope. With all the Lower Creek Indians, Negroes, redcoats, militia, plantation gentry, backwoodsmen, merchants and their wives and children, ranchers, slatterns, and pickpockets in the dusty streets, no one gave travelers from Georgia a second glance. However, Sophie did notice the absence of Spaniards, so some selectivity existed within the community.

They bypassed the Lark and Dove at the heart of the commerce area and, farther south, dismounted near three modest wooden taverns like the Red Rock in Alton. All three were doing brisk business — horses hitched in front, patrons smoking pipes on porches. Sophie gestured to one tavern. "The Wolf and the Dove. Hmm. Sounds too much like the Lark and Dove. That one isn't for me."

"Indeed." David stroked his chin. "The Queen Charlotte. I wonder whether anyone in there is playing cards."

Jacques leered across the street. "Personally, I prefer the implications of the Stocking and Slipper."

Amusement livened Mathias's expression. "We shan't be here above two hours."

"I may be old, but do you think I need two hours?"

In the next second, the report of a pistol from the porch of the Queen Charlotte had all eight adults ready to dive into the dust for cover. They jerked around to discover the source of the shot. David said, "Jesus, Mary, and Joseph!"

Several patrons on the porch guffawed. A fat innkeeper waved his pistol to clear black powder smoke and grinned at them. "Five o'clock, and all's well! Afternoon, folks! You obviously ain't from round here. My clock broke two years ago. Come on in and refresh yourselves. The wife just pulled bread from the oven."

Fresh bread. Sophie's mouth watered. Nothing like a week on the trail to make one appreciate simple comforts.

Jacques nudged Mathias and gave the Stocking and Slipper across the street a nod. "I shall butter my bread elsewhere."

Sophie eyed the Frenchman. "We meet right here in two hours."

Jacques smiled, tipped his hat, and sauntered across the street with his horses. David said to the innkeeper, "Anyone playing piquet inside?"

"Yes, sir, and there's a spot for you at the table."

David sighed, a happy sound. "I'm in." He turned to Sophie and Mathias, a wicked gleam in his eyes, and lowered his voice. "I wonder how much interest I can earn on the rebels' bribe."

Sophie's eyes widened. "Those emeralds aren't yours."

"I've made small fortunes for lenders."

Mathias frowned, his voice also low. "You flash emeralds around, and you won't be leaving here in two hours."

David's smile dazzled. "Come in and watch me manage it."

Mathias cast a look at a smithy next door. "Only while I loosen the dust off my throat. I've another site to visit."

Sophie assented with a grumpy sigh. David turned back to the proprietor. "What about our slaves and Indian guides?"

"Indians come on inside and get fed. Slaves go round the rear." He bustled back indoors.

The party went forward to the hitching post of the Queen Charlotte and secured the horses so each had access to the water trough. After assuring everyone that they understood the timing, the Negroes bowed their heads and shuffled around the side of the inn. The others headed inside the tavern with their saddlebags.

The first thing Sophie saw through the tobacco smoke was a British flag covering most of one wall. Well, after all, Charlotte *was* King George's wife. Next she noticed five redcoats sprawled on chairs around a table, a dice game between them and tankards before them. They directed languid interest at the newcomers, and after David waved a greeting, nodded and returned to the dice. Mathias's cousins migrated to the rear of the tavern and three members of a Lower Creek tribe. David homed in on a corner table populated by three civilians, one soldier, four tankards, and playing cards.

Sophie and Mathias followed him and slid into a window seat nearby. At the next table sat a plump young woman accompanied by an even plumper older woman. Both were fanning themselves and heavily rouged.

The younger woman smiled at Mathias and brushed his elbow. "It's so hot." Mathias scooted closer to Sophie, who could tell the woman's lower leg was rubbing his. "Don't you agree it's hot?" Mathias eyed Sophie and seemed embarrassed.

Sophie grinned at the women. "Forgive him. He's a deaf mute." Beneath the table, Mathias prodded her shoe with his moccasin. She enlarged her smile. "But there's a Frenchman in the Stocking and Slipper looking for some-one to talk to."

The women gaped, having realized only when Sophie spoke that she was a woman. Then they rose, bobbed curtsies, and hastened out the door and across the street. Sophie muffled a laugh. "*Vive le Montcalm.* Don't you dare tell him I did that."

"I'm a deaf-mute. My lips are sealed."

"Good. Are you always so rude to doxies?"

He shook his head. "They usually treat me like I'm a piece of furniture. I cannot imagine what happened in this instance."

"Oh, well, of the two of us, clearly you were the more handsome man. A compliment to both of us, wouldn't you agree?"

"Backhanded flattery if ever I heard it."

Chapter Twenty-Two

KER-POWW! "HALF PAST six, and all's well!"

All was, indeed, well inside the Queen Charlotte. The number of patrons in the tavern had tripled. David had earned the Congress ten percent on its investment. And while Mathias visited the smithy next door, his cousins communicated with Lower Creek warriors in the back of the tavern, despite their different dialects.

Sophie grimaced at the fat proprietor strutting his smoking timekeeper back inside. Powder wasn't cheap. He used the equivalent of an entire box of cartridges each day calling out hours and half-hours. All had best be well.

The excellent English tea, of which she'd been deprived in Georgia due to trade restrictions, was plentiful inside the tavern. By six-thirty, however, it made its presence known to her bladder. She whispered to David, "I'm going to find the vault."

"Not a bad idea. Let me know where it is."

She handed over her saddlebags, squeezed from her seat, and glanced across the street at the Stocking and Slipper. Using up every minute of his two hours, the Frenchman was. But after all, there had been *two* women.

The innkeeper's wife aimed her down the back stair, and she exited the tavern to a circle of a dozen Negroes dancing in the dusk of evening while another fiddled. She skirted them, a pot of corn mush kept warm above a fire, and a beehive oven. Off to the side, Lila sat with two elderly women and rocked her baby to the rhythm of the music. The new mother gave Sophie a mystical smile.

A trail wound through a small citrus grove, and the trees cleared to reveal a barn, watering trough, and vault. Through the planks of the barn Sophie smelled the horses belonging to the innkeeper. A massive Floridian mosquito lazed around her ear and she swiped at it. She rapped on the door of the vault to make sure it wasn't occupied before entering.

Above the serenade of fiddle music, footsteps rustled in the coarse grass outside — likely a tavern patron with several tankards of ale talking in his bladder. Uninterrupted time in a seat of easement was another simple comfort she'd relinquished in favor of the quest. She reached for the corncobs.

No one was waiting when she emerged, but the hair on the back of her neck stood up. She hurried by the trough, and when she passed the barn, he stepped out with a familiar greeting: a huge, raised knife, and a sneer wrapping his mouth and black eyes. She stiffened in horror. "*Adios, hija del Lobo,*" El Serpiente whispered and sprang for her.

A pistol fired, and she shrieked. The assassin howled with pain, the knife knocked from his hand. "¡*Santa Maria!*" He turned toward the grove enraged and shaken, wagging his hand.

At the edge of the grove, Dunstan Fairfax stood at attention, a smoking pistol in his hand, gaze fixed on the assassin. Neither his face nor his voice displayed any feeling. "The devil. I missed." He holstered the pistol.

Loathing carved deeper into El Serpiente's face, and he shook his fist at Fairfax. "The same way you missed Manuel's knee in Alton?"

More horror churned Sophie's stomach. All her suspicions about Fairfax were true. She backed away from both men.

Fairfax encroached on the assassin. "*Señor* Vasquez, or Velasquez, or Alvarez, or whatever your latest alias is, Major Edward Hunt insists on an audience with you. Be sensible and come along with me peacefully."

The assassin spat on the ground, drew his sword, and stepped to the right, the trough looming behind him. "I would rather mate with a demon, *El Teniente del Diablo.*"

"The devil's lieutenant" drew his hanger. "As you wish." Sophie crept toward the grove, having no desire to watch a master murderer and a military machine dismember each other. Fairfax's words iced her spine. "I shan't be but a moment, Mrs. Barton, so don't go far."

She ran. Metal clashed behind her. The assassin cried out, and she halted to look back. Fairfax had maneuvered El Serpiente into tripping over the trough. While she gaped, the lieutenant dragged the other man up off the ground and knocked him out with a solid fist to the jaw. Then he swung around and spotted her.

Terror loaned her legs extra speed. Halfway up the path through the grove, the thud of Fairfax's boots closed behind her. The fiddle music grew louder, as did hoarse breaths of pursuit. A few feet from the exit of the grove, he snagged her arm and hauled her around.

"Lila!" Sophie loosened her arm and swung at Fairfax's jaw. He blocked the swing and pinned her arm. "Lila!"

He clapped a hand over her mouth, pinned both arms, and dragged her back down the path. When they emerged at the barn, the assassin still unconscious, Fairfax released her mouth. "An audience between you and Major Hunt would be a waste of his time. He wouldn't have the slightest idea how to extract information from you."

"I demand that you release me this moment! Lila!"

Angelic radiance suffused his face. "Not until I've expedited the process of extracting information."

He dragged her toward the barn, and dread smothered her. She was going to be flayed alive. "Help! Fire! Fire!"

Fairfax kicked open the barn door. "Scream if you like. No one shall hear you."

"You shall be answerable to Major Hunt for every bone you break, every bruise you give me, every scratch!"

He hauled her inside and pinned her against the far wall, his left arm trapping her right, his right hand clutching her left, as if they'd paired off in a bizarre waltz. A horse whickered in the stall nearest them and shied away. Fairfax's voice softened in the shadows. "Breaking, bruising, and scratching? No, I cannot be bothered with any of that."

In the next instant, her awareness of him jolted to comprehend that one hundred sixty-five pounds of sweating, hard-muscled male pressed her to the side of the barn, her inner thighs heated on his groin. The horror in her stomach curdled. She wasn't going to be flayed alive. Oh, no.

His chest expanded and contracted against hers while his breathing returned to normal. He smiled. "As I was explaining outside, I believe we've gone about this all the wrong way."

He didn't sound penitent. "Take your hands off me, Lieutenant Fairfax."

The warmth of his breath slid along the right side of her neck. "Dunstan," he whispered. "Dunstan."

"Damn you!"

He laughed, his breath a caress on her neck. "You think me a monster, don't you?"

"Torture and violation are two sides of the same shilling."

His lips hovered above her right ear. "I've never forced anyone."

Surely he understood the multiple forms of rape. And he hadn't denied torture. She squirmed for escape but succeeded only in riding higher on his groin. Revulsion roiled in her chest, particularly when she realized that any woman unfamiliar with Fairfax's twisted mind might be aroused by his physical prowess and appeal. Any woman.

"You — you're supposed to be in South Carolina with the Seventeenth Light. You ignored movement orders. You'll be court-martialed for coming to East Florida."

"Court-martialed? Certainly not. I've been authorized to neutralize the St. James espionage menace."

Aghast, Sophie stared at Fairfax. Not only had he covered up his acts of torture and murder well, but he'd schemed his own transfer out of Georgia far enough in advance to whisper seduction in the ear of his future commander and receive his blessing on the pursuit of spies. For the duration of the mission, Major Hunt had been saddled with a junior officer who was manipulative, brilliant, and brutal. Empathy for Edward panged her.

"So here I am." Fairfax grinned. "And here *we* are." He drew his lips along the line of her jaw in a touch so light she barely felt it.

Her skin crawled, a flush of flesh extending from her right ear down into her right toes. Her voice emerged hoarse. "I haven't any information that could be of use to you."

"The flowerpot," he whispered, nibbling her earlobe.

She stared at the open door of the barn over his shoulder. Fairfax was crazy. "Flowerpot?"

"You remember. The daisies. A message buried in the soil, I wager."

It came back to her then. Sunday night over a week before, when she was still under house arrest, she'd received that mysterious flowerpot full of daisies and the second cipher hidden within. She tried to make her tone as dubious as possible, but for some reason, it continued hoarse. "Why do you believe there was a message buried in the soil?"

"Mmm. I haven't understood until now why he's so obsessed that he could chase you across three hundred miles into this worthless hell." He nuzzled her neck, the heat of his lips encouraging her skin to crawl even more and her head to spin. "You're such a spirited liar. Of course there was a message in the flowerpot — one so important that you violated house arrest." He trailed his lips into the hollow of her throat. "You're also lying if you say you aren't enjoying this —"

"And you're doubly damned, Lieutenant." She attempted to thrust him away from her and again only succeeded in enhancing the contact of their bodies. A shudder soared through her. His restraint was so calculated, so *well practiced.*

"How intriguing. Do you realize no woman has ever pretended to fight me before?"

"I'm *not* pretending!"

"If you truly want me to desist, stop lying to me. Tell me about the message. Did it not specify the alternate meeting place for Don Alejandro and the rebels?"

His lips migrated up to her chin, and she thrust her head back, as far away from him as possible, her neck muscles straining. Oh, gods, she didn't want Fairfax to kiss her mouth. She'd as soon tongue a slug. "I don't know what you're talking about." She held her jaw shut.

His lips caressed the curve of her chin just below her lower lip. "Mmm. Tell me the location of that meeting place, and I'll let you go."

Not from the way the fire in his groin was talking. She jerked her head aside again, neck muscles tormented and at the limit of their endurance. "New Orleans. They're supposed to meet in New Orleans if they cannot meet in St. Augustine."

He altered his restraint to seize her head and hold it immobile, his mouth poised above hers. "I'm now thoroughly intrigued with you. Do you realize no woman has ever pretended she didn't want me to kiss her?"

"I'm *not* preten —"

It couldn't have lasted very long, not when she kept her jaw gripped shut and her lips closed, and yet it seemed interminable. He confined the kiss to a series of strokes and nibbles, while she exerted by far the greater effort because she remained rigid and unyielding the entire time. Let him kiss stone for more response. Yet her body hadn't exactly turned to stone in the eight years since Richard's death, damn it. At times it quivered with hunger — not hunger for Fairfax, but he knew widows were bound to be hungry. Outrage surged through her. How dared he invite himself into her hunger? He dared because he knew just how much it disgusted her.

He returned his lips to her jaw line. "If we continue at this, by the morrow I guarantee you'll no longer be considering it torture."

"You're a vile creature."

"And you're still lying, my enchanting Sophie Barton. We know there will be no meeting of Spaniards and rebels in New Orleans. Had you mentioned a location such as — mmm, you've a delightful, throbbing pulse right here on your throat, Sophie, Sophie, Sophie, mmm — a location such as *Havana*, well, perhaps I'd have believed you." He pulled back, gloating. "Let's talk about Havana, shall we?"

If he'd already possessed military intelligence about Havana, why should he toy with her in such a way? "I don't know anything about Havana. Take your hands off me!" Hearing her voice betray a flush of tears just beneath her facade, she felt mortified.

"Another lie. How you flatter me. You *are* enjoying it."

A shadow crossed the barn door, someone passing outside. Envisioning an enraged El Serpiente slicing not one, but two throats from ear to ear in that barn behind the tavern, she thrashed in Fairfax's arms. "Get off me! You disgust me, Lieutenant!"

"No, I fascinate you. I'm in all your darkest fancies."

Her tears spilled through. "Let me go, please!"

"*Please?* How I love the sound of that word — seductive, submissive." In shifting his restraint, he ceased to pin her groin with his. If she could gain a few more inches maneuverability — she relaxed to signal acquiescence. "Ah, it *is* Havana, then, and after your contact on Saturday with Don Esteban Hernandez, I wager he told you the names of some of their agents before he died." Esteban Hernandez? Was that Stephen Hawthorne's real name? "So let's start with St. Augustine, darling." He relaxed a little, granting Sophie the space she needed. "Who are the agents in St. Augustine?"

She heaved her knee up into his groin. When he doubled over and exhaled in shock and pain, she thrashed loose. With a growl he lunged for her. She sprinted for the door, hearing his chase — staggering, raspy-breathed — then a crack of splintering wood as she cleared the trough. A glance behind brought her to an abrupt halt. The lieutenant had collapsed to the ground just outside the barn.

"Miz Sophie!" Lila stepped toward her over Fairfax, who was out cold wandering his twisted mind, and past the remains of the bucket that had ushered him there. The revulsion in Sophie's stomach exploded into a thousand jarring shards, and she squeaked out Lila's name before falling into the younger woman's embrace.

Lila's tone sounded incensed, protective. "There, there. I heard you call. I didn't know where you was at first. Maybe I should have killed him. He be just like the young massuh. What some men think they got a right to be doing with women..." She trailed off in disgust.

"I — we have to get out of here." And oh, how she wanted soap and water to scrub her face, throat, and neck.

"Yessum. That one be madder than a hornet when he wakes up."

"El Serpiente!" Sophie spun about and stared at the watering trough. Clouds from the west had engulfed the setting sun, but she still had enough daylight to discern that the assassin had disappeared. She whirled on Lila. "Did you see him leave? What direction did he take?"

Lila shook her head. "While I watch from those trees over yonder, a Spaniard come along, find him, pick him up, and carry him off."

"A Spaniard?" Another Spaniard! The fifth assassin?

"Yessum."

David's piquet game was over, as was Jacques's fun with the doxies and Mathias's tour of the smithy. They must now fly with the greatest speed to St. Augustine in hopes that ten British soldiers who knew about Havana and two Spanish assassins wouldn't reach the city ahead of them and find André Dusseau. "Tell Cow Ford adieu, Lila. We're leaving."

Chapter Twenty-Three

BY TWO-THIRTY THE following afternoon, surrounding plantations, cattle ranches, and fruit groves and an increase in traffic alerted them that they'd entered the vicinity of St. Augustine. They halted. Sophie, Ulysses, and Lila dismounted, and Sophie retrieved the reins of their horses. "If Fort Mose is still standing, it shouldn't be too far away. Good luck to you."

"Thank you, Miz Sophie." Ulysses bobbed his head. "And good luck to you folks, wherever you going." In seconds, the family disappeared behind clumps of palmettos and moss curtains. A collective sigh of relief spread over the party. Abetting the escape of slaves was punishable by law. No one regretted being divested of the liability.

An hour south, the foliage to either side of the highway cleared, and the party paused to absorb the view. Squarish Fort St. Mark, formerly El Castillo de San Marcos, anchored the northeast corner of St. Augustine, its impenetrable coquina walls creamy as the inside of a bivalve, crenellations etched against the cumulus-and-cerulean sky. White, sandy beaches and the Matanzas River stretched east of the fort. Beyond that, a watchtower protruded from the low foliage on the north end of Anastasia Island, a sentry post with an eye on the Atlantic. Rowboats and fishing sloops lazed along the Matanzas. Beyond sandbars, three vessels lay at anchor: a warship flying the colors of Britain as her ensign, and two merchant brigs.

The King's Highway terminated at gates on the northern wall of the city. Two guards conferred a warm welcome, then Sophie and her party bypassed the public slaughtering pen near the gates. They hadn't traveled far down St. George Street before an exotic thrill teased Sophie's spine. In place of familiar wood buildings of Georgia and Cow Ford was a fusion of whitewashed tabby-shell masonry walls, cypress planks, and thatched roofs of palm fronds — not dwellings of British design. Vine-covered arches beckoned to shadowy loggias, and she imagined ghosts: a black-veiled *señorita*, a tonsured friar, even Pedro Menéndez de Avilés himself, the city's founder. Whitewash slapped on walls almost obscured a non-British coat of arms here, or non-English words there, reinforcing Sophie's impression that the presence of King George the Third was but a hasty glaze over the terracotta of a culture that had persevered through two centuries of hurricane, fire, and massacre.

She shook off her amazement and trotted Samson up to pace her brother's horse. "David, let's find the Dragon and Phoenix Inn, as Hernandez recommended."

"What does it look like I'm trying to do?"

"It looks like you're trying to tour the city. I think the inn is on a parallel street. Ask for directions."

He grumbled. "Why do women always ask for directions?"

"Because men are forever getting themselves lost."

"Well, what did you expect me to do back there, ask one of the gate guards for directions, *Madame* Secret-Keeper?"

Lack of sleep had made him just as irritable as she was. Each of them needed a good night's sleep, maybe several good nights' sleep. But David and the others knew she'd cheated them of details in her fantastic tale of watching Fairfax and El Serpiente duel, then extracting Hawthorne's real name out of Fairfax without receiving injury.

Lila had been of no help to them in poking holes in the story. The Negro woman had stuck to a minimal-detail account of sneaking up behind Fairfax after he'd cornered Sophie and braining him with a bucket. Sophie decided it was simpler if David and Mathias didn't know the rest.

She dismounted and walked her horse over to ask directions from a baker. "Left at the next street, eight shops down on the right," she told David a moment later with a cheery smile.

She spotted the signboard for the inn as soon as they turned the corner. After dismounting and retrieving their saddlebags, they headed into the dim, muggy common room of the Dragon and Phoenix. Most tables were vacant. Three civilians sat engrossed over cards at one table, and two others conversed at another table. A sixth civilian, dark-haired, sat alone in semi-shadow, a tankard before him. Not a soldier in sight. Splendid.

The proprietor emerged from a back room wiping his hands on an apron. Jacques returned his greeting. "*Monsieur*, we are looking for a young Frenchman who may have spent last night here. Perhaps he also had another man for a traveling companion."

Sophie studied the dark-haired man leaning forward on his elbow, listening. He looked Spanish. The proprietor nodded at Jacques. "There was a young Frenchman here last night, and he had an older fellow with him."

André Dusseau and the third member of Hernandez's team! Jacques inched forward. "Are either still here?"

The innkeeper's face grew guarded. "Who wants to know?"

"I am the lad's uncle and guardian. The older man has tried several times to swindle our plantation near Cow Ford from him."

The proprietor studied Jacques and nodded again. "Some young fellows just won't settle down. Alas, he's no longer here. Left early this morning."

"Where did he go?"

"I couldn't say for sure, but I overheard the two discussing business at the wharf."

A breeze of sticky air wafted Sophie, and she swiveled in time to spot the dark-haired man hurrying from the tavern. Mathias, who'd also been observing him, moved to the window to watch his departure. "David," she whispered. "David, that man who just left..."

"I saw him." David also peered out the window.

Jacques waved his hands as if bargaining at the market. "Did they plan to sail somewhere?"

"I didn't hear. I don't ask much if their money is good. I'm sorry I cannot be of more help, sir."

"*Merci.* You have been of tremendous help. We had best get down to the harbor and see whether we can catch him before he sails to Jamaica this time."

Outside, the mystery man had vanished. Jacques looked at David, then at Sophie in question. She said, "A patron who found your story interesting. He left soon as the wharf was mentioned."

Mathias jerked his thumb south. "He went on foot toward the wharf. Hardly a coincidence, I think."

David positioned his saddlebags back on his horse. "I suggest we keep our eyes open for the fellow."

They rode toward the wharf. The street opened up into the town plaza, with the governor's house to the west and a guardhouse before them. Shops, taverns, and the town market rimmed the plaza in between, and the harbor and wharf beckoned east of the guardhouse. Although they spotted dark-haired men along the way, none was the man in question.

The Creek brothers stayed with the horses while Sophie, David, Mathias, and Jacques hastened out to collect information. Since the harbormaster had gone into town and was due back within a quarter hour, they split up to chat with crews from the two merchant brigs. Sophie and Jacques found themselves in the company of mellow, olive-skinned Portuguese from the *Gloria Maria*. Their contribution to the culture of St. Augustine was dark, red wine.

The first mate, a slender fellow in his early thirties named Sebastião Tomás, communicated in broken English. After pointing out the ship's captain, who stood talking farther up the wharf with the merchant *Northwind*'s captain, Tomás informed them the *Gloria Maria* was leaving early on the morrow for Havana with the remainder of the wine in her hold. They thanked *Senhor* Tomás and rejoined David and Mathias in time for the harbormaster's return.

In the company of the sneezing, rheumy-eyed harbormaster, Jacques repeated his tale about the wayward nephew. The harbormaster confirmed the news they'd dreaded: that Dusseau and his older companion had chartered the fishing sloop *Annabelle* out of St. Augustine just that morning, ostensibly for Savannah. But they knew the *Annabelle* had gone south to Havana instead. They thanked the harbormaster, smiles ebbing into exhaustion, and rejoined the Creek warriors and horses. "Damnation," David whispered. "So mucking close."

They stood in silence, the afternoon sun glaring at them like a bloodshot eye. Sophie gazed eastward past the island to the masts and spars of the three ships at anchor. "You know, those Portuguese from the *Gloria Maria* are leaving for Havana tomorrow. The first mate seemed like a decent fellow."

David darted a look at the gig for the Portuguese ship. "Good for them. *Bon voyage* to the *Gloria Maria*."

She studied him with incredulity. The only other time she'd seen her brother give up was with the printing press. "I thought you were intrigued by the idea of going to Havana."

"That was before I realized I could get my throat slit or my skin peeled in the process."

"But we've come so far. We cannot just quit."

"Sophie, we set out on this journey to find Don Alejandro in St. Augustine and question him about the old man and Jonah's murders. I wager he and Dusseau realized the danger of meeting here and fled to Havana. We've done the best we could. Let's go home before the Fates change their minds and our lives become as forfeit as stock back there in the slaughter pen."

"But it looks as though El Serpiente is following them. Mathias and Uncle Jacques have business with him on Jonah's behalf and need our support. And the emeralds are a responsibility we must discharge."

"Oh, sweet Christ, not the Congress's stones again."

"Why assume the stones came from the Congress?" Jacques scrutinized him. "I doubt it could afford to part with such a sum, even for an alliance with Spain. Consider that the money might be Hernandez's personal money, an inheritance."

Sophie observed the captain of the *Gloria Maria*, a whip-slender fellow with graying temples, who was speaking with Tomás at the ship's gig. The captain paused conversation with the first mate long enough to return the inspection, his dark eyes shrewd on her. She looked back at her companions. "If that's the case, neither the Congress nor King George has the right to these emeralds."

"Exactly. With Hernandez dead, the rightful owner becomes his next of kin — his uncle, Don Antonio, in Havana." The Frenchman returned his attention to David. "Surely among all of us there is enough honor to return an inheritance to a family."

David threw up his hands. "Damn Hernandez! We should have left him bleeding to death on the road."

"I agree." Jacques's gaze swiveled to the Portuguese gig. "But how bad can a voyage be with a cargo of Portuguese wine?"

Dubiousness swam in Mathias's eyes. "Don't you get seasick when you cross the Atlantic, Uncle?"

"Bah. Just a bit of queasiness the first day out. Nothing brandy cannot cure."

David grimaced. "Seasickness is the least of it. Out there are pirates. And those massive storms, hurricanes."

Mathias ignored David and regarded Sophie. "Did you inquire whether the Portuguese would take on passengers?"

"No. I was still hoping we'd find Dusseau here." She glanced over her shoulder again. The captain smiled at her, teeth white in a tanned face. "But let's not stand around. That fellow who's been watching us all this time is the captain."

Mathias nodded. "My cousins wish to return to Georgia, having no desire to sail to Cuba. Let us learn whether the Portuguese have room for the four of us. Then we'll find an inn and a place to board the horses."

David's sigh whined with resignation. "Very well. All of you might as well follow my lead on this, too. But I'm warning you, I've seen enough crooked piquet to know we've missed something about Hernandez's shooting. Meeting in the home of his uncle, rather than the Church of Saint Teresa, smells absolutely rancid. If this blows up in our faces —"

"Don't worry." Sophie tightened her lips in annoyance. "We won't say you didn't warn us."

They left the two Creek warriors with the horses again and approached the gig. The captain met them halfway and inclined his head. "Good afternoon. Sebastião mentioned you might have questions for me. Miguel de Arriaga, *capitão* of the *Gloria Maria*, at your service."

David matched the captain's easy smile, and the two shook hands. "Good afternoon, *Capitão* Arriaga. I'm Daniel Hazelton, and this is my sister, Sarah, her husband Mark, and his father, Jonathan. I'm moving to East Florida from North Carolina, taking on an indigo plantation, and thought I'd check into sugarcane as a secondary crop. Have you passage for four as far as Havana?"

"*Sim, senhor.* As for the quality of the accommodations, well, that depends on the depths of your pockets."

David rubbed his hands together. "Excellent. Step this way, and I'll allow you to inspect the payment I have in mind."

David and *Capitão* Arriaga strolled toward the horses. Sarcasm gleamed in Jacques's eyes, and, lingering behind with Sophie and Mathias, he produced what would have been a perfect imitation of a preacher had it been pronounced from a pulpit: "My brothers and sisters, let us give thanks to Measure Travis, Zack MacVie, Peter Whitney, and Donald Fairbourne for their equine donations to our cause."

"Amen," said Sophie and Mathias before the three of them caught up with David and the captain.

Chapter Twenty-Four

THE EXTRA HORSES purchased passages aboard the *Gloria Maria* for Sophie, David, Mathias, and Jacques. In the plaza of St. Augustine afterwards, they and the two Creek scanned posted notices and broadsides before strolling through the chaos of trade. Negroes wearing silver armbands engraved with the word "free" hawked vegetables, fish, and ale next to bartering merchants and peddlers. Magicians delighted children by pulling coins from their ears. A trick dog danced on hind legs for his fife-playing master. No one carried around the baggage of fear and hostility that so characterized residents of the Savannah area. Even soldiers were relaxed.

Amazement softened David's tone. "The war is little more than rumor here."

"*Oui*. They would all rather be taking a *siesta*."

Sophie shook her head. "Deprive them of supplies or business, and they'd feel the tension to the north." Shock speared her when she recognized the mysterious dark-haired man observing them from the porch of a shop bordering the plaza. She gripped David's forearm. "Over there. It's the fellow from the Dragon and Phoenix." All six turned to regard him.

With a congenial smile, he ambled over. "Welcome to St. Augustine. You look a bit lost. Do you need directions?" Intrigue danced in his dark eyes.

A Spanish accent lurked beneath his flawless command of the English language. David pumped his hand. "Hazelton's the name, Daniel Hazelton. And your name?"

"Luciano de Herrera. Ah, you recognize my name. I am not surprised. I am a long-time resident. Got left behind in '64 to round up some escaped horses." He exchanged greetings with passing soldiers. "Wound up helping with property sales and, in general, smoothing out the transition for the governor."

David's easy smile didn't reach his eyes. "How fortunate."
Herrera drilled his stare through David's skull. "So, Mr. *Hazelton*, what brings you to St. Augustine?"

Clever and resourceful, Luciano de Herrera had made himself invaluable to the Britons colonizing St. Augustine for so many years that he was now beyond reproach: the dream of any long-term operative. Sophie wouldn't have been surprised to hear he made regular reports to Spain or Cuba beneath the very nose of Governor Tonyn. Meanwhile, David returned his penetrating stare and lowered his voice. "Esteban Hernandez referred us to you."

"Did he? And how does the young man?"

"Not well, I'm afraid. He's dead."

Amiability evaporated from Herrera's face, and caution crept into his surveillance of the six. "Might I inquire of the circumstances?"

"Stung by a serpent we couldn't kill. We've reason to believe more venomous creatures abound."

Herrera's lips twitched once, and his caution shifted to encompass the surrounding townsfolk. "A wise observation. This land has its share of such creatures. Beware a scorpion that inhabits the same terrain as the serpent."

El Escorpión and El Serpiente. Lovely.

"Thank you for the warning. We'll watch where we walk."

"As I always have." Herrera regarded the wharf. "You've booked passage on the *Gloria Maria*? *Capitão* Arriaga is a fine fellow with a trim vessel. If you don't distract him with talk of poisonous creatures, he will have you in Havana quite possibly in advance of any fishing sloops that departed this morning."

"Excellent. Might you recommend an inn for tonight?"

Herrera's eyes glittered. "Widow Evans's inn on St. George's Street across from the barracks. Next street over, George Garner owns a stable where you may board your horses."

"Thank you."

"Now if you will please excuse me, I have an appointment." Herrera touched the brim of his hat and smiled. "A pleasure to be of help. Good luck in your business, Mr. *Hazelton*, and I hope your stay in St. Augustine is pleasant." The Spaniard turned about and blended with the crowd.

***

At sunset, torch bearing soldiers and administrators paraded north past Evans's Inn in a fife-and-drum flourish to lock the city gates for the night. The six travelers peered out at the parade but otherwise kept a low profile and remained alert for familiar faces. Fortunately, business at the inn was already bustling due to the house specialties of roast beef and good ale. The sweaty, tipsy patrons in the common room provided adequate cover for anyone needing anonymity.

By nine, Sophie had grown sleepy, so Mathias escorted her upstairs past jovial guests to the door of the room the six of them had rented for the night. A reveler bumped into them in the hallway while Mathias was trying to kiss her hand. Irked, she shoved open the door, yanked the blacksmith into semidarkness, and slammed the door shut behind him.

So he could only be her friend, eh? He wouldn't look at her with such longing if he really believed that. As far as she was concerned, the platonic phase of the relationship had long overstayed its welcome. She flung her arms around his neck and planted a full kiss on him, figuring the worst that could come of it would be another rejection. But when he drenched her with return kisses, hefted her over his shoulder, and navigated past everyone's gear to the bed, she, amazed and delighted, thanked her lucky stars the two of them could finally agree on something.

At the bedside, he seized her face in his hands and plunged into another round of deep, wet kisses while she grabbed his hips and pressed herself against his groin, seeking that half-remembered fit rendered perfect and living for a few hours during a summer thunderstorm eighteen years earlier. His hands strayed from her face down her body, caressing her breasts through her shirt, wandering on to stroke the crevice of her buttocks through her trousers. Then he knelt at her feet and kissed her pubic mound.

Her mouth filled with saliva. Oh, heaven, what were his mouth and fingers about? Her vision of the room blurred. Shadows in the far corner rippled. She blinked to clear her vision. A hand rotating a knife blade emerged from the corner. Elemental horror pierced her primal mind when he stepped into full view, as astonished to see them as she was horrified to see him at all, and swapped his knife for a pistol.

She flailed her arms about. "Mathias, behind you!"

"Wha —?"

She sprawled onto the bed with a shriek as the pistol fired. The fiery breath of the ball skimmed hair near her left temple. "It's *him*! A knife!"

Mathias tackled El Serpiente to the floor at the foot of the bed, eliciting curses in Spanish. Limbs swung about, and torsos tangled in the darkness. "Drop it!" Mathias sounded as though he were gritting his teeth. "Mongrel son of a whore, I'll kill you for murdering my —" Mathias began gasping for air.

"Confirm the alternate location for Don Alejandro's meeting! *Rápidamente* — or I choke you! It is Havana?"

By then, Sophie had vaulted out of bed and flung open the door. Surely someone had heard the pistol discharge. "Help! Murderers! Help! Someone help us!" But the din from the common room doused her yell, as it had masked the pistol shot, and she still heard Mathias choking behind her, so she seized a musket.

The opened doorway yielded just enough light for her to whack the barrel across the Spaniard's back. He roared in pain, shoved off Mathias, and scrambled for the doorway. Mathias lurched for him, but the assassin made it out the door stumbling and cursing. The blacksmith bolted out after him, and Sophie pursued both, arriving on the ground floor in time to see El Serpiente lope out the front entrance and Mathias's pursuit stymied by the crowd.

Snarling, massaging his throat, he waited for her. She pulled him closer so they wouldn't be overheard. "He didn't stab you, did he? Good. I cannot say I think much of Herrera's recommendation for an inn."

"Herrera must have let them know about us. Damned Spaniards." Four redcoats squeezed into the common room with thirsty expressions, and Mathias pulled her around so his body shielded her face. "At this hour, I don't recommend that we draw attention to ourselves by leaving and searching for another inn, even the Dragon and Phoenix. We'd best remain alert and keep quiet about the attack. Where in hell did he come from, anyway?"

"Shadows on the other side of the room. I suspect he was snooping." How fortunate that each of them carried their share of emeralds with them, and she also carried the second cipher, its translation, and the copy of *Confessions* in her haversack. "El Escorpión likely isn't far off."

"Let's round up the others so the assassins don't surprise us again." Sleeping in shifts yet another night: exhaustion weighed down her sigh. He braced one hand on the wall behind her and searched her eyes while tension dissipated from his expression. "I heartily regret the interruption."

"As do I."

He kissed her hand, his dark eyes smoldering, and gentle laughter shook his shoulders. "Unrealistic of me to expect I could fight you off the whole way to Havana and back. Don't lose our location on the map, General."

"No, Ambassador, I don't believe I shall."

***

At six-thirty Wednesday morning, the group made their way to the wharf after a final check on their horses, stabled with Mr. Garner. Sebastião Tomás waved them aboard the gig for the *Gloria Maria*. The Creek brothers, who had transferred over their emeralds, clasped arms with Mathias, Sophie, David, and Jacques in farewell. Then they mounted their horses and rode away in silence. Sophie, watching their departure, felt as though a shield had been stripped from her body, and she whispered an entreaty to the universe for their safe return to the Creek village in the familiar forests of the Georgia colony, hundreds of miles away.

Two brawny sailors stashed the passengers' gear and weapons aboard the gig and helped them aboard. Then they shoved off and rowed east of north toward a channel that led around the tip of Anastasia Island, allowing a parting view of the old fort's coquina walls, agleam in a sunrise that blazed over the scarlet uniforms of soldiers on watch.

They pulled alongside the seventy-foot *Gloria Maria*, her hull painted a pumpkin orange, the green and red of Portugal as her ensign. Sailors steadied the gig. Tomás climbed the boarding net, and weapons and gear were hauled up.

Sophie boarded with the help of Mathias and Tomás. On deck, while the crew of twelve echoed commands in Portuguese and made departure preparations with line and shroud, she got a better view of the British ship-of-the-line and merchant brig anchored to the north, both close enough to spot men on deck and up in the shrouds. David, Mathias, and Jacques climbed aboard, and the passengers retrieved their property for Tomás's tour around the deck and down the companionway to their cabins.

In the narrow, lantern-lit corridor below, she noticed Mathias's dazed expression. "Are you all right?"

"Fine." He seemed to be concentrating. "Just fine."

Jacques whipped out his flask. "*Bon voyage, mon neveu.*" Mathias motioned it away. "I see it in your eyes. It is the le Coeuvre curse. We were not meant to be sailors. Lovers, drinkers, and wanderers, *oui*. Sailors, *non*."

"I cannot stay drunk the entire voyage."

"Suit yourself." Jacques swigged brandy.

Their cabins, side by side, both measured all of five feet wide by ten feet long. Jacques and David took the second cabin. By the time Sophie toted in her gear as well as Mathias's — because a greenish cast had settled over his face — she found little room to move about the first cabin. Hands on hips, she surveyed hammocks, blankets, and pillows stowed along one bulkhead, a hinged desk opening out from the opposite bulkhead, and a stool, closed chamber pot, and bucket below the desk. The port light let in daylight, and an unlit lantern hung near the doorway. For *this* they had each paid a horse? The red wine had better be damned good.

Beneath her feet, the ship gave a lurch, and wonder filled her voice. "We're moving!"

But something other than wonder had captured Mathias's face. His mouth made a noise like, "Urp."

"Say, you'd better get back up on deck."

"Urp."

She helped him down the corridor, and they clambered back up the companionway. On deck he dashed to starboard just in time to retch over the railing.

She decided against checking on him. That he could be sick before they'd even reached the open sea didn't bode well. He'd probably have to stay drunk the entire voyage, like Jacques. Any fancies she'd entertained about picking up where they'd been interrupted the night before fizzled. Not that their cabin was conducive to such activity, anyway.

Jacques meandered from aft and offered the flask to his nephew again. Hanging over the railing, Mathias refused. David strolled over to Sophie. "A bloody shame he feels so badly. And how is *your* stomach?"

She inhaled the sun-warmed, salty breeze of early morning with pleasure. "Apparently the St. Jameses are a seafaring lot."

He craned his neck back to gaze at a sail unfurled. "She feels alive, doesn't she?"

Capitão Arriaga paused from striding aft to smile at Sophie and David. "*Bom dia*, my passengers!" He unfolded a spyglass, his smile on them sharpening. "Help me solve a mystery aft."

He continued on his way, and she eyed David. Arriaga's words hadn't sounded like a request. They found the captain aiming the spyglass at the ship-of-the-line. She didn't need it to spot two redcoats on deck watching the *Gloria Maria* take leave of St. Augustine. She and David exchanged a glance, and both swallowed.

Arriaga adjusted his spyglass. "Sebastião says the major and lieutenant queried him this morning, looking for an elderly colonist and a young Frenchman. They have the most peculiar expressions, like hunters who have lost prey." He handed her the spyglass. "See if it is not so."

Dry-mouthed, she aimed the spyglass toward the warship *Zealot*. There stood Edward, sunlight gilding his hair, Apollo determined to capture Daphne. At his right stood Fairfax, his face full of madness and undefeat, his russet hair like solar fire, King George's very own god of war. She clamped her lips together against the scream tearing her soul: *Go back, Edward, and let us be!*

"*Senhor* Hazelton, I remind you that Portugal is neutral in this war. I will not harbor rebel spies."

"I'm no rebel spy, *capitão*."

"But I saw recognition in both your faces just now. You know those soldiers. They seek you, too, do they not? Answer me quickly, or I drop anchor and allow them to board."

Chapter Twenty-Five

FOR ONCE DAVID was at a loss for a lie. Sophie handed the spyglass to the captain and infused her tone with haughtiness. "Yes, Daniel, do tell the captain about Major Hunt's quarrel with you. No doubt the captain can relate. He is, after all, a *man*."

David seized her implication and rubbed his chin with contrition. "I've — er — dallied with his mistress —" The sharp edge in Arriaga's gaze faded. "— for the past two years, and he's just now finding out about it."

"You have been sleeping with that man's mistress for two years, and he is just now finding out about it?"

"What can I tell you? He travels, she's lonely, and —"

"Bah! Britons, masters of the high seas, but what Briton could ever keep a mistress properly?" It was a question Sophie herself had pondered for several days.

David shrugged with one shoulder to convey indifference. "At times, they do seem a bit cold."

"*Cold*?" Contempt curled the captain's lip. "The stories I could tell you, and all from the lips of their ladies."

"Yes, ladies definitely know what they want, but some gentlemen simply cannot accept it when they fail to discern a woman's subtleties —"

"Or when they are ill-equipped to deliver."

The two men regarded each other a moment in silent accord. Then David's tone emerged blithe. "I presume you won't drop anchor and allow them to board."

Arriaga stomped forward, voice carrying over his shoulder. "We go on to La Habana...mistress...two years...bah..."

David muttered, "Thank you, Sophie. I was stumped."

She studied the *Zealot*. "Do you think they'll pursue us?"

"After everything that's happened on this trip, I shan't be surprised." He guided her fore, where the rising sun danced on the Atlantic.

She shaded her eyes. "How many guns has the *Zealot*?"

"Seventy-four. She's a full ship-of-the-line."

And the *Gloria Maria* had but six swivel guns and two signaling cannons.

Across the sparkling water, the *Zealot* was alive with sailor activity. Dread prodded her when she recalled David's warnings from the previous afternoon. She reminded herself that she was responsible for returning an inheritance, but it didn't ease her certainty that none of them had considered the tenacity and connections of two British officers. How difficult was it, then, to imagine them commandeering a warship to seize a sloop bound for Havana — and, as a bonus, a Portuguese brig?

***

Her head abuzz from red wine, her stomach full of beefsteak, Sophie declined Arriaga's offer of tawny port. The ship throbbed beneath her like a giant sea beast. With all the wining, dining, and rolling, her equilibrium didn't feel quite as stable as it had that afternoon.

The captain decanted port into David and Jacques's goblets. "*Sim*, we encounter pirates. With a decent wind, the *Gloria Maria* averages about eight knots." He closed the flagon and offered cheroots to the men. They lit up, and the cabin became even stuffier. "With a beam wind and ideal seas, we cover almost three hundred miles in a day."

Jacques blew a smoke ring. "You outrun them."

"Precisely. Their vessels offer no match for the speed and grace of the *Gloria Maria*. She is a sea goddess."

The men toasted the prosperity of the *Gloria Maria* and her crew. Arriaga regarded his three supper guests with faint humor. "We encounter few other ships while at sea. Often we make an entire run spotting only two or three away from port. I am curious." He pulled off the cheroot and exhaled. Sophie squirmed, certain she'd have to go up on deck soon to clear her head. Arriaga watched them. "I am curious whether there is a connection between all four of you and a sloop sailing ahead and a frigate sailing astern?"

A sloop and a frigate. Sophie was too mellowed from the wine to provide Arriaga with more than a bland expression. She glanced at David's card-playing face and watched him savor his cheroot. Jacques also betrayed nothing with his expression. But she sensed the captain wasn't fooled.

David blew a smoke ring finer than Jacques's. "A sloop, you say? Hmm. My agent heard a rumor that a competitor chartered a sloop out of St. Augustine yesterday morning down to Havana."

The captain smiled. "Did you dally with his mistress, too?"

"The agent's or the competitor's?"

Arriaga's smile sharpened again. "And what of the frigate?"

David sketched a small figure eight in the air with his cheroot. "I've no clue. I don't pay much attention to ships. Perhaps she's that British warship — what was her name? — at anchor just off St. Augustine."

"She is not the *Zealot*. The *Zealot* is a ship-of-the-line."

Sophie withheld a sigh of relief. Perhaps Edward and Fairfax *would* give them up for lost.

"I haven't the slightest idea of her mission or who might be commanding her." David leaned forward. "But might we get closer to that sloop, see whether she bears the name *Annabelle?*"

Arriaga's expression grew sly. "And just how badly do you want us to overtake the sloop?"

Sophie, not relishing the overtones of the conversation, coughed and rose. "Excuse me, gentlemen. I've enjoyed the supper and company, but I must check on my husband."

The three men rose and bowed. "It distresses me when a passenger becomes ill. *Senhora,* I hope he feels better soon."

"Thank you, *capitão.* I shall convey your concerns."

Amidships on deck, Sophie leaned over the port side and inhaled salty air for several minutes until the tobacco-and-wine cobwebs cleared from her brain. Rigging and sailcloth stretched. Block and tackle creaked. In between the Gulf Stream and the coast, the *Gloria Maria* flew southward on a wind from the east.

A gibbous moon, just risen, beamed a radiant road across the Atlantic and sparkled on foam where wood met water. A ghost ring around the moon symbolized for Sophie just how insubstantial her original motive for solving Will's murder had become, especially since Woodhouse's Tavern. To be sure, she'd find her father's killer. But in doing so, she no longer need prove her own worthiness as his daughter. Embracing the adventure had made her aware of another treasure to be claimed.

Aft, past lemon-yellow lantern light swaying with the ship, second mate Jorge and the helmsman wished her a pleasant night in broken, accented English. The ride aft was bumpy, and she held the railing while her gaze followed the luminous trail of the Milky Way. Even washed by moonlight, the sky seemed populated with hundreds more stars than she'd ever noticed on land.

Was that a light out there on the northern horizon, where the frigate had been sighted? She blinked and squinted but saw nothing except stars and sea. Unease nudged her again. Portugal *was* neutral in the war, but cocky frigate commanders had been rumored to not worry about such particulars. She scanned the north horizon again, unable to shake the feeling that something out there pursued them.

A minute later, she strolled forward, encountering the fore watch, who also wished her a pleasant night. Splotched with moonlight, the dark rectangle of Mathias's blankets blotted the pale deck, and on the blankets Sophie spied the shape of his body stretched out, still. "Are you awake?" He stirred and sat up, and she knelt beside him. "Full belly?"

"Yes. An excellent beefsteak."

"And how is it sitting?"

"Every now and then that sick feeling returns, but I'm much better now. José the cook was right. I needed a full stomach." He caught her hand in his. "Sit with me. How was supper?"

"Elegant. Not at all what I was expecting aboard ship."

"I wager Arriaga doesn't eat nearly so well by halfway across the Atlantic."

"No doubt. I left during the port, cheroots, and negotiations."

"Negotiations?"

"David was trying to convince the captain that we should overtake a sloop sighted southward."

Mathias sucked in a breath. "The *Annabelle?*"

"I shan't be surprised. With Arriaga's bragging about the speed of this ship, we could overtake her on the morrow." Exasperation trailed her nostrils in a stream of breath. "I assume David will engage the captain in cards to make him compliant with our request for a change of velocity. But don't think for a moment that he accepts our story about researching sugarcane in Havana, especially not with a frigate behind us."

She felt him tense. "Gods. A mystery sloop ahead, and a mystery frigate behind. Who'd have thought the Atlantic so well-trafficked? And where are the redcoats and the Rightful Blood?"

"Hush. You shall surely tempt the Fates."

"The Fates — bah!" He stroked her cheek once with the back of his hand. "In my next lifetime, I shall become a boulder. Boulders don't get seasick."

She smiled at the certainty in his expression, visible even in moonlight. "You won't recognize me if you're a boulder."

"Of course I'd recognize you. I've known you for thousands of years. If you returned to the world as a squirrel, I'd create hollows on my surface for you to hide your acorns in. If you returned as a tree, I'd roll over and shelter your sprout. And if you returned as another lovely woman, I'd smooth my surface and make it so inviting for you to rest upon — aye, nestle that firm, shapely arse of yours right atop me —"

"You *are* feeling better than you were this morning."

"It's all this fresh air, you see."

"Yes, I do see," she whispered and brushed his lips with hers, where she tasted the ocean. They let the kiss linger, metamorphose into deliberate, soft caresses that swelled the tide in Sophie's loins until her throat and breasts pounded with it. Shared air formed the sigh between them when they separated.

"You're even more beautiful now than you were eighteen years ago," he said, low.

She chuckled. "I don't have a girl's body anymore."

"No, indeed, your woman's body is all gifts of life and spirit, sweat and blood. Just like Earth, the great mother."

Mathias had written eighteen years of poetry to her — simple, clear, and powerful poetry — in his soul. *He does not hunger for wealth of substance,* Jacques had told her the night before they arrived in Cow Ford. *He hungers for wealth of spirit...the companionship of people who appreciate his worth and accept him as he is. A partner.* Someone who believed in what he did. Someone who recognized the way he transformed the poetry of his soul into masterpieces of metal and diplomacy.

She touched his hand. "How have you known me for thousands of years?"

"You've been in the spirit lake." He yawned.

She thought back to the night she'd wept on his shoulder. "What is this spirit lake? Twice now you've mentioned it."

He sounded groggy. "Creator stands on the shore of the spirit lake and withdraws a drop of water. 'What do you want to be in this lifetime?' Creator asks the drop of water, 'a rock, a blade of grass, an otter, a hawk?' The water drop is you or me. We decide what we want to be in the new lifetime, and we take the form of it. Rock, grass, otter, hawk. When the spirit learns what it came to learn and discharges the form, it returns to the lake and disseminates the knowledge to all other spirits so they benefit from the knowledge. That is how I know you, from the lake."

How could the Indians not feel kinship for everything on the earth after being rocks, grass, otters, hawks? "What have you been in your past lives?"

He thought a moment. "A stag. A vein of copper. A hickory tree. A brook."

She smiled again. "Is this your first time as a human?"

"No. I've been a man before. I've been a woman, too."

"You held Lila's baby just like a midwife would."

"And what have *you* been in your past lives?"

She'd never given the idea of multiple lifetimes much consideration, and yet from the way Mathias explained it, it sat far better with her than the Christians' dogma. Heaven had always sounded boring and pointless to her. "After what's happened the last eleven days, surely I must have been a man."

He laughed. "Indeed, a mighty warrior. A general who led armies to multiple victories." He yawned again.

"Perhaps you were my wife or mistress in that lifetime." They both tittered before subsiding into comfortable quietude. She contemplated the spirit lake a moment longer. "The lake must be changing with all that knowledge every spirit returns to it."

"Mmm. Evolving."

"Where is it evolving?"

"Toward the unity of all things, the Great Understanding." He yawned a third time.

She squeezed his hand. "Come back to our cabin."

"Ah, if only I could be certain the seasickness wouldn't return and spoil it for us. The last thing I want is to be interrupted again. Let us see how I feel in the morning."

She kissed his brow, disappointed, and nodded. "How much we both need rest. I'm so weary my hands shake."

"Go rest, then." He kissed her hand. "Good night."

Chapter Twenty-Six

THURSDAY MORNING, SOPHIE awakened with sunlight bobbing on her face, the smells of coffee and tar in her nostrils, and her bed swaying. When she recognized the creaking and straining noises as those of blocks and sheets, she realized she'd spent the night in her cabin on the *Gloria Maria*.

And she'd spent it there alone. Disappointment tugged at her at the sight of the second hammock swaying empty. After disentangling her feet from the blanket, she rolled from her hammock and used the chamber pot. Then she slipped on her shoes and followed her nose in search of coffee.

A haze rising from the east dimmed sunlight on deck. She squinted outward and wrinkled her nose. Gone were merry waves with foam dancing upon their crests, replaced by swells six feet in height, giving the ocean a swollen, feverish appearance. Clumps of seaweed the color of liver rode the swells, hair torn from the head of Tethys the titan. The *Gloria Maria* compensated for crests and troughs, her rhythm pronounced.

A trip fore rewarded her with the sight of a sloop's white sails not five miles ahead. Mathias rose from where he'd crouched beside a coil of rope. "David must have won at cards."

"Good morning to you, too." She hugged him, her body meeting his with a smooth and humid fit.

The proximity of a sailor in rigging nearby restrained their kiss to a peck, but Mathias slid his arm about her waist and whispered against her neck, "I believe my sickness is cured."

"Without a drop of brandy. Amazing." They chuckled.

Scuffing his boots, Arriaga joined them, spyglass in hand. He smelled of port and cheroots and looked as though he'd had no more than three hours sleep. No telling how much money he'd lost to David. Sophie gestured toward the sloop. "The *Annabelle*?"

"Too soon to tell, *senhora*."

"How soon will we overtake her?"

A brief lift of his shoulders communicated ambiguity. "She can sail closer to the wind, but the captain might find himself in the Bahamas before he outran us. If a passenger paid him to reach a destination such as Havana quickly, he would maintain his course and not sail to windward."

Arriaga had the field figured out. Le Comte André Dusseau, seeing his sloop being overtaken, might assume them pirates. "Has she any guns, *capitão?*"

"A small swivel gun." A voracious smile enveloped his face. "The outcome of the day also depends on the strategy of that frigate, now but six miles behind us. Paolo on the main mast identified her colors as Continental. She has thirty-eight guns and is in pursuit of *us.*" His smile grew knife-sharp. "And there is the ship-of-the-line a few miles behind the frigate."

"Gods," Mathias muttered.

Arriaga gauged their reactions. "Shall we wager the warship is the *Zealot,* and she set sail with those two British officers aboard? Ah, I am certain we shall know soon, for she, like the sloop, is running as quickly as possible."

He circled them once, evaluating. "Such an interesting voyage. Here we are chasing a fishing sloop. We are, in turn, being chased by both a Continental frigate and a warship.

"*Senhora*, your brother Daniel — if Daniel is his name, if he is your brother — plays one and thirty as if he were born to gambling. You, *senhor*, are an Indian, and I wager you are also an artisan. Your French uncle — if he is your uncle — has ties all the way back to Montcalm. And you, *senhora* —" Arriaga appraised her from head to toe, intrigued, his dark eyes alert. "You speak with the authority and confidence of one who has operated a business."

She met his stare, uncomfortable as it made her, and the captain sniffed. "I do not expect you to explain yourselves. However, you may consider giving me your true names. No doubt you have noticed the change in the seas today." He gestured eastward. "And observe the sky."

Mares' tails of cirrus streamed from the haze in the east, heralds reaching westward. Puzzled, Sophie looked at Arriaga. "I'm not a sailor. What does all that mean?"

"It means, *senhora*, that you had best pray for the wind to continue from the east, for if it shifts about to the northeast, by tonight, the captain of each ship will have far more to concern him than pursuit." He pivoted and strode astern.

***

While adjusting to the roll of a larger swell, Sophie balanced the tray between her hip and one hand and reached for the door handle just as Mathias opened the cabin door from within. Blotting his face with a towel, he stepped aside to let her in, then shut the door. The stool squawked when he pulled it out. "Ah, food. My salvation." After tossing the towel on his hammock, he reached for the tray. "Have you eaten?"

"Yes. Go ahead. It's all for you."

She sat on the floor, and neither spoke while she cleaned her teeth and he gobbled breakfast. He gestured with a chunk of bread. "You've been aft to look for the other two ships?"

"Yes. I can see the frigate and her colors clearly."

He swallowed the bread. "What business can a Continental frigate have with us?" Naked of moccasins, he wiggled his toes.

"I've been thinking about that. Suppose MacVie managed to inform rebel leaders that their emerald couriers were being menaced by redcoats and Loyalists, in addition to El Serpiente."

Mathias grunted agreement. "So the Continentals were positioned to lend support to the rebel mission after it headed to Havana. We're a threat, and the frigate's captain means to intercept us."

"Yes. I hope the sloop doesn't fire upon us. The frigate captain would receive the wrong impression."

The blacksmith swigged wine and pointed to the flask. "Excellent. I see how Arriaga stays in business. And what of the ship-of-the-line?"

"Spotting her requires a spyglass. Were you too ill yesterday morning to spot that anchored warship?"

"I saw her. Is the same ship following us?"

"She appears to be the same one, yes, the *Zealot*."

"With Hunt and his hellhound aboard." Mathias crammed more bread in his mouth and swallowed.

"I thought he'd give us up."

"Come now. Did you really think so?"

They studied each other. She remembered David's words to her about Edward, more than a week before: *...he's in love with you, Sophie...He may be a mediocre soldier, but he possesses great tenacity and determination...* With a shiver, she also recalled Fairfax's words: *...he's so obsessed that he could chase you across three hundred miles...*

If three hundred miles on land were nothing to Edward Hunt, the ocean wouldn't stop him, either. She licked her lips, salty with sea spray. "I *hoped* he'd give us up. But I suppose not, with an alliance between Continentals and Spaniards at stake."

"And the woman he loves, too."

"I don't love him. Surely he must realize that."

"He wants you."

"You've wanted me for eighteen years, but did you follow me like a dog all that time? That sort of obsession is unnatural."

"Different men, different courtship styles."

"*Courtship*? Is that what you call our relationship all these years? Had we not been thrown together in this adventure, I'd have gone to my grave without an inkling of your affections."

He scowled. "Not so. I'd have said something —"

"*When*?"

"Why do women always want to know *when*?"

She stared at him, dismayed. "After everything that's happened between us for a week and a half, you're still afraid Major Hunt's going to purchase my affections, aren't you?"

"The thought does cross my mind, yes."

"You concluded that since he's chasing me, I must be destined to break your heart again? I don't believe it. I've drawn close to you, and you're so accustomed to orbiting me from afar that you're spoiling for a quarrel to save face. That's how it works for you, isn't it? That's unnatural, too."

His expression as mobile as marble, he corked the wine flask and set the tray down. "Pardon me. My sickness might be returning." Looking not the slightest bit seasick, he yanked on his moccasins and stood.

She pressed her lips together, her heart climbing into her throat and hurting. "And that's your answer. You don't talk about it. You just walk away." He yanked open the door. She rose and found her balance. "With such a strategy, how did you ever manage to negotiate anything for the Creek?"

The slamming door made her wince and brought tears to her eyes that she dashed away. Edward was in her face. Mathias was out at arms' length. Damned if she understood men. She straightened and squared her shoulders. Who needed any of it?

***

With a freshening east wind and the skies lowering through morning, José extinguished the galley fire and served a cold midday meal. Up on deck, Sophie and her companions watched Fate gather momentum: sloop, brig, frigate, and warship converging. Meanwhile, Mathias moved in and curtailed Sophie's conversation with Arriaga about Mediterranean cultures when he overheard the captain say, "In ancient Crete, women did not cover their bosoms. It is the truth. I have seen statues in Knossos." So much for playing aloof. Arriaga's attentions to her made Mathias nervous.

Mid-afternoon, with the sloop identified at last as the *Annabelle* and less than a mile ahead of the *Gloria Maria*, the frigate and ship-of-the-line closed on the brig running parallel to each other. The wind stiffened, thrust waves up near the deck. Sophie seized the railing, swept wind-whipped hair from her mouth, and tugged on Jacques's elbow. "Why don't those two fire on each other?"

The Frenchman studied the ships in pursuit. "The frigate is outgunned. Only under desperate circumstances will she attack a ship-of-the-line. In a fleet battle, by formality, the warship may not attack the frigate unless provoked. But we know how often ship captains follow the rules."

"And this isn't a fleet battle." David threw a look astern.

Arriaga returned forward from conversing with his signaler and said to David, "The *Annabelle* will not acknowledge us."

"Close the distance."

"*Senhor* Hazelton, I remind you of her gun."

"You know the range of that gun. You can get closer."

"Will your competitor acknowledge you even then? For all I know, the two of you hate each other enough to fight a duel."

Sophie watched David and the captain trade glares. "Very well. He isn't my competitor. My sister and I suspect two men aboard the *Annabelle* of complicity in our father's murder."

"Ah." Arriaga's shoulders relaxed. "Finally I have a truth here. And your real names?"

"I'm David St. James. My sister, Sophie. Mathias Hale and his uncle, Jacques le Coeuvre."

"Let us have more of the truth now, *senhor*." His gaze scoured the four of them. "Are any of you spies?"

"With God as my witness, *capitão*, no, and we want no part of this war. Misunderstandings have caught us in the middle. You can get more speed from this brig, can you not?"

The captain gave him an unpleasant smile. "Of course. It is all I can do to hold her back in a beam wind. And I *will* hear more of your truth after we have shaken loose those two behind us." He strode aft, his commands in crisp Portuguese.

Sailors climbed footropes under the yard and bowsprit. Rather than cringe at the sight of maritime acrobatics and wonder how men could hang on in such a wind, Sophie looked astern. The sails of the frigate and warship seemed to fill the sky.

Jacques cocked an eyebrow. "The *capitão* is a slick one."

A grudging smile jerked David's lips. "He kept us from getting closer until I told him the truth."

Jacques patted his shoulder. "Perhaps it was time you met someone who is immune to the stories you spin."

The *Gloria Maria* leaped forward, and David grabbed the railing. "Look lively, Dusseau! Here we come!"

Sophie started. "Say, what's that flash of light?"

The "boom" from the *Annabelle*'s gun reached their ears in the next second, and a ball plumed the water a thousand feet ahead of the *Gloria Maria*. "Bloody hell! She fired on us!"

Portuguese consternation erupted all over the ship. A gust from the northeast whistled around canvas and lines, and a maintopman jabbered about the frigate and the weather. At another explosion, fainter, from astern, Mathias peered over the port railing. "The frigate just fired upon us!"

"Warning us off." Jacques's expression darkened. "And the ship-of-the-line?"

"Still not engaging the frigate, Uncle."

"She will bide her time and scoop up the scraps of battle. *We* will be the scraps if this continues."

In response to additional commands from Arriaga, sailors redirected sails and rigging, and the *Gloria Maria* seemed to take a deep breath before settling back to her previous speed. Nevertheless, the *Annabelle* fired another ball at the brig, and the frigate responded with additional shots. Arriaga barked out more commands and jogged forward. "*Senhor*, accept my apologies, but we will not rendezvous with the *Annabelle*. For the safety of all aboard, we are clearing the field —"

Dire exclamations broke from the maintopman, and Arriaga strode to port for a look northeast. In the next second, the wind veered, and with a groan of timber, the *Gloria Maria* heaved to starboard. Yards, spars, gaffs, and rigging swung wide, sailors aloft howled and cursed while clinging on for dear life, and the fore topgallant blew out in a bang. Everyone standing forward, including Arriaga, tumbled to the deck, and unsecured equipment rebounded amidships.

Arriaga scrambled up and bellowed a new set of commands, echoed aft by Tomás. More hands clawed their way aloft on shrouds and ratlines to stow the thrashing sail.

David, crouching, gaped northeast. "Look at *that*!"

A black shelf of cloud had belched from the haze and was trundling southwest. Sophie, assisted to her knees by Mathias, squinted into a wind that tried to pummel them flat. Jacques propped his elbow and jerked his head toward the approaching squall. "All ships are too close to the coast of East Florida. We cannot lie to and ride it out. We will wreck on the reefs."

Scudding ahead of the squall appeared to be Arriaga's strategy. Moments later, the forestaysail set, the foretopsail set and reefed, and all other sails furled, the brig braced herself in the angry sea. Wood groaned and rigging strained as the two sails filled with the approaching tempest, and the ship steadied in her new bearing.

Wind slapped a wave across the deck. Sophie shielded her face and clung to the railing. "What happened to the *Annabelle*?"

"Over here!" Mathias called from the starboard bow. "Her sails blown out by that first big gust."

Sophie, Jacques, and David joined him at the leeward railing. A scant thousand feet away, the *Annabelle*'s crew worked on their sails. The *Gloria Maria* slipped past, stabilized by foresails and expert hands on the tiller. Three miles northeast, the squall bore down on the frigate and warship, all hands aboard both ships still lowering and furling sails. Sophie shook her head. "The squall will be upon the *Annabelle* in minutes."

A dark-haired young man, likely André Dusseau, appeared on deck to offer what aid he could to the captain and crew of the sloop. An elderly man climbed up after him, the third member of Hernandez's trio. A band of rain passed between the two ships as he turned around, preventing their getting a clear look at him, but Sophie blinked and gasped, her soul brushed by phantasm.

Beside her, Mathias stiffened. "Am I seeing things?"

"*Mon dieu*, not unless I am, too."

"I know what I *think* I saw." Sprayed by rain, David rubbed his eyes and gaped, trying to penetrate the rain.

Wind deposited globs of seaweed tangled with small fish on deck, and tepid rain tasting of seawater soaked the passengers. They gripped the railing. Rain curtained off the *Annabelle*, but not before they spotted the sloop once more, her sails dropped and furled, her mainsail at last set.

Tomás stumped forward drenched, his Spanish sounding soaked. "¡Abajo! ¡Abajo!" He motioned them below. Passengers washed overboard were bad for business.

Just before Sophie headed down the companionway, she spied the squall swallowing the frigate and warship. Tomás shoved the hatch closed behind her and her party. Slammed from one side to the other in the belly of the storm-tossed brig, the four of them traded stunned glances in the gloom of a dingy lantern and gathering night. Bitterness and apprehension carved through David's expression. "God *damn* it all to hell."

Chapter Twenty-Seven

IN THE ADJOINING cabin, where they'd stored their gear at the beginning of the night, a small object bounced on the floor and progressed to smaller and smaller bounces until it, along with other loose objects, clattered to the wall on the port side. When the *Gloria Maria* rolled back the other way, the loose objects in the cabin mirrored the motion. The pattern repeated so many times that Sophie lost track of how long it had gone on.

She imagined powder, balls, and splintered arrows smeared on the floor with the contents of the chamber pot, a sort of storm stew. Amazing that she could hear anything from the other cabin for the shriek of the wind. She and her companions hugged the floor to avoid being flung into each other. They'd puked several times, except Mathias, who must have purged the instinct from his system the previous day. No one spoke.

Through the wind's howl, she heard another band of rain lash the hull. Yanked about like a splinter being pried from Poseidon's thumb, the fragile wood-and-canvas *Gloria Maria* reared up and slammed down what felt like fifty-mile-high mountains of ocean, jarring Sophie until her jaw ached.

Right after the lantern had extinguished, plunging them into night spiked with pink and blue lightning, they'd heard a mast crack, loud as cannon shot, followed by the collapse and wreckage of rigging and spars on the deck. Sophie imagined Arriaga and his crew swept overboard then and the brig — her rudder lost, her two foresails blown out — batted along by the storm like a ball of yarn in a kitten's paws.

Entrenched in seasickness, nothing left in her stomach to vomit after half a night, she no longer cared what became of them. Let the *Gloria Maria* impale herself upon the reefs of East Florida and plunge them to the bottom of the Atlantic.

The ordeal felt worse for her, having glimpsed a specter who looked hauntingly like her father stranded aboard the *Annabelle*, moments away from being pounded by the black squall. Logic told her it couldn't have been Will. She'd seen his burned corpse. But her eyes had contested logic — not only *her* eyes, but also those of her companions. Perhaps they'd each been granted the illusion in denial of death and destruction.

For the odds were against the sloop picking up enough forward speed to stay ahead of the squall. Considering the thrashing the *Gloria Maria* endured, surely the *Annabelle* had foundered hours before, along with all aboard her and two-thirds of the rebels' bribe to Don Alejandro. Likely none of them would ever see the two men who'd partnered with Hernandez again.

On they rose and plunged through the tropical storm, neither capsizing nor running aground, until at length the rain and wind abated from the port quarter and astern. Jacques groaned in the darkness. "It feels as though the wind has shifted."

Mathias squeezed Sophie's hand gently before speaking. "Yes, it seems to be coming from starboard now, but no comfort in that. We're still being walloped in these waves."

"From the starboard — *mon neveu*, do you not understand? If we are still traveling south, a wind from starboard is coming from the west."

David groaned. "Meaning what, Uncle Jacques?"

"Meaning that perhaps we have seen the worst of it. I have heard men speak of riding out these storms. Nearly always the wind switches from the east to the northeast, and then, when the worst is passing, the wind comes from the west, until finally it returns to the southeast or east."

They stayed quiet awhile longer, listening while the wind abated. David broke the hush with what was on everyone's minds. "The visibility was poor, but we all saw what looked like the old man aboard the *Annabelle*. Suppose it really was him. No, no, hear me out. I've gone over and over this. While we were at Zeb's dance, suppose the old man and his cohorts unearthed Elijah Carey's corpse, transported it to MacVie's land, swapped the clothing, then burned it?"

"A *second* masquerade?" Sophie heard the way her tone bit the air. "That's horrendous. I cannot believe Father would torture us in such a way. If that was him on the *Annabelle*, I — I don't know about you, but I feel betrayed. All the heartache we've suffered these weeks, thinking he's dead."

"I cannot reason it, either. Perhaps El Serpiente fouled his plans to slip word to us, and it became a masquerade he never intended to continue."

"*Oui*, but how could the team of St. James and Carey have accomplished a second masquerade with such expertise that they did not leave us a single clue?"

"Suppose we ignored clues."

Mathias stirred. "Indeed. Sunday in the copse on MacVie's property, I noticed a smell from the charred body. It wasn't the odor of burned flesh."

"Decomposition, from Mr. Carey's body!" Sophie felt the energy of discovery and hope ripple through her companions. "I smelled it, too, but I was so distraught that I pushed the thought of it aside. What if Father intended for us to ignore the clues?"

Mathias rose on one elbow. "David, remember I told you I'd noticed that the corpse's arms hung straight, not twisted backwards, as they would have for a living victim who'd been tied to the stake."

A raspy chuckle escaped Jacques. "Even after all my years working for Montcalm, I must admit that I, too, missed a clue. Late Sunday afternoon, I walked the graveyard and noticed that the dirt on *Monsieur* Carey's grave looked freshly turned."

Surprise widened Sophie's eyes. "Assayceeta Corackall visited me Sunday afternoon to bring condolences. He told me the Creek, hearing of Father's murder, had witnessed the passage of his spirit through the forest early Sunday morning."

"His spirit?" David laughed. "Ye gods, if we're right about this, if that really was the old man aboard the *Annabelle*, he left so many clues that we're bloody idiots for not having figured it out. But the committee's ambush suggests that the old man was so desperate to succeed that he'd sacrifice his own flesh and blood. I don't believe it. I cannot escape the feeling that Donald Fairbourne just wanted to scare me back to Alton. And the old man and I didn't always agree, but I know he wouldn't have wanted me murdered."

"I don't think Father had anything to do with the ambush."

The snarl in David's voice was audible. "MacVie?"

"He was second-in-command for the Committee of Safety and probably browbeat the rest of them into the ambush." She paused. "And MacVie told me he wanted to kill me for personal reasons."

"Why, that stinking son of —"

"David, let it go." Mathias lay back sounding exhausted. "Consider this. If we're correct about this wild scheme, and Will was on the *Annabelle*, he planned the ruse with Elijah Carey's corpse to purchase time and cover so he and his two 'friends of John Adams' could slip from town and head to their meeting with Don Alejandro in St. Augustine. And that means we must assume we aren't the only ones who've figured this out. All this time, the redcoats may have been chasing Will, not us or El Serpiente."

Sophie said quickly, "No one else, Arriaga included, needs to know that Father may not have been murdered."

"Agreed." David ejected a hard sigh. "But if Hunt and Fairfax survived the storm, they may as well head back north. Unless a miracle occurred hours ago, most of the bribe for the Gálvez has taken up residence at the bottom of the ocean."

"*We* survived. If the redcoats did also, they've too much at stake to merely return to the colonies." The serene certainty in Mathias's voice surprised Sophie.

"He's right, David. Our part isn't finished. We've these emeralds to discharge, so we go on to Havana. And if we encounter those assassins again, let us not forget that Jonah was almost certainly murdered by one of them."

"Emeralds." Tension tugged on David's voice. "The gods only know where the storm blew the *Annabelle*, how much damage she sustained, and how long it will take her to reach Havana. What impression will we make in Havana without the other two-thirds of the emeralds? I told you this reeks of crooked piquet. If we seek out Don Antonio Hernandez and give him our paltry portion, he might suspect us of robbing and murdering his nephew — maybe even of sinking the *Annabelle*."

Sophie shifted about, encouraged because the ship didn't feel quite so out of control anymore, but flustered by David's logic. "Fortunately we don't have to plan that far ahead this moment. Unless I'm mistaken, we'll be spending the next few days recuperating from the storm."

"Repairing the structural damage," said Mathias. "Pumping out the seawater. Straightening out the hold."

She returned the squeeze to Mathias's hand and took heart. "I wonder how far off course we've been blown."

Jacques chuckled again. "Perhaps to the Bahamas, eh? I have never been there. I should like to see the islands."

She attempted a laugh but curtailed it when her stomach knotted. "I've heard that buccaneers prowl the Bahamas."

"Ehhh. Blackbeard is long dead."

"But there are still plenty of Continental, British, and Spanish warships about."

They heard voices on deck, the hatch thrown open, and footsteps clomping down the companionway. The door to the cabin whammed open, and the four squinted into lantern light. *Capitão* Arriaga's slender frame filled up the doorway with vitality and competence. Rainwater and seawater dripped off and puddled beneath him, and by some trick of lighting, for a second or two, Sophie swore he'd traded his hair for seaweed and his two legs for a merman's tail. "*Bom dia*, my passengers! You are each alive and in one piece, *sim*?"

"Alive, *oui*. In one piece, *non*. My stomach resides in that chamber pot over there."

Arriaga laughed at the Frenchman. "In good spirits, no less! I am honored. You will be pleased to know we have passed through the worst of the tropical storm. José is cleaning up the galley even now so our empty bellies will soon have some relief."

David pushed up to a sitting position. "Where are we?"

"We must have clear skies to know that."

"We heard a mast break. Which one was it?"

"The main topmast. And we have leaks to repair. If we are lucky, we will find safe anchorage for a few days."

Jacques prodded David. "What did I tell you, eh? The Bahamas. *Oui*, I would like to see the Bahamas."

"And well you may, *Monsieur* le Coeuvre."

★★★

Blown east by the tropical storm, the *Gloria Maria* limped south Friday toward the Bahamian archipelago on sails of the bowsprit and foremast but only the mainsail and main staysail on the mainmast. Just before noon, they came upon bobbing wreckage of a ship that had been caught in the heart of the storm — broken masts, barrels, a corpse tangled in timber and canvas. Hammering and sawing aboard the brig stilled while they sailed past. Portuguese crossed themselves and murmured to *Nossa Senhora* Maria.

Captain and crew resumed structural repairs, general cleanup, and pumping the hold, while Sophie and her companions sorted through the chaos in their cabins and cleaned and repaired their gear and weapons. Discouraged from taking a nap by all the noise, they mended clothing, ate José's excellent fare, and avoided the tropical sun. In truth, had they not been aware of the brig's vulnerability, Friday might have felt restive.

Early afternoon, ship's carpenter León, who was on the mainmast, spotted the Abaco archipelago, northernmost islands of the Bahamas. The brig headed southeast, paralleling a string of cays imbedded in a barrier reef to the east of Abaco. They turned southward again, rounding the middle of Great Abaco Island and passing a cove occupied by a brig, her crew finishing repairs of storm damage. Tension dissipated from Arriaga's face after a look through the spyglass confirmed the other ship as a merchant he recognized, not a pirate. About four in the afternoon, farther south on Great Abaco, the *Gloria Maria* entered an empty, quiet cove secluded by royal palms and jungle.

Arriaga unloaded four of his men into a gig and sent them scouting ashore. They returned to report that all was quiet on the beach and in the jungle, and the other brig had already set sail. But human visitors had preceded them to the cove, evidenced by salt-crusted remains of an old campfire. The captain didn't seem concerned or surprised by news of the campfire and had his men tow the *Gloria Maria* deep into the cove, past an island covered with billowing sea oats embedded in alabaster sand. Arriaga explained to the passengers that in the morning, after transporting everyone ashore, the crew would tow the brig in even closer to shore and careen her, enabling sailors to plug leaks in the hull.

Only a few feet of water separated the keel of the brig from the sandy bottom in the cove when they anchored. Never could Sophie have imagined such turquoise water — so clear she could see all the way to starfish on the bottom — or the pristine alabaster sand on the beach, sprinkled with shells of rose, vermilion, taupe, and violet. With the lush verdure, azure sky, balmy sea breeze, and fluffy cumulus, she understood why pirates had favored the Bahamas.

Arriaga joined her on the port side facing east and leaned both elbows on the railing. "Beautiful, eh?"

The breeze rippling through palms and sea oats ashore beckoned a welcome. "In all my life, I've never seen anything to compare with it. Is this what Cuba is like?"

"In some places, sim. But Cuba has more variety. Mountains, waterfalls, and streams. Many mahogany trees like that one over there. Hah. If that were not the only mahogany tree on this island, the Spaniards would be here, too, chopping wood for their ships as they have done in Cuba." He smiled at her expression. "You want to step ashore today, *senhora?*"

"Only if it doesn't interfere with your repairs."

Still smiling, he straightened, the fervor of his gaze like a sultry summer night in the Mediterranean. Behind him, Mathias approached, spotted the two of them together, and drew up short. "I think I can spare someone to tour you and your companions around." Arriaga fingered her sleeve, as if brushing off lint. "But you must be sure to catch some crabs."

Sophie looked from his fingers, to the sensuous curve of his lips, to the surprise on Mathias's face. "Crabs?"

"*Sim.* They crawl out on the beach at night. See the size of my hand? Even bigger than that." Scowling, Mathias strode back the way he'd come, leaving Sophie to wonder whether the storm had siphoned the passion out of him and into Arriaga. "With the moonlight tonight, you will not even need a lantern. I will send Sebastião and twenty sacks with you in the gig."

"*Twenty* sacks, *capitão?*"

"You will have no problem filling them." His laughter was vivacious, hearty with his love of the Atlantic Ocean. "Crabs are stupid."

True to his prediction, the crabs appeared after nightfall, scuttling across the sand. In the moonlight, Tomás demonstrated to the four passengers how to scurry up behind a crab and grab it, keeping fingers clear of the claws. Laughing and kicking sand around, they filled the sacks in minutes. In fact, they might have used a few more sacks. Crabs *were* stupid.

But as they rowed back to the brig, Sophie studied the beach of moonlit silver and the blackened jungle beyond it. This wasn't the *Gloria Maria*'s first visit to the cove. Arriaga had known about the crabs, and Tomás had showed the passengers how to flirt with a group of dolphins familiar enough with humans to venture close to shore. Salt-crusted remains of a campfire: she wondered whether crabs weren't the only foolish creatures in the cove.

Chapter Twenty-Eight

EARLY SATURDAY MORNING the passengers again went ashore, this time to a grove of palm, cocoplum, and pigeon plum trees, where the crew had strung hammocks and provided rum, cheese, fruit, and cakes. The crew even had the decency to set up their bubbling, stinking pitch pots downwind. The arrangement was enough to satisfy the grouchiest of guests. Jacques, who had drunk five sailors under the table the night before, proceeded to the nearest hammock and sprawled in it. Within a minute, his snores echoed through the grove.

Only the fact that Mathias had come to bed long after she'd fallen asleep threatened to skew Sophie's mood, but she was far too interested in Abaco to preoccupy herself with his mood. She watched the crew of the *Gloria Maria* careen the ship with heavy tackle attached near the base of the mahogany tree and ten feet off the deck on the mainmast. After the Portuguese waded out to stuff leaky seams with oakum and cotton and cover the patches with pitch and tallow paint, she, David, and Mathias walked along the beach and explored mollusks and starfish.

Sophie surrendered to the heat just after noon. Belly full of fruit and cheese, head humming with rum, she tumbled into a hammock and snoozed, lulled by the music of tropical birds and palm fronds. Even a distant, grumbly thunderstorm failed to rouse her.

Late afternoon, a fishy smell prodded her awake, and she stared head-on at a grouper working its bloody, hook-torn mouth. With a yowl, she flipped from the hammock and rose, scowling, to the whoops of David, Mathias, and Jacques. The Frenchman slapped his knee. "See you jump, *belle* Sophie!"

Mathias poked David. "She mistook it for El Serpiente."

David, who'd held the grouper in her sleeping face, pondered the fish. "Surely not. This poor creature, god rest its soul, looks too much like Fairfax."

"*Oui*, it is something about the eyes, I think. Cold-blooded. Shall we go ahead and flay it, then?"

The three men swiveled sun-and-rum-flushed grins at her. The prod to her intuition was almost painful, so she glowered. "I hardly think it wise to tempt the Fates with such humor."

"Fates, bah!" Jacques swaggered. "After such a storm, what are the odds that assassins or English pigs are here in Abaco?"

David swelled his chest. "Those louts are food for sharks."

She crossed her arms. "You'd better throw your one little fish back before you give the Portuguese cause for ridicule."

"Hah." David brandished it at her. "Fortunately, we didn't catch just old Fairfax here while you slumbered."

Beyond the grove, they'd strung fourteen fish out on three ropes. David's grouper, which weighed less than five pounds, was the smallest. They toted the catch down the beach to where José was lambasting a sailor for a careless cleanup of the pitch pots. Spying the catch changed the cook's entire attitude.

Whistling, he set to work dressing the fish. In the cove, Tomás and three men rowed the gig and pulled while Arriaga and sailors along shore pushed to right the *Gloria Maria*. To cheers from the passengers, the brig was towed to deeper water. Knee-deep in water and bare-chested like most of the crew, Arriaga faced them with a grin and took a bow for a job well done.

***

After supper on the beach, a sailor fiddled while men smoked pipes, sang, and danced around a bonfire. Each tune, Sophie got passed between Mathias, David, and Jacques. The captain, quick to perceive Mathias's reserve, claimed her for several tunes. While they danced, Mathias slunk off, annoying Sophie. Not that she disliked Arriaga, an accomplished dancer, but it dawned on her that she'd misread Mathias in addition to Edward. Even were Jacques sober enough to reprimand his nephew for inattention, it wouldn't have helped. The blacksmith wasn't ready to change their relationship. Perhaps he never would be.

While the fiddler took a break, and everyone refilled tankards of rum or wine, Mathias reappeared. David slapped him on the back. "Welcome back. We feared the crabs had carried you off, and we were about to send out a search party." He and Jacques guffawed.

"I walked up the beach." Mathias regarded Sophie. "There's a place that's quite lovely by moonlight. You want to see it?"

"Certainly!" David took a step forward before Jacques snagged his upper arm. "Ah. Right. What Uncle Jacques means is that he and I are too busy drinking rum and learning bawdy Portuguese, so we shall defer the walk to later." His leer glittered in the firelight. "But you two run along."

Mathias hadn't taken his eyes off her. She laughed, handed her tankard to David, and hiccupped. "Oh, why not. I'm sure my dear old chum Mathias will come to the rescue if crabs try to carry me off." With another laugh, she looped her arm in his and bounded up the beach with him.

He disentangled their arms after they'd galloped far enough to be out of earshot and caught her hand in his while still matching her stride. "'Dear old chum'?"

With the sensuality of shimmery stars, a swollen moon, and a surf serenade, most men would seduce a woman on that beach. But Mathias wasn't most men, and she had the hunch he'd rather *talk*. "'Dear old chum' is more complimentary than 'stodgy old fart'."

He braked their progress and faced her. "I knew it! You've been trying to make me jealous with Arriaga! All that dancing with him!"

Oh, damn. Mathias didn't want to talk. He wanted to argue. "Well, one thing I'll say about the captain. He knows how to appreciate the company of a woman."

His eyes bugged. "So you were encouraging him!"

By then, she wished she'd drunk more wine. She glanced at the bonfire, then to the deserted beach ahead, a silvery ribbon by moonlight. "I'm sweaty from dancing and a bit drunk. I'm going to walk and cool down. I suggest you return and get yourself thoroughly drunk. If you find a fellow named Mathias Hale, send him after me. I've stored up eighteen years of lewd fantasies to share with him." She strolled up the beach.

The shells went crunch, crunch beneath her shoes. After a quarter minute or so, she heard the echoing rasp of Mathias's shoes. She kept walking and rounded a bend to where there were fewer shells. Just ahead, a blanket had been spread upon sand where the beach widened, and a bottle of wine stood upright beside the blanket.

She stared down at it while Mathias approached, and it occurred to her that perhaps he hadn't wanted her out there to lecture her. The breeze felt marvelous on her sweaty arms, and she looked with longing at the water before facing him.

He bowed. "Good evening, madam. My name is Mathias Hale. Some dolt of a fellow back there told me you wanted to see me."

She removed her shoes and stockings, began tugging off her trousers, and quipped, "Last one in the water is a rotten egg!"

His splash naked into the tepid, thigh-deep water wasn't but seconds behind hers. Since she'd never advanced in swimming past basic dog paddling, he was upon her in two strokes. She squealed with mock protest before wrapping her legs about his torso, anchoring herself against him, and sliding her tongue around his. "My lucky stars," she whispered a moment later, the warmth of his mouth on her throat, "Neptune is poking me with his trident."

His lips wended around to her neck. "One of your fantasies? Tell me more."

She unwrapped her legs and licked his chin. "Mmm. Salty on the surface. Shall I find something sweet inside?" And she trailed her tongue down, into the hollow of his throat, around both nipples, across his flinching stomach, past his navel and abdomen. Salty, yes, they were creatures of salt.

"Sophie — Sophie —" His knees wobbled, and he rolled his head back.

Crouching, she reached behind, grabbed his buttocks, and guided the primordial trident into her mouth. "If you don't stop — Sophie — I shall —" He gasped and shuddered. "Oh, gods, Sophie, yes, just so, oh, oh —"

As his cry faded from the beach, he lifted her into his arms, savored the salt on her lips, and carried her back to the blanket, where he tasted her until he grew engorged enough to swim in the ocean of her body. Suspended on the verge of *le petit mort*, she gazed into her own vulnerability in his eyes, the obsidian depths there reflecting starlight and moonlight the way of a still midnight lake. Over and over she arrived at the brink of rapture, but the lake in his eyes guided her back, so she must hover at the edge and listen to arousal and rawness thundering in her veins, heartbeat and current of the empyrean.

In the instant before she wept with release, her soul recognized the spirit lake in his eyes. *Le petit mort* was but the dénouement of the mighty and fragile ecstasy that fueled the universe. She understood then why she'd climbed out her bedroom window two weeks past and turned her back on a comfortable life in Alton and the promise of opulence in England. She'd found the adventure she'd been seeking her whole life. To her amazement, she need never have looked farther than her own heart.

★★★

Near midnight, David and Jacques tottered up the beach belting out a ditty about three French soldiers and their commanding officer's wife. Consequently, Sophie and Mathias were fully clothed by the time the two men arrived. Arriaga's orders: everyone except sentries must spend the night aboard ship. Sophie looked with fondness at the site of their lovemaking while Mathias folded up the blanket. They hadn't but scratched the surface on her supply of fantasies. How fortuitous that the trip to Havana wasn't even half over.

On deck late Sunday morning, she squinted north. Sentries had reported the arrival of a storm-damaged fishing sloop — alas, not the *Annabelle* — in the neighboring cove the previous night, hence Arriaga's caution. Abaco as a refuge must be on every sea captain's nautical charts.

Aboard the *Gloria Maria*, sailors assembled the new main topmast. Sails had been hung out to dry in the light breeze. She followed their shade until noontime sun denied her cover. On the verge of ducking below to evade direct sunlight, she spotted the captain headed her way from amidships beaming his approval. He extended a folded parasol to her. "My dear wife left this aboard in March. Please, you make use of it."

"Thank you, *capitão*."

He caught her hand and kissed it. "My pleasure, *senhora*."

She opened and extended the parasol and watched him amble away, his flattery flushing her cheeks. Not impervious to his charm, she considered all the *Gloria Maria*'s ports of call and bet herself that the captain had a dear wife in every one.

That evening, while Tomás inventoried repairs to confirm their completion, second mate Jorge accompanied the passengers ashore to bag more crabs. The dolphins put in an appearance but seemed nervous and kept their distance, so Sophie blew them a kiss of encouragement from shore. Poor creatures, having their cove turned into a shipyard.

Aboard the brig, she sat back-to-back with Mathias, drank Portuguese wine, sniffed cooking crabmeat, and listened to fiddled shanties and folk songs while the remnants of vermilion sunset emptied from the west. The crew wasn't as eager to wallow in rum as they'd been the previous two nights. Excessive consumption of spirits had made several of them sluggish. Still, sentries were back aboard, the brig was seaworthy again, and everyone was in good cheer.

She turned in after another exquisite supper, too sleepy to chat with her companions and the captain, sat on the blankets, and thought of Hernandez's final moments. Again, she heard him implore her to give the emeralds to Don

Alejandro and meet at the home of his uncle in Havana.

Since David's warning on St. Augustine wharf, something about Hernandez's last words had niggled the back of her brain. The logistics of the young Spaniard's shooting *were* wrong. How could El Serpiente have shot him from the front and his horse from behind? Weariness fuzzed her focus. She stretched out on the blankets.

Jerked awake from a dream about gunfire, she heard footsteps pounding down the companionway and dragged a blanket over her torso just as Mathias burst into the cabin. "Sophie, wake up."

"I'm awake." She heard a firearm report in the distance. "What the blazes is going on?"

He closed the door. Moonlight through the port light illuminated him. "Someone's shooting at the ship from the beach." He knelt beside her, having scooped up his rifle, powder horn, and pouch. "Stay here in the cabin while we resolve it."

"Of course, but —" Foreboding clawed her chest. "— but who's shooting at us? Pirates? Arriaga will weigh anchor to get away, right?"

"No pirates. We'd have seen their ship by now. It's one person wasting shot at us from different spots on shore."

Someone from the sloop in the northern cove, perhaps? Sophie's foreboding deepened.

"Arriaga probably won't weigh anchor yet. The shot's falling short, and we need daylight to navigate our way out of the islands safely."

David knocked on the door. "Is Sophie all right?"

"I'm snug in bed, dear brother."

"Stay there, *belle* Sophie." From Jacques's growl, his fingers itched for his tomahawk.

Mathias pecked her cheek and rose. She covered her torso until he'd exited and shut the door. Then she dressed. Although she had no desire to make a target of herself up on deck, she wouldn't sleep again until the matter was resolved.

In the moonlit cabin she listened. Sporadic shots continued every thirty seconds to two minutes from the beach, not from the island, which was closer. She envisioned a man firing at the brig, relocating to another spot on the cove, and reloading his musket for another shot. Who would do such a thing? Why? For how long would he continue? Was it someone from the sloop?

Footsteps in the corridor outside drew her attention, and the hinges on the other cabin door squeaked. David and Jacques were up on deck with Mathias, so who was entering their cabin? She tiptoed to her door, heard the other door squeak closed, and had just enough time to squeeze into the corner at the door before her cabin door eased open.

A man garbed all in black and smelling of seaweed crept in, light from the corridor glinting on a dagger in his hand. Horror and panic leaped through her. The person on shore had created a diversion to allow an intruder to slip aboard the *Gloria Maria*. Moonlight in the cabin would reveal her presence. She slid to the floor and groped, her hand closing about the parasol.

Before she could grab anything more substantial, the man turned about. She sprang upward with a shriek.

The second of surprise that the shriek bought enabled her to swing the parasol by the fabric end. Air whooshed with its descent, curtailing when the solid mahogany handle whacked his temple. He grunted and collapsed. She dropped the parasol and bolted out.

The first person she saw upon scrambling up the companionway was Tomás, who registered the terror on her face in an instant. "¡*Un extraño — un cuchillo — en mi cabina!*" she blurted in Spanish.

The first mate stared with incredulity toward the diversionary musket fire ashore, comprehension flooding his expression. He signaled her to wait there on deck, checked his pistol, and ordered two sailors with cutlasses to accompany him below. Seconds after they disappeared, David spied her and trotted over. "We told you it's much safer below!"

"Safer? Hah! A man entered my cabin with a dagger, so I hit him in the head with a parasol. Tomás just went down there."

"Wait here. Keep your head down." His fowler gripped, he clambered down the companionway after the Portuguese.

Another musket report sounded from shore. She crouched on deck steadying her nerves, considering with irony that she'd complied with Arriaga's request to make use of the parasol. The musket ashore fired once more before David emerged from below, followed by Tomás. She stood, her knees shaky. Behind the first mate, the two sailors carried a sea-dampened, semi-conscious man. They dumped him on deck, and he groaned. Tomás trotted off to find the captain. The sailors stood guard.

Tension and incredulity gripped David's face. "Damnation. I don't believe it!"

"Especially after we came through the storm," she murmured, by then all too familiar with the man's dark features. The prisoner of the Portuguese was none other than El Serpiente.

Chapter Twenty-Nine

CAPITÃO ARRIAGA CLOSED El Serpiente's grappling hooks into a sack along with the assassin's daggers and rope and addressed David. "The American rebels do not like you. The redcoats do not like you." He handed the sack to Tomás and glanced at the bound, silent assassin on the deck. "And the Spaniards do not like you. Does anyone like you, *senhor?*"

"I told you we were caught in the middle of this. Had I known that tracking my father's murderer would make me a target of assassins, I'd have stayed in Williamsburg playing cards."

Hands clasped behind him, Arriaga paced around El Serpiente. "I have not heard of *Casa de la Sangre Legítima.*" Another shot fired from shore. Still operating the diversion, El Escorpión had no idea his partner was in custody. El Serpiente maintained silence and a face devoid of expression. A smile carved through Arriaga's features. "But if these assassins are the menace you believe, there must be a handsome bounty awaiting those who release them into custody of the governor of Cuba."

Jacques's scowl exploded. "You do not mean to take him with us? These are assassins, not altar boys! They butcher innocent people. They tried to kill us, believing we stood in their way. They will kill *you* without compunction. Execute this man without delay, or you will regret it."

"Need I point out that I have had occasion to regret taking *you* aboard? The Spaniard is my prisoner. You will not lay a finger on him unless he becomes aggressive. Those are my orders. Am I understood?"

All for money. Disgust permeated the assent of Sophie and her companions.

El Escorpión fired another shot. Sophie gestured to shore. "And just how much longer must we listen to that?"

Arriaga flapped his hand toward shore. "The assassin frequently announces his location. We are hardly at a disadvantage."

"But who can sleep for all the noise? Do you want your crew exhausted on the morrow?"

"Ah, so you suggest I send men out there to capture him?"

Arriaga had the attitude of someone who was trying to educate a fool. On the verge of retorting that she detested being treated in such a manner, she swallowed her words. Showing her to be a fool just might amuse Arriaga to no end.

Instead, she frosted him with a glare. "An intriguing idea. Since bounty money warms your blood, there's a second source of it out there on Great Abaco." She heard her traveling companions suck in breaths. Arriaga's eyes hardened with her rebuke, but she held her glare. "Your four passengers cannot sleep. Resolve the problem."

No one spoke for several seconds. In the background, El Escorpión got off another shot. Then the cackle of El Serpiente scratched the air like the sound of ice on winter-brown branches. "*Sí, capitán*, go ahead and try to capture my colleague — but I suggest you send at least five men so your dead may be buried properly. For two years, agents for the French, British, Dutch, American rebels, and Spanish government have failed to apprehend us. Fortune continues to favor the Rightful Blood, for the storm blew our ship right to you." He cackled again. "But who knows? Perhaps a Portuguese pig of a ship captain can succeed where everyone else has failed, eh?"

"Miguel!" Tomás stepped toward the assassin, a dagger clenched in his fist.

Jacques's upper lip curled. "What did I tell you, *capitão*? Kill the Spaniard now, and be rid of the menace."

In Portuguese, Arriaga ordered the first mate to sheath his dagger and instructed Jorge and three sailors to secure the assassin. Hoisted to his feet, El Serpiente glowered at everyone. Arriaga's men shoved the assassin on to the hold.

A shot sounded from shore. Arriaga returned his attention to Sophie. "Tell me how *you* would resolve the problem with the other assassin."

He hadn't given up trifling with her. "Fire a cannonball into the jungle. If the assassin survives, you will have communicated your message for him to begone."

Arriaga's nod verified that her suggestion had been the action he'd intended all along. While he and Tomás supervised a three-man gun crew readying a cannon with powder, wads, a ball, and a cord dipped in saltpeter, El Escorpión fired again.

The crew waited. El Escorpión's next shot allowed the team to get a bearing on the musket flash. A sailor ignited the match through the touchhole. Sophie covered her ears.

The cannon vomited a yard-long tongue of flame, and the *Gloria Maria* quivered with the force of it. Out in the jungle, the ball smacked trees and chewed into branches and bushes. The echo of the blast faded from the cove, and Sophie fanned away the sulfurous stench of burning powder.

A minute of quiet elapsed, then another. Five minutes went by, and they still heard nothing from shore. El Escorpión had understood Arriaga's message.

The captain strolled back to the four, his expression and bearing dignified.

"*Boa noite*, my passengers, and may your sleep be restful at last." He inclined his head and returned forward.

Sentries took up posts around the deck, pistols and cutlasses in their sashes and belts. Jacques lowered his voice. "A pity we have not the money to pay Arriaga to hang El Serpiente. I will sleep tonight with my gear blocking the door and all my firearms loaded."

"I won't argue that." David jerked his head toward the companionway. "Let's talk." They clambered down, and in the cramped corridor, he turned a grim face to Sophie. "I thought you'd get us all abandoned ashore."

She regarded him with a cool eye. "Why?"

"Catholic women don't enjoy the liberties of American Colonial women, and they don't challenge Catholic men."

She cocked an eyebrow. "To the contrary, it appears that Catholic men indulge women who stand up to them."

"Only when it *amuses* them. Watch your tongue with Arriaga — and in Havana."

Jacques shifted from one foot to the other. "Enough of the cultural lesson. We have a Spanish demon in the hold. Let us hope the captain and crew take adequate precautions."

David massaged his temple. "Those assassins must have chartered that fishing sloop in the cove to the north of us and headed out around the same time as the *Zealot*. The rotten luck of it all — that the storm blew them our way."

Jacques's face torqued. "Who else did the storm blow here?"

David swatted the Frenchman's shoulder. "Sophie was right yesterday. Cease tempting the Fates. Imagine the frigate and ship-of-the-line on the bottom of the Atlantic, and thank the gods we're leaving Abaco on the morrow."

★★★

Predawn on Monday, the report of a pistol awakened Sophie. Shouts and running on deck pumped disorientation through her head. She found the empty blanket beside her still warm and heard Mathias sliding on his trousers. A man on deck screamed in agony. She groped for her clothing.

"Stay put, Sophie!"

In the corridor outside, Jacques pounded to the companionway with a war whoop. David's voice roared after him. "You damned old fool, get back here!"

"Uncle! Damn his eyes —"

"Mathias, *you* stay put, too!"

A second man on deck hollered with pain. Sophie, hopping into her trousers, heard a body-sized splash out in the cove, followed by pistol shots from deck. Barefoot, she leaned against the bulkhead, trying to steady her breathing.

Mathias found her in the darkness and stilled her in his arms. "Listen." The gunshots tapered off. Harsh voices faded into murmurs. "Whatever happened is over."

An occasional murmur of Portuguese punctuated the pacing footsteps overhead. She envisioned El Escorpión swimming across the cove, climbing aboard to rescue his fellow, and slitting sailors' throats before the rest of the crew chased him, empty-handed, back into the cove. The sky paled. She heard commands, more footsteps on deck, the splash of the lowered gig, and the creak of blocks. The brig was underway. Mathias released her. They finished dressing.

Footsteps down the companionway preceded David's voice. "Jacques le Coeuvre, what in hell did you think you were doing by running up there into all that?"

"Had my old bones been a few seconds quicker, David, one sailor might still be alive."

Mathias shoved aside their gear and opened the door. "Come in and give us your account, Uncle."

His thumb hooked in his belt near his tomahawk, Jacques strutted in. David stood in the open door with an occasional glance toward the companionway, his fowler in hand. Backlit by the lantern in the corridor, the Frenchman swung his beady gaze about the cabin. "El Serpiente killed two sailors and escaped. Right over the rail into the water I saw him fly, and he but ten feet from me." His fist gripped the head of the tomahawk.

David scowled. "This is madness! How did he escape? Arriaga left him bound and under guard."

"*Oui.*" Jacques shook his finger. "I tell them last night to search him thoroughly. He manages to conceal a blade smaller than the length of my little finger — see here, eh? He uses this blade to weaken his bonds while the attention of the guard wanders. He pretends to fall ill or be in pain. The guard comes close to investigate. *Sssslck.*" Jacques swept his forefinger across his throat. "Then he takes the guard's cutlass and runs for the deck. A man on deck spots him and sounds the alarm by firing a pistol. Another man tries to stop him. *Sssslck*, two blows take off his arm and slice his neck. The assassin also kicks Tomás in the groin. Men converge on him, but even more menacing, Jacques le Coeuvre, warrior for Montcalm, charges him with his tomahawk." The Frenchman gestured out the port light. "Over the side the coward goes, into the water and the night. The captain should have hanged the cur last night."

"Uncle, don't remind Arriaga of your advice. He lost his bounty and two men. I'm sure he'd rather lose *us.*"

Since the Portuguese were using the gig to tow the brig into deeper water, the travelers headed out. Forward on deck, they stood at the rail and squinted into orange sunrise warming their faces. Dawn trimmed the edges of cumulus with gold and rose, and a breeze played with the sails of the foremast and repaired mainmast. After the sailors climbed back aboard and stowed the gig alongside, the island of Great Abaco slipped into shadow behind them, its jungle still mottled with the gloom of early morning.

Sophie shielded her eyes and squinted westward. "Cuba is southwest. Why are we headed east?"

Jacques rested his elbows on the railing. "Perhaps the captain decided to go through the Bahamas, rather than to the west of the islands. Here he comes now. Ask him."

From amidships a somber-faced Arriaga headed their way, a rolled map in his hand. They waited in silence for him, and Sophie resisted squirming at the hollow look in his eyes. "You must be curious about our bearing. I plan to avoid much of the Gulf Stream by sailing through the Bahamas. Let me show you."

He unrolled the map and pointed with the forefinger of his other hand. "After we tack to south and clear Abaco, we head west, passing north of Eluthera. We continue south-southeast along the eastern side of the Andros Islands and round the southernmost of those islands. From there, with continued winds from the southeast, Havana lies almost straight west, and the trip takes but another day or two." He rolled up the map, tucked it beneath his arm, and looked east again.

Mathias pitched his tone low, gentle. "Thank you for updating us, *capitão.*"

Arriaga studied the sunrise, his bearing formal. "I have been captain of the *Gloria Maria* for six years. Never have I lost a man at sea. At noon today, we will give Juan and Carlos to the Atlantic." He looked at Jacques. "Would that I had listened to you last night, *Monsieur.*"

He walked away, his shoulders back and his head high, yet Sophie nevertheless felt him diminished. She regarded her companions. "Gentlemen, we have a ceremony to attend today at noon."

"Indeed." David's fist braced on the railing. "We certainly do."

Chapter Thirty

THE SWEET SCENT of tobacco carried in the morning breeze. Pipe in hand, Jacques sauntered forward to join Sophie. "My nephew is about to checkmate your brother."

"What's new? After the captain declined playing cards with David, he needed *some* mountain to climb."

"Chess is definitely not his mountain, but I admire his perseverance. It must be a St. James trait."

"Hah. I've persevered at little but eating and sleeping since Monday." She raised her arms overhead and stretched her ribcage for a few seconds. "Granted, four days of indolence feels delightful after two weeks of hell, but really, I've been quite dormant."

"Not so." Jacques puffed his pipe. "You are preoccupied."

Perplexity wound through her sigh. "I keep thinking about what David said in St. Augustine. Mathias found no sign that El Serpiente had an accomplice the morning he shot Hernandez, but how else could he have shot Hernandez and his horse from opposing directions? Even if he galloped past — bah!" She threw her hands up. "And how coincidental is it that Hernandez sent us to Luciano de Herrera, who sent us to Evans's Inn, where El Serpiente found us?"

"Let us leave the peculiarities of the shooting for a moment, for I admit that puzzles me, too. What does the incident at Evans's Inn suggest about *Señor* Herrera?"

"That he's a triple agent for the rebels, the Spaniards, and the Rightful Blood." Jacques smiled in agreement. "Gods, what lies he lives. And this Don Alejandro de Gálvez character." She flushed. "I've a certain fancy running through my bones about him, but it cannot be correct —"

"*Non, non*, trust your instincts. Tell me what you feel."

She hesitated. "Don Alejandro is an impersonator." She burst into laughter. "Absurd, isn't it?"

Jacques growled. "*Why* is it absurd?"

"The Gálvez wouldn't send anyone except a family member to so important a meeting because sending an impostor indicates they're playing games with the rebel couriers. That's hardly a display of trust from them."

The Frenchman dripped contempt into his voice. "Trust? Your thinking is as closed as that of a pig in Parliament."

"Then you believe Don Alejandro is an impersonator and the Gálvez are toying with the rebels? Spaniards! I cannot abide with such sneakiness. The idea makes no sense."

Jacques smoked his pipe with fury, and his eyes hardened. "Britons — fools! Ironic that they will not trust an honest native, but if a dishonest man extends what *they* consider civility to them, they will give him their very entrails.

"The French and Spanish may have spilled each other's blood, but we understand each other. After all Spain lost in America in the Treaty of Paris, after she just extinguished a rebellion in her colony in Peru, after Britain crushed the American rebels in Charles Town last month, do you think any Spaniard, let alone the great family Gálvez, would be quick to trust and support disorganized, slovenly, and irresponsible rebels?"

Sophie worked through the conclusions in her head. "You're suggesting that the Gálvez are testing the rebels, seeing if they're truly capable of following through with a critical task? And if the rebels persevered through extreme hardship to bring a bribe of emeralds, they'd be considered worthy?"

Jacques nodded to the horizon. "Worthy of Spain's alliance, *oui*, and the Gálvez would speak favorably of them to King Carlos." His eyes narrowed. "But the Gálvez would never send one of their own flesh and blood to such a meeting — *non*, not with the threat of *Casa de la Sangre Legítima*. They would send an impersonator." He looked back at her. "In all I have heard of the contemporary Gálvez, never have I heard mention of a family member named Alejandro."

"Zounds," she whispered. "Lieutenant Fairfax said as much."

Jacques thumped her on the back. "Well done."

In the background, she heard the cry of "*Terra!*" from a sailor on the mainmast, but she ignored it. Don Alejandro an impostor. Dazed, she rubbed her neck. "Would Don Antonio know?"

"Why not?" He pressed a finger to his lips signing silence.

Sophie spotted Arriaga headed their way. "He looks chipper. He's all but ignored us since we left Abaco."

Jacques grunted. "With certain feminine exceptions."

"*Bom dia*, and good news, my passengers! Paulo aloft has spotted Cuba."

Sophie comprehended the captain's convivial spirits. By noon, he'd be rid of an evil-omened set of passengers. She shifted around to peer forward. No sign yet of the Pearl of the Antilles, as Columbus had labeled Cuba.

Mathias and David joined them forward — David's expression glum, Mathias's neutral. Arriaga clapped David on the shoulder and steered him for the railing. "Chess was never my game, either, *senhor*, but look to port, and within a quarter hour, you will have forgotten the tournament."

David's eyebrows rose. "Cuba?"

"*Sim*. With this fine wind, we will arrive in La Habana by noon." A fist on his hip, Arriaga stepped back and allowed Mathias room. "I know the city well. I can recommend a decent inn." He eyed Jacques from head to toe. "Or a tailor."

"We brought a change of clothing."

"Ah, good." He smiled at Sophie.

She smiled in exchange. "Except for a black veil. I've been told women wear them in New Spain, and I hardly had time before my departure to consult a clothier in St. Augustine."

"Calle O'Reilly is filled with tailors." Arriaga switched his gaze to David. "And your destination in La Habana?"

"The Church of Saint Teresa."

"Ah. La Iglesia y Convento de Santa Teresa de Jesús is east of Plaza del Cristo, midway along Calle Brasil at Compostela. You will find it a beautiful monastery, built by the Carmelites at the beginning of this century." His study of David grew shrewd. "But surely you did not make this voyage just to visit a monastery?"

"We've a meeting with Don Antonio Hernandez. Do you know where to find him?"

Surprise flooded Arriaga's expression before he could conceal it. He moistened his lips with his tongue. "You should have no problems locating the chief assistant to the royal treasurer. During the day, he works in the house of the Marqués de Arcos, near Castillo de la Real Fuerza. Any *volanta* driver will know where to find his home, not far from the monastery."

"Thank you, *capitão*."

"Let me know if I may be of further assistance." Arriaga inclined his head before bustling off amidships.

When the captain was out of earshot, David grinned at Sophie. "We dress like rustics, are chased by Spanish assassins, the redcoats, and the Continentals, and plan to visit the royal treasurer's assistant in Havana. Arriaga doesn't know what to make of us."

"Our truth is stranger than anyone's fiction."

She took the opportunity then to explain her hunch about Don Alejandro. They based their primary plan of action on their most logical expectations. If they saw no sign of the *Annabelle*, the *Zealot*, or the Continental frigate, Jacques, David, and Sophie would locate Don Antonio and turn over his nephew's emeralds to him while Mathias booked their passage back on a ship headed for the Colonies. They'd rendezvous at the city gates at four to look for decent lodgings. David and Jacques insisted on staying at least one night to partake of Havana.

They discussed strategies in case they spotted the *Zealot* or discovered that the *Annabelle*, the Continentals, or the assassins had preceded them to Havana. Then, because the northern coastline of Cuba was visible off the forward port side, they packed up their belongings below, changed clothing, and transferred all the emeralds into Jacques's saddlebags.

Sophie emerged first back on deck. In her shift, jacket, and petticoat, she headed forward and shaded herself from the sun with the parasol. Arriaga met her and unfolded a delicate black lace veil. "Please, you make use of this, *senhora*."

"Oh, no, I cannot. It's much too costly, and besides, your wife will miss it."

Conspiracy crept into his smile. "My *wife?*" She glanced away, flushing. The Mediterranean bred sorcerers for charm. "It is worn thus." He draped lace over her head, down her back, and across her torso, avoiding snagging it on the parasol. Appraisal swelled in his eyes when he finished. "Sublime and exquisite."

"Thank you." From the veil arose the scent of cedar and a fainter, exotic essence like that from Ceylonese floral gardens. The veil most certainly hadn't belonged to a sea captain's *wife.*

He fondled lace near her throat, his expression sober. "Spaniards have ever been too senseless to suspect lovely ladies of espionage."

"*Espionage?*" Her laugh didn't sound at all convincing.

"I know nothing, *senhora.*" He lifted her free hand to his lips and, with impeccable timing, released her, bowed, and left ahead of Mathias's arrival.

Mathias took in her appearance. "Lovely." He leaned forward, brushed her lips with his, and paraphrased the second cipher: "The woman in the black veil awaits you in the Church of Saint Teresa."

She fingered the veil. "A parting gift from Arriaga."

"Beware the serpent." His eyes twinkled, and he stroked the veil. "And do inform me if the good captain tries to fit you with more intimate apparel."

During the final hour of the voyage, Cuba swelled from a smudge on the horizon into a formidable land of mountains, jungle, rolling hills, and white beaches. Sunlight sparkled on wavelets, fair-weather cumulus dotted the azure sky, and a southeastern breeze held steady, speeding them onward. In the end, the *Gloria Maria* sailed past fishing and merchant ships and a Spanish warship before rounding the headland where Castillo de los Tres Reyes de Morro squatted on guard. After saluting the fort with cannon and swivel gun, the brig slid into a channel, entrance to Bahía de la Habana.

Off the starboard sat Castillo de San Salvador de la Punta, guardian at the city walls. Sophie had heard that each night, when the city gates closed, the Spaniards pulled a heavy chain up across the channel between the two *castillos,* thus sealing the entrance to the harbor. She imagined enemy ships sunk in crossfire between the two *castillos.* The city walls, made of rock from the surrounding hills, were five feet thick and thirty feet high and still bore scars from British cannon bombardment in 1762.

As the brig sailed farther into the harbor, Sophie stared in amazement, for an enormous fortress loomed on the cliff to port less than half a mile east of Castillo de Morro: Castillo de San Carlos de la Cabaña, built following the British invasion during the Old French War. All the *castillos* represented Spain's most powerful defense complex in the New World. Erected to guard treasures plundered from the Aztecs and Incas, they made the Castillo de San Marcos and the walls of St. Augustine look like a child's model.

And how did St. Augustine compare to Havana? Sophie peered again at the city walls, this time through masts and spars of ships lining the harbor. Even thirty feet high, the walls couldn't block her view of bell towers from dozens of *iglesias,* roofs of nobles' *palacios,* and a multitude of royal palm trees. Havana must rival Boston and Philadelphia in population. In comparison, St. Augustine looked like Alton.

Even from without the city, she felt the way Havana beckoned to them with dark-lashed eyes and lush lips, despite the meter imposed on Spaniards' lives by the Catholic Church. And she imagined that Havana, gateway to both sanctity and sin, groaned with ghosts of enslaved aboriginals and Negroes who had been extinguished beneath the rapacity of the Spaniards. Fascination rippled through her at the thought of setting foot in such a city, and she saw her own wonder reflected on the faces of David and Mathias. Jacques's expression was one of recognition and satisfaction.

The harbor tangle of merchant and fishing vessels diademed by screeching seagulls included three Spanish warships in desperate need of cleaning and structural repairs, and two French warships in better condition — but no Continental frigate. Neither did the travelers spot the *Annabelle* — although they might have missed a sloop in all the congestion. The *Zealot* wouldn't have risked venturing into Havana's nautical traffic. Sophie experimented with breathing easier, but instinct nagged her not to relax.

Arriaga awaited them when they debarked, humidity and searing sun not fazing him in the slightest. He shook hands with the three men and dropped a wistful kiss on Sophie's hand. When she folded the parasol and tried to return it, he insisted that she keep it.

David sidled up to her and pointed to the parasol after they walked away from the brig. "Something else to remember dear old Miguel by."

She smiled and reopened the parasol. A thoughtful something it was, too.

Chapter Thirty-One

LOCKED IN COMBAT over a dead fish, a cat, rat, and seagull created a flurry of activity without equal among the humans on the wharf. In Havana's heat and humidity, *mañana* was the motto for sailors; *tomorrow* I'll paint, make the repair, unload cargo.

Outside warehouses near the city gates, whores solicited sailors. Sophie's nose quivered, detecting stenches far less savory than seawater, fish, and tar. A cacophony of church bells erupted from within city walls, pealing the noon hour.

While a white-coated gate guard roved a sleepy glance over them, Jacques spun a fictional account of their business. Waved through the gates by the guard's yawning partner, the trio carried their gear into a world dappled yellow-green. Bougainvillea proliferated everywhere, as did almond, Poinciana, and royal palm trees, filtering the harsh sunlight, capering it off baroque exteriors of buildings and their stained-glass *ventrales* of blue, red, and yellow. Birds fluttered among branches and bell towers.

Sophie took a deep breath and coughed, her taste buds violated by the stenches of mildew, excrement, and putrefaction. David grimaced, fanned his face, and guided her around a dog carcass. But Jacques grinned with familiarity. "Ah, Havana, she smells like Paris!"

"Look out!" David yanked the enraptured Frenchman from the avenida to avoid his being trampled by a *volanta* racing over the cobblestones. The lightweight carriage of a Spanish noble, steered by a liveried Negro on horseback, clattered north. "They drive worse here than in New York. Watch where you walk."

Sophie stepped away from goat turds. "An excellent idea."

Two more *volantas* zoomed past before a *volanta* for hire rolled to a stop before them. The driver, a Spaniard, tipped his hat. "*Buenas tardes, señores*

y señora. ¿A donde van?"
David nodded. *"Estamos buscando a Don Antonio Hernandez."* Over her shoulder, Sophie glimpsed Arriaga striding for the gates and waving off the approach of several whores.

"Ah, sí, señor." The driver dismounted and reached for their gear. *"No problema, no problema. Vamos primero a la casa del Marqués de Arcos."*

"Un momento." Jacques elbowed David aside with a growl for the driver. *"¿Cuánto?"*

David backed away next to Sophie. "Let Uncle Jacques haggle a rate for us on the king's pence." Arriaga entered the city. *"Capitão,* would you care to share the fare for a *volanta?"* In the background, discussion heated between Jacques and the driver.

Interest raised Arriaga's eyebrows. "You are headed for La Iglesia de la Santa Teresa, then?"

"We're going to the house of the Marqués de Arcos first."

"No, thank you, *senhor.* That is north. La Iglesia de la Santa Teresa is west, very near La Iglesia Santo Cristo de Buen Viaje, where I am going to give thanks to *Nossa Senhora."*

"I presume this is a tradition for you after a voyage to Havana." At the street, fare rate negotiations intensified and incorporated plenty of hand gestures.

"Sim. La Iglesia de Buen Viaje is favored among sailors." He inclined his head to them. "Good luck to you."

David tipped his hat. "Thank you, *capitão."*

Arriaga looked both ways and darted across the street before a *volanta* driver could make a target of him. The rate exchange had quieted. Victory in his posture, Jacques beckoned them aboard. The Spaniard, sullen, loaded their gear, including the parasol, atop the carriage, then cut west on a side street before trotting the *volanta* north.

Despite the stink, Jacques poked his head out the window often to look around. Sophie longed to gawk, too, but it wasn't the action of a black-veiled lady. It surprised her how much she did experience of Havana from inside the *volanta*, especially when wood smoke or the scent of a bakery managed to rise above the reek. Peasants plodded past leading mules laden with baskets of yucca and papaya. Vendors hawked their wares. Spanish soldiers in white patrolled the streets. Verdant foliage and scarlet flowers proliferated. All in all, Havana made Cuba seem a land of clear green and burning crimson.

Nearer their destination, packs of black-robed ecclesiastics roamed Calle Obispo, and merchants swarmed Calle O'Reilly, the business hub of the city. The absence of women on the streets, even whores, reminded Sophie of David's lecture about the place of women in Catholic countries. The house and offices of the Marqués de Arcos were located near a plaza dominated by a massive cathedral. From the *volanta*'s parking place out front, Sophie could see the north city walls and a guard tower.

Jacques inquired inside for Don Antonio. Sophie and David listened to enticing songs of tropical birds. An intermittent breeze chased off flies and cooled the inside of the *volanta*. Church bells pealed another quarter hour before the Frenchman returned scowling. He yanked open the carriage door, ordered the driver to the Church of Saint Teresa, stomped inside, and slammed the door. The *volanta* jolted into motion, and he flopped onto the seat next to David. "Disorganized, inefficient Spaniards."

David cocked an eyebrow. "Don Antonio wasn't in?"

"*Non.* We just missed him. I spent most of my time inside waiting for someone to inform me that he had returned to his mansion near Plaza del Cristo. As it is not far from the Church of Saint Teresa —"

"— why not visit the church before calling on him?"

"*Mais oui.*"

"After all, there must be some reason Esteban Hernandez directed us to his uncle's home instead of the church."

"Some reason, indeed." A nasty smile pinched Jacques's face. "And why not give those mongrels following us just as high a *volanta* fare as we are incurring?"

Sophie gasped. "We're being followed?" The nagging in her instincts ratcheted up to a wail.

David grinned at Jacques and gestured behind them. "It's the *volanta* with the brown trim, right?"

Jacques mirrored his grin. "You have sharp eyes."

"A skill acquired when one has rivals."

Sophie's glance skittered between the men. "What can we do about our pursuit?"

David settled back in his seat. "They'll reveal their intent soon enough."

The trip south took nearly twenty minutes. They stopped twice for farmers herding cattle and pigs across the narrow, cobbled Calle San Ignacio. During the time, Jacques coached Sophie and David on passing for Catholics and explained what they could expect from the interior of a Catholic church.

Before their own *volanta* pulled up in front of Iglesia de Santa Teresa on Calle Brasil, their pursuit turned off. Alert, the trio entered the cool, musty dimness of the nave through a handsome doorway bearing curvilinear ornamentation. The remnants of incense from the Sexte office tickled Sophie's nose. Sunlight filtered through stained glass and splotched cobalt, scarlet, and saffron across the shadowy shapes of a dozen parishioners praying in dark wooden pews. Along the sides, small, squat candles flickered on saints' altars. Near the main altar, light from larger candles softened the motions of acolytes. Murmurs in Spanish and Latin reached her ears, as did the click of wooden rosary beads.

David sat in a pew at the back. Jacques led Sophie to the middle of the nave, where she slid into a pew and settled onto her knees. The black veil shaded her face and caressed her cheeks. Jacques slid into a pew near the altar and knelt.

Eyes adjusted to the dim interior, she glanced over the parishioners, mostly women in black veils. In the pew ahead, an idiot with unkempt gray hair rocked himself. Pity prodded her. Another man five pews forward rose from near a veiled woman and stepped to the aisle.

She gaped, and her heart hammered. It was Will St. James!

So they *had* seen him aboard the *Annabelle*. He was alive! Love, heartache, and relief flooded her eyes. She blinked back the tears. Not yet.

David was studying sputtering candles to the right. She stared at Jacques, willing him to turn around, but the Frenchman remained facing forward. In exasperation and panic, she sat back and scooted across the pew toward the side, freezing when Will slid into the third pew in front of her, a couple of feet from another woman. He was approaching every black-veiled woman in the church for his contact. Sophie fought back a burst of laughter and knelt again. Well, then, let him come to her.

Very soon, he stood. Now David was contemplating archangels carved into the beams. She relaxed, reached in her left pocket, and withdrew her father's wedding band. The pew quivered, accepting his weight, and the idiot in the pew ahead rocked faster. Will scooted over within two feet of her and murmured, "Saint Augustine, deliver my immortal soul from sin."

Was that some kind of code greeting or password? She muttered, "I'd as soon deliver your infernal hide to the redcoats for printing those broadsides."

"Sophie!" Will managed to hold his voice to a whisper, even as he gripped her extended hand. She slid the ring into his palm, not daring to look straight at him for losing her composure. He fumbled the ring on and emitted a ragged sigh. "Good gods, my child, what are you doing here?"

"Jacques, David, Mathias, and I are trying to give the emeralds to you or Dusseau so we can exit this nightmare." Her attention caught on the idiot. Had he moved closer?

"*Hernandez's* emeralds?"

"*Sí* — er, yes. He's dead."

"And he gave *you* his stones? He never permitted us to touch them!"

So Hernandez had lied when he told them the bribe was split between three couriers. How much of his story had been truth? "To give to Don Alejandro, he said."

"Dear gods, not to him, you mustn't —"

"We won't. We're giving them to you instead. Where's André Dusseau?"

"Outside. Staying out of sight."

She sucked in a breath of alarm. The idiot was, by then, sitting only about three feet to the left of Will. "Uncle Jacques has them. He's up in that front pew. Go quickly."

"We don't want those emeralds, and good gods, I cannot believe all of you have risked your lives for this spider's web of double-crossing Spaniards —"

With a shriek, she shoved away from him just as the "idiot" swung around, candlelight glinting on polished steel in his hand. The dagger of El Serpiente embedded in the wooden back of the pew above where Will's heart had been not a second before.

Women screeched. Acolytes at the altar gawked. Will backhanded El Serpiente, knocking him onto the pew and sending his wig askew. Then Will bolted toward an exterior door near the altar. Sophie clambered for the aisle at the opposite end of the pew. The assassin leaped the pew and raced for her.

More women screamed. Men shouted. David lunged up the aisle for her, and Jacques sprinted back, a snarl of protection on his face.

Daylight pierced the nave, the front door opened by several Spanish soldiers. El Serpiente vaulted over a couple of pews and sprinted for the exit taken by Will. Black-veiled women hemmed in the soldiers, each wailing in Spanish about having her widowly virtue threatened by a horde of pirates with cutlasses.

A priest emerged from a door behind the altar and hustled down the aisle toward the soldiers and women, indignation on his face. David and Jacques seized Sophie's arms and marched her past the knot of panic, out the front door and gates, into their waiting *volanta*. Jacques's voice whipped out at the driver. "¡A la casa del Don Antonio Hernandez — rápidamente!" The Frenchman banged the door shut. The *volanta* sped out into the street.

Sophie pushed away Jacques's offer of brandy. "I mustn't dull my wits. Give me a moment to calm down."

The snarl erupted on his face, and he shook his fist. "Five seconds more, and I would have wrung that assassin's neck."

David's snarl looked just as menacing. "What, and deny me the pleasure?"

"Both of you be quiet and listen!" She steadied her breathing. "To misquote the Bard, 'Something is rotten in Havana.' Father is alive, and he was back there in the church, but he doesn't want the emeralds. He was appalled that Hernandez told us to take them to Don Alejandro. But he was neither surprised nor upset to hear that Hernandez was dead."

The *volanta* squealed to a halt before the private entrance of Don Antonio's tree-shrouded mansion near the city's west wall. Sophie's gaze roved across to a church on the Plaza del Cristo: La Iglesia Santo Cristo, where Arriaga had spoken of visiting. A French sailor entered at the front door after crossing himself.

The gate at Hernandez's private entrance opened to reveal four large, liveried slaves, who marched to the door of the *volanta*, opened it, and stepped aside, waiting. David's tone lacked emotion. "This is finally beginning to make sense in a very twisted way." *Twisted*, Sophie considered, as in a s*pider's web of double-crossing Spaniards*.

They exited the *volanta*. Three other carriages were parked before the mansion. Jacques ordered their driver to wait. While one slave shut the carriage door, the others made sure Sophie, David, and Jacques were unarmed before gesturing them to the gate. All four slaves accompanied them within.

Jacques lowered his voice. "I have a theory about Hernandez's shooting."

David nodded. "I wager I have the same theory."

"El Serpiente had no accomplice on that part of the road. He could not have shot both Hernandez and his horse."

David muttered, "He had an accomplice of sorts — someone who shot Hernandez because he'd discovered Hernandez had betrayed him and his fellow traveler to *Casa de la Sangre Legítima*."

Disbelief swirled through Sophie's soul. "Father or Dusseau." Hernandez's pistol shot at the abandoned trading post north of Darien had been meant for *her*, not the assassin. "And the emeralds aren't a bribe. They're a lure."

David whispered, "Yes, a lure for those who are in bed with the French. I wonder, do the Gálvez actually have stakes in this game? Did they send this Alejandro person? Are they entangled with *Casa de la Sangre Legítima*? Or do the Gálvez know nothing of the scheme, and *Casa de la Sangre Legítima* is merely borrowing their name?"

Jacques rubbed his hands together and kept his voice low. "We will learn soon enough, as it appears we now have an interview with the Rightful Blood. I suggest that we begin by playing the innocents, although in truth, I have not much faith that all the innocents in heaven weigh enough to tilt the odds in our favor."

Chapter Thirty-Two

A CHAMBERLAIN LED them across marble floors past an office with a mahogany *escritorio* to a patio at least twenty-five feet wide surrounded by galleries, balconies, and iron railings. In the courtyard jungle of tropical foliage and flagstone, they waited, the four slaves unobtrusive but present, enough sunlight piercing the overhanging branches to shadow the perimeter.

A trim, aristocratic man in his fifties entered with a younger noble. Both wore powdered periwigs. They scrutinized the travelers, dark eyes communicating half an eon of nobility. Even wearing the fine veil, Sophie, in her coarse petticoat, jacket, and mobcap, had never felt more out of place.

"I am Don Antonio Hernandez. You have business with me?"

"Jacques le Coeuvre." The Frenchman bowed. "David St. James. Sophie Barton. We bring word of your nephew, Esteban Hernandez. We apologize for being the bearers of ill news. He was killed in the Georgia colony two weeks ago."

Don Antonio showed no interest. He wasn't just toughing out bad news. Rather, it wasn't news.

"Before he died, he begged us to deliver the contents of his saddlebags to you, his uncle. We altered our travel plans to accommodate his request." Jacques extended the saddlebags. "Here is your nephew's property."

The younger Spaniard's eyes glittered. Expression harsh, Don Antonio signaled a Negro to retrieve the saddlebags. After a glance inside and whispered instructions from his master, the slave left with the saddlebags. Don Antonio's eyes iced. "*You* murdered Esteban."

Sophie stiffened. It looked as though the three of them would be allowed no leverage in the matter and must finish out a futile script. Jacques kept his voice even, although she knew he and her brother were also shocked. "We did not. Had we done so, would we have brought you his property?"

"Yes, if it availed you of the opportunity to murder Don Alejandro de Gálvez." He looked at his companion.

Silence wrung the patio while the travelers regarded Don Alejandro, the impersonator. The time for playing innocents was over. David lifted his chin. "See here. We are *neutrals* in the American War. We set out three weeks ago from the Georgia colony to track down our father's murderer. We found your nephew on the road, badly wounded, and tried to make him comfortable.

"Since then we've come through a tropical storm and assaults by madmen to honor his final request and deliver his property to you because *we have integrity.* Yet you cannot even thank us for our trouble. No, you accuse us of murder most foul. Well, please, don't let us take up any more of your time."

"*Señor* St. James, we all know your father and André Dusseau are alive, so cease the play. Where are they?" Sarcasm twitched Don Antonio's lips. "They were to have met Don Alejandro."

David's card playing expression slid into place. "We haven't seen my father in weeks."

"Where is the half-breed Creek Indian?"

Damnation. Someone had preceded them with news not only of Esteban Hernandez's death but also with intimate knowledge of their party. Jacques's tone was subdued. "My nephew was washed overboard during the storm." Sophie heard tears in his voice and lowered her gaze to the patio in pretense of grief. "He was like a son to me. You are also an uncle. I did not understand why you showed no grief at the announcement of your nephew's death. It is clear to me now that someone brought the news prior to our arrival."

Dry-eyed, Don Antonio sniffed. "A Continental frigate pursued you aboard the *Gloria Maria.* Marines from the frigate arrived here two days ago with news of Esteban's death. They conclude — and I agree with them — that you murdered him."

Eight men in the green uniforms of Continental marines emerged from shadowy foliage around the patio and surrounded them. Cotton-mouthed, Sophie clutched David's hand.

This was horrendous, the world turned upside down.

Don Antonio's sneer deepened. "They will place you under arrest and take you back to the Colonies for execution, for attempting to obstruct a meeting between the Gálvez and couriers of General Washington. Capitán Carlton, please join us and apprehend your prisoners."

A Continental marine captain stepped from a doorway hidden by foliage. His carriage, even in the shade, was so familiar that terror blossomed in Sophie's gut. Daylight shone like fire in his russet hair, and that appalling angelic radiance consumed his face.

"General Washington thanks you for your assistance, my lords." Victory and delight fueled Dunstan Fairfax's smile. "Indeed, the general has a noose for each and every traitor."

Jacques voice roared across the patio. "That man is Lieutenant Dunstan Fairfax, a Briton! You have been deceived!"

Fairfax rolled his eyes at Don Antonio with an I-told-you-so expression. The Spaniard shook his head. "The papers identifying the capitán and his mission are in perfect order, as are those for his men. You three have no identification."

Sophie didn't recognize the men with Fairfax and had no idea how he'd obtained such papers. Stolen? Forged? What happened to the soldiers from Alton? How had Fairfax found recruits for what was essentially a suicide mission? Where was Edward? Perhaps no forgery was needed, and it wasn't a suicide mission, because Don Antonio was in bed with Britain from the start.

David voiced his theory. "The frigate wasn't the only ship chasing us. Lieutenant Fairfax's warship, the *Zealot*, was also in pursuit. The frigate and warship were less than a mile apart when the storm caught us. The redcoats may have gained control of the frigate and appropriated uniforms and commission papers —"

"In the midst of a tropical storm, *Señor*?" Don Antonio snickered. "Do you realize how mad that sounds?"

"Uniforms and documents may be stolen, falsified." David swept a circle in the air with one hand. "You've been deceived. The redcoats have set a trap for all of you!"

From the set of Don Antonio's jaw, his mind was made up. Fairfax gestured to the marines. "Take them."

Derision contorted Jacques's face. "I will be damned to hell before the get of an English whore and a poxy sheep takes me prisoner, English pig." He spat.

Sophie gasped. "Uncle Jacques, no!"

Fairfax looked up from spittle smudging the shine on his black boot to the Frenchman, and his face emptied of expression. "Don Antonio, you're a man of distinguished birth. Before I remove the spies, grant me the opportunity to seek redress for the slur inflicted on my family name just now."

"Of course, capitán."

"Shall we dispense with it here on the patio, *Monsieur*?"

"With pleasure, pig."

"You issue the challenge. I select the means." Fairfax turned to Don Antonio. "May we have the use of your pistols?"

"Oh, gods," whispered David. Had Fairfax selected swords, he'd have conveyed his intent to be satisfied at drawing blood only. But Fairfax was finished with Jacques.

The Spaniard signaled one of the slaves. "*Mis pistoles para duelo*." The slave bowed and strode from the patio.

"Thank you, Don Antonio." Fairfax regarded Jacques. "Select your second, *Monsieur*." He gestured for one marine to join him and the others to withdraw. The slaves and Spaniards also withdrew from the patio to observe from a gallery.

David gripped Jacques by the shoulder and, with Sophie trailing after, steered him to the opposite side of the patio. "You're mad, or you'd realize what you've gotten yourself into."

Glory sparkled in the Frenchman's eyes. "Do you imagine this to be Jacques le Coeuvre's first duel with one of *them*?"

"The Old War was over seventeen years ago!"

"*Au contraire*. It has lasted since the dawn of time." Jacques gave him a tender smile. "And it gives me great honor to have you as my second, *mon ami*."

David flushed, one of the few times in his life Sophie had ever seen him do so, and glanced across the patio at Fairfax's second. "He's waiting for me so we can pace out the field and draw lots. I'll be back." He left them.

Jacques took Sophie's hand. "You know Fairfax is broken inside his head. The monster should not be suffered to live and visit terror on people. None will dispute me killing him here."

She blinked back tears. "That's why you challenged him."

"*Oui.* I have been waiting on a clear shot at the animal. If I fail, you and David must find a way to extinguish him."

"I? Kill Fairfax?" Her hands began trembling. "It's far more likely to snow in Havana this moment!"

"Find a way, or you will live to regret it." He gripped her hand. "You never told us what happened to you in Cow Ford, but it will seem miniscule in comparison."

She tensed, grateful again for Lila and that bucket. Don Antonio's slave returned with powder, balls, and an ornate case containing dueling pistols. By then, David and the marine had measured ten full paces and cast lots. David would give the order to fire, but Fairfax had won the right to fire first.

Determination etched Jacques's face. He drew a purse from his waistcoat pocket and pressed it into her hand. "In the event that I fail to exterminate that English pig, Don Antonio should have no difficulty giving me a decent burial with this."

"Oh, no," she whispered. Having endured the death and resurrection of her father, she couldn't bear to lose Jacques. "No, Uncle Jacques!"

He leaned closer, his voice almost inaudible. "I love Mathias as *hopwiwa*, son of my sister. Tell him so."

Panic stormed through her soul. "No, *you* tell him so!"

"It has done my old heart much good to know you two have finally found your way back together." He stroked her cheek and walked over to load his weapon.

Tears closed her throat. Pale-faced, her brother returned to her side after embracing Jacques. She shoved the purse at him. "Here. He wants a decent burial."

David compressed his lips and fit Jacques's purse inside his waistcoat. Then he guided her off the patio near one of the marines. "Wait here until it's over." She nodded, voice gone.

Pistols cocked, Jacques and Fairfax took their stations. David, at the edge of the patio equidistant from them, cleared his throat. "Gentlemen, are you prepared?"

"*Oui.*"

"Yes."

David took a deep breath. "Present!"

Both pistols came up and aimed. Jacques's fire answered Fairfax's with but a half-second delay, yet through clearing smoke, Sophie saw only Jacques collapse.

Denial ripped from her throat. "No!" She flew from the gallery and knelt at the Frenchman's side, David crouching opposite her.

Crimson heart blood seared through the hole in the left upper section of Jacques's waistcoat. His eyes searched the sky through the clear green of overhead leaves, and his voice emerged raspy. "*Est-ce que le Québec est le nôtre?*"

Sophie didn't know how David kept his voice steady for the response: "*Oui, mon ami, le Québec est le nôtre.*" Yes, my friend, Quebec is ours.

Joy buoyed Jacques's expression. His gaze still fixed on the sky, he took a deep breath, as if reaching for something. Then his entire body relaxed, and his eyes glazed over. Clear green and burning crimson.

Sophie bowed her head, closed her eyes, and pressed the heels of her hands against her eyelids. Too soon, she heard the scraping of multiple boot soles around them on the stones of the patio. When she opened her eyes to look at Jacques's peaceful expression, her peripheral vision encompassed that ominous pair of cleaned, black boots. Fleeting impulse urged her to dull the shine with her own spittle.

David rose, his voice detached and firm. "*Monsieur* le Coeuvre requested that he receive a decent burial with this."

Coins jingled. "Of course, *Señor*," said Don Antonio.

David walked around Jacques's body and assisted Sophie to her feet. The marines encircled them again, Don Alejandro standing aside with Don Antonio. Fairfax turned to Don Alejandro. "If you and your attendants will proceed to your *volanta*, it will be my great honor to escort you safely to your meeting with Mr. St. James and *le Comte* Dusseau."

"*Gracias, capitán.*" Fanatics, the Rightful Blood. Even surrounded by Britons, they'd attempt to kill alliance members.

"Don Antonio, I thank you again and regret that this action has delayed our departure. We shall leave now, that you may mourn your nephew in peace."

Fed up with the sham, Sophie glared at Don Antonio. "*Mourn?* I doubt you'll shed one tear for your nephew. He disappointed you. He bungled an ambush on a rebel and French spy so badly, your own assassin had to kill him." The Spaniard's face blanched. Fairfax gazed at her in amazement, then with an intensity she didn't want to consider.

"The overall scheme was brilliant. Use the Gálvez name to lure alliance members to Havana and execute them. But then these Britons showed up." Fairfax stiffened, and the Spaniard worked his mouth in rage. "To preserve your cover as a loyal Spaniard, dedicated to the alliance with France, you pretend to believe Lieutenant Fairfax's story and hand us over to them so *they* can execute us. Do the Gálvez support *Casa de la Sangre Legítima*, or did you merely steal their name for your purposes?"

Don Antonio's voice hissed. "How dare you speak to me that way!"

Fairfax shoved David. "Take them outside!"

Marines closed around Sophie and David and marched them to where the *volanta*s parked in the street. While everyone waited for Don Alejandro and his four bodyguards to situate themselves in their *volanta*, Sophie looked across the street to the mariners' church.

The front door opened. Out walked Miguel de Arriaga. The commotion piqued his curiosity, and upon closer attention, he made eye contact with both Sophie and her brother. She watched the way his gaze landed on the proximity of the soldiers. From his initial expression, he realized that they had been taken prisoner. From the subsequent emotion on his face, she could almost read his thoughts: *None of my business. Portugal is neutral.*

Damn.

Arriaga's eyes bulged at the sight of Fairfax, and his gaze clambered over the lieutenant's Continental uniform. The last time the *capitão* had seen Dunstan Fairfax, he'd been a redcoat standing on the deck of the *Zealot*, anchored off St. Augustine. Once again, Arriaga's expression composed into, "No, Portugal is neutral." However it took more of a struggle getting there that time.

Damn.

Fairfax jutted his jaw toward the Spaniard's *volanta*. "Habersham, ride in the third carriage with Don Alejandro for his protection. Jones, McDonald, McCoy, ride with Mr. St. James in the second carriage. Mrs. Barton and I shall ride in her carriage up front. The rest of you bring up the rear."

Panic sliced frost through Sophie. Fairfax planned to be alone with her in the *volanta*. Jacques's reminder about the incident at Cow Ford spun through her head, and she knew it was time to play the card she possessed. She allowed cold fury to elevate her voice. "You have lost your wits if you think I will willingly ride alone with you in that carriage. You tried to force me in Cow Ford!"

Wrath congested David's face. He took a step toward Fairfax. "Why, you son of a dog —"

"Gag him," snapped Fairfax. "No — bind and gag both of them." He rubbed his temple as if a headache brewed there. Then he produced a conciliatory smile that made Sophie wonder whether his lip muscles had ever attempted such a gesture. "Mr. St. James, I assure you that I'm of entirely human stock."

David snarled when the gag came around his mouth. "If you touch my sistmmmflngmth —"

"And I also assure you that I've never harmed your sister."

Two marines half-dragged and half-shoved a glaring David toward one of the *volantas*. Fairfax pushed the lace veil off Sophie's head and onto her shoulders to make room for her gag, which he whisked from the marine in attendance and wrapped and knotted himself. Then he snatched rope from the marine and yanked her arms behind her back.

With her voice silenced and her hands being tied behind her, she watched honor and determination flood Arriaga's face. No longer was the predicament about Portugal's neutrality in the American War.

Just before Fairfax propelled her toward their *volanta*, she had the satisfaction of seeing the Portuguese slip away to the east. Silent. Sneaky.

Chapter Thirty-Three

FAIRFAX JERKED OPEN the door to the *volanta*, whamming it into the carriage body. The driver yelled imaginative conjectures about Fairfax's parentage, accompanied with hand gestures guaranteed to transcend the language barrier. Fairfax shoved Sophie. "In there." She stumbled. Scowling, he heaved her in.

Her impact on the floor shook loose her left garter and popped open her jacket, exposing her shift. Since the irate driver consumed Fairfax's attention, she squirmed and attempted to make her bosom look less inviting while being treated to Fairfax's communication skills: "*No hablo Español bueno. Vamos* — what's that you say? See here, I don't give a damn what your mother eats with sailors. *Vamos* to the harbor — uh, *la puerto,* no, damnation, it's *el puerto,* you lazy lump, you know exactly what I mean, so make it so! And *rápidamente!*"

He leaped in and slammed the door. "Imbeciles." The *volanta* swung into the street, pitching him atop her, his face in her petticoat, his hat knocked off.

When he struggled up and assessed her disarray, she focused on loose trim above the door. Quiet descended on her. The ride to Havana harbor could take ten minutes, more than enough time for Fairfax to finish what he'd started in Cow Ford. Bound and gagged, she saw no point in exhausting herself with struggle.

He pushed up and slid the veil off her shoulders. After taking a seat and peering out the window, he replaced his hat. Then he studied her, snaking lace between his fingers. "How courageous you look lying there half-naked. From the expression on your face, you're resigned to the inevitability of violation." He brushed lace on his lips and cheek. "Many goodwives approach the marital bed with the same attitude." He silkened his voice. "Does that make it truly rape, then?"

His gift for contorting reality went with his broken head. A pothole jolted the *volanta*, jamming her jaws together.

In her peripheral vision, he cocked his head. "What the devil are you staring at? Ah, that loose piece of trim. Come now, I *must* be more interesting to look at." With his forefinger, he prodded the hat into a jaunty angle. "Don't I make a dashing rebel? Oh, pardon me, you're *patriots*, not rebels. That makes us the oppressive, tyrannical brutes — never mind that we represent the lawful government."

Her right shoulder throbbed against the floor. The gag made her jaw ache. She concentrated on the trim. In no way must she appear to agree with Fairfax about the rebels, even though she did agree. He'd twist her interpretation until she lost confidence in her ability to reason. Besides, if he'd wanted her opinion, he'd have removed her gag.

"Your brother's imagination amazes me. Such a masterful conjecture about the frigate and the *Zealot*. The two actually collided during that wretched storm. Naturally both lost men, but we gained the frigate. The Yankee Doodle Navy makes for such splendid humor. Warships are a waste of your money."

He leaned forward, elbows on his knees. "Here, now, I suppose you're wondering about Major Hunt."

Her focus on the trim broke. Edward represented the three-week-long nightmare's anchor of sanity on the redcoat end. Were she his prisoner, the fear of rape would never have clutched her heart. In question and hope, she transferred her attention to Fairfax.

He sprawled back and fondled the lace some more. "Of course you're wondering about him. But don't squander your energy doing so."

Blast. He'd lured her into that trap. She yanked her focus back to the trim, her self-confidence as jarred as her shoulder.

He draped the veil across his thighs, set his hat on the seat beside him, and indulged in a stretch that popped joints. "Since I'm the villain, I'm entitled to review a villain's repertoire of measures I might take with a captive to ensure submission. How long do you suppose it'll take us to reach the harbor? Eight minutes? Alas, that isn't enough time. I shouldn't have said *rápidamente*." With the toe of his boot, he nudged her petticoat up a few inches to reveal her naked calf. "What's the Spanish word for slowly, Sophie? S-l-o-w-l-y." He slithered the edge of the veil over the tender skin behind her knee. Revulsion rode a wave through her. "Is it *lentamente*? How much might I have to pay the driver to make this ride last two hours? You and I have unfinished business."

He wadded up the veil, flopped back with a sigh, and slapped his forehead. "Damn, what's gotten into me? It must be the sight of you lying there half-naked that made me forget about our rendezvous with your father and Dusseau. This has all come together in such splendid fashion. Those two have been skulking about Havana between the harbor and the Church of Saint Teresa. I imagine seeing you and your brother bound and gagged in the company of Continental marines will be sufficient to speed them our way and clear up misunderstandings. We shall all return to the Colonies, then all of *you* shall make the acquaintance of the gallows. Why do I get the impression you aren't paying attention to me?"

Church bells pealed the quarter hour. After laying the veil beside his hat, Fairfax lifted her to the opposite seat with gentleness. He pulled up her stocking and refastened her garter. Then he straightened out her petticoat and brushed dirt and dried grass off it. "Darling, I've a job to perform, and I'd dearly love your cooperation. How it would predispose me in your favor if you helped me." The soft, damp kiss he dropped on her bare chest above the top of her shift sent her skin crawling.

"The five in that carriage behind us expect to thwart nine of the king's finest and kill your father and Dusseau. Cheeky of them, eh?" He loosened her gag, lowered it, and nuzzled her ear. "Intelligent women enthrall me. I was bewitched when you flung Hernandez's Rightful Blood connection in his face. Questioning the Gálvez involvement was a brilliant stroke. That's one family I'd love to topple — ah, but for some solid evidence against them. By the by, the two assassins arrived here late yesterday. I wager you've an idea where they are this very moment."

If she'd known El Serpiente's whereabouts, she'd have felt far better herself. Still, she saw no reason to inform Fairfax of her Havana encounter with him. From all she'd experienced, the assassin might accidentally help her escape Fairfax. She worked her mouth. "Is that the only piece you haven't figured out yet?"

He ran his tongue around the outside of her ear. "Allow me to explain. I ask the questions, and *you* answer them." He caressed his cheek across her bosom, the heat of his hands enclosing her ribcage. His breathing hoarsened with arousal. "Where are the assassins?"

Her stomach knotted at the prickle of saliva on her ear and the pressure of his hands on her waist. "We last encountered them Sunday night, on Abaco. The captain captured one of them, but he escaped."

Fairfax sat up and stared, his hand on her waist. "Abaco?"

She wiped her ear with her shoulder and scooted away. "The storm blew us there. We stayed for two days repairing the brig."

He reeled her against him, fascination sparking his eyes. "I enjoy your lies." He brushed his lips over her lower lip, and she jammed her jaw shut. "It isn't that your skills at deception are lacking, you enchanting coquette. It's knowing that you lie to play with me. You're just as eager as I to consummate what we started back in that barn —"

"Damn you! I told you the truth about the cipher at my home that Sunday night, and you didn't believe me then, either."

"You lied to me in Cow Ford."

"You don't want my cooperation. You want to push me about."

"My, how you hate me for executing the French spy, despite how merciful I was. He hardly suffered at all, *belle* Sophie."

Tears stung her eyes. She turned her head and blinked them away. How wicked, to taunt her about Jacques.

"We should all be that lucky. Some live lives of so violent a nature that we court violent ends, often even sobbing for death to release us from the torment our souls earn for our bodies. Considering the life le Coeuvre led, he was one of the fortunate ones." His hand around her jaw, he forced her face to his. "I gave him the glorious end he wanted, and I made it merciful and quick just for you. Thank me."

Did Fairfax believe her head was as broken as his? "Hell shall freeze first."

He smiled, his tone tranquil. "I said, thank me." His fingers trailed down her neck and over her collarbone, pausing to cup her left breast through the fabric of her shift. Then he lowered his mouth to her breast and rooted for her nipple. She'd imagined enduring rape, perhaps even battery, with passive resistance: her body limp, her soul closed off from her body and unsurrendered. But when his teeth teased her nipple out to an aching point, her womb quivered in response, and she gagged with horror. Her body wouldn't cooperate in passive resistance. She could no more close off her soul than she could control the moon. He pulled back, gloating. "You're so welcome, darling."

Nauseated, she looked at the piece of trim again, unable to block out his smile. He brought her jacket together and fastened it closed. "Shall I leave off the gag? You must promise to keep quiet after we arrive at the harbor."

The gag tasted foul and hurt her jaw. Beneath the shift and jacket, her nipple relaxed into the humidity deposited by his mouth. "I — I promise."

He scrutinized her before yanking the gag back in place. "Promises can be extracted from many layers of sincerity, but yours hardly scratched the surface just now. Not to worry — we have at least five days at sea ahead of us, and by the end of that time, I'll have taught you more than your wildest dreams about sincerity." He grinned. "*I* promise."

After draping the veil about her shoulders, he sat opposite, replaced his hat, and redirected his scrutiny on Havana, moving little and saying nothing. Spared his attention, Sophie clawed her way through grief, apprehension, and terror.

Not thirty minutes before, Jacques had sat in the carriage, cantankerous and full of life. How could he be dead without even a shred of damning or beseeching in his last look? And dear Mathias was at the harbor arranging their voyage home, ignorant of the horror bearing down on him. Aware of the double-cross, had Will and Dusseau enough sense to stay out of sight?

What was Arriaga plotting? Where were the two assassins? Had Edward perished in the collision between the ships? If Fairfax succeeded in escaping Havana with her, by the end of the return voyage, when he was done with her, would she even care whether she lived or died?

The four *volantas* pulled up before the city gates. Fairfax assisted her out, signaled marines to unload their gear, and tossed the driver of their *volanta* a purse. Someone dropped the parasol. Fairfax scooped it up and shoved it under his arm.

While the lieutenant paid the other drivers, David scoured Sophie from head to foot and blasted Fairfax with a glare, intuiting everything said and done during the carriage ride. Without his gag, David would have challenged Fairfax. Fairfax knew that. Only Jacques had he wanted to kill outright.

Bored gate guards waved the group of fourteen through. How grand of Continentals to capture spies — and the Spaniards hadn't needed to lift a finger. Clouds scuttled over the sun. A breeze picked up in advance of a thunderstorm.

The group tromped out to the wharf past whores and starving varmints, ships and boats, cargo crates and boxes. Through a break in the clouds, the steamy, afternoon sun bore down on Sophie, and the smells of tar, paint, seawater, and fish assailed her. She heard French and Spanish: give me the hammer, give me the rum. Strains of fiddle music wafted over the wharf, competing with the screams of seagulls. Any sailors they passed who weren't too busy or too apathetic to eye them displayed the same expressions as the gate guards: Good of the Continentals to have done all the work. But when they marched past the *Gloria Maria*, the snatches of merry Portuguese on deck dwindled off. León, José, and Sebastião Tomás paused from their chores to gape at them in perplexity and disbelief.

At a dilapidated thirty-five-foot schooner, three non-Spanish sailors on deck transferred their gear aboard. Inside the city walls, church bells pealed. Had another quarter hour gone by?

David emitted a muffled yell, his eyes bulged northward. Sophie followed his gaze, helplessness flooding her at the sight of her father and André Dusseau striding toward what they thought was a group of Continental marines. Fairfax pivoted to present his back to the approaching men and gave Don Alejandro a knowing smile. "You see, we didn't have to search far for St. James and Dusseau, did we?" He gestured to a marine next to him. "Habersham, take these two spies below, so they won't interfere."

With a *shlick*, a Creek arrow sliced the humid air and pierced Habersham's throat. He collapsed gurgling, and everyone gaped. In the next instant, another arrow lodged in Fairfax's right buttock. He dropped the parasol. "Bloody hell!" After seizing the shaft, he yanked the arrow out.

David and Sophie sprinted for the approaching men. David outdistanced her. His gag loosened. "Run, old man! Redcoats disguised as Continentals!" Thunder rumbled to the south.

Sophie heard pursuit and Mathias's yell from near a warehouse. "Run, Will, it's a trap!"

Will and the young Frenchman dashed back the way they'd come. Two marines bolted past Sophie, and a third hauled her back around. She thrashed, losing the lace veil in the process, and gaining a horrified glimpse of both assassins from *Casa de la Sangre Legítima* descending on her father and the Frenchman, knives drawn. Fairfax stormed past her with the remaining men. "I want all of them aboard — St. James, Dusseau, the assassins!"

Don Alejandro and his men retreated for the city gates, unable to reach their targets through the knot of marines. The church bells were still pealing — not proclaiming a quarter hour, but ringing alarm over Havana. From the gates, musket-bearing Spanish soldiers spewed onto the wharf. Leading the way ran Arriaga, pointing at Fairfax. "¡*Británicos, allí, allí!*" Sailors gaped. Merchants dove for cover.

A Creek war whoop followed a pistol shot and more thunder. Half-thrown into the schooner, Sophie squirmed around in time to spot Mathias, his tomahawk raised, bowling El Serpiente off her father. André Dusseau lay unmoving on the wharf. One marine had tackled David, and the other had squared off with El Escorpión. El Serpiente's screech of terror ended with one sharp tomahawk blow. Just before the marine hauled her below, she heard a splash and glanced out into Bahía de la Habana. Her father was swimming for his life toward Castillo de San Carlos de la Cabaña.

The marine flung her into a grimy cabin stinking of rotten fish. A quarter minute later, David stumbled in, his gag in place. The door slammed shut. Bruised and sweating, they staggered to the salt-crusted port light and peered out. After more pounding footsteps and shouts from Fairfax to cast off, the schooner was free of the dock, drifting out into the harbor, gathering the thunderstorm's gusts in her sails.

From up on deck came bumps and thumps and a groan of agony. The cabin door whammed open again. "I ought to kill you for that arrow, you half-breed bastard." Fairfax, his breeches bloody, shoved a bound, gagged, and semi-conscious Mathias into the cabin. "Perchance I'll change my mind soon enough. The Straits of Florida is full of sharks." Fairfax sealed them into the cabin.

With another moan, Mathias rolled onto his side, his nose bleeding and one eye swelling. Sophie and David knelt at his side. Musket fire erupted from the dock. Fairfax and his men returned fire. The church bells grew more faint. Wind gusted. Thunder boomed across the bay. The schooner picked up speed.

Swivel guns fired at them from the decks of docked ships, somehow missing the schooner's masts, spars, and hull before she slipped from range. Sophie rose and returned to the port light. Through salt spray and filth, she saw Spanish soldiers swarming the wharf. Two raindrops streaked the glass. A man, not a soldier, stood still in the midst of activity where the schooner had docked, holding something and gazing out at the schooner. From his dignified carriage, she recognized Arriaga, the parasol and veil in his hands. Tears sprang to her eyes.

She peered forward, expecting the schooner to be caught in lethal crossfire between the two *castillos* at the mouth of Bahía de la Habana. But a Spanish warship was entering the harbor at the same time the schooner exited. The Spaniards wouldn't risk catching their own ship in that crossfire, just to capture a handful of redcoat spies. No, the schooner was free.

Fairfax had passed himself and British soldiers off as Continentals deep in enemy Spanish territory. He had killed an enemy Frenchman in a duel, captured what he believed were rebel spies, and escaped with them in his custody. His actions had crippled, if not crushed, the chance of a formal alliance between Spain and the American rebels — if such an alliance had ever been more than the Rightful Blood's clever ruse.

Fairfax was the stuff of which national heroes were made. Months after his captives had ended their lives upon the gallows, the *London Chronicle* would still be praising him. Sophie bowed her head and wept.

Chapter Thirty-Four

HALF AN HOUR after the schooner escaped Havana, a marine entered the cabin to deliver food and water and remove gags and bonds. The schooner would rendezvous with the *Zealot* around sunset. Unless the prisoners desired to be placed in irons, they must remain in the cabin for the voyage and not resist.

After the marine left, they regarded each other and worked cramps from their shoulders and jaws. Each passing second of silence tightened the tension for Sophie. How would she and David break the news to Mathias about Jacques?

The blacksmith fingered his nose and fumbled in his waistcoat for a handkerchief. David whipped out his own, his voice soothing. "Here, have mine."

Sophie whisked the handkerchief from David, dribbled water on it, and dabbed it beneath Mathias's nose. "Does that hurt? I don't think your nose is broken, but you'll definitely have a black eye." She wiped the corner of his mouth. "Your lip is cut. You didn't lose any teeth, did you?"

Mathias guided her hand away from his face. "Enough." His voice hushed. "My uncle is dead, isn't he?"

David scowled. "Fairfax killed him at Hernandez's mansion."

"Then I shall kill Fairfax. Jonah was *tcusi*, younger brother. I was expected to take care of him. But my uncle was *pawa*, my mother's brother. The people respect *pawa* the way you respect your father. *Pawa* teaches a boy much of what he needs to know as a man, looks after him, disciplines him. My uncle was the only father I knew, the man I respected above all others. I *must* avenge his death."

Sophie reconsidered the afternoon at the swimming hole and Mathias's scarred shoulder. She'd never understood why he tolerated Jacob's abuse and wondered if he was afraid of Jacob. But cowardice didn't inhabit Mathias's soul. His Creek perspective enabled him to disregard Jacob because he wasn't of consequence. Neither "father" nor "stepfather" mattered as much as "uncle." Jacques, *pawa*, was the man who had mattered.

David growled. "You'll have to beat me to Fairfax first."

Sophie's heart sank. Mathias frowned at David. "Why so?"

"I learned what Sophie was reluctant to tell us about her encounter with him in Cow Ford. He tried to force her —"

"David, please —"

"Please, my arse! The mongrel threw you in the *volanta* with him this afternoon and had his way with you for the entire ride."

Mathias glowered. "Sophie, is that true?"

Chivalry was alive and well. "Did I look as though I'd been abused when I stepped out of the *volanta* at the harbor?" But she didn't sound convinced, even to herself.

"I know he pawed you, and the gods only know what hell he put your mind through."

"Your brother's right. The son of a whore needs to die in the most excruciating manner possible."

Greater than her fear for herself was her fear for David and Mathias, who were taking the bait Fairfax had set for them. She gripped an ear on both men. "Listen to me! He cannot destroy my integrity." Perhaps if she said it often enough, she might believe it. After all, in three weeks, she'd learned much about freedom, dignity, and honor from her traveling companions, Ulysses, Lila, and Miguel de Arriaga. Somewhere in that repository, there must be a lesson on how not to surrender her soul.

Mathias and David squirmed when she pinched harder. "His worth before the world and in his own eyes depends on him hauling *someone* back to the gallows after this chase."

"Dash it all, Sophie, that hurts! Stop it!"

"Indeed, let go of my ear. Do you fancy us little boys?"

She released them. "I'd far rather have you both alive and with me on the morrow than have you waste yourselves on a monster that lusts to fight with anyone. Oh, how he desires it. He bloats off blood like a mosquito. Deny him that satisfaction, and watch him diminish.

"And one more point I must emphasize." She crossed her arms. "Fairfax is *not* Britain."

David massaged his ear. "What are you getting at?"

"Britain has taxed us and lodged soldiers in every city and town, and I've seen the thought in your eyes. Britain is the only beast in this conflict. Surely you realize Fairfax has his counterparts in the other armies, though I've not had the misfortune to make their acquaintance."

Mathias nodded. "War grants all manner of demons permission to slither into the upper world."

"Exactly." While the blacksmith walked to the port light and peered out, David gave Sophie a rueful smile. The schooner swayed in the cradle of the Florida Straits. She said, "Mathias, you'd best have a bite to eat."

His voice sounded distant. "I'm not hungry."

She walked over beside him. His eyes had focused on something remote. Her heart ached. "You killed El Serpiente, so you've taken care of Jonah, *tcu-*

si." Mathias wasn't satisfied. She slid her hand up his arm to his shoulder. "Although my way is not your way in this matter, I respect your need to avenge your kinsmen. I'm sure you know that Jonah won't be coming back, no matter how many assassins you kill." When he tried to pull away, she flung her arms around him, her eyes shut. "Hear your uncle's final words: 'I love Mathias as *hopwiwa,* son of my sister. Tell him so.'"

He stiffened. "No, not yet —"

"'It has done my old heart much good to know you two have finally found your way back together.'"

A whisper tore from his throat —"No!"— before the tension in his body released into a sob. He crushed her to him. David wrapped an arm around his shoulder, and they stood that way for a long time, triumvirate grief in a current too sweeping for them ever to have swum. At length, Mathias's swollen whisper emerged from the embrace. "Tell me Will escaped."

David nodded, his tone subdued. "Yes, he did."

She stroked Mathias's face. "You saved his life." And she, gazing into her brother's damp eyes, wondered whether they'd see their father alive again.

★★★

Just after dusk had gloomed over their prison, the cabin door banged open, and three marines entered. The prisoners blinked in lantern light. Behind the men limped Fairfax. "Good news, rebels. In ten minutes, I shall have the honor of escorting you aboard the *Zealot* and housing you in the customary style for prisoners of war." He gestured toward the door. "Your presence on deck is now mandatory."

Sophie exited the cabin, and with her first breath of fresh air, realized that the foul stink had permeated her hair, clothing, and skin. At the railing she inhaled, purging her lungs. Through dusk she spotted blotches of islands to the north and the approach of the *Zealot* from the northeast. She brushed David's elbow. "Any idea where we are?"

"The Florida Keys. We sailed north all afternoon."

Fairfax paused behind them, raising her hackles. "I'd no idea that you paid as much attention to maps as you do to strategies for piquet. We shall rendezvous with the *Zealot* approximately twenty miles south-southwest of Key Largo — if that means anything to you."

The lieutenant walked past them. David lowered his voice. "It means we'll arrive at St. Augustine within five days, if the weather holds well."

The gallows in five days. Her shoulders sagged. "Might they put in at Savannah and take us back to Alton?"

"I doubt it. The *Zealot* was stationed off St. Augustine. She must return to her original mission as soon as possible." Grim humor ground at his mouth. "Besides, we don't carry the importance of Ben Franklin or John Hancock, so there's no point in parading us around." He sighed. "No, indeed. It shall be a quick and simple noose for the three of us."

Sophie gazed east to hide her desolation. If Fairfax had his way, the noose would be the only quick and simple part of it.

The vessels drew alongside each other, and sailors from the *Zealot* rowed a gig over. Fairfax ordered the prisoners, two marines, and their gear and weapons transferred to the gig. Sophie descended the schooner's boarding net into the gig after David and Mathias and sat staring at the starlight-speckled water while sailors rowed them to the warship. Then she climbed up the *Zealot*'s boarding net.

Surrounded by marines, forced to wait on the deck of the *Zealot*, she brushed off her filthy petticoat, straightened, and watched the gig cross the water for Fairfax and the other men. She overheard a seaman say that the three sailors aboard the schooner were being left behind to pilot her and follow. The prisoners watched the gig return, by starlight discerning Fairfax from the boat's other occupants by the victory in his posture.

David grumbled. "He'd have walked across the water if they hadn't sent a boat for him."

Mathias muttered, "Where's a waterspout when we need one?"

Aboard the *Zealot*, Fairfax's gaze landed on them and swelled with satisfaction. Sophie's hopes for finishing her life with dignity withered. He limped over to them, exultant.

"Lieutenant."

He pivoted and stood at attention in response to the familiar voice. Sophie caught her breath. Lantern light shone like white gold in the hair of Edward Hunt, who had made his way amidships through clusters of sailors and marines, his carriage taut with fatigue. Justice presided in his expression, not vengeance or cruelty. She nearly wept with relief.

"Sir." Fairfax saluted.

Edward returned the salute and assessed them. "What of Dusseau, Gonzales, St. James, le Coeuvre, and the two assassins?"

Sophie frowned. Gonzales? Who was Gonzales?

Still at attention, Fairfax displayed no emotion. "Gonzales escaped, sir, as did St. James. Le Coeuvre and El Serpiente are dead. If not dead, Dusseau and El Escorpión are mortally wounded."

Edward frowned. "You aren't certain?"

"No, sir. There was a commotion on the wharf. We departed Havana in great haste to avoid capture by the Spaniards."

"I see."

Sophie saw, too. Edward was disappointed with Fairfax. Although the lieutenant's actions had surely muddied water between Spain and the rebels, he'd spent a great deal of resources and time and hadn't brought back a major player.

"I shall take them to the brig, sir."

"No. These three are my personal responsibility."

"But sir —"

"I shall expect a full report from you in my cabin on the morrow at seven o'clock. You'd best see the surgeon about your injury straightaway. Divest yourself of *that* uniform as soon as possible. Dismissed, Lieutenant."

Fairfax saluted. "Sir." He limped aft.

Edward passed a visual inspection over them one by one without lingering on her, as if he were wary of touching hot metal. A host of regrets cascaded through her — that she'd hurt him, that she'd been unable to return his love or accept his offer of protection, and that soon he must witness her execution. But Edward was a creature of the air, Apollo of sunlight and justice, while she was a creature of the dark earth. Not in a lifetime could he have lavished the kind of wealth upon her that her soul craved. She averted her gaze. The god of sunlight didn't want her apologies.

"Ye gods. How did the three of you come by the stench of rotten fish?" David cocked an eyebrow. "I suspect that spending six hours in the hold of that schooner would confer similar redolence on anyone. Do we reek too much for the brig? Well, please do turn the hawse pipe on us. I can hardly stand the smell myself. Five days hence, even the hangman will thank you for it."

Edward curbed appreciation for David's vivacity from his expression — a difficult maneuver when even she wanted to laugh with black humor. "I daresay he shall. For tonight, however, if I am assured your utmost cooperation, I shall part with orthodoxy and ask the captain where I might lodge the three of you that you might remedy the problem of that reek with some amount of privacy."

David inclined his head. "Many thanks, Major. I shall comply with all your demands."

Gratitude wandered across Mathias's face. "As shall I."

She mustered all the sincerity she could. "I promise."

Edward's nod was curt. "Bring your gear and follow me."

★★★

In a closet adjoining Edward's cabin, the three took turns bathing and washing hair and clothing, tasks impeded by the cramped conditions. They didn't complain, however, not when they, ears pressed to the bulkhead, overheard conversation between Edward and the ship's captain.

They never discerned enough detail to make them viable informants for the rebels, a condition intentional on Edward's part. But while the *Zealot* slipped past Key Largo and the Biscayno Reef and found the Gulf Stream on the night of June 24, the names of Charles Lord Cornwallis and Continental General Johann de Kalb figured in the adjacent cabin. The prisoners learned of Cornwallis's activity fortifying a base in South Carolina from which the redcoats could subdue the Carolina backcountry — and of the Congress's desperation to halt him, wolverine in the South. From nearly a thousand miles away, the thunder of something damned monstrous brewing in South Carolina was already audible.

The three whispered of it, wondering what other than British victory could result from a ragtag Continental encounter against well-fed redcoats. Convinced that they were rebel spies, Edward had instilled those very speculations in them. Spies mustn't go to the gallows believing that their actions mattered in the great scheme of things.

Discussion of the war subsided, then they each spoke a special memory of Jacques le Coeuvre into the darkness, spilling tears again and bidding him adieu as best they could. Jacques wouldn't have wanted a fancy wake. But the belly of a British ship-of-the-line didn't strike Sophie as a seemly place to tell the Frenchman goodbye.

David dropped off to sleep, having squished himself against one wall of the closet out of courtesy. Against the background of his slumbered breathing and the *Zealot*'s creaking, Mathias drew Sophie atop him, and they bade each other a silent, sad adieu to the rhythm of the ship's swaying in the Atlantic Ocean. The speculation about military action in South Carolina had served as a shield against the crush of reality. But in the naked aftermath of lovemaking, as they kissed away each other's tears, they were certain — certain as the sun would rise a few hours later in the eastern sky — that they would never know the outcome of the American War.

Chapter Thirty-Five

ON DECK SUNDAY morning, the *Zealot*'s captain read from the Bible while sailors and soldiers shifted about, sails stretched in the briny breeze, and the mangrove-covered coast of southern East Florida slipped past to leeward. He recited the Articles of War to remind sailors of offenses such as mutiny and sodomy that they were forbidden to commit. Then Sophie, David, and Mathias were escorted back to the closet by the two soldiers who had delivered breakfast and swapped out their chamber pot and lantern.

The closet was in disarray. Their belongings had been ransacked. Sophie seized her haversack and emptied the contents on the deck. No cipher, translations, or *Confessions.*

"Jolly. Now they've proof we're rebel spies."

She sighed, miserable. "Would that I'd thought to destroy the messages after committing them to memory."

David shook his head. "Would that any of us had thought to do so. What fools we are. I hardly see how we're worth the noose."

Mathias signed for silence. The tread of boots to the end of the corridor was followed by a rap at the major's cabin door. David groped for his pocket watch. "Seven o'clock," he whispered. "It's Fairfax with his report."

They pressed their ears to the bulkhead, privy to the conversation. "At ease, Lieutenant. How's your injury?"

"Well enough, sir."

"You're fortunate the arrow wasn't poisoned."

"No time," whispered Mathias. David mouthed, "Too bad."

"Sir."

"I require a moment to read this. Remain while I do so."

Realization shot through Sophie. She blurted a whisper. "Fairfax doesn't know we're in here. Major Hunt's the one who searched our belongings."

A smuggler's brazen smile swaggered across David's mouth. "Dunstan, laddie, you've botched the job. You let spies escape, and you didn't search your captives. For shame. What will your next commander say?"

Mathias grinned, too. "Slovenly job in Havana, Lieutenant. We shall withhold that promotion for awhile."

They sniggered. Edward's cabin stayed quiet about five minutes. Then stool legs squawked on the flooring. "Let's go for a walk on deck, shall we, Lieutenant?"

"Sir?"

"I require your clarification of some points in the report, and I should like fresh air in the process."

The prisoners pouted at their door while the two officers exited and walked past the guards. David voiced their shared sentiment. "Dash it all. Hearing the major's evaluation of Fairfax would have brightened the rest of my short lifetime." No doubt Edward had figured the same.

The morning dragged with little to stimulate them. Mid-afternoon, they were served salted beef, Pease porridge, hard biscuits inhabited by weevils, and stale beer — a stark contrast to their meals aboard the *Gloria Maria*. They amused each other by tapping their biscuits and seeing whose weevils scurried out the quickest.

Minutes after they'd finished the meal, a knock came on the door. Mathias opened it to a soldier at attention. "The captain requires Mr. St. James and Mr. Hale on deck for fresh air."

Sophie frowned. "What of me?"

"Mrs. Barton is ordered to Major Hunt's cabin."

Edward wanted David and Mathias out of earshot while he questioned her. She rolled back her shoulders. "Well, then, I certainly hope to join you gentlemen on deck afterward."

They filed out. She waited for her companions to exit the corridor before she knocked on Edward's door.

At his invitation, she entered a cabin the size of those aboard the *Gloria Maria* to find him perched on a stool before a desk. He set down his quill, rose, inclined his head to her, and resumed his seat without expression. The deadlight let in a bit of daylight, but a candle on the desk conferred the hue of fresh blood to his coat. She closed the door and waited.

He laid the paper aside, pulled a clean sheet from a portfolio, and dipped his quill in the inkwell. "For the record, please state the full names of your daughter, your sister, and a third blood relative in addition to their spouses' names and where they reside."

Next of kin. She swallowed, wondering when the diameter of her throat had shrunk. "My daughter is Elizabeth Anne Sheridan nee Neely. Her husband is John Clark Sheridan. They reside in Augusta. My sister is Susana Margaret Greeley nee St. James. Her husband is John Roger Greeley of Alton. And my cousin is Sarah Margaret O'Neal nee St. James. Her husband is Lucas Hezekiah O'Neal. They live in Augusta."

His quill scratched across paper. He replenished the ink. "Your full name?"

"Sophia Elizabeth Barton nee St. James."

Finished writing, he laid down the quill and sprinkled fine sand upon the document. Then he turned to her and crossed his legs. "On Saturday June 24 in Havana, Cuba, Lieutenant Fairfax was witness to you, David St. James, and the now-deceased Jacques le Coeuvre, delivering emeralds to Don Antonio Hernandez, an enemy Spaniard. Lieutenant Fairfax witnessed you telling Don Antonio that you had accepted the jewels from his nephew, Don Esteban, one of three known spies prepared to intercede with the Spaniards in the interest of the Continental Congress.

"Lieutenant Fairfax also confirmed our intelligence reports that Don Diego Alejandro Gonzales, also present during your meeting yesterday, was impersonating a Gálvez in a hoax to assess whether the American rebellion was organized enough to deserve formal support in King Carlos's court. Fortunately for His Majesty King George, the fouled delivery of the emeralds will confirm the rebels' disorganization to the Spaniards. However, your possession of a coded message and translated cipher and your participation in the delivery of the emeralds are sufficient evidence to identify you as a rebel spy and mandate your death upon the gallows. Have you comment in your behalf?"

"I'm not a rebel spy."

"I knew you'd say that."

"You know I'm not a rebel spy."

He pushed up from the desk in anger. "No, I don't know that! What I've *seen* is that a woman that I loved — a woman I fancied marrying — rejected my offers of protection and apparently fell in with rebels."

"Marriage? Yes, perhaps you fancied marrying me. I don't doubt you wanted me for your mistress. But while you and I enjoyed each other's company here, in America, such an arrangement never would have worked for us in England. You've realized that, but perhaps it makes it easier for you to accept if you envision me a rebel."

He tightened his lips, granting her assertion weight. "If you aren't a rebel, why did you sail to Havana with the emeralds and meet with enemy Spaniards instead of waiting for me in St. Augustine?"

"I couldn't give you the stones. They weren't King George's any more than the Congress's. The name Don Esteban gave us was that of his uncle, Don Antonio. Unless Lieutenant Fairfax lied to you, you'll see in his report that we delivered the stones to Don Antonio, *not* to Don Alejandro, and it was Don Alejandro whom the rebel couriers were supposed to present with the emeralds. However, we four operated under the assumption that the emeralds were part of Esteban Hernandez's inheritance, meaning their only rightful owner was another Hernandez family member.

"Edward, this had nothing to do with the American War. It had everything to do with the personal integrity of each of us. We could have divided the wealth among ourselves, returned to Alton, and been quite well off for many years, and no one besides us would have been the wiser about how we came by such fortunes." She shook her head. "But we couldn't do that. We're honest human beings, each of us, and sometimes an honest human being must look past convention of law to complete a duty that he or she knows is right, deep in the soul. Sometimes the law is *wrong*.

"I understand what the evidence looks like against us. I know how far you've bent convention to grant us comfort in our final days, and I thank you for it."

His sapphire eyes burned from a face gone too pale. He walked from her, hands clasped behind him, and faced the bulkhead in silence, staring as if he saw the ocean through it. At least a minute elapsed before she heard his voice, low, and while he spoke, she sensed he'd forgotten her presence and thought aloud, voicing issues he'd struggled with a long time.

"This war, this damned war. What a waste. We don't want to be here killing our brethren, and we don't want to spend another day in a land that resists us with every natural weapon it can unleash." Bitterness tainted his tone. "The casualties are men and women of integrity. The survivors are fanatics with no sense of decency. It isn't justice." He glanced at her. "Have you read that Declaration of Independence?"

"Yes."

"A masterpiece of philosophical persuasion. I agree with the Congress on many grievances. But why should I agree with them about anything? Doesn't that make me a traitor?" He pressed his right palm to the bulkhead. "Across that ocean, many members of Parliament sympathize with the colonists.

"And I hear regret in the Declaration, voices of delegates who didn't want to sunder ties with Britain: 'We have appealed to their native justice and magnanimity, and we have conjured them by the ties of our common kindred, to disavow these usurpations, which would inevitably interrupt our connections and correspondence'."

Edward turned back to her. "Men of the Congress and Parliament hold the same values dear to them, yet they're at each others' throats, labeling each other godless heathens. This war sucks the blood from everyone, no matter the color coat we wear. Years from now both sides of the Atlantic will still be weakened from its feeding. We have all cast ourselves to it as oblations. I see no way out of it."

She took a step toward him. "Go back to England. Speak in Parliament. Tell them what you've told me just now."

"I spoke my mind in Parliament last year." He shook his head, the movement diminutive, as if to emphasize the extent of his influence within Britain's government. "They told me to reseat myself."

"Return and try again. Yours isn't the only voice of reason. Surely they must hear you someday."

"My voice is too small by thousands of acres, one generation, and at least two titles. It's best heard at the local level among the common people."

Sadness swept her — not for herself, but for Edward, a natural statesman with talents ignored and unrecognized by his peers. "Yours is a voice of justice. In Alton we listened to it for four months and felt far more secure." She walked to the desk, picked up the paper scripted with information about her kin, and showed it to him. "But is *this* the justice you administered in Alton and Hampshire?" He stared as if she'd struck him. "Is it the justice sought by the Congress or even that administered by much of Parliament?

"No, I think it's something else." Bitterness infiltrated her tone. "How did the Declaration word it? 'Under absolute despotism, it is the right and duty of the people to throw off such government and to institute new government'. Could this be one of those grievances where you and the Congress agree?"

"I take your point. I believe we're finished for now."

"Of course we are. Much as His Majesty courted the illusion that the American colonies would always be content as dependent children of Britain, we courted the illusion that I might be content as your mistress. But you've realized it cannot work — not for us, and not for Britain and the colonies."

In the dimness of the cabin, emotion on his face folded into inscrutability. She jiggled the paper. "What do you call this: duty? An order? Honor? I realize that you're a man of duty and so must complete what you believe is your duty. In a few days, I will go to the gallows with my head held high — not because of politics, but because I was guided by my conscience and am an honest woman. In a few days, it will be over for me, but I suspect you'll spend the rest of your life sorting out this duty, order, and honor."

His expression thawing, he returned to the desk, removed the paper from her hand, and spread it flat with care. "Always outspoken and forthright, never deceptive: Sophie Barton."

"Please understand that I never meant to hurt you."

"I know you didn't."

Tension mounted across the space between them. She felt the impulse to embrace and comfort him, and from the sentiment sifting into his face, he wouldn't have resisted. But it was as if a pale wall had materialized between them, a barrier that dissuaded their meeting in the middle.

He rolled his shoulders back. "As I said, we're finished for now. Accept the escort outside, take some fresh air up on deck, and send Mr. St. James or Mr. Hale down to see me next."

Lost for words, she stared at him. Then she let herself out of the cabin and sought her escort.

Chapter Thirty-Six

PREDAWN THE FOLLOWING Thursday morning, Sophie awakened to feel the *Zealot* at anchor east of St. Augustine. She lay still and, with calm and thankfulness, experienced what she believed to be her final morning on the earth — appreciation for Edward's clemency, awe and delight for the bond she shared with David, and gratitude for the gift of trust, joy, and ecstatic union she had discovered with Mathias. Then she woke her companions.

They lit the lantern, dressed, assembled gear and waited for the inevitable knock on the door. It came minutes later, along with a breakfast of biscuits and tea and the order that they be ready to leave in a quarter hour. On deck in the sunrise, she regarded the distant coquina walls of Castillo de San Marcos. Just fifteen days earlier they'd sailed forth from St. Augustine aboard the *Gloria Maria*.

The prisoners were lowered into a gig with Edward and Fairfax and rowed across the Matanzas River. No longer limping, Fairfax paid them the same regard he'd grant a load of lumber. Not being an object of his attention felt liberating, a blessing. In contrast, Edward's face was sunken and gray. Demons had stolen sleep from his eyes and crushed his soul.

At the wharf, the soldiers from Alton met them and escorted the prisoners — minus possessions except clothing on their backs — to jail. One of three prostitutes sharing Sophie's cell scratched at scabs on her arms. The fifth woman in the cell was an Irish pickpocket who reminded her too much of Mary, the St. James's servant. David and Mathias shared the company of eight drunks sleeping off a night of vandalism. The other cells were full of male inmates. The jail stank of sweat, piss, and puke.

An hour after Edward left to learn the city's protocol for rebel spies, Sophie glimpsed Fairfax through the door grate, pacing in the front room. Another hour passed, and he departed the jail, leaving the soldiers from Alton with the jailer and his assistants.

Not until after ten did the lieutenant return. He marched straight back to the cells. "Attention Mr. St. James, Mr. Hale, Mrs. Barton. Due to a backlog in processing criminals, the justices of St. Augustine cannot hear your cases and schedule your executions for at least three weeks. It behooves us to transport you to Georgia so we may complete the business with due haste." He paused. "I trust you find the news as distressing as I. Therefore, I insist upon having your utmost cooperation in the matter."

The whine in David's voice masked his glee. "Will we get dinner before we leave? Tea and biscuits doesn't go very far."

"This morning Major Hunt had business matters to resolve, the nature of which he didn't disclose to me. As a consequence, we shan't leave until the morrow. I assume you shall be fed whenever and whatever the other wretches in this jail are fed. Have you stabled your horses somewhere in the city, or did you sell them prior to your departure for Havana?"

David sounded bored. "They're stabled with Mr. Garner."

"You three haven't much money to retrieve them."

"We shouldn't owe much after our payment. We used the name Hazelton. And don't forget Jacques le Coeuvre's horse." Fairfax stomped out, followed by David's voice. "Come now, lieutenant, you can find me something decent to eat before dinner, can you not? You don't want me perishing of hunger before you stretch my neck on the gallows. Lieutenant, are you there? Well, how do you like that, Mathias? He's ignoring me."

Sophie caught David's eye through the grate on the door and motioned for him to cease the banter. Then she sat on a bench grinning, aware that her cellmates regarded her with a mixture of fear and awe: a woman marked for execution, for whom Fate had granted a few more days of life.

***

Early Friday morning, she and Samson the gelding became reacquainted, and the horse's affection and loyalty cheered her. Mr. Garner had taken good care of the beasts. When Sophie mounted the gelding, he pranced about, eager to take on the day, hot and muggy as it portended. How she wished she could have shared his enthusiasm. A night spent serenaded by the scratching and snoring of her cellmates had left a crick in her neck. Still, she counted her blessings. Two of David and Mathias's cellmates had taken turns retching all night.

Before departing St. Augustine, Edward, his expression inflexible, lectured them about the dangers of the road and assured them that if they tried to escape, they'd be executed on the spot. At one point, he paced upwind of Sophie, and she smelled tobacco on him — peculiar since she'd never observed him to smoke. She sniffed again. The tobacco had been blended with something else, and the combined scent nagged her with its familiarity, even while eluding identification.

She forgot about it after the soldiers set a steady pace that made excellent time and didn't exhaust the horses. By late morning, owing to the good condition of the King's Highway, they'd covered more than half the distance to Cow Ford.

On occasion they journeyed more than a quarter hour at a time meeting only a startled deer or wild hog and surrounded by the whisper of wind in the live oaks, pines, and palmettos. In just such a deserted stretch of highway about eleven o'clock, they rode over a rise to find a Lower Creek warrior beside a horse in the road, examining the horse's shoe. The Indian eyed them with wariness and led the horse to the side of the road to allow them to pass.

Edward signaled a halt. "Everyone dismount and stretch. Mr. Hale, be so good as to examine the horse's shoe for that fellow."

"I may not be able to communicate well with the warrior, Major. They have a different dialect here."

"Still, you can try."

Sophie dismounted, stretched her arms over her head, and turned her head from side to side. Mathias had almost reached the warrior when the Creek vaulted on the horse's back, dug heels into its sides, and sped from their midst with a whoop.

David frowned after the warrior. "Touchy fellow, eh?" Then he sucked in a breath. "Ye gods."

She followed his stare, and chills chiseled her back. More than thirty warriors on horseback emerged from concealment, muskets and arrows trained on them. Fairfax and the privates looked about in astonishment.

In a calm voice, Edward said, "Steady, everyone. Take no aggressive action." He walked within plain view of most of the Creek. "What do you want?"

A warrior spoke in their dialect, pointed to Mathias, Sophie, and David, and signed for them to come with the warriors. Fairfax sounded annoyed. "Mr. Hale, what are they saying?"

Mathias wagged his head in wariness. "They seem to believe we three owe them a debt and insist that we come with them."

"A debt? What sort of debt?"

"I've no idea. I've never seen any of them before." The spokesman grew irritable and made more hand gestures, punctuating them with strings of words. "It's something about theft."

Edward's tone hardened. "Did you steal from them?"

"Certainly not. I told you I've never seen them before."

"Nor I," said Sophie, and David agreed.

"Well, then, I suggest you convince them of their error so we may be on our way."

Mathias scowled. "Major, I barely understand their dialect. Why should I interpret for someone who intends to execute me?"

Edward regarded him sensibly before addressing the spokesman. "Do any of you speak English?"

The warrior twisted about and signed behind him. A Negro on horseback walked his horse forward into clear view and halted it to the right of the warrior.

Sophie stiffened, saw David do the same, then lowered her gaze to the ground until she could look back up at Ulysses, the former slave, without recognition screaming from her expression. "I don't believe it," David whispered to her.

The warrior growled, pointed to Edward, snapped out more dialect, then gestured to the prisoners. Ulysses scanned them with no recognition and addressed Edward. "Bear Up The Tree say these people stole a horse from our village more than two weeks ago. He say they also steal weapons and lie to Mico. We take the stolen weapons and bring the thieves back to the village for justice."

Edward shook his head. "Tell Bear Up The Tree that he has mistaken them for others. These people claim they've never seen any of you before."

Ulysses made the translation. Bear Up The Tree responded in a belligerent tone, and Ulysses addressed Edward again. "Bear Up The Tree say a third man was with them more than two weeks ago, an old Frenchman."

Accusation narrowed Fairfax's gaze on Mathias. "Mr. Hale, you've lied to us."

Wide-eyed, Mathias spread his hands and shot a glance of bafflement at Sophie and David. She saw from his expression that he understood enough of the dialect to comprehend subcurrents of a scheme the redcoats didn't perceive. David said under his breath, "What the devil are these Indians trying to do?"

"Lieutenant, as you were." Edward pinned Bear Up The Tree with the commanding expression of a statesman. "Our people have a treaty with yours. These three are Mico George's prisoners, spies for the rebels, our enemies and yours. They have the sentence of death upon them. We are transporting them to the Georgia colony for execution. You must allow us to pursue Mico George's justice in this matter."

Ulysses translated. The warrior bared his teeth at Edward and raised his musket. Sophie backed half a step from the Creek leader, her breath reedy in her throat over his response, venom that needed no translation.

"Bear Up The Tree say our justice more important. You release the thieves and weapons to us, or he shoot you."

Fairfax stomped the road. "Sir, this is absurd! The savages are supposed to be allies! I say this is a trick! Mr. Hale is a liar. All along he's understood them. They're his friends who would rescue him."

Edward never took his eyes off Bear Up The Tree. Pragmatism entered his voice. "Look around you, Lieutenant. Tell me their motivations matter. We're very much outnumbered."

A snarl exposed Fairfax's teeth. "You're just going to give them up? After more than four weeks, you're going to surrender to rebels?" Etched into his expression and voice was his contempt for Edward's mercy toward prisoners and acquiescence toward savages. And Fairfax clearly believed the Creek bluffed with their threat to shoot.

Edward reached to his side, drew his curved sword, and held it up, striking a courageous and indomitable figure. To Sophie, his actions seemed to create less of a challenge than a signal to Bear Up The Tree, for the warrior's belligerence faded into resolution and understanding. She shrieked, "No!" the second before the warrior fired his musket.

"Aaaaghh!" The sword clanged to the road. Scarlet blossomed across Edward's right thigh and he collapsed, rotating his torso as he did to make eye contact with her for one second, enough time for his expression to communicate the command, "Go!"

Stupefaction speared Fairfax's surliness. "Major Hunt — sir!" The lieutenant sprinted to Edward's side, knelt along with several privates, and raised his fist to Bear Up The Tree. "You filthy, traitorous savages! Treaties and honor mean nothing to you, do they? Take your thieves, then. Be welcome to them.

We shan't stop you."

David shoved Sophie toward Samson, uprooting her from her paralysis. "On your horse," he muttered in her ear. "Nothing here is as it seems. The sooner we're away, the sooner we'll find out the real story."

Chapter Thirty-Seven

THEY RODE WEST hard, permitting no leisure to dwell on the shooting. Bear Up The Tree signaled a halt in the middle of the swamp. Muck sucked at Samson's shoes, turkey buzzards circled, and insects found the taste of sweat irresistible. Bear Up The Tree gestured south. All but he, Ulysses, and four Creek abandoned Sophie's party and trotted their horses in that direction.

The leader nudged his horse over to where his prisoners caught their breaths and fanned away bugs. Sweat slicked his bronze, tattooed skin. His eyes were the color of onyx. "We go north now. Ground soft here." He guided his horse away.

Sophie gaped to hear English spoken where she'd never expected it. Above the stink of grease on the warrior, she recognized the familiar scent of the tobacco-herb combination the Creek smoked during discussions. Shock flooded her brain.

Edward's business Thursday had been with the Lower Creek. While passing the pipe around, he'd arranged their escape. He'd taken a ball in his leg to allay Fairfax's suspicions. Never would he have done so had he believed them rebel spies, or had he trusted the courts to deliver the correct verdict. In silence, she implored any deities listening to allow him to survive his act of justice and mercy.

Her gut roared by the time they paused in a copse of pines for corn cakes and dried venison. Nothing had filled her stomach since the predawn slop that passed for corn mush in jail. Soon after they finished eating, Ulysses, who had helped several warriors confiscate their weapons from the redcoats, ambled over and returned their weapons. David produced a smile fit for a cotillion and motioned for the Negro to sit cross-legged with them. "My good man, how are Lila and the baby?"

"They fine. Lila be helping the women in the fields, sharing some things we know. That child be growing like a weed."

Mathias gestured to the Negro's horse. "You've done quite well for yourself in just a few weeks."

"Yessuh. I teach English to folks who want it. They teach me to hunt, find my way round. Got my first deer with the musket two days ago. Ain't no mas-suh ever going to find us."

He lowered his voice. "We taking you to the Georgia colony so as them red-coats don't find you at least as far as the St. Marys River. Yesterday the major ride into the village to talk to Mico. Mico ask me and Bear Up The Tree to join them, make the English words. We smoke the pipe, and I wonder where I seen this redcoat before. I remember the night Lila have the baby, just before we met you folks, we sneaked round their camp.

"The major say he be escorting three prisoners that he know be innocent, but he afraid Mico George rule otherwise and they get executed. He throw money on the mat before Mico. More money than I ever seen in my life. He say help me save them, Mico. They got to escape.

"He describe you. They plan the ambush. He say things may go bad, so if I give you the signal, you shoot me in the leg to make it look better. I think, man, how bad do things got to get when you want somebody to shoot you? Then I see. The lieutenant want all of you dead." He regarded Sophie. "Or maybe worse. Lila tell me what happen in Cow Ford."

Mathias and David glowered. Sophie waved it away and thanked Ulysses, but she knew Mathias wasn't finished with Fairfax.

After Ulysses left them, Mathias spoke up sounding chagrined. "I mis-judged Hunt. He's truly a warrior."

David scraped venison from between his teeth. "I called him 'a mediocre soldier.' Zounds, how wrong I was."

She flicked her gaze back and forth between them — brother of her blood and bones, brother of her heart and spirit — two of the most remarkable men she'd had the fortune of knowing. And Edward — never would she have ex-pected him to step so far outside regulations. In the final look he'd given her, she'd recognized that his actions hadn't been based solely on his convictions of their innocence and the court's shortcomings. The agony it brought him to let her go ripped him as much as the musket ball.

David snorted. "We've returned a fortune to an ungrateful Spaniard and escaped the gallows. Where do we go? We're in exile."

"To my home village." Mathias held up a hand to divert their protests. "My aunt communicates with Beloved Women from Cherokee villages in the Caro-linas. The Cherokee may be able to hide us."

David eyed Mathias as if he'd hit his head and wasn't thinking clearly. "Aren't the two tribes at war?"

"It depends upon our perception of the enemy. I'd like to try strengthen-ing relations between my people and the Cherokee. I shall be honored to have your company in such an endeavor."

How welcome did the Creek feel in the land of the Cherokee? Sophie imag-ined Mathias an ambassador among them. A thrill of apprehension and antici-pation spiraled through her.

David scratched his head. "Sounds interesting, however, I have a plan of my own. I haven't visited a card table in weeks. Fairfax, rot his soul, denied me the pleasure of cleaning out the Spaniards in Havana. I've always enjoyed cards in Williamsburg, and there's a widow there whom I'd like to visit."

Sophie smirked at him. "Abby, right?"

"No, Nancy."

Mathias nodded. "Williamsburg is far enough away that you shouldn't be conspicuous."

"Of course, I need to visit a widow in Augusta before I head to Williamsburg."

Sophie grinned. "Martha, right?"

"No, *Abby's* the widow in Augusta."

Mathias frowned. "That visit will put you at risk."

"So I won't advertise." He studied Sophie, sobered. "Betsy must be frantic about you. Come with me. You could see her in Augusta. And Nancy's family owns the press in Williamsburg. With your experience, you'd be a tremendous help to them."

She was spared making a decision when Bear Up The Tree signaled for them to resume traveling. David rolled to his feet, and Mathias helped her up. "No matter where we three end up, let us have a few days' respite among the people first."

She smiled at him. "Agreed."

"I've no objection." David braced his hands on his hips and gazed southward. "But someday after all this is over, I must discover just how easily the Spaniards in Havana lose their purses."

***

They arrived exhausted in the Creek village just before sundown on Friday, July 7. Within a minute, Sophie and David were shown to the guest portion of Laughing Eyes' hut. Mathias and his aunt sought a conference with the mico, and the travelers' horses were led away to receive care. David began snoring almost before he'd flopped into the hammock in the guest hut.

On a mat at the other side of the hut, Sophie lay awake, her belly full of beans, corn cakes, and melon, every muscle aching. Her mind gyrated with the adventure and flashed places, faces, and events through her memories.

Zack MacVie's ambush. Wolves and peddlers. Fairfax's attack on the outlaws. Esteban Hernandez. El Serpiente and El Escorpión. Ulysses and Lila. Cow Ford. Luciano de Herrera. Miguel de Arriaga and the *Gloria Maria*. A tropical storm and a moonlit beach. Imperial haughtiness on Don Antonio's face. Jacques's dying words. Her father's swim for safety. Edward's mercy.

The journey from East Florida had been as placid as the trip down to St. Augustine had been horrific. She'd spend the rest of her lifetime sorting out June 1780. If the people of Alton but knew what they'd been through — ah, but they'd never believe it.

After Mathias slipped inside the hut, they lay side-by-side on the mat, listening to David's snores intensify. Mathias snickered. "Listen to him. He's pushed the past four weeks clear from his mind so he can make room for card tables."

"A remarkable skill, eh?"

"Indeed. Here, now, I've much news. Most importantly, Will spent last night in this very hut."

She gasped and pushed up on her elbow. "Uninjured?"

"Yes, except for his being travel-weary."

"Thank the heavens." She felt jittery with relief, love, heartache. "We must find him. Where did he go?"

"All my aunt knows is that he's meeting rebel friends in the Carolinas."

Sophie lay back, frustration emptying her in a sigh. "Father wouldn't have said more. Protect the people."

"Yes. So do you truly want to pick up his trail and follow him?" Mathias sounded reluctant.

She considered a moment, trying to find a path through her swirl of conflict, at last deriving insight from what Runs With Horses had once said to her: *The journey of Will St. James separates from yours for awhile, but Creator will again unite your paths.* For now, she'd continue her own journey. "No."

"Wise woman." Mathias stroked her brow. "Tomorrow at dawn, my aunt shall dispatch a messenger with information about us. He'll ride to a Cherokee village in northwestern South Carolina. They should be able to give us refuge there.

"Locally, Alton's been quiet beneath the command of Captain Sheffield, although tongues still wag over how Will dug up Mr. Carey's corpse. The official finding of the murder investigation is that the Spaniard was flayed alive by his Spanish partner."

From Sophie's brief contact with Lieutenant Stoddard, she'd judged him astute enough to figure out who really murdered the Spaniard. A pity if the official statement meant the redcoats intended to protect their own. Fairfax had acquired a taste for dispensing his own "justice."

"A convenient finding for all parties. El Serpiente won't be contesting it. Has there been word of Major Hunt and his men yet?"

"None."

"Excellent. And how is the war going?"

"Mid-June, General Horatio Gates was commissioned by the Congress to assume command of the Southern rebel army from Johann de Kalb. Aside from a skirmish in North Carolina, the southern colonies have been relatively quiet. Perhaps everyone's being reasonable about the heat and lying low. Too bad Major Hunt didn't let us hear more of his conversation with the captain of the *Zealot*. With Gates's commission and all of Cornwallis's activity, something enormous must be building in South Carolina."

"Do you think it's wise to go there? My concern is less about relations between the tribes. I don't want to get underfoot when Gates and Cornwallis stomp about."

He took her in his arms. "Honestly I don't know what we shall encounter in military action. I do know that the word of one Beloved Woman to another will grant us hiding, so at least we shan't be found by anyone from Alton, particularly the redcoats.

"Yes, there's danger in South Carolina. I suppose an option would be to head west, but that's even more dangerous. Unless you know kin elsewhere who would hide us for awhile —"

"They're all in the Carolinas."

"Well, there you have it." He stroked her cheek in the darkness. "If someone had asked me a month ago at Zeb's dance, I'd have told them I never expected you at my side. But having you there has made the hell of the last month more bearable for me. If you will come with me into South Carolina, help and guide me, I shall be the most content man on earth."

Oh, how she wanted to see her daughter again. No bond on the earth equaled the intensity of that between mother and daughter. But playing a part in the formation of an alliance between the Creek and Cherokee called her from beyond her boundaries of comfort and thrilled her with a challenge to both heart and intellect.

Help and guide me. Her soul had come to rest in Mathias as it had never rested in her life. No man's decoration, she was Mathias's partner. A line from *The Iliad* came to her then: *If even in the house of Hades the dead forget their dead, yet will I even there be mindful of my dear comrade.* She touched his lips with her fingertips. "I shall go with you."

★★★

"Hold the lantern closer, will you?" David strapped his bedroll behind his saddle and grumbled at the paling sky. "Bugger that son of a poxy whore. Fairfax must have run several horses to death galloping up here two days behind us."

Mathias entered the circle of light. "Are we ready?"

"Surely, when icicles hang from Satan's breeches."

Sophie gave David a cheery smile and turned to Mathias. "We're ready." She handed the lantern to Runs With Horses and mounted Samson.

Mathias clasped his cousin's arm. "With any luck, Fairfax won't remember to visit the people for at least half a day."

Runs With Horses smiled. "Go. The wind will take your footprints."

The trio walked their horses from the village. Soon after they crossed a brook to the northeast, David halted and dismounted. Mathias and Sophie did the same, and she read her brother's intent in the dawn. Time to part company.

Mathias prodded his shoulder. "Are you sure your widow is worth it?" At David's keen look, he grinned. "Never mind."

"David, I'm going with Mathias."

His eyes twinkled with approval. "Of course you are."

"If you can safely do so, give Betsy my love and tell her I'm all right. And give us a good hug. It shall have to last awhile — oof!" The hug buried her nose in his shoulder. "That feels much more like a bear than a brother." She clung to him. "Oh, please be very careful. I shall miss you terribly."

"And I shall miss you at least as much." He whisked her hat off her head and kissed her forehead. "Musket Woman. Swamp Woman. Ocean Woman. Paper Woman." He dropped the hat back on her head.

She released him, adjusted her hat, and watched him embrace Mathias. A grin split David's face. "You two are so like a couple of peas in a pod. If you decide to make it official, don't forget to invite me. I'm jolly fun at weddings —" He winked. "Just as long as it's someone *else's* wedding."

Finis

Historical Afterword

History texts and fiction minimize the importance of the southern colonies, Florida, Spain, and the Caribbean during the American War of Independence. Many scholars now believe that more Revolutionary War battles were fought in South Carolina than in any other colony, even New York. Of all the wars North Americans have fought, the death toll from the American War exceeds all except the Civil War in terms of percentage of the population. And yet our "revolution" was but one conflict in a ravenous world war.

Many history texts and fiction also claim that those who identified themselves as patriots were in the majority during this war. Many scholars now believe that *neutrals* were in the majority, pinioned between two minority and radical opponents and often getting caught in the crossfire, a pattern we see played out in current events. Those who do not learn from history...

Propaganda was a mighty weapon wielded by both sides in this conflict. On 29 May 1780, British Lt. Colonel Banastre Tarleton led a cavalry charge against militia and regulars commanded by Colonel Abraham Buford in the Waxhaws region of South Carolina. Although Buford galloped away, leaving his leaderless unit to be devastated, the bloody outcome of the battle was seized upon by patriots and wrung for every ounce of anti-British propaganda they could twist from it.

The impact of women during the American War, especially those on the frontier, has been minimized. Women during this time enjoyed freedoms denied them the previous two centuries and the following century. They educated themselves and ran businesses and plantations. They worked the fields and hunted. They defended their homes. They ministered their folk religion at gatherings. They fought on the battlefield. Although unable to vote, women did just about everything men did.

Contrary to popular belief, Jamestown, Virginia was not the earliest European settlement to survive in the United States. Don Pedro Menéndez de Avilés established St. Augustine, Florida in 1565, decades before the British built Jamestown.

Established in 1738, Gracia Real de Santa Teresa de Mose (Fort Mose) was a community of freed slaves sanctioned by the Spanish. Destroyed twice by warfare, the concept of Fort Mose remained a beacon into Revolutionary times, drawing many escaped slaves to Florida.

The city of Galveston, Texas is named for Bernardo de Gálvez of the powerful Gálvez family. In the final years of the American War, the Spaniards, led predominantly by Gálvez, battled the British and forced them from outposts such as Pensacola and Mobile along the Gulf of Mexico. Long before Yorktown, Cornwallis's military strategies were already being hampered by Gálvez and the Spaniards.

Luciano de Herrera acted as a Spanish operative in St. Augustine for almost twenty years. When British governor Patrick Tonyn pierced his cover and sent soldiers to arrest him in 1781, Herrera was clever enough to have escaped to Cuba the day before. And when St. Augustine was returned to the Spaniards a few years later, Herrera was granted a leading government post in the city.

Selected Bibliography

Dozens of websites, interviews with subject-matter experts, the following books and more:

Abbott, Shirley. *Historic Charleston*. Birmingham, Alabama: Oxmoor House Inc., 1988.

Baker, Christopher P. *Havana Handbook*. Emeryville, California: Avalon Travel Publishing, 2000.

Bass, Robert D. *The Green Dragoon*. Columbia, South Carolina: Sandlapper Press, Inc., 1973.

Boatner, Mark M. III. *Encyclopedia of the American Revolution*. Mechanicsburg, Pennsylvania: Stackpole Books, 1994.

Campbell, Colin, ed. *Journal of Lieutenant Colonel Archibald Campbell*. Darien, Georgia: The Ashantilly Press, 1981.

Gilgun, Beth. *Tidings from the Eighteenth Century*. Texarkana, Texas: Scurlock Publishing Co., Inc., 1993.

Harland, John. *Seamanship in the Age of Sail*. London: Conway Maritime Press Ltd, 1984.

Harvey, David Alan and Elizabeth Newhouse. *Cuba*. The National Geographic Society: Washington, 1999.

Hudson, Charles. *The Southeastern Indians*. Knoxville, Tennessee: The University of Tennessee Press, 1992.

Kemp, Peter and Richard Ormond. *The Great Age of Sail*. New York: Facts on File, Inc., 1986.

Lane, Mills. *Architecture of the Old South*. New York: Abbeville Press, Inc., 1993.

Manucy, Albert. *The Houses of St. Augustine: Notes on the Architecture from 1565 to 1821*. St. Augustine, Florida: The St. Augustine Historical Society, 1962.

Morrill, Dan L. *Southern Campaigns of the American Revolution*. Mount Pleasant, South Carolina: The Nautical & Aviation Publishing Company of America, Inc., 1993.

Mullins, Lisa C., ed. *Early Architecture of the South*. Harrisburg, Pennsylvania: The National Historical Society, 1987.

O'Brian, Patrick. *Master and Commander*. New York: William Collins Sons & Co. Ltd, 1970.

Padron, Francisco Morales, ed. *The Journal of Don Francisco Saavedra de Sangronis*, 1780-1783. Gainesville, Florida: University of Florida Press, 1989.

Scotti, Dr. Anthony J., Jr. *Brutal Virtue: the Myth and Reality of Banastre Tarleton*. Bowie, Maryland: Heritage Books, Inc., 2002.

St. Augustine. *Confessions*. Trans. E. B. Pusey.

Steen, Sandra and Susan Steen. *Historic St. Augustine*. Minneapolis, Minnesota: Dillon Press, 1997.

Suchlicki, Jaime. *Cuba From Columbus to Castro*. Washington: Pergamon-Brassey's International Defense Publishers, 1986.

Swager, Christine R. *Black Crows & White Cockades*. St. Petersburg, Florida: Southern Heritage Press, 1999.

Tunis, Edwin. *Colonial Craftsmen and the Beginnings of American Industry*. Baltimore, Maryland: The Johns Hopkins University Press, 1965.

Waterbury, Jean Parker, ed. *The Oldest City: St. Augustine, Saga of Survival*. St. Augustine, Florida: The St. Augustine Historical Society, 1983.

Woodman, Richard. *The History of the Ship*. London: Conway Maritime Press, 1997.

The Blacksmith's Daughter

A Mystery of the American Revolution

by Suzanne Adair

The patriots wanted her husband dead. So did the redcoats. She took issue with both.

In the blistering Georgia summer of 1780, Betsy Sheridan uncovers evidence that her shoemaker husband, known for his loyalty to King George, is smuggling messages to a patriot-sympathizing, multinational spy ring based in the Carolinas. When he vanishes into the heart of military activity, in Camden, South Carolina, Betsy follows him, as much in search of him as she is in search of who she is and where she belongs. But battle looms between Continental and Crown forces. The spy ring is plotting multiple assassinations. And Betsy and her unborn child become entangled in murder and chaos.

Please turn the page to follow Betsy Sheridan's journey.

Chapter One

SERENADED BY PREDAWN cricket chirp and frog song on July 11, Betsy Sheridan paced in the dining room, already dressed in her shift, short jacket, and petticoat. Her stomach uneasily negotiated the collision of oily pork odor from Monday night's supper with leather's rich pungency from Clark's shop. She knew better than to blame the queasiness on being four months along with child.

News delivered at suppertime had driven nettles of anxiety into her soul. Her mother and uncle captured by Lower Creek Indians in East Florida — good gods. The Lower Creek didn't treat their prisoners to tea parties. Imagining her mother Sophie and her Uncle David tortured in creative, native ways made her gut feel like a blazing spew of grapeshot.

At the window, she breathed in familiar morning scents wafting from the back yard on a cool breeze: sandy soil entwined with red veins of Georgia clay, wood smoke, pine resin. "Pregnant nose," the midwife had called her heightened sense of smell. Out back, King Lear the rooster crowed. With Clark's apprentices arriving at seven, Betsy had best fetch the eggs and start breakfast soon. Perhaps the morning routine would ease some of her anxiety.

Her lit candle held aloft, she paused outside the cobbler's shop to peer up the stairway. Annoyance rifted her anxiety at the soft snores issuing from their bedroom. Clark wouldn't have overslept had he not stayed up for that midnight delivery of Cordovan leather from Sooty Johns. Betsy had never liked Johns, a greasy little peddler. Because she, curious, had tiptoed downstairs to watch the two men unload the leather, and they thought her asleep the whole time, the delivery had felt illegal.

In the shop, she lit and hung two Betty lamps. Her gaze skimmed over the counter where she kept the ledger and lodged on the workbench piled with Cordovan leather. Magenta by lamplight, it almost assumed the hue of coagulated blood. *Spain.* Why should Spanish leather be delivered early Tuesday morning to John Clark Sheridan, a British sympathizer, ostensibly one of Spain's enemies? A shudder rose in her, and she wondered whether she should hide the leather.

Not that she needed more to worry about. Shaking off her concerns over the delivery, she walked to the workbench and pushed aside an awl and two cowhide boots to make room for her candle beside a small mirror. The action of settling her mobcap atop her braided dark hair eased her stomach. After a final inspection to ensure a trim appearance, she stood.

One of the cowhide boots slid off the bench, so she leaned over and snagged it. When she propped it beside its mate, she spied a sliver of paper between heel and sole. Curious, she pried it out and read *Mrs. Filbert's daughter is Sally* in her husband's handwriting.

Odd. Who was Mrs. Filbert?

Betsy tilted the paper closer to the candle. Here, now — what was that? Writing appeared on the edge of the paper nearest the heat.

Amazed, she passed the rest of the paper above the flame. Bluish script gibberish and three-digit numbers filled in the page, some sort of cipher. She waved the paper around. It cooled, and the writing vanished.

A chill brushed her neck. Clark had planted a secret message in the boot. Should she tell him she'd found it?

More anxiety wound through her. Bad enough that her family on the St. James side was in so much trouble lately, but now her husband was involved in questionable deals. When they'd married in January, she'd dreamed of leading a normal, uneventful life: helping him with his business, raising children, tending the garden and house. By the lamplight of that Tuesday morning, though, her optimism looked as naïve as that displayed by fifty-six Congressional delegates who'd signed their names to a declaration of independence from George the Third's rule. Four years later, thousands of redcoats still occupied the thirteen North American colonies.

Another crow from King Lear prompted Betsy's attempt to wedge the paper back in the heel. Unsuccessful and exasperated, she shoved the note into her pocket, lit a lantern, and bustled from the shop with it. The back door squeaked when she exited from dining room into garden, and Hamlet and Horatio loped around from the front yard, tails awag in greeting. She paused to scratch behind the hounds' ears, and memory caught up with her.

Almost two months earlier, during her mother's last visit to Augusta, they'd sat in the dining room sipping herbal tea, and Betsy told her the news: *You shall be a grandmother before Yule.* They'd laughed and embraced through tears of joy, and for the first time ever, Sophie had talked with her as one mother to another, dissolving the physical distance between them that seven years of living apart had imposed. But now, captive of the Lower Creek...Betsy blinked away the salty mist of misery, her stomach afire again with apprehension.

She stumbled a few steps before righting herself and continued down the path to the henhouse. The dogs bounded away to the front of the house. A sparrow began his reveille. The earth smelled cool, damp, and ripe. Inside the henhouse, she hung the lantern on a hook and grabbed a basket. The hens welcomed her with soft clucks, the acrid odor of their droppings magnified by her nose.

"Well, Titania, have you an egg for me this morning?" The hen shifted to allow Betsy's groping fingers access to straw only. She proceeded to the next hen. "You, Desdemona? Alas, no egg." She straightened. "Strange. Perchance you need a change in diet. Well, I'm sure to find something from Portia. No? Oh, very well, you did lay two eggs yesterday." She fumbled beneath more hens without success, and an eerie sense of familiarity spread through her. The only other time this had happened was when all the eggs had been collected as a *prank* just prior to her arrival.

She lowered her voice, not daring to believe. "Uncle David?"

She heard amusement in his voice outside the henhouse. "I cannot play that trick on you twice, can I?"

She raced out and flung her arms around dark-haired, lanky, handsome David St. James who'd no doubt passed the night in the arms of a certain wealthy, lovely widow in town. Small wonder the hounds hadn't alerted her to his familiar presence. "Great thunder, it *is* you, and you're all right!" She smacked his cheek with a kiss. "Oh, gods, when I heard the news yesterday, I could scarcely eat or sleep for worry." She tugged him toward the house. "Clark has been so worried, too. But you've escaped the Indians!"

David braked their progress toward the house. "Don't tell your husband or anyone else that you've seen me."

"Why not?" She noticed her uncle's hunting shirt and trousers and checked herself. "You're running, aren't you? Mother, too."

"Yes."

"Just like Grandpapa Will."

She watched David's stare home on her. "What do you mean?"

"*He* was hiding in the henhouse yesterday morning."

David darted a look around. "Where is the old man?"

"Probably in South Carolina." Cynicism seeped into her voice. "That's where he seemed to think he could lay low with rebel friends because he landed himself in all that trouble with the redcoats last month. Running a spy ring from Alton, printing incendiary broadsides, escaping to Havana to intrigue with the *Gálvez* family. The Gálvez family. Zounds. How did a printer from a frontier town ever catch the eye of people so high up in the Spanish court? And what did he expect from all that intrigue? Surely not a pardon. I don't suppose he'll ever learn, will he? So I fed him breakfast and sent him on his way before it grew light. And where's my mother?"

"On her way to a Cherokee village in South Carolina." He glanced at the sky. "And since I don't want to be recognized on the road, I must away to Williamsburg before it gets much lighter." His tone became shrewd. "I'm here only to assure you your mother is safe and well, and she sends you her love."

The unreality of the situation descended on Betsy. She felt as though cotton stuffed her head. "A redcoat from our garrison came by last night to relate the news. You and Mother had been arrested as rebel spies after chasing Grandpapa to Havana. Then you were captured by Indians north of St. Augustine while the redcoats were escorting you back to Georgia. You and Mother, rebel spies? Hah. Perchance if men bore children, yes. Why don't you tell me what really happened."

David ejected a soft laugh. "Well, we did go after the old man, but it was for his own good. We aren't rebel spies, and it's a great misunderstanding that would take me too long to explain. Rest assured, though, that your mother is safe for now."

Betsy frowned. Of course it was a misunderstanding, and no one could dance a reel around the truth like her uncle. "When shall I have the full story?"

"When someone has the time to explain it."

Ah, no. He wasn't going to escape without explaining the greatest mystery of all. "Surely you can tarry long enough to clarify *one* detail. Wait here while I fetch what arrived by post yesterday and show it to you."

"Very well, but hurry."

She bustled up the path, flung open the back door, seized the package from within a cupboard, and trotted back out to David. "See here, this was addressed as follows: 'To Mrs. Betsy Sheridan in Augusta, Georgia.' Well, go ahead and see what's inside."

Stupefaction and recognition flooded his voice when he examined the parasol and lace veil within. "I don't believe it."

She set the box and its contents down next to the basket of eggs David had collected. "There's a brief letter here somewhere. Who is Miguel de Arriaga, author of the letter?"

"Captain of a Portuguese merchant brig, the *Gloria Maria*."

"So you and Mother had quite an adventure!" Awed and envious, Betsy straightened and handed him the letter. Then she leaned inside the henhouse, unhooked the lantern, and held it to illuminate Captain Arriaga's script on the page.

David skimmed the letter, and she followed the path his eyes took over it, having already memorized the contents:

MADAM:

Your Uncle and Parents were Passengers aboard my Ship, the Gloria Maria. I gave this Parasol and Veil to your Mother, a remarkable Woman, and she lost them in Havana when British Soldiers captured her. If you see her again, please give them to her and tell her I tried to help.

I am Madam
Your humble Servant
Miguel de Arriaga

"How did Captain Arriaga find me?"

"Your mother told him about you." Her uncle folded the letter with haste and handed it back to her. "Here you go. Now I must away."

She'd once seen a large-mouthed bass wiggle off a hook with greater finesse. "Oh, no you don't." After tossing the letter into the box, she seized her uncle's arm. "You tell me what the captain meant by my 'parents.' No more pretense. Look at me. Dark hair and eyes, olive skin. And these cheekbones! Both my mother's husbands had blond hair and blue eyes. I couldn't be the daughter of either of them. So who was — *is* — my father?"

David squirmed, trying his best to get off that hook. "Your mother's the one who must have this conversation with you."

"But she's on her way to South Carolina, and you're here." Betsy released him and set the lantern down. "She's with my father, isn't she? I shall go looking for *both* of them so I may have a proper explanation."

"Come now, you've more sense than to travel into a war-torn colony."

She jutted her chin forward. "You tell me, then."

He sighed. "Your father is Mathias Hale, a blacksmith from Alton."
Astonishment shot through her. "Hale?" She had a vague recollection of
the Hale family as respectable blacksmiths in her hometown of Alton, south of
Augusta. The wonder of discovery began arranging perplexing pieces of her
past into a logical picture. "*That's* why Mother sent me here to be fostered with
Lucas and Sarah seven years ago. I must resemble my father or someone in
his family, and she wanted me out of Alton." Confusion trailed off her words.
She blinked at her uncle "Why didn't Mother marry Mr. Hale? Was shame or
hardship involved?"

David held up his hands. "Another long story which I've no place or leisure
to explain. Forgive me, but I must begone." He strode to the back of the henhouse and unhitched his horse.

She tracked him, her thirst unquenched. "Is he a good man?"

"Yes, a very good man."

"Well, then, I truly don't understand why she didn't —"

"Betsy." He turned to her and seized her shoulders. "You must leave it for
now."

"But can you not imagine what it's been like for me, Uncle David, to never
have had a father? In all my seventeen years, I've had uncles, a stepfather, and
grandfathers, but they haven't been my *father.*"

"You shall meet him someday, I know it. He's that kind of man. But now
isn't the time to look for him." David pressed a kiss to her forehead, released
her, and climbed into the saddle with his fowler. "*Don't* go to South Carolina."

Betsy stepped back, certain she exuded defiance in her stance. "Why not?"

He wagged his finger at her. "I mean it, Betsy. *Don't* go to South Carolina.
And, for that matter, stay clear of Alton for awhile, especially a lieutenant by
the name of Fairfax."

Oh, faugh. Her uncle's "enemies" were all cuckolded courtiers of wealthy
widows. She sweetened her smile. "Not to worry."

The paling sky outlined perplexity in her uncle's posture. As much as he
enjoyed women, he'd never figured out what to do with those who were head-
strong. "I cannot command you to anything, can I?"

"Good luck in Williamsburg, Uncle David." She blew a kiss.

He shook his head, reined his horse around, and trotted it from the yard
with a final wave. Betsy watched until the gloom of dawn swallowed him before retrieving the lantern, eggs, and box. Then she ambled back to the house
escorted by the aria of a mockingbird.

So. Her kinfolk had evaded the Crown's "justice" upon the gallows and
torture at the hands of Indians and were *en route* to sanctuaries in other
colonies. And for the first time in her life, she had a father: a blacksmith, a
"very good man." At the back step, she paused to address the sky, her shoulders back, her face aglow. "Mathias Hale," she whispered, "expect me soon."

End of Chapter One

Made in the USA
Columbia, SC
11 June 2022

61486913R00148